THE
DRIVE

TYLER KEEVIL

Myriad Editions

Published in 2013 by

Myriad Editions
59 Lansdowne Place
Brighton BN3 1FL

www.myriadeditions.com

1 3 5 7 9 10 8 6 4 2

A CIP catalogue record for this book is available from
the British Library.

ISBN: 978-1-908434-31-9

Printed on FSC-accredited paper and bound by
TJ International Ltd., Padstow, Cornwall

MIX
Paper from
responsible sources
FSC® C013056

For her

'A fast moving car is the only place where you're legally allowed to not deal with your problems.'

Douglas Coupland

PART I.

chapter 1

I wandered into the rental car agency on a Monday morning, carrying a backpack filled with supplies: socks, boxer shorts, T-shirts, my sleeping bag, and six beers. Originally it had been eight beers but I'd drunk a couple of road pops on the bus ride over. The agency was out at the airport. It was called Budget or Thrifty or something like that. I'd found it on the net. They were the only company in the Lower Mainland that offered unlimited mileage, as a kind of sales gimmick. I guess they expected you to pay your money and putter around the city for a few days. That was obviously a huge mistake on their part.

The office was a dimly lit cubicle with four glass walls, like an aquarium, built into the airport's underground parkade. As I approached the counter, the clerk on duty looked up and smiled. He was an Asian guy wearing horn-rimmed glasses and a gold hoop earring. His hair was gelled into this retro quiff that stuck up stiffly at the front.

He said, 'How are you this morning, sir?'

I hadn't really slept for two weeks. Or eaten much. Eating was hard.

'Peachy.'

I gave him my driver's licence and reservation number. He started tapping the keys on his computer. His fingers were long and elegant, like spider legs. One had a ring on it.

'You married?' I asked.

He stopped typing.

'I'm engaged.'

'I didn't know men wore engagement rings.'

'It's fairly common, these days.'

He began typing again, keeping one eye on me – as if he already suspected I was going to be a problem. 'Today's your lucky day,' he said. 'We don't have the car you reserved, but for the same price we can offer you an upgrade.'

He rattled off a list of vehicles I could choose from: different makes, different models, different manufacturers. The names floated in the air around us, meaningless as vapour. I'd never owned a car and didn't know much about them.

'Are you interested in any of those, sir?'

'Sorry – what was that last one?'

'A Ford Expedition.'

He said it like it should mean something.

'Great,' I told him.

He handed me a bunch of forms to fill out. As I did this, he received a text on his cellphone. He read it, smiled, and began texting back. I tried to peek at the screen without him noticing, but he caught me.

'Is that your fiancée?' I asked, still scribbling.

He frowned. 'Why?'

'No reason. It's just nice to see other people happy.'

He turned his phone face-down, hiding the display from me. When I'd finished filling out the forms, he swiped my credit card and handed me the key, being careful not to actually touch me in any way.

'That's five hundred and eighty dollars and sixty-three cents.'

'My reservation said it was three hundred-something.'

He blinked. 'I asked if you wanted our Loss Damage Waiver Plan and you said yes.'

'Did I?'

'I can remove it, if you like.'

'No. I might as well keep it. There's a fairly good chance I'll crash this thing.'

He didn't smile. He pointed to the lot and told me where the car was parked.

'Thanks – and say hi to the fiancée for me.'

As I left, I could tell he was still watching me.

The underground parkade was lit by cheap fluorescent tubes that flickered and hummed like lightsabers. My vehicle sat in the corner of the lot. It was a monster SUV with tyres as high as my waist, running-boards, and a crash bar jutting out from the grille. I ran my palm across the hood, feeling that smooth-metal sweetness, and imagined rumbling along the American highways. I would be wearing Ray-Bans, and listening to Springsteen. I'd have my windows rolled down and my sleeves rolled up. My forearms would be tanned, my hair tousled by the wind. I'd have a cigarette tucked behind one ear.

I climbed up into the driver's seat to see how it felt. I sat gripping the wheel for about thirty seconds. Then I got out and walked back to the office. The Asian guy was talking on his phone. As soon as he saw me, he hung up and stuffed the phone in his pocket.

'Is there a problem?' he asked.

I explained that the Expedition was too big, and too fancy. He looked at me in a way that would become familiar in the following weeks: with a certain wariness, as if I were a dog that seemed friendly but might snap given provocation.

'I'm driving it a long way,' I said, 'and through some fairly shitty areas.'

'I see.'

'I need something that's good on gas, and won't get ripped off.' I pointed out the window. 'That thing wouldn't last two minutes where I'm going.'

I said it theatrically, and it worked. He took the key back from me and gave me new forms to fill out. I signed my name in all the same places and ticked all the same boxes.

'Where *are* you going?' he asked.

'To the States,' I said. 'I need to get away. It's pretty hard to explain.'

'Right.'

He took the form from me, pinching it carefully, as if it was a piece of evidence.

'Have a good trip,' he told me.

The new car was a Dodge Neon, cheap and sleek, with pizza-cutter wheels and a lame little spoiler on the trunk. It was the kind of sedan my stepmom would drive. Actually, it was the kind of sedan my stepmom *had* driven. A few years back, she'd owned an earlier version of this same model. That car had been green. This one was maroon red. There were glittering flecks and sparkles ingrained in the paint job. It had been freshly waxed, and I could see a distorted version of myself reflected in the panelling.

I walked around the car, checking it out. I kicked the tyres a couple of times, just to feel as if I was giving it a proper going-over. I also popped the hood and examined the engine – a gleaming tangle of hoses and wiring and machinery. It looked good to me. The clerk was watching all this through the glass wall of his office. I gave him the thumbs-up, but he didn't respond.

I figured I'd better get going.

I put my backpack in the trunk and got in the driver's seat. It was an automatic, with only seven thousand kilometres on the clock. The interior still had that new-car smell of upholstery, plastic and glass cleaner. I eased the key into the ignition, feeling that satisfying click, and started the engine. It shivered to life. I bent forward to kiss the wheel.

'This is it,' I said, to my car and myself. 'The start of our epic journey.'

I put her in gear and backed out. The tyres squeaked on the concrete as we circled the parkade. I was so excited that I kept missing the exit, but eventually I found it. Then my car and I emerged from underground into a world full of heat and light and noise and fury.

The terminals at Vancouver International are laid out in a horseshoe formation, with the parkade in the centre. The parkade is encircled by a one-way traffic system that forms a kind of crescent. I slid on to the crescent and accelerated around it, leaning into the curves. Other vehicles were pulling in and out, making drop-offs or pick-ups. The windows of the Arrivals lounge flicker-flared in the sunlight. I left all that behind, and at the airport exit the road flung me out like a stone from a sling, unleashing me on to Highway 99.

chapter 2

Two weeks before, I'd been working on an independent film. By coincidence, we were shooting out at the same airport, Vancouver International. We'd set up on an access road near the landing field. There were planes all over the place: lumbering around on the ground, roaring down the runways, banking and circling overhead. The sky was coated in swirls of cirrus cloud, creating a blue-marble effect.

'Can you use a longer lens for this scene?' the director asked me. He clapped a hand on my shoulder and squeezed. He was a scrawny guy who wore skinny jeans and always drank soy shakes on set. A total hipster.

'You got it.'

Officially I was the camera operator, but he'd only hired me because of my camera. Six months before, on my twenty-first birthday, I'd bought a five-thousand-dollar video camera with money I'd saved up cutting lawns. I'd been hiring myself out with it, as a way of gaining experience. To start with, it had mostly been on spec. This was my first paid job, at a hundred bucks a day. The director didn't have much faith in me, though. Neither did the DP. He hovered at my shoulder, checking every shot and constantly adjusting the frame.

'All right, people!' the director called, striding on to set. He'd parked the car we'd been using for the shoot – a cherry-red '57 Chevy – at the side of the access road. 'In this scene, our leads are lying on the hood, watching the planes land.'

There were two main actors. One was an ex-hockey player who did push-ups between takes and liked changing his shirt in front of everybody. The other was this girl with white skin and green hair. She never talked to me or any of the crew, unless we were in her way. Their characters were supposed to be on a road trip together to break her heroin habit. I think that was the idea, anyway.

'Trevor, let's shoot this from the front. A medium two-shot.'

I got in position, still fiddling with my lens. The actors were already sprawled on the hood, sharing a cigarette. The director made sure they were good to go, then nodded at me.

'Rolling,' I said.

'And... action!'

Right away, the sound guy put up his hand, signalling that something was wrong. He was a teenage volunteer who wore sweatpants and had moustache fuzz, like a patch of mould growing on his upper lip. 'Hold it,' he said. 'I got a blip.'

'What's a blip?' the director asked.

The sound guy gave him the headphones, so he could listen for himself.

'Shit,' the director said. 'That's weird.'

After that the DP wanted to hear, and everybody else. They all took turns trying on the headphones. I went last. I pressed one headphone to my ear and listened. You could hear the drone of plane engines, which the director had expected. But behind it, every three or four seconds, there was a little blip in the audio – almost as if somebody had tapped the microphone.

The sound guy was already fiddling with his wires, and checking his connections.

'Maybe it's low on batteries,' the jock said.

The sound guy shook his head. 'This mic doesn't use batteries, okay?'

You could tell he was panicking a little, since it was his equipment. The rest of us milled in a herd, looking around and trying to figure out what could be making the blip. I noticed a radar tower near the runways. The antenna dish on the top was slowly rotating.

'Hey,' I said, pointing. 'It could be that radar tower.'

They all looked. The antenna went around, and around, and around, every three or four seconds. The rhythm was the same as the blip. We couldn't hear it – you can't hear radar, obviously – but somehow the microphone was picking it up.

The director grabbed the headphones to listen again, while studying the antenna.

'He's right,' he said. 'Good job, Trevor.'

The sound guy came over and gave me a high-five. People congratulated me. Not that it made any difference to the shoot. It wasn't as if we could stop the radar tower. Our sound would still be screwed, and the editor would have to fix it in post-production. But at least we knew what was causing it now.

'Positions, people,' the director called out. 'Let's shoot this fucker.'

He loved saying stuff like that.

During our coffee break I was eating a stale jelly doughnut when the director came over to join me, which he'd never done before. He squatted down on my camera case and thanked me again for solving the riddle of the radar tower. He said he was stoked on the shots we'd got so far, and told me he was going to use this short to apply for a grant from the National Film Board. If he got it, they would be making a feature in the fall.

'How'd you like in on it?' he asked.

'That would be awesome, man.'

He grabbed a doughnut from the tray, took a bite, and kept talking with his mouth full. 'None of this indie bullshit. I'm talking union wages, real equipment. I'm even planning a few helicopter shots. Imagine that. You could shoot that scene for me.'

'I'm great at helicopter shots.'

'I know. I know you are.'

We talked like that a little more, daydreaming about our make-believe future together. He wanted to take his film on the festival circuit: Sundance and Toronto and Venice and South by Southwest. Then he'd get a distribution deal, and it would blow up huge.

'What's your feature going to be about?' I asked him.

'Like this – only longer.'

'Oh.'

The director popped the last bite into his mouth and licked his fingers, as if it was the greatest thing he'd ever tasted. He had icing sugar all over his lips. 'Another road movie, I mean,' he said. 'Like *Easy Rider* crossed with David Lynch. It'll be about one character's journey. A personal odyssey. But with all these trippy and surreal elements thrown in.'

'Road movies are tough to do. They're so episodic.'

'You can get around that. I'll give him some companions.'

I told him it was a great idea. It would have been fairly awkward if I'd told him how uninspired it sounded. Also, I thought he might get mad and fire me.

As it turned out, it didn't matter either way.

chapter 3

From the airport I drove south on Highway 99, past grain silos and wheat fields and a Sikh temple decorated with big yellow spires, like onion bulbs. I dropped through the George Massey tunnel, then shot out into Ladner. At the junction with Highway 17, I passed the turnoff for Delta and Tsawwassen. The sign above the road showed a little pictogram of a ferryboat floating on water. Until then I hadn't considered how many memories lay along this route. It was riddled with them, like sinkholes, ready to draw me down.

Tsawwassen was one of the places I'd been with her. On her first visit to Vancouver, I took her to Saltspring Island, and to reach it you have to go via Tsawwassen. When we arrived, we'd just missed a ferry. The next one departed an hour later, and while we waited we wandered down one of the wharves that runs alongside the berths. People were fishing out there. A dozen or so men stood in a row, making casts and cranking their reels. The lines, strung from the rods to the surface, glistened in the sun like spun silk. She got talking to this Chinese guy and somehow convinced him to lend her his rod. That was just like her.

'Five minutes,' the guy said, holding up five fingers. 'You fish five minutes.'

You could tell he didn't expect her to catch anything, but she did – on the first cast. The rod bent right to the handle and she got yanked towards the edge of the wharf. There was no railing, so me and the guy grabbed her. We held her by the waist and she braced herself and let the line whizz out, slowing it every so often with the reel. It must have surprised the guy to see her handle it so expertly, but her father had taught her. He was an ex-factory worker with a mangled hand who fished every morning off a jetty in the Vltava.

'Good, good!' the Chinese guy cried. 'Let it run!'

From up and down the dock, the other fishermen flocked towards us and gathered around. They shouted encouragement and advice, shoving each other and jostling to stay at the front. Directly opposite us, in the adjacent berth, was the ferry to Nanaimo. It had begun loading and the first few passengers stood on deck. They were watching, too. Tourists were pointing, taking pictures, calling out. One of the straps of her dress had slipped off her shoulder, exposing the tan-line of her breast. She didn't notice. She was totally focused.

'*Sakra*,' she kept saying, swearing to herself in Czech. '*Sakra!*'

The fish cut back and forth, tugging hard on the line. She moved with it, following the rod like a diviner, and the whole crowd moved with her. Whenever the fish relented, she took in a bit of line. She fought it like that for maybe fifteen minutes. When the fish finally breached the surface, everybody gasped in unison. It was a huge salmon, a Chinook, and it was going crazy – twisting and convulsing on the hook. From the wharf to the water it was about a ten-foot drop. She reeled the fish up slowly, and when it cleared the edge of the dock it was still flapping, scattering water and scales everywhere. All the fishermen whooped and applauded and moved in closer.

She lowered the salmon to the dock, and looked at me.

'I caught it,' she said, panting, 'so you have to kill it.'

'I do?'

The Chinese guy nodded gravely, as if he understood the logic of this. Among his gear he had a wooden club, like a child's baseball bat. He handed it to me. The other fishermen stood in a semi-circle and watched. We knelt together. She pinned the flopping fish in place and I brought the bat down on the back of its head, hard. It quivered and went still. One of its eyes had popped out and blood began leaking from its gills. We stood up, holding the fish between us, and the fishermen cheered again. Even the foot passengers cheered. It was as if we'd sealed something, or signed a pact. Then the boat horn sounded, the ferry pulled away and the fishermen dispersed. We thanked the Chinese man and carried our catch back to the loading area.

We didn't have a cooler to store it in but we had our camping gear, so we decided to cook the salmon, on the beach next to the terminal. Zuzska knew all about cleaning fish. She hacked off its head first, then slit open its belly. Its heart and kidneys spilled out, glistening like gems. While she scraped away the rest of the guts I got the camping stove going. We cracked open a couple of Kokanees, sat down in the sand, and fried up chunks of salmon.

'It's just like Christmas,' she said.

'Nobody has fish at Christmas.'

'We do.'

Instead of turkey, apparently her family always had carp. They would keep a carp in the bathtub in the weeks leading up to Christmas. They'd feed it and name it and treat it like a pet. Then, on Christmas Day, they would kill it to eat.

'Poor fish.'

She shrugged. 'Fish are stupid.'

She plucked a piece of salmon from the pan, popped it in her mouth, and licked the oil off her fingers. We stayed there, eating and drinking, until the ferry arrived, then had to pack up and go get in line with the other foot passengers. The people around us kept staring at her. She'd washed her hands but her forearms still shimmered with slime and water. Blood streaks stained the front of her dress, and fish scales sparkled on her cheeks, her neck, her chest. She stank of the sea, and she looked like a beautiful and particularly brutal mermaid.

That was Zuzska for you.

Somebody was honking at me. I checked the rear-view. There was an SUV behind me, riding my ass and flashing its lights. Without meaning to, I'd slowed down to forty klicks. I could see the driver hunched over his wheel, snarling at me. He was a bald guy wearing tinted glasses and a flat cap. Instead of speeding up I tapped the brakes – just to mess with him.

He swung into the other lane, pulled alongside me, and started screaming through his open window.

'What do you think you're doing, asshole?'

'What does it look like I'm doing?' I shouted back. 'Driving!'

'You mean daydreaming!'

'Yeah – I'm daydreaming about your sister!'

We argued like that for a while, shouting and swearing and swerving erratically in our lanes. Partly I was pissed off because I knew he was right. I'd come on this trip to forget about her, to get away from her, to get over her, and I was already sinking into sentimentality.

'Pull your head out of your ass!'

'I hear you, okay?' I screamed. 'Now fuck off!'

I hit the gas, leaving him and Tsawwassen behind.

chapter 4

We filmed at the airport until dusk. The sky melted into marmalade and the planes continued crawling around in it. The director said, 'That's a wrap,' and handed out call sheets for the next morning. The actors were allowed to go. The crew stayed behind to pack up the gear. Afterwards the DP dropped me off at a bus station on Marine Drive, and I caught the No.10 up Granville. The bus was crammed with commuters – all of them shuffling, rustling, shifting – but I found a seat near the back. I sat and cradled my camera case and gazed out the window.

I remember I was still thinking about those blips, transmitted from the radar tower. I tried to imagine the way they pulsed through the air – wave after wave of them, washing over the planes, mapping their locations on traffic control screens. If those same signals had been hitting our microphone, maybe they carried on even further, lapping at cars, trees, buildings, streets, people, everything. And, if you had some kind of ultra-sensitive detector, you might even be able to create a radar map of the entire city – a glowing green grid that charted the progress of day-to-day life in Vancouver.

Then my phone rang. It was Zuzska, calling from Prague. We normally talked a bit later because of the time difference, but I didn't think that meant anything.

I answered. 'Hey, *kočka*.'

She was crying. She told me that she'd slept with somebody, or been sleeping with somebody. It was hard to hear – she kept choking on her words – but the meaning trickled through to me. I felt around for a cord or button to stop the bus, and accidentally pulled the emergency lever instead. An alarm went off – this steady droning, like a shotclock buzzer. The bus lurched. The driver was pulling over. I stood up, with the phone still mashed to my ear. All the passengers were looking at me. I walked down the aisle between them, stunned and helpless, like a groom going to the altar. The driver didn't get mad, or demand to know what was going on. He just opened the automatic doors for me. I'll always appreciate that.

I stumbled past him and stepped off the bus.

'Say something,' Zuzska said. 'Say anything.'

But I couldn't. My larynx had seized up. I made an odd, pathetic noise, like a cat mewling, and ended the call. The bus was pulling away. It had left me next to a chain-link fence, and a field full of weeds. I threw the phone into the field, flinging it as far as I could. Then I bent over and put my hands on my knees, feeling sick. I didn't actually think I was going to puke, but I did. I puked in the gravel at the roadside. All those jelly doughnuts came back up, along with the ravioli we'd had for lunch. The puke was thick, red and slimy – my blood and guts, lying there for all the world to see.

I sat down on my camera case. Cars hummed past, zipping about the city's grid, still being mapped by the blips. They carried on and I stayed there, in a kind of catatonic stupor, until the sun went down and the sky grew dark and I started to shiver. Then I remembered something: my phone. It was still out in that field. I climbed the fence and thrashed around among the nettles and dandelions, hunting blindly for it, crying like a child.

chapter 5

On my left the big white arch rose up, looming over traffic and straddling the centre of the boulevard like the legs of an albino colossus. I'd arrived at the Peace Arch Border Crossing. There were seven lanes open. Going into the States, choosing a good lane is crucial. If you get the wrong border guard, you can end up being hassled, interrogated or searched – all the things I wanted to avoid. I'd drunk a couple of beers and I had some weed on me – enough for maybe three joints. I'd packed it all into the straw of a slurpee. This way, if they searched me, I could suck the weed up through the straw and swallow it – there'd be no trace. But I preferred not to have to do that, for obvious reasons, and it all depended on the line I chose.

'Left is always right,' I said, and turned that way.

My whole life, I've put faith in that nonsensical motto. I sat in the left lane, tapping the steering wheel, and inched along behind a station wagon. The sky sagged down, heavy with cloud, and there was a mugginess to the summer air. I opened my window. The other drivers were listening to their stereos, and the mixture of tinny pop tunes drifted between the vehicles. My rental car had a stereo, too, but I left it off. I didn't feel like playing music.

The line shifted. I moved forward.

I'd been over this border countless times – first with my old man when I was a kid, and later with my friends, as teenagers. Cross-border shopping trips were a great Canadian tradition. I knew all the tricks: smile and nod, hand over your passport, address the guard as 'sir' or 'madam', politely answer his or her questions. Be specific, but not too specific. It had always worked when I'd gone down to pick up Zuzska. Sometimes, for her visits, she would fly into Seattle, since flights were cheaper to the US than to Canada, and I would drive down to meet her. It was two and a half hours one-way, and by the time I reached Sea-Tac airport I would be sickened, shaky, quaking with lust and anticipation. I developed my own set of rituals to calm down. I would drink two beers at the airport bar, brush my teeth in the bathroom, and win a stuffed animal for her from one of those grabbing-claw games. After her flight landed, I'd stand and count the passengers emerging from Customs, telling myself that before I reached a certain number she would appear. When she finally did, it was like being jolted with a defibrillator.

The line shifted. I moved forward.

Our ride home from the airport had its own rituals. En route we'd be kissing and touching, laughing and chatting. I'd struggle to keep the car straight, to stay on course. At the border we would have to explain what I was doing, bringing a foreign body back into my country. We would smile and tell them our story: how I'd gone to live in Prague, how she'd been my Czech language teacher, how we'd fallen in bilingual love. The guards always smiled back, won over. *Ah*, you could see them thinking, *young love*. They would stamp both our passports, as if confirming the validity of our relationship. A few weeks later, on the way back down, we'd go through the whole process again with the American guards.

The line shifted. It was my turn.

I rolled down my window. As I pulled up at the booth I could see the guard inside, watching me. I smiled and handed him my passport. He had pale, spotted cheeks and puffy sacs under his jaw, like a toad. He was sitting on a high stool.

'Where are you going?' he asked.

'Just down to the States, sir.'

He stared at me as if I'd told him the sky was blue.

'On a little road trip, I mean. Through Washington and Oregon.' That sounded fairly specific. Was I being specific enough? 'And maybe on to San Francisco.'

He leaned forward, peering at me. He had those crazy bubble-eyes that bulge out.

'San Francisco?' he said.

'I have a friend who lives there.'

I could tell I shouldn't have mentioned San Francisco. It was full of hippies and liberals and potheads and queers. In his mind, anyways.

'This your car?'

'No, sir. It's a rental.'

He held my passport up to his nose. 'You live in Vancouver but you rented a car?'

'I don't have my own. And I really wanted to go on this road trip.'

That clinched it. He handed me back my passport without stamping it. 'Could you pull over beside the Customs office?' he asked, pointing it out.

It was a white building just beyond the border. The windows were tinted and you couldn't see inside. I parked next to it and turned off my car. I knew the drill because I'd been searched before, on one of those shopping trips with my old man, before my stepmom was on the scene. We'd gone down for the day and were smuggling goods back: toys and T-shirts and video games. A lot of families did the same, and occasionally the guards searched people, hoping to slap a customs charge on them. But we'd been ready for them. We had cut the tags off the clothes and opened the toys and gotten rid of all the receipts and boxes and packaging.

This time, I was ready for them too.

I reached for my slurpee. At first it seemed as if the straw was plugged. I couldn't get any suction going. I sucked harder, and it all came up at once – a burst of cherry slurpee and weed that made me choke. I coughed and spluttered, trying to get it down. Bits of bud got stuck between my teeth. I had to rinse out my mouth with slurpee, working the

20

slush around my gums, but managed to swallow most of it. I figured I had maybe half an hour before a devastating body-stone kicked in.

The door to the Customs office opened. A woman in a blue uniform came out with a dog. She was a small woman but her dog was very big. A German shepherd, I think. I got out of the car, still holding my slurpee.

'We're going to give the vehicle an inspection, sir,' she said. 'Would you mind opening the trunk for me?'

As I went to do that, her dog started sniffing around the hubcaps. Apparently the hubcaps were a hotspot. The woman held one hand low on the dog's leash, near its collar. I'd left my door open, and the next place they checked was the front seat. The dog put its paws where I'd been sitting and snorted at the upholstery, getting closer to the cup-holder.

'The trunk is open,' I said, hopefully, 'if you want to check there.'

The woman ignored me. Her dog now had its nose right inside the cup-holder, poking around like a pig snuffling for truffles.

'What is it, Herbie?' the woman asked. 'What's there?'

Herbie made a sound in his throat, uncertain. I'd walked around the side of the car to watch. Herbie glanced over his shoulder at me. He was obviously a smart fucking dog. For a few seconds we sort of had a staring contest. Then his ears went back, flat on his head.

He roared and jumped at me.

'Holy shit!' I cried.

His paws thumped my chest and I fell over backwards, screaming. But Herbie wasn't going for me. He'd clamped on to my slurpee cup. He held it in his teeth and shook it back and forth, as if he'd caught a rabbit. Slurpee sprayed everywhere.

'Easy, Herbie.' The woman pulled hard on the lead. 'Easy, boy.'

Herbie sat back and panted, his tongue lolling out the side of his mouth. Pink slurpee juice dripped from his jaws.

The woman crouched down to examine the mess he'd made. She looked from the cup to me. I was still sprawled on the concrete.

'Maybe he just really likes slurpee,' I said.

chapter 6

The night she called was the night I stopped sleeping. I came home from the film shoot and slunk into my suite. I was living in my dad's garage conversion and didn't want to face him or Amanda, my stepmom.

I dropped my camera case and stood in the centre of the living room. The floor was covered in cinematic detritus: film canisters and video tapes and memory cards and lenses and filters and scrims and hard drives and scraps of paper filled with storyboards, character sketches, dialogue notes. I'd been cultivating this creative nest, a den full of story, but none of it could help me now. I was completely off-script. I just stood looking around, panicky and disorientated, like an actor trying to remember his lines.

I had three full-size movie posters on my walls. One showed Al Pacino in *Carlito's Way*, holding a handgun. The other two were for *Casino* and *The Godfather*. The first time she'd visited, Zuzska had jumped all over me about them. 'What is the point of this?' she'd said, striking a Pacino pose. 'You like guns? You want to be a gangster?' Then she'd told me that guns were a phallic symbol and that I obviously had middle-class masculinity issues. She was taking these night courses in psychology and thought that made her an expert.

At the bottom of the *Casino* poster, the Las Vegas cityscape sparkled like a distant galaxy. The year before, Zuzska and I had driven down to Vegas, and almost gotten married in secret. We'd thought it would help sort out all the immigration difficulties if I ever moved to the Czech Republic, or she ever moved to Canada. I thought about that for a few minutes, and then went over and ripped that goddamn poster off the wall. I attacked it like a demented house cat: tearing it into strips, and tearing the strips into bits, and scattering the bits all over like confetti. Then I dropped to my knees and pounded the carpet with the soft underside of my fist – once, twice, three times – and clutched at my skull, as if it was about to burst open.

I whimpered.

Eventually I crawled over to my kitchen table. It was a lime-green laminate table that doubled as my work desk. I got out a pen and some paper and started writing: *How could you do this to me, to us…* Then I stopped. The words were too familiar. I tried again, and again, but it was always the same – lines I'd heard in films, or read in books. I had none of my own. I filled seven pages of loose-leaf paper and the best I could come up with was this: *It's as if you've reopened Pandora's Box, and let all the evil in the world out again, but this time you shut the box on hope. Worse, you shut the box just as hope was trying to get out – so hope got caught between the lid and the edge of the box. Hope got crushed. Hope has broken ribs, a burst spleen, a shattered sternum. Hope's back is broken. There is no hope for hope.*

Even that was just a reference to something else. Also, it made me sound insane. So I didn't send it. I didn't send any of my letters. Most ended up on the floor as balls of paper. When the ink ran dry I put on some Miles Davis and got incredibly sentimental. I watched *Cinema Paradiso*, played solitaire, and drank half a mickey of absinthe. I read the first page of *The Unbearable Lightness of Being* over and over, trying to get the words to make sense. She'd given it to me for our anniversary, and told me she'd always be my Tereza. At dawn, I made myself coffee and sat on the back porch, beneath the pine tree. I could smell the brine of the Cove. It was quiet out there. I trembled in the quiet, quivering like a leaf.

Finally I called her, but we didn't really talk. I couldn't talk. It was like the letters. Everything sounded second-hand. Regurgitated words. My tongue felt thick and useless.

I remember asking her why. *It just happened*, she kept saying, *it just happened*. It was as if she was blaming it on a tornado, or a hurricane – a natural disaster that had blown us apart.

I hung up and broke my cellphone. I didn't break it when I hung it up, but after. I broke it on the floor, deliberately, with a hammer. I'd decided it would be the last time I talked to her. Then I added absinthe to my coffee. It tasted bizarre. At one point I tried to masturbate but couldn't. There was nothing happening down there. She'd cast some sort of spell on me, or a curse. I was paralysed from the balls down – a penis-plegic. I ran a bath and lay in it, fully dressed, until the water went cold. That didn't help, either.

chapter 7

They made me wait in a whitewashed room with an American flag on the wall. I sat and stared at the flag until the stars began to spiral and the stripes seemed to ripple and bend. A body-stone was creeping over me, like a slow-growing fungus. They must have let me stew in there for nearly half an hour. The whole room reeked of perfume and body odour and fear.

Then an official came in and sat down in one of the chairs across from me. He had a sprinkling of pimples on his forehead. He asked to see my passport and driver's licence, then opened my passport and thumbed through it. There was a form on the desk in front of him. He began copying my details into the form, frowning in concentration.

'How long will I be in here?' I asked.

He looked up, still frowning. 'That depends.'

'On what?'

'If they find anything when they search your car.'

'I thought they already searched it.'

'This time they're *really* searching it.'

That shut me up. I wasn't worried about the car. I was worried about the slurpee. I thought there might be flakes of bud left inside the straw, or in the cup. When my friend had been searched at the border one time, they'd found resin on his Swiss Army knife. He'd been banned from going to the States for the rest of his life.

The guy finished copying down my details and slid my passport back to me.

'What's the purpose of your journey to the United States?'

He had his pen poised, ready to write.

'I'm going on a road trip.'

He looked up. 'By yourself?'

'I'm trying to get my head together.'

He jotted something down in a box on his form. Then he scratched out what he'd written and stuck the end of his pen in his mouth. He gnawed on it for a while. He looked like a high-school kid who'd turned up for an exam totally unprepared.

Eventually he said, 'Stay here.'

He left, taking the form with him. I waited. Directly above me hung an incandescent light bulb, dull and yellowish, blazing down like a heat-ray. I was getting hotter and hotter, sweltering, melting into my chair. I felt as soft and malleable as a chunk of clay. It was hard not to squirm and shift around. Mostly I was worried about my eyes. Pretty soon they would be bloodshot and cherried, from being so body-stoned, and that could easily give me away.

The door opened again and the guy came back. He had two people with him. One was the woman who had searched my car – the dog-handler. The other was a Latino guy in a pinstriped suit, who reminded me of a professor. He even wore little wire-rimmed spectacles. He peered at me over the lenses. He had my form on a clipboard in his hand.

'Sorry to bother you, sir,' the first guy said to him. 'It just seemed a bit odd.'

'No worries, Shooter,' the professor said. 'We'll take care of it.'

The guy's nickname was Shooter, apparently. Shooter looked relieved.

The professor studied me. 'So you're the kid going on the road trip.'

'Is that a problem?'

He glanced at the woman. 'Search turn up anything?'

She shook her head. 'Not yet. They're running some tests.'

I knew she meant on the slurpee. I tried to look indifferent, and innocent. That wasn't easy, since I wasn't really either.

'Let's wait on that,' the professor said.

He sat down opposite me, with Shooter and the woman on either side. All three of them had pens and pads of paper. The professor clicked the end of his pen and twirled it around his finger – first one way, then the other. It was obviously something he'd practised a lot.

'What's the purpose of your trip?' he asked me.

'Does a trip need to have a purpose?'

'If it doesn't,' he said, 'it looks suspicious.'

I rubbed my hand over my face. My cheeks felt sensitive, as if they were sunburnt.

'I'm going through a tough time,' I said. 'It's personal, okay?'

None of them wrote that down. They just looked at me. Dubiously.

'What?' I asked, holding out my hands, beseeching them. 'Is that so unbelievable? Isn't that what young guys do? We've been doing it for decades, ever since *Easy Rider*. Ever since Kerouac, actually. You know – traversing America, being free, finding yourself and all that shit. *That's* the purpose of my trip. Except I'm doing it in a budget rental car, instead of on an awesome chopper.'

They were taking notes now. The three of them scribbled furiously, as if I'd given them some sort of solution, or equation, a breakthrough scientific formula: the new $E=MC^2$.

Then the professor said, 'You taking any drugs on this road trip?'

He said it super-quick – as if he wanted to catch me by surprise.

'No way, man.'

He frowned at that. I probably shouldn't have called him 'man'.

'Nothing at all? Even for personal consumption?'

'Nope. I'm not into that stuff. I'll probably buy a few beers on the other side.'

He wrote down each of my answers. The other two weren't writing any more. They were watching. The woman was, anyways. Shooter had started nibbling on a hangnail.

'And where exactly are you going?' the professor asked.

'Nowhere in particular.'

He sat back, smiling. His glasses flashed once beneath the light, as if he'd taken a picture of me with his eyes.

'Not San Francisco?'

I'd forgotten that I'd already mentioned it to the guard in the booth.

'I might end up down there.'

'So you *are* going somewhere.'

'Maybe – but it's not official or anything. I mean, I'm trying to keep my options open. Go with the flow. I have a friend down in San Francisco but haven't told her when I'll be arriving.'

Shooter had started doodling on his paper pad. I noticed he'd written 'Gay' at the bottom of the page, followed by a pair of question marks.

'Wait a minute,' I said. 'I'm not gay, okay?'

The other two looked at Shooter, who put his palm across the page, hiding it.

'I'm not gay,' I repeated, karate-chopping the table for emphasis. 'I just can't have sex at the moment. I can't get it up or something. I've lost my libido, my sex drive. It's a perfectly legitimate physical condition. Impotence. I'm impotent, okay?'

Shooter dutifully crossed out 'Gay' and wrote 'Impotent'. I'd made my point, at a price. I'd started to sweat. My fingers felt stiff and I could no longer feel my feet. I was being baked in that kiln-hot room, slowly hardening like fired clay.

'Are you all right?' the professor asked, peering at me. 'You're white as a sheet.'

I licked my lips. If they decided to take a blood test, I was fucked.

'Maybe you should tell us what this is all about.'

'All right.'

29

I closed my eyes and bowed my head, as if in prayer. I figured I had to toss them a scrap of truth. People respond to authenticity.

'It's my girlfriend. She… died.'

I have no idea why I told them that. It just popped out, like a burp. Shooter was so surprised he dropped his pen. The three of them drew back and glanced at one another.

'I'm sorry.' That was Herbie's handler. She seemed the most sympathetic – maybe because she felt guilty that her dog had busted me. 'That must be incredibly hard for you.'

'It is,' I admitted. I'd started tearing up. I was really getting into it. Hopefully that would explain my red-eye. 'It is, but I'm trying to cope.'

She pushed back her chair and said, 'I'm going to check on those tests.'

When the door slammed behind her, I jumped. Seeing that, the professor smiled.

'Take it easy. You've got nothing to worry about – so long as you're clean.'

chapter 8

The next day we were shooting at a rest stop on the Sea to Sky Highway, near Squamish. My dad agreed to drop me off up there before work if I bought him a six-pack of beer. My dad's great at cutting deals like that. He'll do you a favour, so long as you pay him back – usually with a six-pack.

On the drive over, he asked me, 'How's the shoot going, boy-child?'

'Oh, you know.'

We were both drinking coffee: him because he always drank it, me because I didn't want him to smell the absinthe on my breath.

'Script any good?'

I had the script in my lap, open to the scene we were shooting.

'It's a bit avant-garde.'

'That's the problem with these film school graduates.' He gestured with his cup of coffee, slopping a few drops on his tie. He didn't notice. 'All they want to make is navel-gazing art-house flicks, without a real story.'

I hadn't been allowed to go to film school – mostly because it was so expensive. A year at Vancouver Film School costs over twenty grand. That's partly why I ended up going to Prague, and the language school, after graduation.

'What's it about, anyways?' he asked.

'A road trip.'

'That's it? A road trip?'

'And relationships, I guess.'

31

He snorted. 'I bet this director hasn't even heard of *Zen and the Art of Motorcycle Maintenance*. That's a real road-trip story for you. What did you think of it, by the way?'

I had to admit I hadn't read it yet. He'd given it to me for my birthday.

'Jesus, Trevor.' He slapped his forehead. 'I'm telling you, you'd love it. It's about the contrast between the romantic and the rationalist world view, the need to find a middle ground. It's the real deal, a proper philosophical text. None of this flaky new-age garbage.'

He started rambling on about these things called gestalts and Chautauquas. I pressed my forehead to the window and felt the cool tingle of glass. Eventually my dad noticed I wasn't listening.

'You okay?' he asked.

'I should probably read this over before we get there.'

'Whatever you say, boy-child.'

He turned up the radio. I pretended to study my script.

Most of the scenes in the film were the same. The jock and the junkie would pull over at a random location. They would get involved in some kind of incident, and then they would hop back in the car and keep going. That day, the incident was her throwing up. She was in withdrawal, and apparently junkies become nauseous when they're in withdrawal. She was going to puke in the road and we were going to film it.

I was the first to arrive. My dad pulled over and popped the trunk so I could unload my camera gear. He didn't help me. He was still mad that I'd ignored his road trip lecture.

'Remember my beers,' he said before he drove off.

Across from the rest stop was a little tourist shop and a gas station. I bought a pack of Player's at the gas station and sat on my camera box to wait, and smoke, and be miserable. Inhaling made me cough, so I ended up puffing and faking it. I was so tired my vision had gone blurry. I was crying a bit, too. I closed my eyes and sat like that, resting my eyes.

The DP showed up next. He was a tall, gangly guy with shaggy brown hair. He loped over and perched next to me, drawing his knees up to his chin.

'Hey, bro,' he said. That was what he called me. 'Can I see your camera?'

He loved my camera. He knew more about it than me. I got it out for him, and he fiddled around with the settings until the other crew members started to arrive. The director showed up last, with the actors. The rest of us sat around while he talked them through the scene. Then he swaggered over to me and the DP.

'How's my camera crew this morning?'

The DP said, 'Wicked, bro.'

He called everybody 'bro', now that I think about it. I nodded at the director, took a drag, and let smoke slip out between my lips.

'I didn't know you smoked, Trevor.'

'I'm trying to start.'

'Great.' He smiled like a ventriloquist's dummy and shook a sheaf of storyboards at us. 'Let me show you guys what I have in mind for this scene.'

He squatted down with us. He had half a dozen shots scheduled for that morning. The first was a long shot with a telephoto lens, of the jock and the junkie pulling over into the rest stop. As the car stopped, she stumbled out and puked. That was an easy one. We popped it off in under half an hour. The second one wasn't so easy. It was from inside a moving car. The director thought it would be artistic if we swept by and filmed the actors at the roadside. We were going to use the DP's car – this beat-up Volvo station wagon that steered erratically.

'Okay, Trevor,' the director told me. 'I want you shooting from the back seat. As we pass, you swish-pan to the right, finding them in the frame. You get me?'

It seemed a tricky shot to pull off, especially on an absinthe hangover and no sleep, while doing sixty in an old beater.

'I get you.'

We piled into the station wagon to try it out. With the DP driving, we headed up the highway and doubled back, but when I went for the swish-pan I missed the actors entirely.

'Cut!' the director cried.

He had a handheld monitor wired to the camera, so he could see what I was doing.

'Sorry, man,' I said.

'No worries. We'll do that again.'

We did. I screwed up the next take, too. My hands were jittery and I had no feel for the camera – it wouldn't do what I wanted. After five or six takes, the DP offered to give it a try. I passed my camera to him, and the director took over at the wheel. He kept glancing at his watch. It was only the second shot of the day and we were already behind schedule.

'Fuck,' he said absently.

Somehow, the DP nailed the shot on the first take.

'Finally,' the director said. 'We should have just done that in the first place.'

The DP handed the camera back to me. I started cleaning the lens and the director turned the car around. Nobody said anything as we drove back up to the rest stop.

We managed to squeeze off one more exterior shot before breaking for lunch. The catering lady – who was also the producer – popped the trunk of her car and handed out slices of pizza, with paper plates and President's Choice cola. When she offered a piece to me, I shook my head. I felt too sick to eat.

'Thanks anyway,' I said.

The DP looked over. 'Aren't you having any, bro?'

'I'm a vegetarian.'

'It's vegetarian pizza.'

'Great.'

I took a slice. It was home-made pizza, with mushrooms and green peppers. She'd kept it in tinfoil and it was still warm. I gnawed on it for a bit but swallowing made me gag. I wandered away from the group. When I thought nobody was looking, I flung my pizza across the highway. I was aiming for the woods on the other side, but a gust of wind caught the slice and slapped it down in the middle of the far lane. Cars started running over it, smearing it out like a piece of roadkill. I looked back. The rest of the crew was staring at me. I waved at them. Then I ducked into the souvenir shop beside the gas station.

A Native guy with a crew cut stood behind the counter. He had a piece of wood in his hands, which he whittled as I wandered around. I studied his carvings and his dream-catchers and his pewter jewellery. A set of wind chimes dangled above the door. I listened to them tinkle and breathed through my mouth until I stopped trembling. I still had no appetite, but I decided I no longer needed to eat. I'd become one of those people you hear about that exist only on water and sunlight, like plants. Except, in this case, I'd get by on booze and smokes. It would be like a fast. An extremely unhealthy fast.

On my way out, the Native guy nodded at me, as if in approval of my plan.

chapter 9

For a while we sat in silence, awaiting the results of the tests. By then the heat in that tiny room had baked me dry. My arms and legs had hardened, my joints had seized up, my body-stone had slowly solidified. Shooter started drumming his fingers on the tabletop. Then the professor looked at him, frowning, and he stopped.

The professor asked me, 'Tell us about this friend of yours in San Francisco.'

I stared at him. I was so blasted, it took me a moment to digest the question.

I said, 'She's a lesbian.'

Shooter sat up straighter. He looked interested for the first time. 'A lesbian?' he asked.

'An absurdly beautiful lesbian, with so much natural charisma she's practically off the charts. She's like an angelic *femme fatale*, and my one true friend. I love that woman.'

The professor was smirking now, as if he had me all figured out. Shooter just sat there with his mouth hanging open.

'Not in a dirty way, though,' I said. 'In a platonic way.'

'Of course,' the professor said. 'You want her pity.'

'You're hoping for a mercy lay,' Shooter added.

It was no use trying to explain it. Not to these guys.

'Even if I did – she's got a girlfriend, okay?'

Shooter was taking notes again. At the bottom of his page he'd written 'LESBIAN' in capital letters. Now he changed it to 'LESBIANS' and circled it.

'Is her girlfriend hot, too?' he asked.

'I've never met her.'

The door opened, and Herbie's handler came back. The three of us started shifting around, like kids who'd been talking behind the teacher's back. The professor picked up his papers and shuffled them together, acting all official. Then he cleared his throat.

'What's the verdict?' he asked her.

She was looking at us, trying to figure out what the hell was going on.

'Five more minutes,' she said.

The professor nodded and turned to me. 'What else will you be doing on this trip?'

'Well,' I said. I had to think about it. 'I'm going to Trevor, for one.'

He checked the form he'd been filling out. 'But that's your name.'

'It's also a town near Spokane. My dad took me there as a kid.'

He didn't believe me. He made Shooter go get a map, and I had to point out Trevor for them. The fact that I wasn't lying, that it existed, made them all a bit uncomfortable.

'Fine,' the professor said, folding up the map, 'you're going to Trevor. Where else?'

'Reno, I think.' I didn't mention Winnemucca, or my intentions there, since I wasn't sure if it was strictly legal. 'And at some point I want to shoot a gun. You can do that, can't you? In the States?'

'With a licence, sure.'

'What if you don't have a licence?'

He looked at Herbie's handler. She was the weapons expert, apparently. She said, 'They'll issue you a temporary one at the shooting range, if need be.'

I nodded. 'I guess those are pretty common down here.'

'There's a good range in northern Nevada.' She tapped a spot on the map. 'Near the Oregon border, if you're going that route. It's way out in the middle of nowhere.'

'Do you mind if I write that down?'

The professor shrugged. Herbie's handler tore a piece of paper off her pad and let me borrow her pen. She gave me more specific directions, and I jotted them down. It wasn't easy. My fingers were still numb and the pen felt as big and awkward as a rolling pin.

'Thanks,' I said. 'You guys are awesome.'

I hadn't really considered the details before. Having to articulate it was helping me sort it out. I could almost see the whole trip unfolding in my head, now – like a vision.

'What about Reno?' I asked. 'Do you know any good casinos?'

'Hold on,' the professor said, raising his hand like a traffic warden. I'd taken it too far, obviously. 'We're the ones asking the questions here, remember?'

But he didn't actually have any more. After another minute or so there was a knock at the door. Herbie's handler stepped out and exchanged a few words I couldn't really hear with somebody I couldn't really see. When she returned, she said, 'Tests came back negative. Nothing in the car or the slurpee.'

I held myself still. I didn't want to overreact. I could feel a prickling sensation across my shoulders and down my back, as if my body-stone was beginning to crack. The professor considered me, tilting his head forward to peer over his glasses.

'What do you think?' he asked the others.

The woman shrugged. 'Herbie could have overreacted to some other scent.'

'True.' The professor was stroking his chin. 'But there's something a little off about him, isn't there? Something not quite right.'

He had good instincts, the professor. But not good enough.

'Of course there's something wrong with me,' I said. 'I'm hurting. Bad. I can't eat, I can't sleep, I can't hump. I'm a wreck, sir.' I looked up, showing him doe-eyes. 'And I'm hoping this trip to your country will help me, somehow. Help cure me or make me better.'

That got him, especially the way I'd called him 'sir'. He signed off on the form. He even let Shooter tell me the name of a casino: the Nugget. After that, when they said I could go, I got pretty emotional. It must have been all that weed. I kept thanking them and giving them hugs. I was bawling, too. I could hardly stand. Herbie's handler had to walk me to the door of the Customs office. Herbie was waiting out there, tied to a post. He whined at me. I held out my hand to stroke him, but he bit it instead. Not hard, just a little nip. I guess he was pissed off that I'd pulled one over on them.

'Bad Herbie,' his owner said, smacking his nose. 'Bad dog.'

She apologised, and I told her it was okay. He hadn't drawn blood.

'Have a good trip,' she told me, 'and stay out of trouble.'

I told her I'd try. As I headed for my car, Herbie was still growling.

chapter 10

Our crew showed up, en masse, at this pub on the Eastside, near Cordova. The floor was covered in floral carpet, mottled by decades of spilled beer, spit, and probably blood. One corner of the bar-room had been partitioned off with glass walls to serve as a smoking area. Overhead fans sucked the smoke straight up through the ceiling. Considering it was mid-afternoon, there were more people in there than I'd expected. Mostly old guys in jean jackets and baseball hats, nursing bottles of Molson, keeping it pretty real. They stared at us as we ferried in all our film equipment.

'Let's do it quick, guys,' the director said. 'In and out.'

In this scene, the jock and the junkie were supposed to have stopped off somewhere along the road. They had a few drinks at the bar and they left. That was the whole scene.

'I want you to drink left-handed,' he told the jock.

'But I'm right-handed.'

'The left side represents the unconscious. It'll be symbolic.'

The DP and the grip were busy setting up the lights. The sound guy busted out his boom and shotgun mic and ran a few tests. The manager of the bar couldn't believe it. She'd agreed to let us shoot because the director had promised her a bit part, and no hassles. Now her bar was filling up with sandbags and lighting stands and tripods. Our thousand-watt baby was shining right in her customers' faces. They pulled down their baseball caps to shield their eyes. The floor was a mess of cables and cords that the bar staff kept tripping over. The manager wandered around, gawking. She was a thin woman

40

with twig-like legs and no breasts. I think she was half-cut. She kept saying, 'I didn't know it would be like *this*.'

Finally the director was ready to do a take. He called me and the DP over and described an elaborate shot he had in mind, with the camera drifting down the bar and panning around and coming to settle on the actors. It sounded like a real bamboozler. 'You with me, Trevor?' he asked.

'No.'

They both looked at me. 'No?'

'Not really.' I yawned. I hadn't slept in over forty-eight hours. 'But I've got an idea. It seemed to work pretty well with the captain here operating the camera yesterday.' I clapped the DP on the shoulder. 'Why doesn't he take over for this shot?'

The director fiddled with the brim of his beanie. 'I'm sorry. Was I being unclear?'

'He just seems to understand your vision better.' I offered the camera to the DP. 'She's all yours, captain.'

The DP took the camera. You could tell he didn't like it, but he didn't say anything. Neither did the director. By that point I had a certain look about me. It was a look that seemed to say, keep me happy or I'll walk out of here and take my camera with me.

'Okay,' the director said. 'Positions, everybody.'

The DP clambered behind the bar and started rolling. I stood beside the director to watch the shot on his monitor. When he called action, the DP walked forward, panning along the bar. My camera didn't have a shoulder mount or harness, so it was hard to keep it steady.

'Cut,' the director said. 'That didn't quite work.'

'It's way too shaky,' I said.

The DP and the director huddled together to discuss how they could fix the problem. The rest of us had to wait. The sound guy fiddled with his cellphone. The manager lady muttered about the hassle and poured herself some wine. The customers sat and watched and drank. I squatted on the floor in front of the bar. Then, after a minute, I lay down on my side.

The carpet was hard and filthy and had a sour smell. I closed my eyes.

'Trevor?'

The director was standing over me. They'd finished their little pow-wow.

'We're ready to do another take.'

'Go ahead.'

'You're in the frame.'

I didn't move. I didn't want to move.

'It's impossible to get that shot,' I said. 'You need a Steadicam to get that shot.'

'Maybe you should take a little break, Trevor.'

'I could use a break.'

I went into the smoking area to hack a casual dart. I still hadn't learned how to inhale properly, so I took timid little puffs as I watched them. They ran through five or six takes, trying to get that shot. The last time, the director announced, 'Excellent – we got it.'

You could tell he was lying, though.

My break lasted for the rest of the day. The director didn't ask me to come back to help, and I didn't offer. Instead I watched them shoot the scene with my camera. After finishing my smoke, I'd sat down at a table with a bunch of old-timers. I bought a round of Bud Light and they started telling me about their jobs. They all worked in the shipyards. Considering I'd basically been fired I was feeling pretty good: giddy and dizzy and euphoric, almost as if I was high. It was the lack of food, I think. I've heard fasting can do that to you.

'You getting paid for this?'

One of the old-timers asked me that – this guy with no teeth and sandpaper skin.

'A hundred bucks.'

'Beats a kick in the balls.'

The scene wasn't long, but it took a long time to shoot – mostly because of the director's shot list. He wouldn't settle for a basic shot. He had my camera swooping and spinning

42

around the place like a rabid fruit bat. On top of that, there was the manager lady. When it came time to film her scene, instead of just letting her deliver the lines, he had to explain his artistic vision to her.

'For your role,' he said, putting his hands on her shoulders, 'I see you as a kind of succubus.'

'A succu-what?'

'A succubus, or dream-demon. This scene is very Lynchian.'

All she had to do was serve the jock and junkie drinks, but, as soon as he said that, her face went blank and she began fiddling with her necklace. 'I don't know if I can do it.'

'You'll do fine. Just remember: dream-demon.'

They started rolling, and she prowled into frame, with her fingers curled up as claws – like the vampire from Nosferatu. Then she glared at the two actors and declared, in this Bela Lugosi voice, 'Perhaps you lovebirds would like to try our special – the Bloody Mary!'

'Cut!' the director cried.

He couldn't get her to tone it down. It took almost as long to finish that shot as his art-house establishing shot, and both would probably end up on the cutting room floor. By then, me and the old-timers were about six beers deep, and feeling a bit mutinous.

'The guy's wasting time,' I told them. 'Not to mention my camera.'

'If it's *your* camera,' old sandpaper face said, 'then *you* should be the one in charge!'

They all pounded the table in agreement. They were right. I shoved back my chair and swaggered over to the bar where the DP and director were setting up the next shot.

'So far so good, eh?'

I punched the director in the shoulder, as if we were old friends. He looked at me warily. The evening crowd was coming in and the manager was nagging them to wrap up.

'I think we've done some great work today,' I said. 'But do you mind if I handle this final shot?' I put my hand on

43

the camera. Possessively. I had that look in my eye again. 'It would mean a lot to me. I think I could really bring something special to it.'

'It's only a steady shot,' the DP said.

'On the tripod,' the director added.

'Great,' I said, saluting the old-timers. 'Let's shoot this fucker!'

The whole table cheered. I switched on the camera, peered through the eyepiece and fiddled with the focus. The jock was doing his usual push-ups between takes. Then he sat back down at the bar next to the junkie. She stretched and brushed her hair out of her eyes.

'Rolling,' I shouted.

'Action!'

The two of them stood up and left. It was the end of the scene – the last shot of the day, the last shot of the film. It looked good and solid. I gave the director the thumbs-up.

'That's a wrap,' the director called, raising his arms, in a champion pose.

'Better get a safety,' I told him.

His arms came down. He knew I was right.

'One more, people.'

I made a twirling motion with my finger. 'I'm still rolling.'

The actors got back in position. I had my own reasons for wanting the safety. It was such a basic shot that they weren't using the monitor, and I'd noticed that you could see the director's reflection in the bar taps. As soon as he called 'action' I zoomed in slowly, until his face filled the scene. His features were stretched and skewed by the curve of the metal. He blinked like a bug-eyed goldfish. Blink. Blink.

'I'm the director,' I whispered into the camera's mic, 'and this is my movie.'

He kept blinking, oblivious.

chapter 11

As I pulled into the supermarket parking lot, my body-stone finally broke. It just seemed to crack open like an egg. The high oozed down my neck, my spine, my legs – infusing me with this mellow-yellow feeling. I got out of the car and hopped up on the hood and stood with my hands on my hips, surveying the landscape on the US side of the border. I saw a few low-lying buildings, a grassy verge, and some mud flats leading to the sea. Blaine didn't look much different from Surrey, but it felt different. I felt different. I savoured that feeling for a few minutes before jumping down.

Above the store's awning was a multicoloured sign, with block capital lettering: WE BEAT DUTY-FREE PRICES ON SNACKS FOOD LIQUOR CIGARETTES GIFTS. I strolled underneath it and through the revolving door. A cool wave of conditioned air washed over me. Near the entrance they had food displays to entice the weary traveller. The shelves were stacked with puffy bags, as big as pillows, of various American snacks: cheese balls and pretzels and nachos and pork rinds. I reached out, zombie-like, for a package of beef jerky, and squeezed. The cellophane crinkled deliciously, and I could feel the tenderness of the meat beneath. My stomach shuddered. I loved beef jerky. Zuzska had always hated it.

'You're fasting,' I said aloud, to remind myself. 'No more lapses.'

I got a shopping cart and wheeled it up and down the aisles. The store was huge and high-ceilinged, like a warehouse. I'd forgotten how big everything in America was. Not just the food and snacks but the shops, the cars, the highways, the people. The liquor section was the same. They had enough booze to fill up a swimming pool: two long aisles stocked with mickeys, twixers and forty-pounders. The overhead lights gave the glass and plastic a jewel-like glitter – an Aladdin's Cave of alcohol. I parked my cart and considered all the treasures, fondling the bottles in passing. They felt cool and smooth to the touch. I loaded my cart up with a shit-mix of twixers, mostly whisky and bourbon and gin.

I needed road pops, too. Beer and wine were in the next aisle over. There was a sign hanging over the shelves: *Is This Your Lucky Day?* If you bought a flat of Lucky Lager and a carton of Lucky Strike, you got ten bucks off. I grabbed one of each and lowered them into my cart, then explored a little more. The remaining aisles contained souvenirs: mugs and flags and playing cards and fake licence plates and stickers that said *Land of the Free.*

'That's where I am,' I said, slapping a sticker on my chest. 'The Land of the Free.'

I stood on the back bar of my cart, like a kid, and coasted around the store – gliding up and down the aisles. Other customers stopped to stare. The cashier must have seen me, too. She had her arms crossed as I cruised up to her till. Like everything else in the store, she was big: a big lady with big, frizzy hair and a big mole in the centre of her forehead.

'I suppose you've got ID,' she said.

That was something else I'd forgotten about the States. In Canada, the drinking age is nineteen. In the US, it's twenty-one. I fumbled around for my wallet. I had some difficulties getting my driver's licence out. When I did, the woman stared at it for a long time. It was a BC licence, and the backdrop was a Canadian landscape: forests and mountains and the sun shining over the sea.

'This looks real,' the lady said.

'I'm a real person.'

She looked from me, to my photo, and back to me. 'But it says you're twenty-one.'

'I am. Twenty-one and a half.'

'No kidding. Hey, sis – come look at this.'

Another employee was stocking shelves nearby. She waddled over and went around behind the counter. She looked exactly the same as the till clerk except she didn't have a mole. She had a mullet instead – a big grey mullet, like a dead squirrel lying on her head. They both studied my licence, tilting it back and forth to check the hologram and lamination. In their matching uniforms, leaning close together, they looked like a set of conjoined twins.

Finally, the one with the mullet declared, 'Yep – it's real enough.'

'Ain't that something,' the other said. She glanced at my photo one last time, then handed the licence back to me. 'Guess we're in business, son.'

'Thanks,' I said.

By that point a few other customers had got in line behind me. The mullet-headed sister stuck around to help bag my purchases. As she did, she was still looking me over.

'What a cute baby-face he's got,' she said.

'Uh-huh,' her sister agreed. 'He's got to be the youngest-looking twenty-one-year-old I've ever seen. I wouldn't mind taking him home and teaching him a thing or two.'

She winked at the mullet, who laughed so hard she started wheezing. Behind me the other customers were snickering, too. The sisters insisted on helping me place all the bags in my cart, one by one, carefully arranging them. I paid in Canadian cash. The exchange rate was terrible but I didn't have any American money yet and just wanted to get out of there.

As I was turning to go, they offered me a keychain. Apparently you got a free keychain if you bought enough booze. The keychain was in the shape of a baby soother.

'I don't need that.'

'Sure you do, baby-face.'

'Okay,' I said, grabbing it. 'Whatever.'

They told me to come back soon. As I pushed my cart away from the till, I heard them joking and chuckling with the other customers about me. Outside I could still hear them, as if their voices were following me, floating around my head.

I loaded my beer and smokes and booze in the trunk, keeping a twixer of whisky with me as I got in the front. Near Tsawwassen I'd stopped for coffee, and the empty cup was still lying in the footwell of the passenger seat. I shook the dregs out the window, then opened the whisky. The cap made that satisfying cracking sound when the seal broke, and the bottle went glug-glug-glug as I filled up the cup. I was still stoned enough to think that what I was doing was vaguely awesome in some way.

'Show *you* who's young,' I said, and took a swig.

I turned on the car. It trembled beneath me, like a horse at the starting gate. I pressed the gas down a few times, revving the engine. In the rear-view, peering back at me, was a smooth-cheeked, cherub-faced boy. I angled it away, so I didn't have to look at him.

chapter 12

I was lying face-down on the floor of my suite. That was what I did every night, waiting for something to happen, wanting something to happen. I fantasised about the walls of our house falling down, the roof collapsing, the floors giving out. I daydreamed about a tornado tearing through town, and carrying away the remains of my old life.

'Trevor?'

I rolled over. My stepmom was standing by the door that connects the suite to their house. She still had on her work uniform – this white skirt and blouse – and looked like an apparition, hovering there.

'Hey, Amanda,' I said, as if everything was totally normal. That's what we do in our house: pretend everything is normal, even when it's not. 'What's up?'

'Your father and I thought you might like to have dinner with us.'

I didn't, obviously. But I could tell the whole thing had been orchestrated for me – probably by Amanda. Since she's not my real mom, she tends to overdo the mothering part.

'I'll come over in a bit.'

When I got there, they were already sitting down at the table in their kitchen. Above the table is an overhead fan. The fan doesn't keep anything cool. It's mostly decorative. It just goes around and around and around, like the hands of a very fast clock.

'Prince boy-child,' my dad said, rolling his eyes. 'Thank you for finally gracing us with your presence.'

I took my usual seat between them. They'd ordered Szechwan. In the centre of the table sat styrofoam containers stuffed with spring rolls and chow mein and moo shu pork.

'How's everything going with your film?' Amanda asked.

'Oh, so-so.'

She smiled, ladling a nest of noodles on to my plate. She still had her name-tag pinned to her blouse. She works downtown, at an injection site, handing out free needles to heroin addicts and helping them shoot up. They all adore her.

'How many days do you have left?' she asked.

'We finished today. The wrap party is on Friday.'

My dad grunted, which meant he had something to say. He just couldn't say it yet, because his mouth was full of spring roll. We waited while he chewed and swallowed.

He asked, 'What are you going to do after that?'

'Go back to Ecological, I guess.' That was the landscaping company where I worked cutting lawns: Ecological Lawn Care. 'And wait for another film job to come up.'

'What about Prague? I thought you had your ticket booked.'

'I do have my ticket booked. That's a couple of weeks off, though.'

I poked at the pile of food in front of me, like a ragpicker looking for scraps. I was pulling that old trick, where you shift things around without actually eating much. I couldn't get away with it entirely, though. Amanda was staring at my plate.

'Aren't you hungry, dear?'

I managed to swallow a mouthful. 'Not really. I think I had some bad food on set today.'

'I'll make you some tea,' she said.

'Peppermint would be nice.'

She was already up, rooting through the tea drawer. My dad gave me one of his looks – a kind of exasperated, 'how dare you?' look. He thinks I take advantage of her trying too hard to be my mom. Which I do, obviously.

'Your food will get cold,' he told her.

'It'll just take a minute.'

My dad started attacking his food again, as if he wanted to eat enough for the both of them before it went to waste. He stabbed at the plate with his chopsticks. The ends made little clicking sounds, like the mandibles of a ravenous insect.

'How is Zuzska, anyways?' he asked.

'Not so good,' I said.

He stopped eating. Amanda brought me the mug of tea. She sat back down and they waited for some kind of explanation.

'We're having problems.'

I put my hands around my mug, cradling its warmth, and blew on the surface of the tea. Swirls of peppermint steam spiralled up in front of me.

'I mean, we're having a break, I guess.'

I couldn't bring myself to tell them more than that. It seemed like enough.

'So that's it.' My dad crossed his arms, shook his head and chuckled – like a doctor who had finally diagnosed a tricky case. 'That's why you're staying up all night listening to Leonard Cohen and raiding my liquor cabinet.'

I nodded. He had me there.

'Poor Zuzska,' Amanda said.

My dad tilted his head, as if he'd misheard. 'Poor Zuzska?'

'Poor both of you.'

After that, neither of them said anything for a minute or so. It was fairly awkward. The overhead fan whipped around and around. Then my dad picked up his chopsticks and started eating again.

'Anyways,' he said, between bites, 'I hope you don't use this as an excuse to do something stupid and irresponsible.'

Until then, I hadn't really considered it. But he put the idea in my head. I began thinking: I should probably do something stupid and irresponsible…

chapter 13

South of the border, Highway 99 becomes an American interstate, the I-5. There's this long stretch before Ferndale where the highway divides, so that the southbound and northbound routes separate. I followed the southbound side as it looped through hills covered in scrawny spruce trees and pipe-cleaner pines. There was hardly any traffic and the blacktop had been freshly paved and the Neon wanted to gallop, so I opened it up and let her run. I had my cup of whisky in the cup-holder and took a swig every few miles. I don't think I was going that fast. If anything, I was probably under the speed limit. But the tarmac felt slippery and the car had a tendency to wobble. I kept overcorrecting, weaving back and forth. It was like trying to steer a canoe.

I wasn't listening to the radio. I'd decided not to, as part of my fast. I wouldn't eat any food and I wouldn't listen to any music for the entire trip. As I drove I held my arm out the window, spread my fingers, and felt the wind slide between them. Then I leaned all the way out there, sticking my head in the slipstream. The air blasted back my hair, made my eyes water. I felt like an explorer, standing at the prow of his ship, arriving in the new land.

'Here I come, America!' I shouted, shaking my fist at the landscape. 'You beautiful country! I'm going to conquer you and plunder you and make you mine! Do you hear me?'

A white car pulled alongside me. It was an old box-style sedan driven by a woman with a shaved head. She honked and waggled her finger like a schoolteacher, chastising me. I was encroaching on her lane. I swung back and gave her a mock-salute as she passed.

'I am a *conquistador*!' I shouted.

I reached Bellingham in less than half an hour. From the highway I spotted the factory outlet stores where I'd often shopped with my old man, and the Best Western where I'd stayed with Zuzska the year before. By that point my throat had gone dry and my tongue had shrivelled up. I also had a brutal headache that felt like a hairline fracture at the base of my skull. I was burning out, big-time. I tore open a pack of Lucky Strike and smoked a few, but the nicotine didn't help at all.

'I need more juice,' I yelled, banging the steering wheel.

On the outskirts of town I pulled into a gas station. I thought I might be able to pick up an iced coffee or an energy drink, but when I got inside I found something even better. In the dairy section they had canisters of whipped cream. That would get me going. I gathered up an armful of cans and carried them to the till. When I put them down they clanked and rolled all over the counter. The clerk was a girl about my age, with short pigtails that stuck straight out from the sides of her head. She wrinkled her nose and began scanning my cans.

'Huffing whippets is dangerous, you know,' she said.

'I'm just making a big birthday cake.'

'My friend knew somebody who died doing it.'

Nobody dies huffing whippets. That's a total urban legend.

'I'm sorry to hear that.'

She shoved the cans in a bag and took my money.

Back in the car, I popped the cap off the first canister, but the clerk was watching me through the window so I didn't try it out until I'd left the lot and pulled on to the highway. I had to steer with one hand. Putting the nozzle to my lips, I thumbed the trigger and inhaled. If you hold the canister upright, you don't get any cream, only gas. I hadn't huffed whippets since I was a kid. The sweet chemical taste was like a blast of *déjà vu*, and the effect was instantaneous – as if some-body had lopped off the top of my scalp.

I kept the canister in the cup-holder, next to my whisky. Every few miles I'd take a sip of booze, or a dose of nitrous. Whisky and whippets was an ingenious combination. They seemed to balance each other out. Each time I hit the nitrous, I imagined it was like *real* nitrous – the kind they use in street-race movies to give the car an extra kick. I'd take a huff and hold it in, making my head spin, and accelerate until I had to breathe again.

Doing that, I blew past Mount Vernon and Stanwood and Arlington and Marysville. I'd been through all those places before, some of them with her. They were sinkholes like Tsawwassen: memory swamps that threatened to draw me in, bog me down. I didn't stop at any of them. I didn't even look at them. Whenever I was tempted, I just went faster.

chapter 14

Technically, I didn't get invited to the wrap party – I'd just overheard the DP and grip talking about it. I didn't really want to go, either. But being around people was better than being on my own. They held the party at this hotel downtown. I can't remember the name, but it's close to English Bay, just off Denman Street. The bar has wall-length mirrors and crystal chandeliers. Forty years ago it would have been in full bloom. Now the décor is fading, the furniture is wilting, and the barflies have begun to arrive. It's pretty much a dive. But it's cool to go to dives, if you're hipsters or indie filmmakers who've just wrapped a shoot.

When I arrived, our group was standing in the centre of the room, beneath one of the chandeliers. I got myself a Molson and sidled over. Most of the cast and crew were there, along with some people I assumed were their friends. They were all dressed in skinny jeans and scarves and beanies.

The director was telling the story about the bar manager he'd cast.

'And then,' he said, 'she kept calling them "lovebirds". I mean, who says that?'

Everybody laughed. I lingered on the outside of the group, wishing I'd worn a beanie too. Then I thought, I'd rather shoot myself than wear a beanie.

'You'll see it later,' the director was saying. 'Her performance is priceless.'

'You're screening the rushes?' I asked, as casually as possible.

'Sure – in the conference room.'

He looked surprised to see me. He'd be even more surprised when he saw the close-up I'd shot, of his face in the bar taps. I wouldn't be sticking around for that.

Eventually the one big conversation broke into a bunch of little conversations. The DP noticed me standing alone and came over to talk to me. He was all right like that. He wasn't a full-on hipster, either. He had the scarf, but not the beanie.

I said, 'This shoot has been tough for me, man.'

'You were a little off your game.'

'I was way off my game.'

I wrapped an arm around his shoulder, drawing him in.

'I haven't been sleeping or eating. That's why I threw away the piece of pizza. You remember when I did that, on the highway?'

He said he remembered.

'Well, that's why.'

'That was good pizza, bro.'

'It's all because of my girlfriend. She lives in Prague.'

'Ah.' He started shaking his head, even though I hadn't told him what had happened, or what she'd done. 'There you go, bro. The long-distance thing never works. I've tried it. Trust me. You've got to let go and move on.'

'Move on how?'

He shrugged. 'There's plenty of other fish in the sea.'

I'd been waiting for somebody to feed me that old chestnut. I had my answer ready.

'There's other fish, but none like *this* fish. She's rare and exotic. A real catch.'

'I hear you, bro.'

He patted me on the shoulder, and moved off to talk to somebody else. I stood on my own for a bit, then wandered over to the bar and ordered three shots of whatever whisky they had on special. Famous Grouse, I think. I drank them one after another – as if I were holding a one-man drinking contest – and chased with the rest of my beer. I'd been nursing a mickey of gin on the bus ride over and by that point I felt pretty tanquerayed.

At the other end of the bar, the green-haired actress and the jock actor were standing with their friends. She made the mistake of glancing in my direction. That was my cue. I barrelled over and butted into their little circle. They all stopped talking and stared at me.

'I like your hair,' I said to her.

'Thanks.'

'Is that dyed or natural?'

I think I was trying to make a joke. Nobody laughed, though.

'Do you mind if I smell it?'

Before she answered, I leaned in and sort of sniffed at her hair.

'It looks like seaweed,' I said, 'but it smells like flowers.'

She arched her eyebrows at her friends, as if to say, who *is* this asshole?

'Hey, buddy,' the jock said, shooing me away. 'Go walk it off, eh?'

They turned their backs and tightened their circle, like a herd of elephants.

Later on, all the cast and crew vanished. I guess they went off to watch the rushes. I sat at the bar alone. Then, after a while, I realised I was no longer alone. Two guys had appeared on the stools next to me. I first noticed them in the mirror behind the bar, and glanced over.

'You look like you could use a drink,' I said.

They nodded without looking at me. One of them was stockier than the other, but they both had shaggy hair and crusty clothes and half-grown beards, like curly black moss.

'I'll have more rum,' one said.

'Same,' the other said. 'More rum.'

I ordered rum, too – since it seemed appropriate. The bartender splashed out some Havana Club for us. We raised our glasses and clinked.

'Tonight,' the stocky one said, 'is the worst night of our life.'

'The very worst,' the other added.

They told me that the two of them were brothers. That didn't surprise me – they looked like brothers. What surprised me was that they also happened to be filmmakers.

'Weird,' I said. 'Me too.'

They claimed they'd been driving across America, shooting a documentary. They'd spent eighteen weeks on the road, in the company of a drug-dealing motorcycle gang.

'Like the Hell's Angels?' I asked.

'Crazier than the Hell's Angels.'

It had taken them months to find a gang willing to let them document its activities. Even then, there were certain conditions. The leader told them they could only go on the road with the gang if they underwent the same initiation rites as any other member. They had to slit open a live cobra and drink its blood. They had to pierce their balls and take a tonne of mescaline. They even had to get the gang's sign tattooed on their biceps.

'You're shitting me.'

They both rolled up their left sleeves. They had matching snake tattoos.

'That was just the beginning.'

In Montana the gang had ripped off a truckload of industrial chemicals. They used the stuff to make drugs, apparently. At some bar in Texas, there had been a shoot-out with a bunch of Mexicans, and a big chase through the desert. The two brothers had filmed all that, and a bunch of other weird shit. They'd seen meth labs and gangland executions and crooked politicians paid to look the other way. They estimated that they'd shot five hundred hours of footage, maybe more. It was supposed to be the definitive documentary on biker gangs.

'Then we got to Vancouver,' the stocky one said.

'We were only going to spend one day here,' his brother added, 'before heading home, to start editing our footage. We decided to visit Gastown, to see some sights.'

I lowered my head. I could already see where this was going. All the tourists get lured to Gastown. It's this historic area near the water, with souvenir shops and a steam-powered clock. But it also happens to be two blocks away from Hastings and Main, which topped some poll as the worst area in Canada. That's where my stepmom's heroin addicts hang out, along with all the other nutjobs in the city.

'We parked on the street…'

'…and somebody broke into our van.'

'No,' I said. 'Please don't tell me they took – '

'Everything,' they said together. 'They took everything.'

All their camera gear had been stolen, and all their footage of the gangs. Thinking about that, and about what they'd gone through to get it, actually made me sick to my stomach.

'What are you going to do?' I asked.

They raised their glasses and drank. I imagined them sitting there forever, watering themselves with rum. They would put down roots, like plants, and slowly grow into their stools.

'You could print up flyers,' I said. 'Pin them around Gastown. Offer a reward. Say you don't even want the equipment back, just your footage.'

They shook their heads in unison.

'That won't work.'

'This is Canada, boys. It's full of congenial criminals and gentle junkies. Appeal to their soft West Coast hearts.'

I don't know if I convinced them or not. By then all three of us were swaying at the bar, like cattle drinking from the same trough. We downed one more round together.

'Fuck,' I said. 'That must have been something, eh? Being on the road.'

They were both staring into their empty glasses, like mirror images of each other.

'Best time of our life.'

That was when I first started thinking of doing something similar. Not joining a biker gang, obviously. But hitting the road. I'd been filming a movie about it. Then there'd been these guys. All the signs seemed to be pointing in one direction: away from here.

chapter 15

Somewhere past Everett I hit the traffic jam. It was one of those insane traffic jams that spring up instantly, like a booby trap. I was taking a sip of whisky when all the cars in front of me just stopped in a solid wall. I dropped my cup and grabbed the wheel and stomped on the brake pedal. The tyres skidded and I fishtailed back and forth, sliding to a halt at a wonky angle, inches from the car in front of me. The driver noticed, too. She turned around to glare at me. It was that same bald-headed lady that had passed me before – the one in the white sedan. I waggled my fingers at her, just to acknowledge that I'd almost rear-ended her.

'Sorry,' I mouthed.

I'd spilled whisky all over my lap. It looked as if I'd pissed my pants. I didn't have anything to sponge it off with, so I had to wallow in my wet jeans as more cars pulled up behind me. Like everything else in America, that traffic jam was big. Ahead of me, I could see four endless rows of cars, trucks, SUVs, trailers, eighteen-wheelers, camper vans, RVs and motorcycles. All the vehicles shuddered and quivered, as if waiting for some signal that would start a gigantic race. But the signal never came. I rolled up my windows to keep out the exhaust fumes, and stared at the back of the bald lady's car. It was an ancient Dodge St Regis, with one of those silver fish-shapes stuck to the bumper.

We were in the lane next to the shoulder. Behind me was a Ford pickup truck, and on my left was a mini-van, filled with kids, all of them bouncing around like balls of flubber. People were smoking, listening to music, playing games, doing the kinds of things you do in a traffic jam. I smoked, too. And every so often I sucked on my canister of whipped cream.

One time, as I was doing that, I noticed the lady eyeing me in her rear-view. Then she got out of her car, and came towards me. I managed to stash the whisky under the seat before she reached my door. She rapped once on the window. I rolled it down an inch or two.

'I passed you before,' she said.

She had a pale, perfect face, like a plaster cast. She was wearing a beige gown and robes. I think she must have belonged to some sort of religious cult or sect. A real zealot.

'You were swerving all over the place.'

I sunk lower in my seat, glanced around. People were staring at us.

I said, 'I thought I saw something on the road.'

'There was nothing on the road.' She sounded both certain and conciliatory – like a nurse accustomed to giving patients bad news. 'Nothing at all. We both know that.'

'There was a rabbit. A little white rabbit. I didn't want to hit a rabbit.'

'You're drunk.'

'I don't drink, ever. I'm a monk.'

'I can smell it on you. And you're huffing on *that*.' She sighed and shook her head. 'If it was just you, fine. But you could hurt somebody. I'm going to have to report you.'

'Wait – report me to who?'

But she was already walking away. She got back in her car. I sat with my hands on the wheel, watching. She dug her cellphone out of her purse and dialled. She was serious.

'Shit,' I said.

There was a bit of space between me and the truck. I backed up, threw the Neon in drive and pulled on to the shoulder. It was wide enough to drive on, so I did. I floored it and took off. In my wing mirror I saw the lady scrambling out of her car. She shielded her eyes and stared after me. She might have been trying to read my licence plate, but I couldn't tell if she got it. I just kept going, zipping past all the gridlocked traffic. I flicked on my hazard lights in case anybody wondered what the hell I was doing.

Half a mile along, the traffic started moving again. I pulled back into the lane. The guy behind me honked at me for cutting in, but that was it. We crawled through a work zone, past diggers and pylons and men in high-vis bibs. On the other side, it all opened up again. I got in the fast lane and grabbed my nitrous and took a couple of long, dizzying hits. I sucked the can dry, then tossed it out the window. It landed on the shoulder and danced around.

'Fuck you, America,' I shouted, laughing. 'Is that all you've got?'

From somewhere ahead, I heard a rumbling noise. It might have been a jet plane, or it might have been thunder. Either way, it freaked me out a little. I rolled my window back up.

chapter 16

The sole on my right shoe was peeling off at the toe, and I could hear it slapping away as I walked down Granville Street. After getting hammered with those two brothers, I'd left the wrap party. It was just after ten and the sidewalks were crowded with drunks and clubbers and bar-stars. I passed all the other people without really seeing them. Instead I was seeing her. I saw her smoking in the line-up outside the Commodore, her silhouette back-lit by the club's strobe lights. I saw her on the ice rink at Robson Square, gliding in figure-eights and performing perfect pirouettes. I saw her sprawled on the art gallery steps, soaking up sun, and I saw her in a bubble-tea café by the library, peering at me through the window. Near Cambie Street I saw her floating along, completely candy-flipped, her mouth open wide as she tried to catch a snowflake on her tongue. I saw her everywhere. I couldn't shake her.

'Demons begone,' I said, flailing at the air.

I fled. I rushed along with my head down, forcing everybody else to get out of my way. If they didn't get out of my way, I'd bulldoze them and shoulder them aside. I didn't do it to the girls, obviously. You don't bulldoze girls. But I was bulldozing all the guys.

'Easy, there,' one warned me.

'Watch out, man,' another called back.

Then, out of nowhere, this guy bulldozed *me* – so hard that I spun sideways and fell back flat on my ass, getting one of those electric, funny-bone jolts of pain, right in my coccyx.

'Hey,' I shouted after him. 'Watch where you're going, shit-dick.'

The guy turned around. He was wearing black boots and a leather jacket and looked like the kind of biker those brothers had been making a film about. He also had on this pair of super-dark aviator shades. I don't know why he was wearing them at night, but he was.

'What are you gonna do?' he said.

I stood up. This was it.

'I'm gonna kick your ass, Cory Hart.'

The guy laughed and palmed my face like a basketball and shoved me back. I tripped and fell over again. I was beginning to feel like one of those inflatable punching clowns that bob up and down.

'Don't waste my time, kid,' he said. 'Come find me when your balls drop.'

He kept walking. I stayed sitting on the ground, hanging my head. Eventually I picked myself up. I'd skinned my knuckles and there were bits of grit stuck in the cuts.

'Maybe I will,' I called after him.

The restaurants and bars gave way to strip clubs and all-night pharmacies and sex shops with half-naked mannequins in the windows. One of the sex shops advertised peepshows for a dollar. I went on in. Big plastic dildos and vibrators dangled from the ceiling, and hanging from the walls was all kinds of bondage gear: crotchless pants and leather chaps and gimp masks and other stuff I didn't even recognise. At the back of the store I saw a viewfinder and a coin slot. I put a loonie in the slot and looked through the viewfinder. A screen flickered to life. It showed a lady giving a Chinese guy a massage. Then she started giving him a handjob. It was just a video, not a real peepshow. I could've watched the same thing at home for free.

Somebody coughed behind me. An old man in a chequered suit was waiting to go next. He spat some phlegm into a napkin. A single strand lingered, stretching from the napkin to his lips.

'You done?' he asked.

'It's all yours,' I told him.

The peepshow had given me an idea – one of those ingenious ideas you only get when you're hammered. I went up to the till. The guy working had a spiky mohawk and piercings all over his face. He even had one of those fat discs in his lower lip like an African bushman.

'Is there a place called Madame Cleo's around here?' I asked.

'The massage parlour?'

'I heard they give other stuff. Extras.'

It was a rumour that had gone around in high school. I didn't know if it was true, but figured it might be a way of getting over the little plumbing problem I'd developed.

He shrugged. 'It's on Richards. Two blocks up.'

'Wicked. Thanks.'

I didn't have trouble finding the place. It was right where he said. It was open, too. The lights were on, but you couldn't see inside because the windows were foggy and opaque. A neon sign hung next to the door, with a glowing rose beneath the words *Madame Cleo's*.

I knocked on the door. After a minute it opened. A middle-aged lady stood there, in a pink blouse and pencil skirt. She looked me up and down.

'Are you okay?' she asked.

'Can I get a massage?'

'Of course. You don't have to knock.'

'Sorry.'

I walked into a kind of lobby area. It smelled as if it had recently been carpet-cleaned. Hanging on the walls were abstract paintings of bathers at the beach. The secretary-lady had a desk, which she sat down behind. Across from it, two men in suits were waiting in chairs.

The secretary opened her book.

'It'll be a fifteen-minute wait. What type of massage would you like?'

'What type can I get?'

She smiled. 'We do shiatsu and Swedish and Indian head massages, among others.'

'Just a regular massage. A back massage.'

She asked me if I had a preference of masseuse, and I said no. Then, as she was making a little note, I added, 'I'd prefer not to have a redhead, or a Czech woman.'

She looked back up, her mouth pursed to a rosebud.

'I'm not really picky, though.'

I took a chair beside the two other men. Neither of them looked at me, or talked to me. I stared at them and sort of sneered. I was thinking, at least I've got a good reason for being here. I'm young and drunk and I've lost my sex drive. What's *your* excuse?

'Been here before?' I asked the nearest one.

He mumbled something and shook his head. He was reading the *Sun*. He rustled the pages and raised it, putting a barrier between us.

After about ten minutes a blonde woman came in from the hallway. The secretary nodded at me. It was my turn, apparently. The two businessmen must have been waiting for a particular masseuse. That was fine by me. This one was wearing white slacks and a crisp white blouse. She looked like a military nurse and was fairly hot, in a severe sort of way.

'Come with me,' she ordered.

I followed her down the hall and into a room about the size of a doctor's office. It had a massage table in the centre and a laminate counter off to one side. On the counter, bottles of oil and tubes of lubricant lay scattered around a portable stereo system. She instructed me to take off my jeans and shirt and lie on the table. I stretched out on my stomach, in my boxer shorts. I hadn't been planning on coming to a massage parlour, so I was wearing really lame boxers – these red Christmas boxers decorated with cartoon reindeer.

'Let's see,' she said. 'A back massage, yes?'

She had a European accent. Maybe that was part of her act.

'To start with,' I said.

The table had a faux-leather cover that stuck to my skin like clingfilm and squeaked whenever I moved. I waited, shifting and squeaking, as she popped open the CD player and put some music on. It was choir music – an all-male voice choir. It wouldn't have been my first choice, but I could roll with it.

'Is that Mozart?' I asked.

'Is Bach,' she said.

She was rubbing her hands together to warm up the oil. Then she leaned over me and started doing things to my back. She smoothed it out with her palms and pounded it with her fists and kneaded it with her knuckles, working it over like fresh dough.

'Oooh,' I said. 'Ahhh.'

The choir started singing louder.

'Is nice, yes?'

'Very nice.'

It went on like that for a while. I didn't know what the protocol was when it came to getting extras. I figured it might be up to me to ask, so next time she stopped to get more massage oil, I rolled over on to my side.

'Is something wrong?' she asked.

'I was just wondering if I could buy some extras.'

'What do you mean?'

'You know. Extras. Fringe benefits.' I propped myself up on my elbow. My face had gone as red as my boxers. 'A hand release. Is that what you call it? Like a handjob.'

I was trying to act extremely casual about the whole thing, but lying like that made it tricky. Plus, 'handjob' is one of those words that happen to sound very funny. I smiled when I said it, and she smiled when she heard it. It was like a little joke between us. She took me by the shoulders and eased me back down on my stomach.

'Who told you we did that?' she asked.

'Some guy I know.'

She ran both her hands from my shoulders to my waist, on either side of my spine – using my back like a washboard.

'A lot of people think that,' she said, 'but it's not true.'

'Oh.' I figured she was probably lying, but I didn't want to get in an argument about whether or not she would give me a handjob. 'I guess that's my mistake, then. Sorry.'

She kept massaging me. Partly I was relieved. I mean, even if she had agreed I might not have been able to get it up. On the CD, the male voice choir was going crazy and singing at the tops of their lungs – almost like they were all getting the handjob I'd missed out on.

'Where *can* a guy get a handjob?' I asked.

'Beats me.' By then, she'd dropped the fake accent. 'Down on Dundas, I guess.'

She meant this super-sketchy area, east of Gastown, where all the junkie hookers hang out.

'I mean a trustworthy handjob. A safe and legal one.'

'The only place it's legal is Amsterdam. Or Nevada. The brothels.'

She started karate-chopping my back, super-fast, to finish things up.

'Ouch,' I said. 'Oww.'

It cost me a hundred and twenty bucks, that back massage – more than I got in a day for shooting that goddamn film. But it was worth it. I knew where I wanted to go, now.

chapter 17

As I neared Seattle, I saw that it was enveloped by fog. Some kind of sea-mist had crept in off the bay, obscuring the skyline. Tendrils of vapour curled between office towers, wrapped around apartment blocks, encircled overpasses – as if a giant squid had settled on the city and subdued it. The only thing free of the mist was the Space Needle, jutting up like a lighthouse beacon. The red light at the top flashed every three or four seconds, warning travellers away. *Don't come here*, it seemed to be saying. *Keep going*.

The Space Needle was another place I'd been with her. We'd passed it every time I picked her up from Sea-Tac Airport. I'd kept promising to take her up there one day. She had a thing about heights so I planned it out as a surprise. I booked us tickets to the Space Needle and a night in a four-star hotel that overlooked the harbour.

When we got to the Space Needle, it looked closed. Only half a dozen cars were in the parking lot. There was nobody going through the doors, and nobody inside, either. The interior had a sci-fi design and was constructed entirely out of steel and glass, with curved staircases and abstract shapes hanging from the ceiling. It was cold and empty and creepy.

'Where are all the tourists?' Zuzska whispered.

'Maybe they're at the top.'

They weren't. The observation deck was just as empty. When we stepped out of the elevator, a security guard was standing by the doors. He was shaped like a bowling pin, with a tiny head and huge hips. As he checked our tickets, I asked him if it was always this quiet.

'Not really.' He smiled, in an embarrassed sort of way, and handed back the tickets. 'We received a terrorist threat yesterday, so I guess most people are keeping their distance.' When he saw our faces, the guy added, 'You can get a refund at the bottom if you want.'

I asked Zuzska what she thought, but she said she wasn't worried about terrorists.

'Attagirl,' the guard said.

We had the whole observation deck to ourselves – except for this family of Sikhs who apparently hadn't heard about the terrorist threat either. They were on the side facing Mount Rainier. We went to the opposite side, overlooking Elliot Bay and Olympic Park. The deck was exposed to the sky. Safety wires were strung crosswise around the perimeter to keep people from jumping. In places, though, there was a slight gap between the wires and the guard rail. It was a fairly bad design: a child could have slipped through. Or a skinny girl.

'I bet I could get out there,' Zuzska said.

'I bet you could, too. Look – there's a telescope over there.' I tried to guide her away. In Italy, on Capri, she'd walked right to the edge of this hundred-foot cliff and stood there, on a crumbling outcrop, staring down. When it came to heights she was absolutely fearless.

'Hold my bag.'

'Zu – '

She was already on her belly. She wriggled under the wire, soldier-style. There was a safety platform on the other side, about four or five feet wide. She stood up on it.

'Jesus Christ, Zuzska.'

'I just want to look.'

She said it as if I was the one being unreasonable. I clutched her bag and watched her creep towards the edge. From there it was a straight drop to Seattle – over five hundred feet.

As she peered down, I heard somebody cry out behind me, 'Don't do it!'

It was that guard – the bowling pin guard. He rushed over, waving his arms. 'It's okay, man,' I said.

'Stay back! I'm trained to handle this kind of thing. Everybody stay back.'

There was nobody around. Just me and him.

'She's only looking.'

He wouldn't listen. He shoved me to one side and held out his hands to her. 'You don't want to do this.'

Zuzska had turned around. She gazed at me and the guard. She was only six inches from the edge. A low-lying cloud drifted by, wrapping her up like a shroud and obscuring the platform beneath her. For a moment it looked as if she was standing on air, on nothing.

'However bad it is,' the guard said, 'it will pass. People care about you. People love you.' He put his hand to his chest, over his heart. 'I love you. Now come back, all right? Just come back and we'll talk.'

Zuzska stepped away from the edge. The guy kept encouraging her, convinced he was talking her down, and raised the safety wire so she could slip back under. When she stood up he grabbed her in a bear-hug. She looked at me over his shoulder, her expression poker-faced and priceless.

'You're okay now,' he kept saying. 'It's all right.'

'I wasn't going to jump,' she said.

'I know. I know you weren't.'

By that point the Sikhs had come over, too. Eventually two other guards showed up. They took Zuzska aside and gave her a real grilling. If she hadn't been Czech, they probably would have taken her in, but it would be a pretty big hassle to charge a foreigner for something like that, and I guess they decided not to bother. Plus there was the issue of liability. They've changed the design of those safety wires since then, and I'm sure it was because of her.

I'd reached the edge of the mist. Up ahead, long tentacles of fog snaked across the lanes and twisted between the other vehicles. Everybody was going slow to avoid crashing. I'd tried to stick to the highway and skirt around the city, but the mist was drawing me on, luring me in.

From out of the haze a hotel materialised: the Harbourside Inn. That was where we'd stayed, after the Space Needle fiasco, as part of the package I'd booked. We got a suite on the top floor, overlooking the marina. There was even a private balcony. As soon as she saw that, Zuzska stripped down to her underwear and went to stand out there. The sun had gone down and against the night sky her body was slender and pale as a candle flame. I studied her and sipped the champagne I'd bought, feeling pretty damned romantic.

'Come here,' she said.

'It's raining.'

'Rain is good for you.'

I took the champagne out to her. We drank from those cheap hotel glasses and leaned against the rail, gazing down at the water. We could see the lights of various boats, bobbing above the waves like will-o'-the-wisps. When the champagne was gone, we had wild, feral sex. We did it all over the place: on the floor, the balcony, the dresser, up against the walls. Afterwards we collapsed on the bed, with the balcony doors open and a warm breeze curling the curtains. On the bedside table was a hotel pen and pad of paper. I picked up the pen and began drawing on her: tracing her ribs and ribcage, outlining her belly, her breasts, mapping the entire terrain of her body. As I did, I asked her, 'What were you thinking?'

'While we were fucking?'

'When you were standing on that ledge.' I ran the pen up, encircled her nipple, and brought it back down to her solar plexus.

'I was imagining what it would be like to jump.'

'You'd fall and hit the ground and die.'

'No. I would float. I would turn into vapour and float away like a cloud.'

I stopped drawing, and imagined that. For her, I could almost believe it was possible. 'What about me? How would I find you again?'

'You'll have to use your map.' She stretched, arching her back, so that the body-contours I had created shifted and rippled like tattoos. 'It's the only map you'll ever need.'

I believed her at the time.

chapter 18

I didn't tell my friends what had happened. It would have been like confessing that I'd been castrated. They'd never understood me and Zuzska, anyways. Most of them were involved in casual relationships that lasted for a few months. Then there was me, with my long-distance, long-term thing – a kind of romantic anomaly that seemed a bit unnatural, even suspicious. I knew exactly the kinds of advice they would have given me. They would have said to suck it up, that I was better off without that chick, that she had me completely pussy-whipped.

The only person I could think to confide in – the only person I trusted enough – was Beatrice Carmen. She'd studied at the same language school as me in Prague. Zuzska had been her teacher too. The three of us had hung out together, along with the other students and expats and tutors that had made up our surrogate family in the Czech Republic. At one time or another, Beatrice had been a professional surfer, an actress, an animal rights activist, and a trauma counsellor for shell-shocked army vets. Then she got this job working at a women's shelter in San Francisco. I called her up on Sunday morning, a couple of days after the wrap party.

'Trevor,' Bea said, as if she'd been expecting to hear from me, 'how are you?'

I was huddled up in bed with the last of my absinthe, cradling the bottle like a baby.

'Not so good,' I said. 'It's Zuzska.' I couldn't say any more. It was as if saying the words aloud would make it real.

'I heard,' Bea said. 'She called.'

That figured. If I'd done what Zuzska had, I would have wanted to confess it, too.

'Talk to me, darling,' Bea said.

I told her about not sleeping. I told her that I was finding it hard to do anything, even simple things, like brushing my teeth or dressing myself. I told her that I'd been having murderous dreams and apocalyptic visions. I told her that I was drinking too much and thinking too much, that I'd started talking to myself like a schizophrenic. Eventually I ran out of things to tell her. On her end of the line, I could hear a metallic rasping sound.

I asked, 'Are you cooking?'

'I'm making hash brownies. I'm being a pot-headed Julia Child for the day. I've even got my apron on.'

'What's the weather like there?'

'Sunny. Twenty-three degrees. Offshore breeze of four knots. Low tide.'

'Could you keep talking?'

'Of course, darling.'

She talked to me as she made her brownies. She told me a story about a psychology professor who had fallen in love with her in Baja, and followed her up the coast to propose. As I listened I stared at the photos on my wall. They were all from my year abroad. There was one we'd taken at a photo booth in the Perpignan train station. I was posing between Zuzska and Beatrice and they were both pretending to bite my neck, like vampires.

'Bea?' I asked. 'Did Zu say anything about this joker?'

There was a pause. That meant she had.

'Is she in love with him or what?'

'I can't really talk about that, Trev.'

I closed my eyes and burrowed my face in my sheets. They smelled like me.

'Because you're taking her side.'

'I'm on both your sides. I love you both.'

'Then tell me,' I said. 'What am I going to do?'

'You're going to do whatever you need to do,' Bea said, 'to make things right. To make yourself better. Go crazy. Get drunk. Get high. Break something. Hell – break yourself. And remake yourself. Drop everything and get adventurous.'

I opened my eyes and sat up, like a corpse coming back to life. 'I'm thinking of going on a road trip.'

'Do it,' she said. 'Don't think about it, do it. If you think too much, nothing will ever happen, nothing will ever change. Hold on a sec – I've got to pour this batter.'

There was a clattering sound as she put the phone down. I listened to her humming and puttering about. I could picture her in her apron, with flour dusting her face and globs of batter on her hands. The sun would be streaming through the window, lighting up the scene like a snapshot from hash brownie heaven.

Then she picked up the phone. 'Where are you going on this road trip of yours?'

'I haven't decided yet.'

I didn't want to tell her about my Nevada brothel idea. Beatrice was cool, but not *that* cool. Actually, it was the idea that wasn't cool – so I saw no reason to share it with her.

'Come visit me and Venus in San Francisco,' she said.

Venus was her new girlfriend – the one I hadn't met.

'Can you heal me?' I asked.

'Are you wounded?'

'You could say that. I need a new heart.'

'Like the tin man,' Bea said.

'Wasn't that the scarecrow?'

'The scarecrow needed a brain, and the lion needed courage.'

'I need all three. Not to mention a new penis. Mine's gone limp.'

She laughed – this deep-bellied, lumberjack laugh. 'Okay, honey. Come on down and we'll see what we can do.'

'Maybe I will.'

I heard the creak of her oven door opening and closing, and Bea said, 'Zuzska told me you're not talking to her.'

'Why would I?'

I was still thinking about my trip, wondering if it was actually feasible.

Bea said, 'She's pretty broken up about all this, too.'

'I'll call her eventually,' I said. 'When I'm ready.'

chapter 19

South of Seattle, the mist looked as thick and grey as sour milk. I couldn't see the landscape, but I already knew what lay in that direction. I'd followed the I-5 out of Washington State before, with Zuzska. The previous year, we'd barrelled down in an old Chevy van to meet Bea and her then-girlfriend in Eugene, Oregon. Together, the four of us had roared south on the 101 – the famous highway that winds along the coast – and careened through Northern California, moving from campsite to campsite, consuming as much Americana as we could. We'd seen everything, done everything: sea lion caves and isolated surfing beaches, redwood forests and legendary vineyards, drunken dune buggy rides and Paul Bunyan's colossal, forty-nine-foot statue.

If I took that route, I'd be able to stop at those places, and retrace our steps. All I had to do was keep driving, and let the Neon continue deeper into the mist. It was getting thicker and thicker, caressing the sides of my car, slowly absorbing us. The other vehicles were now just vague shapes. Along the roadside, telephone poles rose up and floated past like the masts of long-lost ships.

'Come on,' I said, slapping my face.

Through the fog, I spotted a turn-off east for the I-90. I reefed on the wheel, making an erratic transition on to the exit ramp. As I merged, another driver honked at me, but it didn't matter – I'd broken clear. The mist fell away, withdrawing and retreating in the rear-view. I tapped the gas and the Neon picked up speed, as if relieved to be leaving Seattle behind.

The sky was still cloudy, the air still charged with the static that precedes a storm, but at least we were heading in the right direction.

A mileage sign swept by. We were 274 miles from Spokane and 262 miles from Cheney and 251 miles from Trevor. It gave me a little thrill, seeing my own name up on the sign like that. It had been the same when I'd passed through with my old man, all those years ago. I was about seven, I think. Mostly we went for the novelty value. There were stores in town with names like Trevor Grocery or Trevor Pharmacy or Trevor Gas Station. My dad took photos of me in front of all those places. Then, at Trevor Toys, he bought me a visor. The visor was made from clear blue plastic, with a rainbow headband and flashing lights all along the brim. I wore that visor everywhere: to school, to soccer practice, to bed. I even wore it in the bath. Part of the reason I wanted to go back to Trevor was to find a visor just like that one.

'Trevor,' I said, raising my coffee cup. 'Get ready for the arrival of Trevor.'

For about half an hour I meandered along, drinking whisky and huffing whippets. But the nitrous wasn't having as much effect. The backs of my eyeballs ached and cloudy patches appeared in my vision, as if some of the mist from Seattle had infiltrated the car. Amid the haze of fatigue, I began to imagine seeing a female shape. I couldn't help it. I pictured her sitting next to me, in the passenger seat, where she should have been. She was dressed in the same outfit she'd worn on our previous road trip: shorts and sandals and these Jackie Onassis sunglasses that were way too big for her but looked incredibly awesome. I turned on her.

'How could you?' I yelled, pounding the dashboard. 'You cheating bitch.'

She just smiled. She was pleased with herself, all right.

'Who is this asshole, anyway? A Russian gangster? A shitty art fag? Who?'

She shrugged, gazed out the window.

'Does he tell you he loves you? Does he wake up early to sketch you while you sleep? Does he carry you home when you're too drunk to walk? Does he know that spot at the nape of your neck where you like to be kissed? Does he have a bigger dick than me?'

I went on and on like that, grilling her ghost and getting no answers. To shake her, I tried to focus on the bad times, the arguments. One of the things we'd argued about on that trip was food. Zuzska hated American food and American restaurants, but I always wanted to stop and eat.

'I won't eat that pig slop,' Zuzska would say.

'Zu-Zu,' I'd say. I knew she didn't like it when I called her that, and she knew I knew it – which was exactly why I called her that. 'We're going to have to eat some time.'

'I don't have to eat.'

'Everybody has to eat.'

Usually I would drag her to Taco Bell or Wendy's or A&W. Once I even took her to Hometown Buffet. It was filled with frighteningly fat Americans – the kind who spill out of their own clothes and overflow the edges of their chairs and seem to jiggle and roll when they move. Strung above the buffet tables was a limp vinyl banner: *$10 Mother's Day Special*.

'I'd forgotten it was Mother's Day,' I said.

'We barely celebrate Mother's Day.' She stared at the other diners the way you might stare at overfed animals in the zoo, with a mixture of pity and disgust. 'It's like Valentine's Day – one of those capitalist holidays that we didn't even have before 1989.'

'We never celebrated it, either,' I said, 'since I didn't have a mother.'

'Poor boy.'

But she said it sarcastically – still pissed I'd lured her in there. At the buffet, she only served herself a small plate of salad. I loaded up with ribs and fritters and coleslaw. I ate all that in about five minutes and then began picking lettuce off Zuzska's plate.

'Yours wasn't enough?'

'I'm just sharing.'

'By sharing you mean taking.'

I took another piece. Deliberately.

'That's how we do things in my family. I guess you Czechs aren't into that, either.'

Zuzska stabbed at her salad as if she wanted to kill it. 'It's because of your stepmom. She pampers you more than any real mother would. Do you want me to pamper you, too?'

She always had to overanalyse things.

'I just wanted a bit of salad.'

'Here.' She shoved the salad plate towards me. 'Help yourself.'

I grabbed a handful, stuffed it in my mouth, and stared her down as I chewed. Lettuce leaves were sticking out between my teeth. A slice of cucumber dropped out and splatted on to the tabletop.

'You're just like them,' she said, gesturing at the other diners. 'A big pig.'

From then on, whenever she wanted to tease me, she'd make these little piggy noises at me, and call me pig-boy. I could almost hear her making them right then as I drove along.

'Is that why you did it?' I asked. 'Because you got sick of me being a pig?'

In the passenger seat, her phantom seemed to nod.

'I'm different now.'

No. You're still a pig, and still a boy. A little pig-boy.

I told her that was bullshit. After what she'd done, I'd overcome the need to eat. My metabolism had shut down, and everything inside me had ground to a halt. She'd turned me into some kind of tin man, my guts and heart rusting away.

'Now I don't need food, and I don't need you!' I was shouting at an empty seat, swerving all over the road. 'All I need is this!'

I brandished my whisky cup. Like the seat, it was empty. I tossed it on the floor and took a slug straight from the twixer instead. The clouds were getting darker, turning black. Somewhere behind them the sun must have been going down, but I couldn't see it.

chapter 20

The first thing I needed to sort out was the brothel. I didn't know anything about brothels, so I looked them up on the net. I Googled 'brothels in Nevada', and found a map. It was a handy map. Red pins marked all the hotspots. There was a scattering of pins around Vegas, and a smaller grouping near Reno. There were also a couple of pins in Northern Nevada, on the outskirts of a town called Winnemucca. It was on the way to Reno. I stared at all the pins. My pointer hovered on the screen.

'Trevor?' my stepmom called, from the top of the stairs. I could see her feet up there, in dirty pink slippers. I was using their computer, since I'd broken mine. I'd been breaking a lot of things. 'Are you still up?'

'I'm writing a script.'

In a way, I was – the script of my road trip.

'I'm making tea. Would you like some?'

'Sure, Amanda,' I said, still staring at my map. 'Tea sounds good.'

I clicked a pin by Winnemucca and a second browser window opened. This one had pictures of what the brothel looked like. It was called the Pussycat Ranch. It had a bar, a strip club, and a few pool tables. It even had a hot tub. Apparently you were allowed to take the prostitutes into the hot tub, which sounded pretty rad. By scrolling over the thumbnails you could view the various bedrooms. Each bedroom had a woman in it, wearing glossy lingerie. They were stretched or draped or bent over the beds like strips of flesh-coloured taffy. The tagline in the sidebar read *Come visit our sex-kittens. Mreowr.* All the kittens looked like models. I couldn't believe places like this existed. It was like the Playboy Mansion, only better because any asshole could go there. Even me.

I clicked on the 'directions' link. It took me to a map of Winnemucca, with street names and addresses. The brothel was near the northeast corner of town, on Riverside Street. There was a banner at the top of the page: *Private and discreet – a place for everyone to cum. The perfect stop on your way through Nevada.* That clinched it. I selected print. As our printer whirred to life, I heard footsteps on the stairs. My stepmom. I'd forgotten about her and her tea.

I clicked all the windows to close them. Then I opened a word document and typed: INT. HOUSE – NIGHT. It wasn't much of a script, but it was something.

'Here you go,' she said, placing the mug of tea down by the keyboard.

'Wow. Camomile.'

I stared hard at my imaginary script, as if trying to figure out what came next. What could be happening in this house, at night? Amanda sipped her tea and hovered. She has a tendency to do that. Hover, I mean. The printer was still printing. Then it made a whining sound and spat out the page.

'What's this?' she asked. She picked it up and peered at the picture, trying to read the small print without her glasses. 'Pussycat Ranch? Is that some kind of pet store?'

'Yep – in Nevada. I'm doing research for my film.'

'How are you going to film in Nevada?'

'We're just going to pretend it's Nevada. We'll cheat the location.'

'Oh. That's nice.' She put my map down, and placed a hand on my shoulder. 'I'll be upstairs, in the kitchen. I was about to call your grandpa – unless you need the phone?'

She kept hoping that I'd phone Zuzska and patch things up.

'No – go ahead. When's he coming again?'

'On Wednesday.'

She padded back upstairs. I picked up the map. The paper felt thin and flimsy in my hands. I folded it once, twice, and slipped it in my pocket. My screenplay document was still open, the cursor blinking at me. I started typing: *Trevor sits in his parents' basement, sipping the camomile tea his stepmom made him, planning a trip to a faraway brothel.* I typed that, then immediately deleted it.

chapter 21

There was no moon and no stars – only a sky smoked black by clouds. I drove along with the twixer squeezed between my knees, and took a swig every few miles. I hadn't passed another car for a long time. It was just me and my Neon. The headlight beams dug a tunnel through the dark for us to follow. Cat's eyes winked from the roadside, and on the centre line striped lane markings zipped by, each one blending into the next.

Ever since Seattle – ever since the border, really – I'd sensed rain coming. You could feel it hanging up there, like a guillotine waiting to fall. Every so often I would hear a distant rumble, as if America was letting me know that she wasn't particularly impressed with me. I couldn't bear to wait any longer. I rolled down my window and stuck my head out.

'If you're going to rain on me,' I cried into the night, 'then rain, damn it!'

And it did. The sky split open, like a water bladder slashed by a razor-blade. All the rain fell at once. It splattered across my windshield, my hood. It pounded down on my roof. Fat drops pummelled the blacktop, bursting apart like small grenades. The road flooded and became a flowing river. I almost expected to see frogs dropping from the sky, limbs spread like parachutists. It was that kind of rain: torrential and epic and biblical. Apocalyptic rain.

I threw the whisky on the floor and grabbed the wheel with both hands. My wipers couldn't keep up with the downpour. A permanent glaze coated my windshield, blurring the world. I hit a deep patch and hydroplaned for a few seconds, slowly drifting towards the ditch, before the wheels found tarmac again and straightened out. I probably should have stopped, but I didn't. I kept ploughing ahead, trying to out-race the rain. The highway had narrowed to two lanes. I must have turned off the interstate somewhere, but I don't know if that happened before or after the rainstorm started.

From out of the murk, I saw a dark shape emerging. It was a car, to the right of the road, overturned in the ditch. The tail-lights were still on, glowing red. That was all I could make out. I slowed down as I drew level with it. There was nobody standing by the road, and nobody else around to help. There was just this car.

'Fuck,' I said, and pulled over.

I got out my dad's cellphone – an old Nokia brick – and thumbed it on. It took a while to power up.

'Come on,' I said, smacking it.

There was a signal, at least. I wasn't that far off the beaten track. I dialled 911 and held the phone to my ear, waiting. I could hardly hear the other end ringing over the rain.

Then somebody answered.

'911 – what's your emergency?'

I think it was a woman, but it was difficult to tell. Her voice was a deep contralto.

'I'd like to report a car accident,' I said. 'A crash.'

'Where are you, sir?'

'I don't know.' I had to yell over the rain. I felt like a soldier reporting in a war zone. 'I was heading east from Seattle on the I-90, but I think I turned off at some point.'

'Were you involved in the accident, sir?'

She sounded unnaturally calm. I guess they're trained to be like that.

'No,' I said. 'It's another car. In the ditch. I was just driving by.'

'Is anybody injured?'

'I don't know. The first thing I did was call you.'

'That's good, sir.' She spoke slowly and carefully, as if to a child. 'I've notified an emergency crew. I'd like you to stay on the line with me until they manage to find you.'

'What's that?' I said.

I held the phone away from my mouth, so she would think the signal was fading. If the cops came and found me in that condition, drunk out of my mind, I was fucked.

'Please stay on the line, sir.'

'I can't hear you. What?' I was shouting now. 'I'm losing you...'

Then I hung up.

I opened my door. As soon as I stepped out of the car, I was drenched. That's how hard it was raining – so hard it got in your eyes, your ears, even your mouth. It was like falling into a swimming pool.

The blacktop was covered in puddles that spat and popped, simmering with raindrops. I splashed through the puddles, making my way towards the wreck. The car was wedged in the ditch, resting on its roof, at a forty-five-degree angle to the road. It was a mid-size sedan, with four doors and a square trunk. One of the headlights was broken, but the other was still on and pointing at the surrounding forest, illuminating pine trees, fallen logs and old stumps. As I got closer, I saw that the car was a Dodge Neon, like mine. It was exactly like mine, actually – only black instead of red.

I slid down the side of the ditch. The bottom was filled with water, which was warm and came up to my knees and smelled muddy and oddly wholesome. I waded over to the car. Steam was hissing up from the undercarriage. The interior was dark and half-submerged, but I thought I could see somebody in the driver's seat. I yanked on the door. It was locked, or jammed. I tried the other doors and they were the same.

I sloshed around to the passenger side and lay down in the ditch, on my back. The ground beneath the water was soft and mucky. I braced myself like that, put my feet against the window, and kicked, using my heels. The glass cracked and spiderwebbed. It took a few more kicks to knock it in completely. Pawing the water from my eyes, I crawled forward to check inside. But there was nobody in the driver's seat. There was nobody in any of the seats. The car was empty. I stayed kneeling there, making sure, then scrambled up out of the ditch, slipping clumsily on the mud-slick sides. I peered up and down the highway. Nothing.

I cupped my hands to my mouth and called, 'Hey! Is anybody there?'

The only answer was a tirade of rain. I gave up. I slogged back to the car and fell into the driver's seat. I was soaked, dripping, with smears of mud on my face and forearms, all over my jeans. It took me a while to notice that my phone was ringing.

I answered it automatically. 'Hello?'

'Is this the gentleman who reported an accident? Are you okay?'

It was that same woman. They were on to me.

'Yes,' I said. 'I told you – I didn't crash. Somebody else did.'

'You may be in shock, sir.'

'I can't hear you.'

I hung up again. But they had my number now, and they could call me whenever they wanted. They might even use the phone to track me down. I was convinced they could do that, via the signal, so I turned it off. Then, just in case, I removed the back cover and took the battery out and shoved the pieces into the glovebox.

I looked behind me. The wreck was still there, sitting in the ditch. The rain smearing my rear window made the image shift and shimmer, like a watery reflection. I put my Neon in gear and got out of there. I could see the other car's tail-lights dwindling in the rear-view, as if it was driving away from me rather than the other way around.

chapter 22

Money. That was the final obstacle, if I was really going to do this road trip. I couldn't fund any of it – the car, the brothel, Reno – without money.

I started by cancelling my flight to Prague. It was harder than I thought. Zuzska had written me a poem once, about the vapour trails you see behind jets. In the poem she described them as threads, connecting me to her. Now I had to cut the thread. It was pleasurable and painful, like tearing off a hangnail. It was also the point when I began to realise that this damage – the damage she had done, the damage I intended to do – was irreparable.

I only got fifty per cent of my money back, because it was such short notice and I hadn't bought travel insurance. I had another couple of hundred left over from the film shoot, which would just about cover a rental car. I needed more, though, and my parents weren't an option. Amanda might have given it to me, but there was no way my dad would have agreed.

I decided to talk to my grandpa instead, since he was coming to visit.

'When's his flight get in?' I asked my dad.

He rustled his paper. 'Six o'clock.'

The two of us were waiting upstairs in the living room. He was reading the sports and ignoring me. We hadn't been talking much, lately – and I hadn't told him or Amanda about my road trip idea. I knew how they'd react. My dad would get all cynical and sceptical and tell me it was a total cliché. And Amanda would start worrying, instantly, about all the things that might happen to me: that I'd crash my car or get shot or have some kind of breakdown, nervous or otherwise.

'That's him,' my dad said.

I heard the car in the driveway, the shutting of doors. Then I heard him coming. He's a big man, my grandpa. When he walks, he kind of rumbles. He rumbled right up our front steps and into the entrance hall, smashing aside the door. His silver hair was tousled, as if he'd been sleeping on the flight. I straightened up, standing taller.

'How's my grandson?' he said.

He offered his hand – a big bear-paw – and we shook. Grandpa doesn't do hugs.

'So-so,' I said. 'And you?'

'Still ticking.'

We sat down in the living room. Amanda put on some music and my dad got out the beer. That's what we do with important guests: we sit in the living room and listen to music and drink beer. And talk, of course. Amanda did most of the talking. She wanted to hear about her relatives in Alberta, and my grandpa's latest project. He designs environmentally friendly engines for buses and trucks that they use in developing countries. He was on his way to Peru to discuss some new contracts. For a while she asked him questions about that.

Then he looked over at me. I hadn't been saying much.

'How's that lady-friend of yours? The Czech girl.'

I stared into my beer. I hadn't noticed, but there was a bug in it. A gnat.

'Not so good,' I said, trying to fish the gnat out. 'We hit a bit of a bad patch.'

'Hmm,' he said.

In the kitchen the oven timer went off, bleeping repeatedly.

'That's the chicken,' Amanda said.

Since my grandpa was having dinner with us, I was kind of obliged to eat something. I had a few lapses like that during my fast, before I hit the road. It was a fairly casual fast, I guess. After dinner I went to sit on the back porch. It was cool, quiet, secluded. Birds flitted from tree to tree, making little flute-like sounds. The evening air was ripe with the scent of brine and recent rain. I knew that smell so well. It was the stench of Deep Cove, of my home and childhood – rich and sweet and stagnant.

The back door opened. My grandpa came out. He rumbled over, making the porch quake, and hunkered down on the step next to me. At first he didn't say anything. From the front pocket of his shirt he fished out a pack of Belmonts. The pack looked small in his hand. So did his lighter. It was an old Zippo that had lost its sheen.

'I didn't know you smoked,' I said.

'When I hit eighty, I figured a couple a day couldn't hurt.'

He lit up and exhaled, squinting through the smoke. When he squinted, the lines in his face were accentuated, like symbols carved into rock.

'Well, then,' he said, and paused.

We'd never talked much, Grandpa and I. He isn't a hugger and he isn't a talker.

'A rough patch, you said.'

'Pretty rough.' I wasn't much of a talker, either. It was all that Nordic blood, running cold through our veins. 'The long-distance thing caught up to us, I guess.'

'You like this girl?'

'I do. I really do.'

'That's tough,' he said, 'but sometimes these things – they don't work out. I had a girl, before I met your grandma. We were going to get married when I got home from my peacekeeping tour, overseas.'

I nodded. I'd forgotten he'd worked with the peacekeepers, back in the day.

'But a year is a long time. Things had changed when I got back. You get me?'

'I get you.'

We sat silently for a few minutes, in the evening stillness, as the sky faded to lilac. Over the fence one of our neighbours was splashing around in his pool. Every night the guy swims twenty laps, wearing goggles and a swim cap, like a real champion. Down the block somebody was having a barbecue. I could hear music and voices and smell the roasting meat.

'This must all seem pretty cushy to you,' I said.

'Depends on what you're used to, I suppose.'

'I'm thinking of getting out of here, going on a road trip.' I was staring at the deck, worried he'd think I was a total wingnut. 'Just to clear my head, think some things through.'

He clamped a hand on my shoulder. 'Distance is good. It gives you perspective.'

'The thing is, I don't know how to pay for it. I'm pretty broke.'

I didn't have the guts to ask him outright for money. That was as close as I could get.

'Hmm,' he said. 'Do you have any assets?'

'What's an asset?'

'Something you can sell. When I was getting my company off the ground, I had to sell my Chevy. First car I ever owned. I loved that damn car. But I needed capital.'

I thought about that for a bit. Then I said, 'There's my video camera.'

I'd saved up for two years to buy that camera. I once calculated that I'd cut over eight hundred lawns to get the money together. But, as far as I could tell, it was my only real asset.

'If you sacrifice something,' he said, 'it'll make the trip more real.'

His cigarette was almost finished. He twisted it out on the ground. Then he heaved himself up, his knees popping as they extended. For a moment he towered next to me, and from my low vantage point he looked so gargantuan I felt as if I was three years old again.

'Your dad wanted to have a nightcap with me,' he said, and turned to go.

'Hey,' I said, picking up his lighter. 'You forgot this.'

He stopped to look back, then waved it away.

'Keep it. If you like.'

I was stoked, obviously. I was even more stoked when I looked at the lighter. It was the lighter he'd been given in the peacekeepers. It had his service number on it – so faded it was hard to read.

'Thanks, Grandpa. That's wicked.'

He shut the door behind him. Since he had to catch a plane to Lima the next morning, I didn't see him again on that trip, but the day after our chat I took his advice. I placed an ad for my camera in the classifieds, and sold it to some kid from West Van. He was chubby and smelled like strawberry perfume and wore a Cuban beret. On the phone he told me he was attending Vancouver Film School. When he drove out to our house, his mom came along with him. There was no haggling or negotiating involved. She just handed over a certified cheque for thirty-five hundred dollars.

It seemed like a dangerous amount of money.

chapter 23

The Neon slid on, propelled along the water-slick highway like a log in a flume. I had to put some distance between myself and the wreck. I was convinced of that. Every thirty seconds or so I checked my mirrors. I kept expecting to see the cherry lights and hear the siren of a highway patrolman coming after me. The emergency crews had probably reached the site of the crash, and would be analysing my tracks, searching for evidence, scanning the clues into their little computers. I'd seen the films and TV shows. I knew how cunning these people could be. It was possible they were already following my progress with a satellite camera.

'It's a fucking duck hunt,' I said. 'A dragnet conspiracy.'

Even the rain was in on it. It wouldn't let up. It just fell and fell and fell, like waves washing over my Neon. I pushed on, clutching the wheel, crashing through the tide.

'A little further,' I chanted, over and over. 'Just a little further.'

Ten minutes later, I saw a sign for a rest stop. I put on my signal. The exit ramp was thick with water. As I descended, it sprayed up around my windows in shimmering fans. I floated on, into the parking lot. It was empty. I pulled over next to the toilets and yanked on the handbrake. Then I stumbled out and slumped across the hood. Rain pummelled my back. I rolled over, offering myself up to it. Fat drops slapped my face, spat in my eyes.

'All right,' I said, holding up my hands. 'You win. I'm done.'

The rain stopped. Instantly. America had proved her point. I lay there, sprawled on the hood of my Neon, completely waterlogged. I could smell the night, the wetness, the pine trees. In the woods, water was dripping off the branches, like an echo of the storm.

'You okay?'

Somebody was poking me.

'Hey – are you dead or are you sleeping?'

I opened my eyes. It was bright and chilly. A woman stood over me, wearing a trucker's hat. I was spreadeagled on the hood of my car, and my clothes were still wet. I gazed at her. My head hurt and I was shivering. I felt completely sodden and wrung out.

'I hope I'm not dead,' I said.

'I saw you lying here.'

'I got caught in the storm.'

She reached up and adjusted her hat. 'Well – so long as you're breathing.'

She ambled over to the snack machines in the rest stop shelter. Behind it I could see her rig – a big green eighteen-wheeler. On the side of the semi-trailer was a logo of a turtle, and their slogan: *Martha's Movers. Not the fastest. Just the best.*

I peeled myself off the hood and sidled past her to the men's washroom. It was tiny, with three urinals, two stalls and one sink. I grabbed on to the sink with both hands, bracing myself, and puked straight down the drain. Since I hadn't been eating, not much came out – just bile that seared my oesophagus. I wiped my lips, and cupped handfuls of water into my mouth. The water tasted sweet, in the way it does after you throw up. I rested on a toilet in one of the stalls for a few minutes, then got up and drank some more. Finally, after all that, I looked in the mirror. My face was pale as a china plate.

'You piece of shit,' I said.

I shuffled back to the car. The bottle of whisky was lying in the passenger footwell. Only a thimbleful was left. I'd managed to drink nearly the whole twixer. I grabbed it by the neck, as if it was a pet animal that had been misbehaving, and locked it in the trunk with the rest of the booze. There'd be no more of that. I had a new vow, to add to my list of vows. America had made it clear that there was certain shit she wouldn't put up with on this trip.

'All right,' I said. 'I'll drink, and I'll drive, but not at the same time.'

To seal the pact, I sparked my grandpa's Zippo and lit up a Lucky Strike. While I puffed away on it, I got out my map – one of those folding road maps that are a pain in the ass to open and close. I unfolded it and spread it across the hood of the Neon. It took me a while to find Seattle, and trace my route along the I-90. There were a bunch of little roads to the north and south of it. I could have been on any of them.

The trucker was still deciding on her snack. I waved to her.

'Could you tell me where I am?' I called.

She came to stand beside me and stared at my map, jingling her coins in her palm.

'Uh-huh,' she said. She pointed to a little yellow road in Washington. Her fingernail was clipped and clean and pink, without any nail polish. 'We're here. On Highway 28.'

Highway 28 ran parallel to the interstate. I wasn't that far off course. This route would take me to Trevor, too. It was just smaller and slower and meandered around a bit.

She said, 'The I-90's faster, if time's an issue.'

'Guess I'm not in any real rush.'

'I hear you. I haul freight, but I ain't one of these speed maniacs. I see so many assholes just racing along the highways, like they're trying to conquer the entire country.'

I looked at her. Something about her voice reminded me of the operator on the phone. It had that same calmness. Her face was calm, too – worn smooth by age.

I said, 'But you can't conquer her, can you?'

'Nope. Better to take things slow, enjoy the journey. Got far to go?'

'Trevor, first. Then on to Winnemucca, Reno, and San Francisco.'

She whistled, long and low. 'Big trip.'

'That was the idea.'

'Where'd you start?'

I had to think about that as I folded up the map.

'Here,' I said. 'I'm starting here.'

chapter 24

On the day I left, while I was getting my things together, I received three phone calls, on my landline. The first was from Amanda. I'd told her and my dad that I was going camping for two weeks by myself, up in Northern BC, and she had already started to worry.

She phoned me from her office at the injection site to see if I wanted to borrow one of their cars – the Camry or the Cherokee. It was tempting. It would save me cash, and I knew those cars so well. They were as cosy and familiar as a pair of old mitts.

'No, thanks, Amanda,' I said. 'I've got a rental lined up.'

'You never know with those rental cars.'

'It's a good agency – out at the airport.'

You could tell she wasn't convinced, but by then it was all settled.

'Well, make sure you touch base with us every so often.'

I told her I would. She insisted I take my dad's cellphone, since I'd smashed mine. He was getting another one soon on his plan, anyways.

'And your dad said to remind you not to pick up any hitchhikers.'

'I better get going, Amanda.'

'Drive safe.'

After we hung up, I finished getting ready. I didn't have many preparations to make. I was just taking the one backpack, with a few spare clothes. But after I'd packed, instead of leaving, I lingered in the house. I walked upstairs and downstairs. I checked all the lights. I brushed my teeth twice. I even cleaned my suite, and bagged all the empties. It was like when you open the door to a birdcage, and find the birds don't want to fly away. I'd always wondered about that. Now I knew how they felt.

At about ten o'clock, the phone rang a second time. I thought it might be Zuzska, and couldn't decide whether or not to answer. Finally I did. It wasn't her, anyways. It was the director. He was calling because the funding had come through for his feature. Some of it had, at least. He'd received enough to shoot it, but not on film like he'd originally planned. He wanted me, and my camera.

'I really liked the work you did on my short,' he said.

I guess he'd forgiven me for the close-up of his face in the bar taps.

'I'd like to,' I said. 'But I can't.'

'But this is the road movie, man. Our feature. Like *Easy Rider*, remember?'

'I remember. The thing is, I sold my camera.'

'Aw, shit.' He sounded so disappointed. Almost heart-broken. A lot more so than me – and it had been my camera. 'Why would you do that?'

'I'm going on an actual road trip.' Then, since that didn't seem like explanation enough, I added, 'It's going to be even better than your movie. Because I'll be living it.'

He still didn't understand, but it had felt good to say it out loud. I was ready. I told the director I had to go, and hung up on him. My backpack was in my suite. I went to get it, checked I had my passport, and headed for the door.

Then the phone rang again.

I walked back and approached it. Cautiously. This time, I *knew* it was her – in that instinctive way that happened between me and Zuzska sometimes. It trilled and trilled. I imagined picking it up, and all the things we'd say: reproaches, apologies, ultimatums. I think I even reached out to touch it.

'Not yet,' I said.

I backed away, then turned and walked down the hall. I felt each ring tugging at me like a string. I stepped on to the porch and shut the door behind me, locking that sound inside.

PART II

chapter 25

I drove into the centre of Trevor and parked on the main street. I wanted to announce my arrival in some outlandish manner. I wanted to declare myself, like in the olden days, when travellers had to knock on the gates of a town. We had a connection, Trevor and I. A bond.

Near where I parked, a hunchbacked guy was standing on the street corner, selling papers. I hopped out and went over and bought one: the *Trevor Tribune*. I tapped the header. 'That's my name,' I told him. 'I'm Trevor.'

'Good for you, pal.'

I wandered down the street. I was hoping to have some kind of mind-blowing *déjà vu* experience, but that didn't happen. Trevor just looked like any other mid-sized North American town. It was all stretched out, low and flat, with a couple of apartment buildings squatting at one end. The main strip had been taken over by chain stores: Starbucks and 7-Eleven and Kentucky Fried Chicken. I didn't see Trevor Toys, or Trevor Grocery. I didn't see any of the shops that I remembered from my childhood.

I passed a few other people – the citizens of Trevor. Trevorites, I guess. I smiled at them. Some smiled back, but not many. For them it was just a regular day in Trevor. Then I came up to a middle-aged woman in a floral dress, dragging a boy along beside her. The boy had curly blond hair, hacked into haphazard locks, and looked a little like I had at that age. I figured they might know where the toy store was, so I stopped them and asked about it.

'You mean Trevor Toys?' she said.

'That's it. They sell clear blue plastic visors with flashing lights.'

She shook her head. 'It's gone now. Toys R Us put it out of business.'

'Shit.'

She frowned at me, for swearing in front of her kid, and tugged him on. I kept walking. At the end of the main street, I found Toys R Us. It was the size of an aircraft hangar, with a flat roof and dull concrete façade. I walked through the sliding glass doors, which snapped shut behind me. Inside, the place was filled with conditioned air, chilly as a fridge. The floor tiles sparkled like ice cubes, and emitted cold and empty echoes at each step. My forearms prickled into goosebumps, instantly. There were hardly any other customers, and hardly any staff.

I went up to the only till clerk on duty – this teenage girl in a frosty white uniform.

'Good morning, sir, can I help you?'

She smiled. On her teeth she had some kind of ornate orthodontic brace. Steel brackets and bits of wire filled her entire mouth, like the inside of an android. I made a small, startled sound, and took a step back.

'Good morning, sir,' she asked again, with the same intonation. 'Can I help you?'

'I'm looking for a visor.'

'What kind of visor are you looking for, sir?'

It was so cold I could see our breath in the air. I rubbed at my arms, trying to keep warm, as I described my visor to her. She listened, her mouth frozen in that metallic smile.

'We don't have a visor like that, sir. Nobody sells visors like that any more. But we have sports visors and cartoon visors. In fact, we have a special on our headwear today…'

She started telling me about the special, about all their specials, repeating her pre-recorded sales pitch. I shivered and backed away. Slowly. She didn't seem to notice. She continued speaking to the empty air, and staring at the place I'd been, as I crept out the door.

Outside, the afternoon sun was hitting the street full-on, like a giant laser beam. I sat on the steps of Toys R Us to warm up. Off to my right, near the wheelchair ramp, stood a woman. I hadn't noticed her on the way in. She'd spray-painted her face pink and dressed up in a pink skirt and blouse. A pair of wings hung off her back. She was acting like one of those human statues you see in Europe. Zuzska had been terrified of them. In Barcelona I'd paid one – this guy dressed as the devil – to chase her down Las Ramblas. He'd followed her all the way to Park Güell. She'd screamed and laughed so hard that she'd had an asthma attack.

I got out a handful of coins and tossed them in the lady's bucket. She lurched to life and pretended to notice me for the first time. In one hand she held a wand, which she brought up and waggled in front of my face.

'I'm your fairy godmother,' she said.

'I could use a fairy godmother.'

'I'll grant you one wish.'

'Well, I'm looking for a clear blue plastic visor, with flashing lights on the brim.'

She closed her eyes and jerked her wand around. I guess she was pretending to cast some kind of spell. Then she bopped me on the forehead with the wand, a little too hard.

'Ow.'

'Sorry. Try the old market, in Oak Park. There's a toy stall.'

'Hey – thanks a lot.'

She licked her lips. The pink paint was coming off at the corner of her mouth. 'Once you get your visor, go. I wouldn't stick around – a pretty young thing like you.' She stirred her wand around my head. 'Some local girl will wrap you up and take you home with her.'

She settled back into her original position, pretending to solidify again. I felt I owed her for the advice, so I added more money to her bucket. But she misunderstood and came back to life, thinking I wanted another performance. I explained that it was just a tip.

It was fairly awkward.

Oak Park wasn't really a park. There was no grass, no playground, and no paths. It was an old dirt lot dotted with oil stains and dandelions. At the very centre stood an oak tree, large and gnarled, with a canopy of branches so elaborate it formed a kind of overhead labyrinth. In the air beneath it, cucumber-green caterpillars twisted and squirmed on strands of silk.

Most of the stalls were arranged in the shade of the oak tree. I walked around, checking them all out. One stall was set up on a two-wheeled farm cart, laden with melons and berries and other fruits. Above it a cardboard sign read *Fresh Trevor Produce*. Another stall, *A Taste of Trevor*, was selling pickled vegetables, preserves and local cheeses. This was more like the town I remembered. Trevor – the real Trevor – had gone underground. There was even *Trevor Body Care*, which sold home-made soaps and organic, chemical-free hand creams.

As I passed, the saleswoman asked, 'Something for your lady friend?'

'I don't have a lady friend.'

There was a toy stall, too – just as my fairy godmother had said. Laid out on the table were grubby Care Bears and boxes of loose Lego blocks and a Hot Wheels track with a note on it: *One piece missing*. I knew those toys. They were the toys of my childhood. There were even He-Man figurines, and original Transformers. Some of the toys were still in their packaging, but most were second-hand. The man behind the table nodded at me. His nose was bulbous with veins, and a jelly-bowl belly jiggled over the band of his jeans.

'Did you used to own a toy store around here?' I asked.

'That was Trev, my brother. Trevor Toys.'

'Where's Trevor now?'

'He killed himself when his store closed.'

'Damn. Sorry, man.'

I didn't tell him that was my name too. It might have tripped him out.

'But I inherited some of his stock,' he added.

I pretended to peruse his stuff. Really I was only looking for one thing, and I saw it – hanging on a hook next to a Smurfette baseball cap.

'Is that visor for sale?'

He took it off the hook, brushed a film of dust from the brim. 'Sure is. Good deal, too. They don't make these any more.'

'Does it work?'

He flicked the switch on the headband. Nothing happened. When he saw my face, he said, 'Maybe it's the batteries.'

Rummaging around beneath his table, he came up with a pack of those circular dime-sized batteries. He popped two into the little compartment on the side of the headband, then tried the switch again. The lights across the brim began flashing, like a big rainbow grin.

'How much?' I asked, reaching for my wallet.

He wanted twenty bucks, but I was so eager and grateful that I gave him thirty. As he handed the visor over, I noticed a kid standing next to me. He must have crept up while we were fiddling with the visor. He was wearing ripped Jams shorts and a T-shirt daubed with ketchup stains. No shoes. He stood gazing at the toys, with this Tiny Tim look on his face.

'Where are your parents?' I asked him.

'Dad's at work,' he said.

'What about Mom?'

He shook his head. He was a single-parent latchkey kid, like me.

'Shouldn't you be in school or something?'

'It's summer.'

He went back to staring at all the toys. I couldn't just let him stand there. I pulled out my wallet again. It was bristling with bills. I still had most of my camera money. I'd hardly even spent anything on gas yet. The Neon was great on gas.

'What do you want, kid?'

He looked at me. Doubtfully.

'I'm not messing with you. It's on me.'

He pointed to an X-wing fighter. I paid the guy and he handed it to the kid. The kid stood there, holding it, as if he expected me to take it away, or tell him there was a catch.

'Go on. Go play with your X-wing.'

He scampered off. The old man winked at me. I thanked him and pulled on my new visor, and wandered around the rest of the market. I stopped at a stall called Trevor Video Bonanza, and bought Bea a copy of *The Wizard of Oz*, since we'd been joking about it on the phone. But as I moved off, perusing the remaining stalls, all these other kids in grubby clothes started coming up to me. Word had got around: the guy with the visor was a soft touch. He would get you anything you wanted – like Santa, except in the middle of summer.

'Mister,' one said, 'I want some Construx!'

'Buy me this G.I. Joe, will you?'

I fled the market, hurrying back towards Main Street. A cloud of street urchins followed, swarming after me. I'd become like the Pied Piper of Trevor or something.

As I rushed by the hunchbacked newsie, I called out, 'Where can I go that these kids won't follow?'

'A bar,' he said.

I saw one up ahead: the Trevor Watering Hole. The hunchback was right: the kids didn't follow me inside. Through the window, I could see them on the street, milling about and looking a little lost without me.

chapter 26

'Nice visor.'

'Sorry?'

'I like your visor.'

A girl said that to me, in the bar. After escaping from the kids, I'd decided to stay for a while, and get drunk. It was a sports bar, but not the kind you'd expect to find in America. It had hardwood floors, ceiling beams, and smelled of mildew, like some of the beer halls I'd visited over in Europe. Instead of the usual pictures of baseball stars and basketball players, the walls were decorated with photos of figure skaters, gymnasts and cross-country skiers. Behind the bar hung an ice hockey jersey, signed by all the members of the Slovakian team.

I'd been drinking alone in there all afternoon. Then this girl appeared.

'Do you really like it,' I said, 'or are you just making fun of me?'

'No – really. I like it so much that I'm going to buy you a drink.'

She asked me what I was having, and I held up my beer bottle. I'd been nursing the local microbrew – Trevor Pale Ale – but it tasted watered-down. The girl knew it, too. She pushed my glass aside, waved the bartender over, and ordered two Stolichnayas instead. She said the name differently from how I would have, tasting each syllable on her tongue, using the correct pronunciation. The bartender seemed to recognise her. He tilted his head to her and murmured something in a language that sounded faintly familiar, faintly European.

'Are you Slovakian?' I asked her.

She smiled. 'Something like that.'

'My girlfriend was Czech. But we broke up.'

'Good. We hate the Czechs. That's why there is no longer Czechoslovakia.'

When the vodka came, she sniffed her glass first – as if it were a flower – before taking a sip. Then she nodded, satisfied. 'So sweet and clear. Like water.'

She slid on to the barstool next to mine. She wasn't big, like a lot of the girls in that place. She was thin, with a lean, long face and a lean, long body. Her hair was long, too. It hung straight down to her waist. It looked slightly damp, as if she'd just got out of the shower.

'You're not from this town,' she said.

'It's that obvious?'

She pinched the brim of my visor, and pulled it down over my eyes.

'This gives you away. Don't you know that saying, about being in Rome?'

I looked around. All the other guys were wearing runners, faded jeans and tucked-in T-shirts – like extras from *Footloose*. Then there was me, with my blue visor and tank top.

'I can get away with it,' I said, pushing the visor back up, 'because this town is named after me. Or I'm named after it, or whatever. Basically, my name is Trevor.'

'And Trevor's come all this way, just to visit Trevor.'

She was teasing me, but you could tell she liked it, too.

'Besides,' I said, '*you* stand out even more. The rest of the chicks in here are either in mini-skirts or leotards or crazy leggings, and rocking hairstyles twenty years out of date.'

She laughed. She was wearing a blue dress, sleek and shimmery as water, with straps that tied up at the nape of her neck. She told me that she was allowed to be different, but that it might get me in trouble.

'Don't worry, though,' she said, 'I'll look after you.'

'I don't need looking after.'

'All men want to be looked after. They want mothers.'

'I never had a mother,' I admitted. 'She died when I was a baby.'

'That's so tragic, Trevor.' She reached up to pat my cheek. Her palm felt cool and damp. 'My little Trevor. I'll spoil you rotten – starting with another round. Mother's treat.'

Two more vodkas appeared on the bar. I couldn't remember finishing the first one. I'd been drinking at a steady canter all day, but this girl wanted to gallop. She took her vodka straight, without ice. Between each round, she would rinse out her mouth with water. They stocked a lot of exotic vodkas, and she insisted I sample them all. We drank like that, sitting at the bar, until the jukebox started playing. The first tune was some hit country song with a boot-stomping beat. A few people whooped and got up to dance. She took my hand.

'Come on, Trevor. Dance with me.'

'I can't dance.'

'You can dance. Mother will show you.'

I had to obey her. She led me on to the dance floor, and I discovered she was right. I could dance. She made it easy. We twisted and turned together. In my arms she felt slim and slippery as a reed, swaying along to the music. After a few songs she made a drinking motion and went to get us more vodka. I stayed out there, shuffle-dancing on my own. At one point I accidentally bumped into the person behind me.

'Looks like we got a live one here.'

It was this guy wearing a jean jacket, straight out of the eighties. He had a bunch of friends with him. They were all wearing jean jackets, too. It was an entire jean jacket gang.

'Nice visor, buddy.'

'Thanks,' I said. 'Your girlfriend bought it for me.'

'What did you say, gaylord?'

They all crowded in around me. The guy started bumping at me with his chest, like a belligerent sea lion. That made me laugh, so he shoved me, and I shoved him back. Then he grabbed me by the collar and was about to deck me when she reappeared, sliding between us to break it up. She had a glass of vodka in each hand. She flung one in the guy's face. I don't mean the vodka, either. I mean the whole glass. It bounced right off his forehead – bonk – and clattered across the floor without breaking. She bared her teeth at him, ferret-like.

'This is my new friend,' she said, 'and you're leaving now.'

She didn't have to say anything else. The guy and his jean jacket gang melted away, like snowmen, and trickled out the door.

'That was awesome,' I said.

She waved it off, as if it was nothing, and told me to keep dancing. So I did. A respectful space had been cleared for us on the dance floor. We danced for what must have been hours. Whenever I got tired, she'd say, 'Don't stop. Dance, Trevor. Dance.' At one point, without my noticing, the music changed. It became jaunty and sad at the same time, like gypsy folk music. The other patrons were in a circle around us, clapping to the rhythm. She took one of my hands and raised it and twirled beneath it, pirouetting like a dancer.

'Now you,' she shouted over the music. 'Your turn to turn.'

I turned, making the bar spin, and it kept spinning even when I stopped. The walls and the dance floor and all the people around us blurred into a kind of kaleidescope. The only constant was her face, floating in front of me, like the centre of a spinning top.

chapter 27

Later the girl was holding me by the hand and leading me down the street. I stumbled along at her heels, still dizzy from all that vodka and dancing. I asked her where we were going, and she said that she was taking me home. I followed her past Toys R Us and out along the highway. There were no street-lamps, no cars. The only light came from the moon – a thin crescent poking up from the horizon like a splinter of bone. In the gloom her hair seemed to glisten green, as if she'd dyed it. The strands swayed hypnotically before me as we walked on and on and on.

'I'm tired,' I said.

'Poor Trevor. Almost there, little one.'

Finally we turned off at a gravel drive that wound up through a forest of willow and cottonwood trees. She murmured to me gently the whole time, telling me to watch my step, that she didn't want me to hurt myself. Overhead the branches arched towards each other, blotting out the moonlight, and in the darkness I could no longer see her. She became a series of impressions: footsteps beside me, her hand in mine, the whisper of her dress, and a heady perfumed scent, citrus and sweet, like water lilies.

At the end of the track we reached her house. It was built in the style of a European château, with faux-stone walls, a gabled roof, and matching turrets on either end. The yard was massive – about the size of a lacrosse field – and divided from the house by a sweeping driveway, where several pickup trucks and SUVs were parked. To reach the front porch we had to cross a wooden footbridge over a small moat or drainage ditch, filled with inky water.

'Wow,' I said. 'You must be loaded.'

'My family are here tonight,' she said, and held a finger to her lips.

'I thought it seemed like a lot of cars.'

'We were having a gathering. Some of them had to sleep over, so watch out.'

I didn't understand what she meant until we stepped through the door and into the foyer. On the floor, lying at our feet, was a man-sized lump that looked like a carapace. I couldn't make out the face or who it was, but I could see it rising and falling and hear the rhythm of its breath. We crept past it. In the hall, and the living room, there were more lumps – all breathing together, all shapeless and featureless. We had to tiptoe our way between them.

'What are they?' I whispered.

'Shhh. They're resting.'

She led me down the hall to the room at the very end. It had an antique dresser in one corner, a four-poster bed, and a picture window with a view of the front yard and forest. I offered to sleep on the floor, like all the other guests, but she told me not to be silly. She was already undressing me. She removed my visor first and hung it on the door handle. Then my shirt slid off and my jeans fell away and I was left standing in my boxers. She guided me to the bed, and pushed me down on it. Beneath me the mattress rolled and sloshed and slurped.

'Whoah,' I said, popping back up. 'I've never been on a waterbed.'

'You'll get a good sleep.'

While she twisted the bracelets off her wrists and unclasped her necklace, I took a look around the room. On the walls she'd hung odd-looking charms, made out of wood and bark and bird feathers. I pretended to study them, but I was aware of her flicking off her shoes, peeling down her tights, shimmying out of her dress. She had a bony body. Her underwear was sleek and black, like her hair, and had a similar velvet sheen. She dived on to the bed, making it ripple, then rolled over and lay back and let her hair fan out across the pillows. 'Come on,' she said, beckoning me over. 'Come to Mother.'

I took my visor from the door handle and put it back on.

'You don't sleep in that, do you?'

I posed for her, with my hands on my hips. 'It's my nightcap.'

She laughed politely. I could tell it bothered her, but she didn't say anything. I slipped on to the bed beside her and she drew the covers over us. They felt a bit clammy.

I said, 'I don't think you dried your sheets properly.'

'That's just condensation on the mattress.'

She reached over to dim the bedside lamp, and we settled down into watery darkness. I felt her wriggling around, heard the hiss of cloth against skin. She was naked now. And so was I. My boxers had vanished. I was stripped and limp and shivering. Her bed was so cold.

'Listen,' I said, 'I've been having a little problem. With… you know.'

'Shhh.' She touched a finger to my lips. 'It's okay. We don't have to do anything. Just this.'

I clung to her, still shuddering.

'You're freezing, Trevor. But I'll heat you up.'

On my chest, I felt something sleek and soft. Her hair. She was rubbing it over me with her palms. The strands slid back and forth, up and down, in a slow-warming massage.

'Hmmm,' I said.

'Sleepy-time for Trevor.'

She started murmuring to me again, this time a sing-song lullaby in her own language. Her hair seemed to be under me, over me, all around me. I'd never held a girl with such long hair. It wrapped me up, enveloping me, soothing and comforting me, until I closed my eyes.

chapter 28

I was underwater and surrounded by seaweed. It covered my limbs, encircled my throat, and filled my mouth – choking me with cold. I didn't know if I was dreaming or awake or in the middle of a waking dream. I thought my eyes were open but it was hard to tell because it was completely dark. The darkness seemed to be pressing in around me, pulsing like a heartbeat.

I was still wearing my visor. I reached up, straining to raise my arm, and flicked the headband switch. The lights came on, warm and multicoloured, illuminating the room. I was in the girl's bed, spreadeagled on my back and entangled in her hair. Locks of it, wet and water-heavy, covered us both in a kind of cocoon. A puddle had soaked through the sheets, which smelled of mould and mildew. The waterbed was leaking.

I peeled strands of hair off my face, and bunches of it off my arms, my torso, my thighs. Each clump was thick and slippery as a snake, and seemed to slither away from my touch. It took a while to extract myself from all that hair, unwrapping my own body like a mummy. When I was finally free, I slipped away from her and rolled to the edge of the bed. My clothes lay scattered all over the floor. I gathered them up and crept towards the door, guided by the light of my visor.

'Where are you going?'

She was sitting up. Her hair was soaked through, trickling down her throat, clinging to her shoulders and breasts. The damp made it glisten, and accentuated the greenish sheen.

'Away from here.'

She blinked and shielded her eyes from the light of my visor, as if it hurt her. 'But you need me to look after you, remember?'

'I'll look after myself.'

I closed the door behind me. In the hall I manoeuvred around the lumps on the floor. They were still rising and falling, breathing and sighing. Even by the light of my visor it was hard to tell what they were, other than shapes that looked vaguely human. They could have been people in sleeping bags, or they could have been something else. Maybe her relatives all had hair like hers: hair to wrap you up, hair to hold on to you.

Outside, I crouched to pull on my shoes. I still had my clothes in a bundle under my arm. I trotted down the drive, naked and shivering. Near the edge of the property I glanced back. At her window I saw a pale figure surrounded by a penumbra of hair that undulated as if underwater. She raised one arm. I couldn't tell if she was waving goodbye, or beckoning for me to come back. I carried on into the woods, using the visor to light my way.

The walk back to Trevor took me a solid hour. At the outskirts of town I stopped to pull on my jeans and shirt. By then the sun was a buttery bulge on the horizon. I'd dried off and warmed up a bit, and was just beginning to realise how truly terrible I felt. That vodka we'd been drinking had shrivelled up my insides. I had no piss or spit or bodily fluid left. It was as if she'd drained it all out of me. I needed a drink: pop or juice or water or beer. Anything.

On the way in, I passed the Toys R Us again. My fairy godmother was setting up out front. She had a compact mirror, and peered into it as she smeared the pink make-up over her cheeks. When she saw me, she shook her head and made a clucking sound with her tongue.

'I warned you, didn't I?' she said.

I held up a hand. I didn't want to talk about it.

On the main street I found a coffee shop – Café Stanley. A tattered awning hung above the door, and a few plastic tables were arranged out front. The kid behind the counter looked almost as hung-over as me. He was cupping a foamy cappuccino between his palms.

'Why isn't it called Café Trevor?' I asked him.

He just shrugged. Whatever. I bought an orange juice from him. Also, I bought a postcard with a picture of the *Welcome to Trevor* sign on it. I sat down at one of the tables and drank my juice. Afterwards I lit a Lucky Strike and started scribbling on the postcard.

> *Beatrice.*
>
> *On my way. Met a Slovakian girl in the town of Trevor. She had green hair and a waterbed. It was a bad scene. I'm through with girls. Not just European girls, but all girls (except you, obviously – but you don't really count, you're more than a girl). I've been making a lot of vows lately and I think I'll add that to the list: no more girls. I'll see you soon, hopefully in San Francisco, hopefully with better stories to tell.*
>
> *From Trevor, in Trevor.*

The postcard had pre-paid postage. I dropped it in a nearby mailbox, then got my map from the car and brought it back to my table. I studied the land to the south, tracing my finger along various routes. If I really wanted to avoid girls, I'd need to avoid all those places that girls typically inhabited, including towns and cities. I'd have to pick the most isolated stretch I could find, a barren part of America. I'd drive into it alone, a man in the wild.

As soon as I'd decided that, and begun to fold up my map, I heard a distant drone – like the humming of locusts. It got louder and louder, crescendoing into a roar. People on the sidewalk stopped to look down the street. Coming towards town, dragging a huge dust cloud, was a motorycle gang. They were all riding identical bikes: black-bodied choppers, crawling along low to the ground, with chrome handlebars that quivered like antennae.

I stood up. The kid from the coffee shop came out to see, too.

'Who are they?' I asked him.

'The Cobras. Bad-ass dudes.'

The Cobras were all dressed in jeans and leather jackets and black boots. Most of them also had on those little hard-hat helmets, with the chin straps dangling loose. They shuddered along in a single row, like a raging centipede. Their faces were completely blank and impassive, except for the one at the front. He led them slowly through town, turning his head back and forth as if he was looking for something. He wore a pair of dark sunglasses – so dark they seemed to swallow up everything. As he drew level with us, he glanced at me and did a double-take, as if he'd recognised me. He slowed down. We gazed at each other.

'Don't stare, man,' the kid whispered.

'I know that guy.'

I wasn't sure, but I thought it might be the same biker I'd tried to bulldoze back in Vancouver. He sneered at me, then gunned the engine and snarled off, burning a wheelie. The others roared after him. They tore down the main street, en masse, and turned into the Toys R Us parking lot. People around me shook their heads and scurried away, hurrying in the opposite direction. I stared after the bikers as the kid started rearrranging his chairs.

'What could they want at Toys R Us?' I said.

The kid snickered, and pointed to the table where I'd left my visor. 'Maybe they want one of those.'

I picked it up. Protectively.

'That's not funny,' I said.

chapter 29

Somewhere south of Trevor I saw a sign for a town called Sprague. It seemed so bizarre that I unfolded my road map while I drove to check. I thought I might have imagined it. But it was there, all right. Sprague existed. I covered the 'S' with my thumb, so that only 'prague' remained. My head was still leaden with vodka and I stared at those letters for a long time, trying to decipher what they meant, what they represented. Then the wind rushing past my window caught the map. It flapped up in my face and started fluttering ferociously, like a giant paper bat that had flown into my car. I swerved back and forth, swinging from the shoulder to the centre line, before I managed to shove the bat-map aside and straighten out.

The thing is, it was the day I should have been flying out to Prague. Somewhere, in another dimension, a different version of me was landing at the airport, and clearing Customs, and striding into Arrivals. Zuzska would be waiting for me there, in one of those hard-backed airport chairs. She would stand and stretch, languid as a cat, and make her way over to me. She would kiss me and call me stranger and ask me if I'd missed her. Then she'd tell me where we were going, what we were doing. She always had a plan, Zuzska did. The last time I'd visited, in February, she'd driven me straight to her place – one of those Soviet-era apartment blocks – and taken me upstairs to the roof. The night before, she had flooded one corner with water and let it freeze, creating a personal ice rink for us.

She'd held up two pairs of skates: white retro figure skates for her, and old-school leather hockey skates for me. I was almost as excited about those skates as the ice rink.

'Your set were my father's,' she said, 'so they might be a bit big.'

We strapped on the skates and glided around up there, twelve storeys in the air. Her building was outside Prague proper, and from the top we had views of the entire city. We skated until evening, then stopped to watch the sunset. Of course, since it was Zuzska, we had to watch from the edge of the roof, within inches of the hundred-foot drop to the parking lot. I stood behind her, gripping her hips, dizzy with love and vertigo, as we gazed out together. The frosted towers and snow-capped spires glowed violet in the dying light. She explained that they called Prague the golden city, the mother of cities, the city of a hundred towers.

'Who calls it that?'

'Mostly travel ads, to lure the tourists.'

'It worked for me.'

She turned to face me, looking up. 'Will you ever move here?'

'I don't know.' I kissed her. Her lips felt cold and hard as marble. 'One day.'

She shrugged and pushed off, gliding away from me. I watched her curl in a circle, one leg stretched out behind in a figure-skater pose, her body forming a perfect 'T' shape. There was a crescent-shaped crack in the ice between us, like a grimace on a frozen face.

At the next exit, I turned off and took a detour through Sprague. On the way in I spotted a stone archway, with the town name painted on the crosspiece. From there I rolled on to First Street. It started with what might have been an abandoned gas station – the sign stripped, the tanks paved over. The next block was just a gravel lot, filled with rusty trucks and tractors. I passed a three-legged dog, which hobbled along after me, and a brick garage tagged with a snarl of graffiti: *Love hurts*. There was also a tavern and a tackle shop, both closed down. The only tower was a decrepit water tower, tottering on rickety stilts, like a broken-down satellite.

At the other end of the drag was an Art Deco building – maybe an old movie theatre – with its windows boarded up. Sitting on the kerb out front was a teenage girl, who looked about fifteen or so. I stopped in the middle of the road and waved to her.

'Do you live here?' I called.

She stood up. She was wearing acid-washed jeans and a Misfits sweatshirt, with the hood cinched tight around her face and her hands buried in the pouch. She peered at my car.

'Are you a cop?' she asked.

'No. The cops might be after me, though.'

She sighed, and pulled out a pipe she'd been hiding in her pouch. The bowl was still smouldering and I could smell the bud. She took a long hoot and said, 'Yeah – I live here.'

'Sprague looks pretty fucked.'

'It is fucked, man.'

'Harsh.'

I stayed there, with the engine idling. She sidled closer. I think she expected me to ask for directions. Instead I asked her for some weed. She didn't have enough to sell me, but she let me take a toke from her pipe – one of those psychedelic glass pipes. I took a hoot and held it and thumped my chest with a fist, feeling the tickle. It was bad weed – stale and dry.

'I'm supposed to be in Prague right now,' I said, coughing.

'Where's that?'

I told her it didn't matter.

I left the interstate at Sprague and headed south on Highway 23. I passed other towns, with names I can't remember. I wasn't paying much attention. I was concentrating on the road and trying not to think about Zuzska. It wasn't easy. Whenever I blinked, or turned my head, I'd catch a glimpse of her in the corner of my eye, the corner of my mind. She'd taken her place in the passenger seat again. I refused to acknowledge her, so she started pestering me.

I don't know why you cancelled your flight.

I didn't answer. I just kept driving.

If you hadn't, we could have made up, made it work.

I glanced at her. She was wearing her green dress – the one in a soft cotton fabric with elastic shoulder straps. I loved that dress. She looked so fucking sexy in it that I actually felt sick with longing, as if my stomach had been slit open.

'That's a lie.'

But instead you stop talking to me and take off on your big trip. What's the point of all this? She gestured at the passing landscape. *You're not going to get me back, you know.*

'I don't want you back.'

So you're doing it out of spite. Like a child.

'Think what you want. I don't care.'

To spite me. To spite yourself. She twisted a strand of hair around her finger, in that way of hers. *What is that saying? That English saying? You would cut off your nose to spite your face. That's you. We don't have a saying like that in Czech, because it is so stupid.*

I told her I didn't care. I called her *kurva*, a whore.

She shrugged. *Isn't that what you found so attractive?*

At one point I began to feel dizzy and had to pull over. It was partly my hangover, partly hunger and exhaustion. I sat with my forehead resting on the wheel and sweat dripping off my nose. I stayed like that for fifteen or twenty minutes, taking deep breaths. I might even have dozed off. I had moments where that happened – where my body remembered that I wasn't feeding it, and tried to shut down. Then at other times I'd feel fine. A little light-headed, maybe, but generally fine.

Poor pig-boy, I heard Zuzska's voice, whispering in my ear. *You should eat.*

I started the engine again. 'I told you I'm not eating.'

125

Later in the day I crossed a bridge over a creek bed, dry and cracked and split down the middle by a thin trickle of water. On the far side lay Oregon. The border was marked by a sign, in the shape of the state: *Welcome to Oregon. We Hope You Enjoy Your Visit.* Somebody had blasted the sign with buckshot.

Oregon looked pretty much the same as Washington, except less developed and more arid. Me and my Neon drifted along through forests of ponderosa and western pine. Every twenty or thirty miles I came upon a rest stop or gas station. The gas stations had posters in the windows, or banners above the awnings, advertising guns and ammunition and hunting licences for sale. It was hunting season, apparently. Other than those places, I didn't see any buildings or communities. I was sticking to my latest vow and avoiding civilisation and people of all kinds – especially the female variety. The back roads and backwoods were the best place for that. There weren't any girls at all out there. Except for the one that kept appearing beside me.

I don't like these woods, she announced at one point. *All the trees look dead.*

She was right – the trees did look dead. Their bark was going grey and the needles had turned stiff and yellow, like the hair of a corpse. But I wasn't about to agree with her.

'Please stop talking to me. Please go away.'

She placed her foot on the dash, flashing a bit of calf. *Don't you like the company?*

'Not yours.'

But you miss me, don't you? You miss your one true love.

'I don't love you. All my love's turned black with hate – like a burnt soufflé.'

She pretended to be shocked, raising her eyebrows and covering her mouth with a hand. She was a great actress, Zuzska. *I don't believe you. You don't really hate me.*

'Right now I do. I hate you so much I could kill you.'

You couldn't kill anything.

'Yes, I could.'

I pointed my finger at her, like an imaginary gun. I tried to imagine it, too. Having her in my power, at my mercy. I pulled the trigger.

'Bang. Just like that.'

She let out a little shriek, and vanished.

chapter 30

The pines outside my window grew thinner and thinner, smaller and smaller, until they lost their needles and shrivelled up and disappeared entirely. I'd left the woods and reached a low, rolling plain of brush and scrubland that stretched south to the horizon. On the other side – way out there – I saw a mountain with twin peaks. It was so far off it appeared almost translucent, like a frosted shard of glass jutting up through the troposphere.

At the edge of the plains was a gas station. I pulled in to fill up. In the parking lot, gathered around a couple of pickup trucks, was a group of men. They were all dressed in camouflage jackets and hunting hats. I was careful not to look at them as I filled up my tank. I could hear them, though, talking and laughing. I thought they might be talking about me, and laughing at my visor. I took it off and tossed it on the back seat. Then I figured they were just talking and laughing, in the way guys do. The longer I listened, the more alone I felt.

After I paid for my gas, I ambled over to their circle. There were half a dozen of them, all smoking and drinking Pilsner. An open cooler sat in the bed of the truck, next to a gun rack laden with hunting rifles.

They parted to make room for me.

'Get anything today?' one asked me.

He had thin legs and a big chest, which he kept puffed out like a bird's. His hat sat low on his head, so the brim shielded his face.

I shook my head. 'No. Not me.'

'Bagged us a couple of bucks.' He jerked a thumb towards the truck. Draped across the hood were two deer, splayed out on their bellies – as if they'd run a long way before collapsing in exhaustion. 'Nice, eh?'

'Yeah,' I said. 'Nice.'

Since they were all smoking, I got out my smokes, too, and my grandpa's lighter. I couldn't do that trick – the one-handed Zippo flick-trick – but I'd been practising striking it on the thigh of my jeans. I tried that. It didn't work. I dropped the Zippo in the dust. I bent down to get it, then flipped it open and fiddled with the flint. They were all watching me.

Finally I got the cigarette lit.

'Can I see that lighter?' the pudgy guy asked.

I handed it over to him. He studied the service number on the side.

'My grandpa was a peacekeeper,' I explained.

He nodded, satisfied, and handed it back.

'My uncle went to 'Nam,' he said. 'Hell of a thing, that. Never got over it.'

They all murmured agreement. For a while, they talked about how messed-up Vietnam had been, and told stories about all the terrible things that had happened over there. Like how this guy had got his dick cut off and stuffed in his mouth. Then one of them said that the shit going down in the Middle East wasn't much better, and that the army was no place to be.

'I tried to enlist,' the pudgy guy said. 'But they rejected me because of my feet. I'm pigeon-toed, see? That's why they call me Pigeon.'

We looked down at his feet. His buddies must have known all about his pigeon toes and his nickname, but they looked anyway. And it was true. His toes angled slightly inwards.

'People with pigeon toes can run fast,' I said.

'That's what I told them!' Pigeon threw up his hands, exasperated. 'See? This kid knows. But the doctor wouldn't sign off on my medical. I could have been a sharpshooter!'

They all agreed. Apparently he was a good shot, this Pigeon guy. He'd been the one to kill the first deer that morning. He started bragging about how he'd shot it from half a mile away. That was far for a rifle, I guess. All the other guys nodded along. In the middle of his story, though, I heard a familiar drone in the distance, zeroing in on us. The dust cloud came next, and then the biker gang, streaking out of the woods like a long black snake. They didn't stop for gas. They just rumbled on towards the lowlands, their chrome handlebars flashing in the sun. Pigeon and the other guys stared at the ground, at their beer cans, at the sky.

After they were gone, Pigeon didn't finish his story. Nobody spoke for a bit. We stood around, spitting in the dirt, until one of them said, 'Fucking bikers. Think they're so tough.' That seemed to make everybody feel better. They got out another round of beers, and offered one to me. We cracked the tabs open together, the sounds echoing each other.

Pigeon pointed at my licence plate. 'You a Canuck, huh?'

'That's right. From Vancouver.'

'Down here for hunting season?'

'I don't have a gun.' I fiddled with my pull tab. 'I've never shot a gun, actually.'

They all gaped at me.

'You're shitting me,' one said.

'No – really.'

'Hell,' Pigeon said. 'You should give it a try, boy. Otherwise you'll never get any hair on your chest. You know what they say – a man's not a man until he's fired a gun.'

I'd never heard anybody say that before, but I guess it's an American thing. 'I want to go to a shooting range, somewhere along the way.'

Pigeon burped. 'Who needs a shooting range? Come shoot with us this afternoon.'

'I'd suck too bad.'

'So what? We're not going after no more deer. Just picking off a few pheasants for kicks, with the handguns. Up in them woods.'

'So long as he doesn't shoot his own pecker off,' one of them said.

Pigeon chuckled. 'Think you can manage that, boy?'

'I'll try,' I said.

chapter 31

In the back of his Jeep, Pigeon had about a dozen attaché-style steel cases. He opened them one by one. Each case contained a different handgun, either a revolver or a semi-automatic.

'Are these all yours?'

'Hell, you should see what I got at home.'

We were up in the woods. We'd driven back from the gas station in convoy, and turned off the main road on to a dirt track that made my Neon buck and shudder. I don't think it was a hunting reserve or anything, but there were pheasants around, apparently. The other guys had wandered off, carrying pistols and cans of Pilsner. Every so often I could hear them shooting in the distance. The reports sounded muffled, like somebody punching a pillow.

'Take your pick,' he said.

'What would you recommend?'

'To start with let's try this little number.'

He selected a snub-nosed revolver. It looked like the kind of gun cops used in old TV shows. Squatting down in the grass, he demonstrated how to load it by thumbing cartridges into the cylinder. They slid in easily, like little metal pills.

'This here is the safety.' He pointed to a switch on the side, then pushed it forward, keeping the gun aimed away from us. 'Now the piece is live, see? And you don't want to be pointing it at anybody – including yourself.'

We stood up. Twenty yards away he'd arranged five beer cans on an old stump. He took aim, one-handed. The gun yipped and one of the cans jumped. I jumped too. Neither of us was wearing earplugs. Pigeon said he only wore them at the range.

'Okay, rookie. Your turn.'

He handed it over. It had a wooden grip, worn smooth and stained with sweat. He showed me how to stand, with one foot forward, and how to aim – holding the gun in the right hand while supporting the butt with the left. I sighted along the barrel.

'Bend your elbow more. Good.'

There was a bead at the end of the barrel, and a notch near the hammer. You just had to line up the bead with the notch. It was the same as the pellet guns I'd shot as a kid.

'Okay. When you're ready.'

I pulled the trigger, and pulled it harder. Nothing happened. Pigeon was smiling at me. I'd forgotten about the safety. I slid the switch forward and took aim again. This time when I pulled the trigger the gun woofed like a dog – a very small dog that wanted to leap out of my hands. Splinters of wood spat off the tree stump, just below the cans.

Pigeon slapped me on the back.

'How's that feel, huh?'

'Good.' I could hear a faint ringing in my ears, like tinnitus, and the grip of the gun felt all slippery. I wiped my palms on my jeans. 'Can I try again?'

'Hell – empty the whole cylinder.'

I did, taking my time. The revolver held eight rounds. I improved as I got used to the noise and recoil, but my aim was still wild. Afterwards I reloaded the cylinder myself, with Pigeon talking me through it. My fingers trembled as I put the cartridges in. I had to take a second to steady myself before I could shoot again. I emptied another seven bullets into the stump. On the last shot – the eighth – I managed to wing one of the cans. It twirled on the spot and fell over, like a demented ballerina.

'Attaboy,' Pigeon said. 'Keep at it.'

I reloaded and fired a few more rounds. While I did, Pigeon prepped another pistol – a semi-automatic. We used that one next. It was the same calibre as the revolver – a twenty-two – and it held more bullets. You loaded them in a magazine that slotted into the bottom of the grip. The shooting action felt fairly similar but I had better luck with it. I hit two cans the first time I tried it, and three on the second.

'I like this one,' I said, hefting it up.

Pigeon grinned. 'My wife carries one like that. In her purse.'

I looked at it. It didn't seem like much, now that I thought about it.

'Do you have anything bigger?' I asked.

He drained his beer can. You could tell he'd been waiting for me to ask. Walking over to his Jeep, he took his time appraising the various gun cases. Then he dipped his hand in one and removed another revolver, holding it with special reverence. It was a beast of a gun, with a hefty chamber and a cannon of a barrel.

'This here is a forty-four Magnum,' he said.

Even I knew what that meant. That was Dirty Harry's gun. Pigeon flicked open the cylinder to load it. The rounds for the Magnum were big and squat and glistening, like slugs. I guess that's why they call them slugs.

'Might want to cover your ears,' he said, raising it.

I didn't. I should have. The other guns had yipped and woofed. This one roared. A dart of flame flashed from the barrel, and one of the beer cans sort of blew apart. The echo resonated through the forest like thunder.

I said, 'Holy shit!'

Pigeon fired off a couple more rounds before switching the safety on and handing the gun to me. It was twice as heavy as the others, and harder to hold level. I kept having to readjust my grip, my stance.

'Hold on tight,' Pigeon warned. 'This baby kicks.'

I stood rigidly and pulled the trigger. The gun bucked and I felt the recoil all the way to my shoulders. I had no idea where the shot went. I was just glad I hadn't dropped the gun.

'Whoah,' I said, offering it back to him. 'That's really something.'

'Go on. Try it again. Don't let it scare you.' He had a fresh can of Pils on the go now. 'Afterwards we can catch up to the others, maybe bag us a couple of birds.'

His voice sounded oddly muted. My ears were humming, as if I'd been punched in the head. I adopted my stance, keeping the gun pointed at the ground, and studied the cans. I took a deep breath, drinking in the scent of pine and dirt, and let the air slip out between my lips.

'You know what I do?' he said. He was right behind me, whispering in my ear. 'I think about somebody I hate. Like, picture their face. Use that as your target.'

At first I tried to imagine the guy – this guy who was dicking my girl. But I couldn't. I'd never seen him. He was a faceless, nameless menace. A shadow. I knew what Zuzska looked like, though. I could picture her easily. Maybe with her mouth half-open, her eyes half-closed, grinding and groaning beneath him. I thought: this is what you get, you *kurva*.

The Magnum came up and the trigger gave beneath my finger and the hammer reared and fell in a way that felt perfectly seamless. The metal can screamed, bursting into shrapnel. I stared at where it had been. My fingers had gone numb on the pistol grip. The howl of the repercussions echoed in my ears.

'Damn,' Pigeon said. 'That sure worked.'

chapter 32

Shooting pheasants was a lot harder than shooting beer cans. The pheasants were bigger, but they were also further away. Plus, they moved. If they saw you or heard you, they burst up into the air and flustered around for a while before flopping back to earth. They never got very far – they seemed to tucker out easily. But all that flapping made them trickier to hit.

'Nice and easy, rookie,' Pigeon told me.

He was standing next to me, with the other guys spread out on either side. We were trudging together through the woods in a staggered line. Pigeon had said it was the safest method. If we all faced the same direction, we had less chance of shooting one another. I picked my way over twigs and fallen branches, cupping the pistol in both hands, keeping it pointed at the ground. Pigeon had lent me his semi-automatic for the hunt.

'Target sighted, rookie,' he said, nodding off to the left.

There was a pheasant squatting on the lowest branch of a nearby pine. Its head jerked back and forth in that curious, lizard-like manner. I took aim with the automatic. Beyond the barrel, I could see the bird's feathered breast pulsing with each breath. I squeezed the trigger. The gun barked and bucked but the bullet whined wide. The pheasant took flight, croaking in alarm.

'Good try,' Pigeon said, patting my shoulder. 'Don't worry – there's plenty of game around here.'

It was true. The scrubby woodland was practically infested with pheasants. Every few minutes one of the other guys would spot a bird and take a shot. They rarely missed. There would be an explosion of blood and feathers, followed by a collective cheer. The pheasant would lie on the ground and twitch, its legs scratching erratic patterns in the dirt. Sometimes the shooter had to go over to finish it off. We weren't keeping any of the birds. We just killed them and left them where they fell. Between gunshots, the forest was quiet except for the rustling sounds we made as we waded through the underbrush.

'Got another bogie for the kid,' one of them said, holding up a fist. 'Ten o'clock.'

It took me a few seconds to figure out what he meant by ten o'clock. Then I spotted the pheasant off to our left, puttering back and forth like a grounded blimp. The rest of them waited politely as I crouched, took aim, and fired. Dirt sprayed across the bird's feet. It leapt up and flapped away, wobbling through the air.

'Fuck,' I said.

'No worries,' Pigeon told me. 'You'll get one.'

But you could tell he wasn't all that sure. Evening was creeping up on us and the sky had darkened to a deep cobalt blue. We didn't have much longer. As the other guys moved off, I lingered behind to check my gun. I thought there might be something wrong with it.

'You coming, rook?' Pigeon called back.

I trotted along in his wake, studying the terrain ahead. Since the trees were well-spaced, you could see fairly far. The ground rose steadily towards the crest of a hill. On the hill was a big Douglas fir, and in the branches near the top I spotted one of the birds. It had to be two hundred yards away – an impossible distance. They'd be completely stupefied if I made that shot. Just for kicks, I tried the trick Pigeon had taught me. I pictured Zuzska's face, instead of the bird. My gun swung up with that same smooth motion and the forest settled into stillness as I drew a bead on the target.

'You *kurva*-bitch,' I said.

Just as I pulled the trigger, Pigeon called, 'Wait!'

I fired and felt the shudder of the bullet leaving the barrel. A second later, the brown bird dropped out of the tree, straight down, like a falling pine cone. A perfect shot.

'Oh, shit,' Pigeon said.

'What? What is it?'

He'd already started up the hill. I hustled after him. I could hear the others following behind, crunching through the undergrowth. At the top of the hill we reached a clearing. In the centre, lit up by a last ray of sunlight, lay my pheasant. Only it wasn't a pheasant. It looked two or three times as big, with a brown body, a white head, and a hooked yellow beak. It was sprawled on its back with both wings extended, as if in mid-flight. A bullet hole, rich and red, gaped in the middle of its chest. Blood had pooled in the pine needles beneath it.

Pigeon clamped a hand over his mouth.

'What is it?' I whispered.

'An eagle,' he said. 'A bald eagle.'

Dropping my gun, I knelt on the ground in front of the bird. I placed my hand on its breast. It was warm and downy and still. I'd never seen anything more beautiful. Or more dead.

'What the hell were you thinking?' Pigeon said. 'No pheasant roosts way up in a tree like that.'

I looked upwards, as if the answer lay overhead. At the top of the tree from which the eagle had fallen, I could see the nest it had built for itself – a massive oval of mud and leaves and twigs. The other guys had arrived by then, but they didn't come too close. They stood at the edge of the clearing, muttering and shifting from foot to foot – not wanting any part of it.

'I'm sorry,' I said. 'I'm so sorry.'

Nobody said anything. We stayed there in the dying light for a long time.

Pigeon had an old camping tarp in his Jeep. He helped me wrap the eagle up – using the tarp as a makeshift body bag. The two of us carried the corpse back to my Neon. At least

Pigeon understood why I wanted to keep it. The other guys didn't. They couldn't wait to get the hell out of there. Bald eagles were the national bird of America, and protected. If a ranger came along, and found us with this thing, we'd be fucked. That was what one of them said, anyway. Those were his exact words. But I couldn't just leave it there, for the wolves and coyotes.

They all watched from a distance as we lowered the eagle into my trunk. By then the sun had set and dusk was closing in, like a casket covering the forest.

'Come on, Pigeon,' a guy called. 'It's getting late.'

Pigeon waved to them in acknowledgement. Then he turned to me. He removed his hunting cap, ran a hand over his scalp, and blew out his cheeks. You could tell he wanted to say something that would make me feel better. But what can you really say to somebody who's just shot a bald eagle?

'Well,' he said, and tried to smile, 'from that distance, through all those trees – that must have been one of the best shots I've ever seen. Or the worst, as it turned out.'

I shook my head. I still had his pistol. I offered it to him, butt-first.

He eyed it uneasily. 'You might as well keep that.'

'I don't need a gun.'

We argued about it for a while, but he wouldn't take it back. He shoved a box of ammunition at me, and told me the pistol was a gift.

'I don't even have a licence.'

'That's okay,' he said, backing away. 'I don't either, for that one.'

By then the other guys were waiting in their vehicles. Engines started up. Headlights flicked on. Pigeon climbed into his Jeep, rolled down the window, and leaned out.

'What are you going to do with the bird?'

'Bury it, I guess.'

'Better do it quick. Otherwise, in this heat, it'll start to rot.' He shrugged. 'And don't be too hard on yourself, rookie. That there was just plain old-fashioned bad luck.'

Then his window was going up, and the vehicles were moving off. I watched them rumble away, bumping and bobbing along the dirt track. The sets of tail-lights got smaller and smaller, fainter and fainter, until they winked out and I was alone in the fading dusk.

chapter 33

Pigeon was right about the bird going rotten. But I had an idea while I was passing the gas station where I'd first met him and his friends. Next to the pumps sat a big white freezer with the word 'ICE' scrawled across the doors. I pulled in and bought two sacks of crushed ice. I also bought a cooler – one of those cheap styrofoam picnic coolers. I placed the bags of ice inside and laid the eagle on top of them, using its tarp as a coffin liner. The bird was already going stiff. I smoothed out its feathers and bent the feet a little to make it fit. When I looked up, the clerk – an anaemic teenager with acne – was watching from the doorway.

I raised a hand to acknowledge him.

'Gonna get that one stuffed?' he called out.

'That's right. It's a keeper.'

As I left the gas station, I bottomed out, grinding the undercarriage on the ramp. I could feel my new load weighing down the rear suspension. That eagle was even heavier than it looked. It was as if it was made of lead, or gold. A Maltese eagle.

I turned on to the two-lane highway. The sky was a purple swath pinned over a black strip of land. At the horizon the two colours met in a crisp and distinct line, like an abstract painting. There was nothing else out there: no lights, no houses, no other cars, no signs of life. It was exactly what I'd wanted. Total isolation. But now that it was in front of me I took my foot off the gas and slowed to a halt, in the middle of the road. I just had a feeling – that shivery, ghost-over-your-grave feeling. Whatever America had in store for me wasn't going to be good. I mean, I'd shot her national bird. She wouldn't be happy about that.

I reached over to fasten my seatbelt.

I floated on alone, in the rolling dark. I'd set the Neon's autopilot to seventy, which meant I could sit back with my legs stretched out and one hand on the wheel, letting her drive herself. I also had the A/C on full and the windows up. I felt completely numb, slipping through the night in my airtight pod, like a spaceman frozen by cryogenics. We were riding low and the Neon had started to whine, straining under the weight of that eagle. I kept telling myself that I hadn't meant to kill it, but it didn't make much difference. I had killed it, and that was that.

I lit a cigarette and rolled down my window. As I smoked, I rewound the sequence of events, and played the 'if only' game. Like, if only my shot hadn't been so good. Or, if only I'd realised it was an eagle. If only Pigeon had warned me a second sooner. If only I'd not agreed to go hunting. If only I hadn't pulled into that gas station. If only I'd never come on this fucking road trip. If only Zuzska hadn't done what she did. If only. If only. If only.

I had one of those starburst moments. I saw all my possible lives, all the choices and paths I could have taken, streaking away from me at light-speed, like the explosion of a supernova. What I needed was a time machine – a bicycle or a DeLorean. Then I could go back and change everything. I'd write a whole new story, and have it turn out the way I wanted. But I couldn't, obviously. I was stuck in this story, with a dead eagle in the trunk, and a girlfriend who was dead to me. It had all happened. It was all fixed. I flicked my cigarette out the window. In my wing mirror, I watched the butt bounce and skitter on the asphalt like a red-hot jumping bean.

Beyond the glare of my headlights and the glow of the dashboard I couldn't see anything, not even the stars. I was trapped in my pod with my thoughts. Hours passed – I don't know how many – and at some point I noticed that the horizon was glowing orange. At first I thought I'd travelled all night, right through until dawn. But it couldn't be dawn. The transition was too sudden and intense and the light seemed to be shimmering like a midnight mirage. Then I smelled the smoke, and understood. It was a brushfire. On either side of the highway, stretching out into the night, the flames rippled and flickered, blurry with heat, like those pictures you see of oil wells burning in the desert.

I followed the road into the middle of the fire, parked, and got out. I was hit by huge blasts of scalding air, as if I was standing in front of a giant hairdryer. Overhead, sparks and embers swirled on the updraughts. The smoke wasn't as thick as I expected, and didn't hinder my breathing. The dry brush was burning clean, purging the landscape in its passing.

I sat down on the ground, overwhelmed.

I'd seen another fire like it, three years before, on the other side of the world. It had been with Zuzska and Beatrice, near the end of my first trip to Prague. The week before I left, we took the train to Catalonia, with a few other travellers and expats. We stopped off in a fishing village called Portbou, on the French border. There were deep-hulled skiffs bobbing in the harbour, and tiny white houses packed together like salt crystals, and a bar called Ca La Feli, with a terrace where we drank Estrella Damm and Mahou and felt very sophisticated.

The first night, a summer solstice festival was taking place. They had a *cobla* band and *sardana* dancers and free sangria and, at dusk, a firework display above the bay. We gathered with the locals to watch. In the middle of the finale, one of the rockets tipped over and went astray. It streaked like a burning snake towards a nearby hill, where it burrowed into the underbrush and began thrashing around, stirring up flames. From there the fire spread, overtaking the entire hillside. Up and down the beach, Spanish children cheered and screamed. The town's only fire engine was dispatched. Volunteers made a half-hearted attempt to tame the flames, while the band kept playing and the party carried on, as if the brushfire was simply part of the festivities.

Down on the dance floor, with all that going on in the background, Zuzska and I started a fire of our own. I can't even remember what triggered it. Some imagined slight, maybe. Or a throwaway remark that caught on and ignited. Pretty soon we were hissing and sputtering, screaming insults at one another, raging among the revellers. Eventually Zuzska blew up and shot off, like a human bottle rocket, trailing a blaze of red hair behind her. I stayed on the dance floor, still smouldering, until Bea came looking for me.

'I'm not letting you fuck up like this!' she shouted over the music. She pressed her forehead against mine, as if she wanted to headbutt me. Bea was capable of doing that, too. 'She's the best thing that's ever happened to you, and you know it. Now go find her.'

I did. It wasn't hard. Zuzska was sitting down at the seashore, weeping like a water nymph. I got it into my head that the only way we could make up was by going swimming. We could douse ourselves and cool our rage that way. Zuzska swore at me, told me it was a stupid idea. Then she started to strip. She peeled off her top and shed her skirt, so fast that I'd barely unbuckled my belt before she'd left me on shore. I undressed and swam after her. A haze of smoke hung above the bay, and the water was filled with phosphorescence. Zuzska streaked on ahead, streaming green from her legs, her arms. She swam into the middle of the bay, hundreds of yards from shore, and stopped to wait. As I drew level she grabbed me and wrapped her limbs around me and started kissing me. I couldn't support us both and we sank down together, all entangled, sharing oxygen. I opened my eyes, and in the underwater murk I saw bubbles, glittering green flecks, her blurred face, the diffusion of flames on the surface. We kept kissing desperately, even after our air ran out, even after we could no longer breathe.

I'd never known love could feel so much like drowning.

Squatting there in the road, and thinking of that other fire, I began to wonder what had caused this one. It could have been lightning, but more likely it had been a moment of carelessness: an untended campfire, a dropped match, or a cigarette like the one I'd tossed out the window. That had been miles back, but if the authorities really wanted to they could add the fire to the list of things to pin on me, along with the car crash, and the eagle. Even if this particular disaster wasn't my fault, it might as well have been.

I eased the car to the roadside, popped the trunk, and grabbed a mickey from my stash of bargain booze. I sat on the asphalt, with my back against the passenger door, and took a sip. Without meaning to, I'd picked gin – Zuzska's favourite. It tasted of her lips, and of her drunken gin-kisses on our nights together.

Next to the road, where the fire must have started, the brush had burned to cinders. Further out it was still blazing. Flakes of ash fluttered down from the sky like black snow. It peppered my face and forearms, landed in my lap and hair. I closed my eyes and stayed like that, relishing the scent of smoke, savouring the crackle-snap of flames. It was so warm and comforting, that fire, smouldering in the dark like a memory.

chapter 34

By morning the fire had burned itself out. Threads of smoke wove up from the blackened ground, and the sky had a milky hue, like a rheumatic eye. I hacked my morning dart and mashed it out in the Neon's ashtray. From then on, I was always careful to do that.

As I drove along, I assumed the wasteland would give way to living brushland again, but that didn't happen. Instead the burnt remains turned grey and crumbled into ash, as if the fire had passed that way long ago. The ash became dust, and dirt, and eventually I realised I was driving through a desert. Not the kind of desert you see in cartoons, with endless rolling sand dunes, but a real desert. The ground was parched and pockmarked by rocks. The only plants were big sagebrush shrubs and clumps of ragweed, bent sideways by the wind.

I pulled over, got out, and unfolded my map across the hood. I'd never heard of a desert in southern Oregon, but there is one, apparently – the Great Sandy Desert. Further south lay Black Rock Desert and Smoke Creek Desert, in Nevada. There were tons of deserts in that area. I folded up the map and looked around. The actual name didn't really matter. It was a desert, and I was in it. That was okay. So long as I kept going, and didn't run out of gas, I figured I'd be fine.

In the desert, I kept expecting to see some typical desert animals: geckos perched on rocks, or rattlesnakes shaking their tails at the roadside, or buzzards gliding in spirals overhead. But there weren't any. The only signs of life I saw were actual signs: road signs and speed limit signs and mileage signs. The mileage signs listed the distances to upcoming destinations in descending order. Reno was always at the bottom. Every road led to Reno, apparently. But it was still nearly five hundred miles away, and I had to drive it alone. A few times, I glanced over at the passenger seat, hoping Zuzska might appear, but she never did. She was gone.

'I wish I had some company,' I said.

My wish came true. Around mid-morning, I spotted what looked like a heap of clothes at the roadside. As I got closer, I saw that it was a man asleep in the sand. He was lying on his back, with a shirt draped over his face and one hand held out, thumb up, as if he'd dozed off while trying to hitch.

I pulled over. The sound of the engine must have woken him, because he sprang up and gathered his things. He had a shoulder bag and a backpack. From the sides of the pack dangled pots and pans, clipped to metal karabiners. As he trotted over to the car I rolled down the passenger window, and he crouched to peer in. He was wearing a pair of aviator shades, with lenses like mirrors. I could see myself reflected back in them. He looked fairly young. About my age, maybe.

'Where you headed?' I asked.

'Where are *you* headed?'

'South.'

'South is good.'

I hopped out to pop the trunk. Then I remembered that I had a dead eagle back there, and a loaded pistol. I told him he could stash his stuff in the back. He laid his backpack on the seat, but kept his shoulder bag with him. It was a faded blue satchel with the US Postal Service logo on the flap. A mailbag. It didn't really go with the rest of the outfit he had on: a linen shirt, khakis, and Birkenstock sandals. All his clothes were covered in a layer of desert dust.

He slid into the passenger seat, and we started driving.

'Man, I'm parched,' he said, fastening his seatbelt. 'You got any water?'

'I got road pops. Lucky Lager.'

'Lucky's good.'

'They're in the back.'

He fished one out, drained it in about thirty seconds, then helped himself to another. As he drank, I angled my rear-view to get a better look at him. His face was lean and sunbrowned, and his lips were a bit chapped. After a minute or so he pushed his sunglasses up, resting them on his forehead. He had a raccoon-eyed tan and boyish features that looked a bit familiar, somehow.

'Say,' he said, 'how about some music?'

'The radio doesn't work.'

'Are you sure? Maybe I can fix it.'

He reached for the dial, and I caught his wrist. I wasn't breaking my vow of silence, even for a guest.

'I said it doesn't work.'

He retracted his hand. Carefully. 'Okay,' he said.

After that, he was quiet for a while. We both were. He sat with one arm folded over his mailbag, holding it against his abdomen. Every few miles he'd fiddle with the buckles and look inside, as if checking that the contents were safe, then close it up again.

'Cool bag,' I said. 'Did you used to be a postman or something?'

'Maybe.' He took a slug of beer, and burped. 'And, if I was a postman, I still might have one letter to deliver.'

I slowed down, glancing at him. 'To who?'

'Somebody important.'

'Can't you just mail it?'

'I don't trust the postal service. The contents are too valuable.'

He caught me eyeing his bag, and shifted it over to his right hip, away from me – as if he thought I might try to snatch it. He said, 'This is one letter I've got to deliver by hand.'

'Is that where you're going?'

'I've got a good game we can play,' he said. 'Let's pretend to know everything about each other, all the boring stuff you

148

ask strangers when you first meet. Where you're from, what you do, where you're going. We know all that. It's like we're already old friends or brothers. So we can only say interesting and refreshing things. How does that sound?'

'Sure,' I said. 'If that's what you want.'

He sat gazing out the window for a minute. I couldn't figure out if he was waiting for me to begin the game or what. But then he put his hand to his forehead, acting like an oracle, and said, 'The only journey is the one within.'

I shifted in my seat. 'That's pretty deep.'

A minute later, he came out with another one. 'Lose yourself and find the key.'

He was good, this guy. He'd obviously played the game before. I tried to think of something that would impress him.

'It's best to take the road less travelled,' I said.

'You didn't make that up.'

'I didn't know that was part of your game.'

'I don't think you really get my game.'

He yawned and slid down in his seat. I kept waiting for him to say something else, but his head slowly sank lower, until his chin was resting on his chest. I assumed he was asleep, until he murmured, almost to himself, 'The road heals all wounds.'

'Don't you mean time?'

He didn't answer. He'd nodded off. As he slept, his head bobbed around like one of those dashboard dolls. For about half an hour or so I drove and smoked and zoned out to the hypnotic movement of the road. I didn't realise he'd woken up until he started talking again.

'I've got a theory,' he announced. Lacing his fingers, he pressed his palms towards the windshield to stretch out his arms and back. 'You know when something really weird happens, and you just accept it and say, "Wow, that was weird"?'

'Kind of,' I said.

'Well, what if you didn't just accept it? What if you *really* thought about it, and searched for the hidden meaning in it?'

'Like what?'

He looked out the window, tugging at his earlobe. 'Say you order a new suit. A blue suit. But the company delivers a black suit instead. And, on the day it arrives, your relative dies.' He turned to me. There were crow's feet around his eyes. He was a little older than I'd first thought. 'Symbolically, the two things are connected. That would be weird, right?'

'Sure. A coincidence.'

'But it's not just a coincidence. It's a *meaningful* coincidence. It's as if the events in your life have aligned. Not through cause and effect, but in some other way. You get me?'

I nodded. 'Sure. It's like when I picked you up. It was weird, finding you like that. You needed a ride, and I needed the company. And it all came together.'

'Exactly,' he said. 'That's it. That is *it*.'

'But as soon as you start thinking like that,' I said, 'couldn't anything be meaningful? Any little coincidence or occurrence? Like, you blow your nose, and on the same day a plane crashes. You can pretend that means something, but it probably doesn't.'

He was peering at me with this shrewd Sherlock Holmes expression. 'Are you a rationalist?'

'I don't think so.'

'You sure talk like one.'

He crossed his arms and stared straight ahead and gave me the silent treatment for a few minutes. Then he said, 'It's not actually my theory, anyway. It's called synchronicity. A really smart guy named Carl Jung came up with it, okay?'

I told him it was okay.

We drove until the sun dropped from the sky and landed in a puddle of red on the horizon. Then the puddle drained away, leaving the world dark. I could see our reflections in the windshield. The yellowish glow of the dials and dashboard made us look like zombies.

'When do you want to stop?' I asked.

'When do *you* want to stop?'

Eventually we stopped. I told him that he was welcome to sleep in the car, but he said he'd rather sleep in his tent. As he unloaded his things, he spotted my visor on the back seat. He picked it up and tried it on. The flashing lights lit up his face, giving it a campfire flicker.

'Sweet visor,' he said. 'Where'd you get it?'

'Up north.'

I walked around the car, took the visor back, and turned it off.

'Want to trade for it? I got lots of cool stuff.'

'No,' I said, putting it in the trunk. 'It means a lot to me.'

'Don't you know what they say about possessions?'

'I have a feeling you do.'

'Hold them in a flat palm, not in a clenched fist.'

Hefting his bag on one shoulder, he trudged about twenty yards off. I cracked open a road pop and sat in the car, watching him through the window. He had one of those camping flashlights that you strap to your forehead. I could see it bobbing around as he worked away. When he crawled inside the tent, it lit up like a paper lantern, floating out there in the dark. I rolled down my window.

'Goodnight,' I called.

A second later, the echo came back. 'Goodnight.'

The lantern winked out. I lowered my seat, and got comfortable. That was when I noticed. On the passenger seat beside me – practically right in front of my face – was his postbag. He must have forgotten it. I stared at it for a long time. Outside my car the desert was dark and quiet and still. I reached over and unbuckled the bag. There was a letter inside, just as he'd said. The envelope was worn and wrinkled, and the seal was open. I could easily have slipped the letter out, read it, and put it back without him ever knowing.

I withdrew my hand and re-buckled the bag.

chapter 35

I heard pounding. Somebody was pounding on the window. I sat up in my seat. The hitcher was outside the car, dressed in his boxers, doing an excited little dance – like a firewalker prancing over hot coals. It was still before dawn and the desert landscape looked dull and grey as porridge. He continued pounding on the glass, using the meaty part of his palm.

I reached over and opened the passenger door for him.

'What's up, man?' I asked.

He grabbed his postbag and glared at me. Suspiciously. 'We'll see what's up, won't we?'

Crouching on the pavement, he unbuckled the clasps, withdrew the envelope, and studied the seal. Then he prised open the flap and peered inside, checking on the letter.

I lit a Lucky and waited for him to finish.

After a minute he slipped the envelope back in the bag, and buckled it. He climbed into the passenger seat and stared at me, his eyes quivering, his nose nearly touching mine.

I yawned smoke. 'How did you sleep?'

He smiled. 'How did *you* sleep?'

We were still friends, apparently.

As we drove along that morning, he got some beef jerky out and starting gnawing on it. He was eating teriyaki flavour – my favourite – and the smells of soy sauce and salt and spices filled my car, my nostrils, my head. Ever since I'd stopped eating, I'd become hyper-aware of food smells, as if my olfactory functions were working overtime.

The hitcher tore off a strip of jerky and wagged it at me.

'No, thanks,' I said.

'Don't you eat breakfast?'

'I'm not really eating anything these days.'

'I totally understand.' He popped the piece in his own mouth and chewed, looking thoughtful. 'You didn't read my letter.'

'I wanted to.'

'But your will was stronger than your desire.' He was staring at me in that intense way of his again. 'I left it there on purpose, you know. I needed to see if I could trust you.'

'And do you trust me now?'

He put his hand on my knee. 'Do *you* trust me? Because I have something to show you. Better than the letter.'

I said that I trusted him.

'Then take this left.'

There was a turn coming up. I hadn't seen it, and don't think he could have seen it, since he wasn't even looking ahead. I guess he just knew that desert incredibly well.

'Left! Go left!'

I turned left.

It was a one-lane road that dissolved into a dirt track. Then the track tapered off, and we were rattling over flat, open ground that was cracked and sun-baked, like old pottery. The hitcher leaned forward in his seat, shouting directions and encouragement at me.

'Go around that rock. Great. Watch out for those cactuses. Cacti, I guess. That's it. Straight through that gap. We're getting close now.'

We came to an old rock formation. There were two hoodoos, sticking straight up like the legs of a giant who'd been buried upside down. Between the hoodoos the ground folded into a crevasse. We got out of the car. Our footsteps raised puffs of dust as we walked over. The crevasse was six or seven feet deep and wide enough to walk in, like a natural corridor.

'What is it?' I asked.

'One of America's secret places. Come on.'

He led me down into the crevasse. The sides were steep and had a rich, ochre colour. Twenty yards along, the ground closed above us and the crevasse became a cave. It grew dark quickly. He'd brought his headlamp and he flicked it on. As he walked, the beam wobbled and bounced off the walls.

'I wish I'd worn my visor,' I said. It was still locked in my trunk.

'You should have.'

Our footsteps echoed off the stone in the enclosed space. The roof got lower, and lower, so that we had to stoop. The walls tightened around us, and I held out my hands to feel my way along. The rock was slick with secretions. He was humming to himself – an off-key tune I'd never heard. When I looked back, I couldn't see the light of the entrance.

'This is cool,' I said, 'but maybe we've gone far enough, eh?'

He just kept walking.

'Do you know where you're going?'

He turned around, so the headlamp shone in my face. 'You said you trusted me.'

'I don't even know you.'

'You don't know yourself.' He sounded angry. 'That's why you're here.'

He got on his hands and knees. There was a hole in the rock down there. He crawled into it. I was thinking, this is how assholes die. Assholes like us. Exploring underground caves, without proper equipment. But I got down and followed him, creeping along, hand over hand. The ground was wet and bits of shale dug into my palms. As we progressed, the tunnel got narrower and narrower, until we had to wriggle along on our elbows, army-style. He was about ten yards ahead of me. I could see his light up there. Then it went out.

'Hello?' I called.

There was no answer. Just the sound of my own ragged breathing. I inched forward. It was completely black. I felt around blindly. The walls and roof of the tunnel were gone.

'This is a darkness that has never seen the sun,' a voice said. 'Now stand up.'

I did. I heard a click, and then there was light. It illuminated the ceiling of a cavern, arching overhead. The rock face was smooth and covered with figures, painted in red. There were animals that looked like deer, elk, and maybe buffalo. As the light flitted across them, their legs flickered and blurred, giving the impression of life. There were people, too – men in the middle of the hunt, with bows and spears, and women standing still. The bodies of the women were big-hipped and shaped like bells, or vessels. They seemed to brim with life.

I gazed up, mouth agape, craning my neck until it ached.

'If you have things to say,' the hitcher said, 'this is the place to say them.'

He was cradling his headlamp in his hands, like a pearl. It lit up his face from below.

'Things like what?' I asked.

'The things that go unsaid. That's what this cave was for. The Natives brought young men here, to purge them of their sins and troubles, and prepare them for adulthood.'

I nodded, pretending I understood.

'We'll try it. Together.' He closed his eyes, took a dramatic breath, and declared into the dark, 'I used to fantasise about making out with my aunt.'

Then he opened his eyes and looked at me. Expectantly.

'Oh,' I said. 'Was she super-hot or something?'

He frowned. 'No – you're supposed to go next. It's your turn.'

'Sorry.'

I thought for a second, and then said, 'I once kicked my own cat, for no reason – and hurt her leg.'

'I was in a gang. A biker gang.'

'I still mooch money from my stepmom.'

'I held up a liquor store at knifepoint.'

Our voices bounced around off the walls, blending and blurring with one another.

'My girlfriend cheated on me.' It was the first time I'd said it aloud. The words just leapt out of my mouth, like a frog. 'She cheated on me, so I imagined killing her.'

'I walked out on my pregnant wife.'

'I'm impotent. Ever since she cheated on me, I can't get it up.'

'I've got a son I've never met.'

We went back and forth like that, working ourselves into a frenzy, trying to top each other's transgressions. Then I came out with it. My trump card.

'I shot a bald eagle.'

Silence. He shone the light on me – so I had to shield my eyes.

'You *shot* a bald eagle?'

'It's in my trunk.'

'Wow. Okay.'

We kept saying things for a while, but none really beat my eagle.

The route back through the caves seemed to take a lot less time than going in. But then, that's usually the case once you know the way and the mystery has evaporated.

When we reached the car, the hitcher asked if he could see the eagle.

'I don't know,' I said. 'It's kind of personal.'

'Come on. I showed you my secret place.'

That was true. I owed him. So I popped the trunk and opened the cooler. 'Here she is,' I said.

The bird looked even bigger than I remembered, crammed into its coffin with both wings folded back. Its beak was open and its tongue stuck out, like a piece of pink taffy. The bags of ice had gone soft and plump, but hadn't melted completely – they were still cold.

We stood side by side, looking down at the bird.

'What are you going to do with it?' he asked.

'I was thinking of burying it. Maybe giving it a proper ceremony or whatever.'

He reached into the cooler and held his palm over the eagle – as if feeling for warmth, or sensing its aura.

'I've got a better idea,' he said.

chapter 36

Our fire looked like a small nest, made out of twigs and sticks that we'd gathered from the surrounding desert. Flames fluttered in the nest and the coals at the bottom glowed orange, like magic eggs. Near dusk we'd parked and set up the hitcher's tent behind a rocky outcrop, maybe fifty yards from the road. Then we'd dug ourselves a makeshift fire pit, and I'd got out my flat of road pops. I knew I'd need them to wash down this plan of his.

'You sure it's fresh enough?' I asked.

We were sitting cross-legged on either side of the fire, swilling beers and waiting for our meal to cook. The flames sputtered and crackled with bird fat.

'I told you – I've eaten tons of roadkill. And you had this baby on ice.'

He'd constructed a makeshift spit out of two forked branches. Stuck on the skewer between them was the eagle, plucked and feathered and slowly roasting. All the feathers lay in a bloody bundle over by the tent, along with the head and the claws, which we'd cut off.

'I won't be able to eat much.'

'That's okay,' he said. 'I'm pretty hungry. But you have to try some of it.'

According to him, this was the only way I could make amends for what I'd done. He'd also said something about absorbing the eagle's strength, or accepting it into me, or whatever – but you could tell he just really liked the idea of eating an eagle. Every so often, one of us would get up to rotate the bird on the spit. Then more juice would stream off into the flames, making them hiss.

While we waited I asked, 'Were you really in a gang?'

'What's said in the sacred cave,' he said, 'stays in the sacred cave.'

I pointed at the spit-roast.

'My eagle didn't.'

'Okay. I was in a biker gang. My brother's gang.'

That was why this guy had looked familiar. He had the same features as the biker I'd seen up in Trevor – the one who'd seemed to recognise me.

'Your brother's gang isn't called the Cobras, is it?'

He was in the middle of turning the eagle. He stopped. 'How do you know that?'

'I keep seeing him. I think he's got a beef with me.'

He was so blown away by that, he had to sit back down and take a big drink. I knew what he was thinking, because I was thinking exactly the same thing: this proved his theory.

'What a coincidence,' I said.

'A *meaningful* coincidence.'

We looked at each other and said, 'Synchronicity!'

He asked why I thought his brother had a beef with me. I told him I wasn't sure, but it was possible that I'd run into him back in Vancouver, and that we'd had a little altercation. When the hitcher heard that, he couldn't believe I'd gotten off so easily.

'No wonder my brother's pissed,' he said. 'You better watch yourself.'

'How can I do that?'

'Just don't mess with him – he's got a gun.'

'I've got a gun of my own.'

We stared at each other in silence for a moment. Then one of the logs in the fire sort of exploded, sending sparks everywhere, and we both jumped – as if we expected his brother to appear out of the darkness. Afterwards we did the guy thing, where you laugh at yourself and act all tough and shrug it off.

'Hey,' he said, and stood up. 'We ought to check on this bird.'

I held the spit while he cut into the thigh with his penknife. The skin had gone brown and crispy, and the flesh inside was cooked through. He sawed off half a dozen thick slices, catching them on a tin plate, then transferred some to another plate for me. I only wanted a small portion. Actually, I didn't really want any portion – but if I was going to take a break from my fast I figured eating eagle was the way to do it.

'Wow,' he said, taking a bite. 'That's good.'

We ate with our hands. I picked up a small piece and blew on it to cool it off. The meat was dark and stringy. I chewed it cautiously, with a kind of reverence. It tasted a bit like turkey, only tougher. I swallowed maybe four or five mouthfuls. That was all I could manage. My stomach felt small as a walnut.

I offered him my plate. 'Want mine?'

'You bet.'

He took it from me and kept eating, shovelling fingerfuls into his mouth. When he finished, he got out a napkin and started wiping the grease off our plates.

I asked, 'Why did you quit your brother's gang, anyways?'

'I just got sick of all that macho bullshit. It's not as if they really do anything, except drive around acting tough, and deal a bit of weed. They want to be like the Hell's Angels, but they're not. I should never have left her to go with them in the first place.'

'Your wife?'

'I missed my own son's birth.'

'You could always go home. To see them again.'

'Sometimes I think I will.' He had his head down, still polishing the plates. 'Just like sometimes you probably think you'll forgive your girlfriend, and get back together with her.'

'Sometimes.'

'And other times…' He shrugged. '*Lo que paso, paso.*'

I gazed at him through the flames, waiting for him to explain. He was finished with the plates. He put them

160

aside, and tossed the napkin in the fire. It flared briefly and died out.

He said, 'What's done is done.'

After dinner we fooled around with my gun. It was kind of inevitable, considering we were two guys, half-cut, sitting around a campfire. He asked to see it, so I went to get it from the car. I checked the clip and safety and handed it over. He hefted it, testing the weight, and sighted along the barrel. He told me it was some kind of Glock.

'Hell,' he said, twirling it around his finger, 'I haven't shot a gun for a while.'

'Have a try, if you want.'

We were lounging in the dirt. He looked around for a target. There was an empty on the other side of the fire. From where he sat, he pointed the gun and casually squeezed off a round. The can popped up and spun into the air. As it came back down – just as it touched the ground – he shot it again. And again. He kept it dancing like that for five or six shots.

'Nice shooting, Tex,' I said.

'Now check *this* out.'

The can had landed on a clump of bunchgrass. He took aim and closed his eyes, shooting blind. For a second I actually believed he was going to do it. But the next bullet kicked up sand.

'Nearly,' he said.

'That would have been so awesome.'

He put the safety on, and handed the gun back to me.

'My wife did that once. We used to go to the shooting range together, as a kind of date thing. One time she stepped up and said she was gonna try it blind. Bam. Bull's eye.'

'That's impossible.'

'Not for her it wasn't.'

'Only a woman could do that.'

He nodded and cracked open another beer. The spray shot up into his face. 'She wasn't even a good shot normally.

I mean, she was all right – for a chick. Not as good as me, or my brother. My brother's insane. He practises all the time, at this gun range south of here.' He twisted off his ring-pull and tossed it into the fire. 'He loves luring people into having a shoot-out. He'll get them to bet something, too. Just so he can win it from them.'

'What a dipstick,' I said.

He took a swig of beer. 'If he's really got it in for you, I'd avoid him.'

'Don't worry. I'm not gonna have any shoot-outs with him.'

He started snickering. He was on his sixth or seventh beer. 'The only way you'd ever beat him is by sheer blind luck.'

'Totally.' I laughed, giving him a high-five. 'Like chick-luck.'

By then the fire had started to sputter. To put out it out, we pissed on it. Not at the same time. He pissed on it first, then me. As we arranged our beds I could still smell our piss, steaming up from the stones. The ground beneath my sleeping bag felt hard and cold. The fire would have kept us warm, but we were both paranoid about starting a brushfire.

We lay on our backs, gazing up. There was no moon, so the stars stood out in thick clumps, like splashes of spilled milk. The hitcher pointed to various constellations, and told me their names. I knew all the regular ones, like Orion and the Big Dipper, but he knew the more obscure ones: the Crab, the Archer, the Lion. He even knew one called the Eagle. Or pretended to know. Sometimes it was hard to tell with him.

As we dozed off, I asked him, 'Where are you going, anyways?'

'Where are *you* going?'

'San Francisco, eventually.'

'Frisco's overrated. I'm going to Sausalito.'

I propped myself up on one elbow. I could see his shadow on the ground. 'Is that far?'

'Far enough.'

He rolled over, turning his back on me. Our little bonding session was finished, apparently. I lay down again. I decided I wouldn't say anything else to him, the prick.

Then he said, 'After tomorrow, I'll go my own way.'

'I don't mind driving you.'

'Yeah – but you know what they say about guests.' He burped, deliberately loud. The smell lingered in the air. 'They're just like fish. After three days, they start to stink.'

chapter 37

I awoke with sore shoulders and numb toes. The sun was already up and so was the hitcher. He was in the process of dismantling his tent, which neither of us had slept in. I huddled in my sleeping bag as he folded up the poles, making them click and clack like giant chopsticks.

Then he noticed me watching.

'You could help, you know, instead of just lying there.'

I got up to give him a hand. First I shook the dew off the fly, then I started rolling it.

'No, no,' he said, grabbing it from me, 'the poles get rolled up *inside* the fly.'

'They'll still fit.'

'I said they go *inside*.'

Eventually I left him to it. I cleaned up the campsite instead. I kicked dirt over the fire pit, gathered up our empties, and stuffed all the eagle feathers in a bag. They felt soft and sumptuous as velvet. When I told him I was thinking of keeping them, he just snickered – as if that was the lamest idea in the world, even though he'd already taken the claws for himself.

'Feathers might come in handy, okay?' I said.

'Handy as a handjob.'

It was the same once we got back on the road. First he complained about me having my morning smoke, which hadn't bothered him before. Then he found my bag of whipped cream canisters beneath his seat. He got one out and gawked at it. 'Have you been huffing *whippets*?'

'Maybe.'

'That's kids' stuff. If this were a real road trip, you'd be doing real drugs. I'm talking *Fear and Loathing*-type shit – ether and mescaline and acid.'

'Nobody does acid any more.'

He couldn't argue with that. Outside, the first waves of morning light washed across the landscape. The cacti and yucca plants glowed coral-red, and the sandy ground glittered like a seabed.

'Dawn is pretty incredible out here,' I said.

He yawned. 'When you've seen one desert sunrise, you've seen them all.'

'How long have you been on the road, anyways?'

'How long have *you* been on the road?'

I was getting so sick of that fucking trick – his little mimicking trick. 'A while,' I said.

'Hah.' He fiddled with the whipped cream canister, trying to pop the top. 'Let me guess. You borrowed Daddy's car to go on a little road trip. For how long? A whole week?'

'It's not my dad's car. I rented it because I needed to get away.'

'Because your girlfriend cheated on you, you mean.'

I eased up on the gas pedal and stared at him – just to let him know I figured that was a pretty low blow. I said, 'I thought what's said in the sacred cave stays in the sacred cave.'

He shrugged, as if the sacred cave, and what had happened yesterday, didn't matter much. He had the top off the whipped cream now. He idly tipped the can back and forth, making the widget clack, then stuck the nozzle in his mouth and took a slow dose of nitrous.

I asked, 'How many times have you been in that cave, anyways?'

'I don't keep count. I go there a lot.'

'But, if it was a rite of passage for the Natives, they would only have done it once. That's the whole point of a rite of passage.'

'What, are you an expert now or something?' When he said 'expert' I felt some spit hit me on the cheek. 'Besides, I could say exactly the same thing about your road trip. Do you know how many assholes I've met out here, trying to find themselves?'

'Sure – it's a rite of passage. Which is why I'll only do it once.'

'That's not what I mean. I'm talking about how clichéd it is. I'm sick of meeting all these middle-class kids in crisis.' He gestured out the window – as if the kids he was talking about were lining the roadside. 'Haven't you seen those foreign people, with stick limbs and swollen bellies? Those people have real problems. Not us. Nobody else in the whole world has it this good. Nobody's *ever* had it this good. Take a look around.'

I looked around. I saw parched earth, and a bunch of rocks and weeds. Also, in the midde of our lane I saw a dead snake, smashed flat as a leather belt. I drove right over it.

He sighed theatrically. 'I didn't mean look around right now. I meant it in a general sense. When you think about that, what does it matter that your girlfriend made a mistake?'

'It was a pretty big fucking mistake to make.'

'About as big as, say, shooting a bald eagle?'

He smiled, as if he really thought he'd put me in my place, and raised the can to his lips. Before he inhaled, I snatched it from him and took a hit myself. 'That was an accident, okay?' I said, and coughed. I'd breathed in flecks of cream with the nitrous. 'An accident is different from a mistake. You can't accidentally fuck a guy.'

'Everything's an accident,' he said. He tried to grab the can back, but I held it away from him. 'You and me meeting like this. Life itself. Just an endless series of accidents.'

'The way you accidentally abandoned your pregnant wife.'

As soon as I said that, he went quiet. After a minute of silence I said I was sorry and offered him the nitrous, but he wouldn't take it. He just curled up in his seat, as if I'd hit him.

Neither of us spoke for about three hours.

Later that day, the hitcher took off his seatbelt and started rooting around in his backpack. He had his food in there, and all his clothing. Also, he had what looked like a rubber mask.

'What's with the mask?'

'Never mind,' he said, pushing it further down. 'I'm looking for... ah. Here.'

He pulled out a clear plastic bag, full of buns. They were wholemeal – the little round kind you buy at the bakery.

'Hungry?' he asked.

'I'm fasting, remember?'

'That's so middle-class.'

He sat with the buns on his lap. Waiting. Every so often, he'd ask me again, and I'd say no again. Other than that, we didn't talk. But in the heat, as we drove, he started farting. He'd let out these nasty eagle and beer farts, then deny it. He was giving off super-bad body odour, too – the dirty, stale stench of the road. By evening it was getting so rank in there I had to lean away from him and breathe out the window.

He'd been right about guests, at least.

'Guess it's time for dinner,' he said, offering me a bun.

'You go ahead.'

He tore off a big bite with his teeth, and chewed it lustily.

'I baked these myself, you know.'

I switched on my headlights, ignoring him. The bun smelled good, though.

'It's important to break bread,' he said. 'To seal a friendship.'

Finally I held out my hand. 'Fine. Give me a bun.'

He did. I tried a bite. It was a bit dry, but had a wholesome, earthy taste. I took another nibble. The eagle meat had reminded my stomach that it needed food. Now it kind of twitched, sensing more. I ate slowly, chewing each mouthful to mush before swallowing.

'Thanks,' I said. 'These are good.'

'It's a special recipe.'

He had almost finished his first bun. He shoved the last bit in his mouth and, before he'd even swallowed it, reached for another. He sprayed the next one with whipped cream, and offered half to me.

'Dessert?'

'All right.'

He ate three or four, I think. I only managed one and a half. They weren't big buns, but they filled me up. I felt as if I'd swallowed one of those expanding towels. It got bigger, and bigger, pressing against the insides of my ribs. I assumed the feeling would pass, but it didn't. It got worse. My stomach started to cramp. I squirmed and shifted as I drove.

'Oh, man,' I said. 'I think I ate too much.'

He was slumped against the car door.

'No – I feel it, too. That's supposed to happen.'

'What's supposed to happen?'

He looked at me. 'You better pull over. It's going to start soon.'

I steered towards the shoulder, driving with one hand and holding the other against my belly. It was spasming now, as if I'd swallowed a live squirrel. I parked and grabbed him by the collar. 'What did you feed me?'

He gripped the back of my neck, pulling me in so our foreheads touched. His pupils were wide and black and I could see the gleaming circle of my own face reflected in them.

'What do you know about vision quests?' he asked.

He'd baked the buns with peyote. I hadn't even known that was possible, but it is, apparently. The nausea was a side effect. Right after he admitted that, I staggered from the car and started gagging up mouthfuls of bun. It came out gooey and wet, as if the bread had reverted to batter in my stomach.

'Try to keep it down,' he said. He was gagging too. Not as much as me, though. I guess he was more used to it. 'It will make the high stronger.'

'Don't want to be high.'

I could barely talk. I was choking and retching and crying a little. He guided me away from the road and eased me down in the dirt, among these little weeds that had furry purple flowers on them. I curled up, clutching my stomach. It was still cramping. I was aware of him moving around me. He was scratching patterns in the dirt with a bent stick.

'You hoodwinked me,' I whispered.

'You wouldn't have done it otherwise.'

It was true. But I couldn't see how that justified it.

'Have you done hallucinogens before?'

'Mushrooms,' I said, and retched again. 'And acid, once.'

'Think of those as appetisers. This is the main course.'

I cleared my throat and hawked in the sand. A spider's web of spit stuck to my lips, hanging down. I wiped it away. I could still taste bits of bun and puke in my mouth.

'Don't worry. It will pass.'

I didn't believe him, but it did – after what seemed like hours. By then he'd finished whatever it was he'd been doing. I managed to sit up. He'd etched a circle around me in the dust. The circle was divided into four and filled with symbols. I couldn't tell what any of the symbols meant, but they looked fairly impressive. He squatted down across from me.

'Now you need to prepare yourself,' he said, 'for the vision quest.'

'I don't want to go on any quest.'

'Remember what I told you? It's only when you lose yourself that you find the key.'

I tried to explain that I didn't want to lose myself – that if I got any more lost I might never find myself again. But he wouldn't listen. He claimed that it was all part of my pathway to individuation. I didn't have the energy to argue. The constant retching had left me feeling as empty and hollow as a gourd.

While we sat there, a desert breeze ghosted past, caressing my skin and cooling my sweat.

'Feel that?' he asked.

I nodded. I was breathing a little more easily. He began talking again. The words came out in a free-flowing stream. He talked about animal spirits and astral space and something called mandalas. It was hard to follow. My mind would get stuck on one particular word or phrase, and by the time I started listening again I'd find that a lot of sentences had flowed by.

'You'll be all alone,' he said. 'Alone with yourself.'

'Aren't you coming?'

'I've been on lots of vision quests. This time I'm your shaman.'

I nodded. I was glad to have a shaman. I listened to my shaman's voice, throbbing between my ears.

'The main thing is not to panic. Stay in your quest area.'

'How do I know what that is?'

'You'll know. Now get going.'

He dragged me to my feet and gave me a push. As I shuffled away, he was digging through the big compartment in his backpack. He waved me on.

'Go – don't look back.'

I walked for a while and found a clearing, dotted with rocks and stones. I didn't know if it was my quest area but I liked it. I kicked off my shoes, stashed my keys inside one of them, and undressed. That was one thing I remembered from what he'd told me: I was supposed to be naked. It felt weird to be naked outdoors, with the wind brushing my balls and tickling my dick. I stared at the rocks. They had mica in them and sparkled like stars in the darkness. I bent down and started to arrange them like actual stars, copying the patterns I saw overhead. I made my own version of the Little Dipper, and the Seven Sisters, and Cassiopeia, and all the other constellations. I don't know how long it took me. A long time, I think. But I enjoyed crawling around in the dirt, naked and alone. I felt like a child again, playing in the sandbox.

Finally, I dusted off my hands and sat in the middle of the clearing. Now there were stars on the ground all around me, matching the stars in the sky overhead. I was at the centre of my makeshift universe. I lay back, spreading my arms and legs out, a starfish among the stars. Time passed. They were bright, those stars – brighter than any I'd ever seen. The light shining off them seemed to hang down in threads. The threads connected the stars above to my stars, and my stars to me. I sat back up. I could see more threads, delicate and wispy as smoke, stretching in an ethereal web between the weeds, the rocks, the landscape, and me. I knew it meant something. I knew it was what I'd come here to see, to know, to understand.

Then I heard a roar.

I looked around. The tendrils of smoke withdrew, like frightened snakes. The roar came again. Closer, this time. It sounded like some kind of animal. I scrambled to my feet, trying to gauge where it was coming from. The third time it roared, I saw it. It appeared out of the shadows: a giant cat that walked on two legs, like a man. A man-cat. It came towards me, growling. The man-cat was naked, too. I could see its dick dangling between its legs.

'You are it,' the man-cat said. It could talk, apparently.

'I am what?'

'You are *it*!' it shouted.

At first I tried to make myself look big. I'd heard that worked with wild animals. I pushed out my chest, raised my arms, and widened my stance like a sumo wrestler. But the man-cat kept coming, muttering and snarling. I had to try something else. I waved my hands and made a lot of noise, hoping to scare it off. That only seemed to enrage it. It growled at me and got into a low crouch. I was thinking, this fucking thing is going to eat me alive...

I turned and ran.

It gave chase. Behind me I heard its footsteps, and its ragged animal panting. Then something hit the back of my legs, and we went down together in the sand. We rolled over and over, like cartoon characters, churning up a cloud of dust. Rocks dug into my back and scraped my shoulders. We wrestled like that, skin on sweaty skin, in a tangle of naked limbs. He was roaring and I was screaming. I wasn't screaming words. I was just screaming.

Something connected with my nose. A knee, maybe. Then my face was wet, and I could taste blood. It clogged my throat. I lashed out wildly with my fists. I got in one good shot. The man-cat howled. His face bent and went all askew. I tried to squirm away, but he pounced on me again, clawing and raking and punching.

'You're only fighting yourself!'

'Fuck you, man-cat!'

I ended up on my back. The cat loomed over me, pinning me down. His eyes and mouth were black: black as the holes cut in a burlap sack, black as space and time, black as oblivion. It was as if I could see right through him to the sky above. I struggled feebly as his mouth came closer, yawning wider. It descended over my head, and swallowed me whole.

chapter 38

I was being cooked on a grill – iron-hard and painfully hot. I opened my eyes. I saw dirt, pebbles, shale, and a beetle that looked enormous as a tank, crawling over the landscape towards me. I was lying face-down, with my cheek pressed into the dust. I got my hands beneath me and eased myself into a push-up position. For some reason, I was naked. My body was lathered with dust and covered in cuts, clotted with dried blood. My head felt like a roasted marshmallow.

Trying to stand made me dizzy. I stayed in a crouch, waiting until it passed, and then straightened up. The sun was directly overhead, pounding down like a pile-driver. I shielded my eyes with one hand. I couldn't remember where I was, what I'd been doing. I hurt all over, but my nose hurt the most. I touched the bridge. The cartilage felt puffy and inflamed. When I tried to clear my nostrils, the pain flared and strands of red snot drizzled into the dust.

A little way off, I found a pile of clothes on the ground. I recognised them as mine. Nearby lay a rubber animal mask. A tiger mask. I recognised it, too. Things started coming back to me. I took the clothes, left the mask, and followed my own footprints – retracing my path and recovering memories of the previous night. There was another set of footprints next to mine. He'd come after me. Both sets led back to the circle he'd scratched in the dust. By the light of day, I could see that the mysterious symbols it contained were just spirals and swirls. I doubted they were authentic. Like most things with that guy, my vision quest had been half-baked.

My car was at the roadside where I'd left it. There were some scratch marks around the lock on the trunk, as if he'd tried to jimmy it. He hadn't found my keys, which were still in my shoe. I dug them out and popped the trunk. My stuff was all there, including my visor. I'm pretty sure that was what he wanted. I tossed it on the back seat and sat sideways in the front, with my feet flat on the road, letting the cooked air clear out of the car. I checked my face in the rear-view. My nose looked swollen and dried blood surrounded my mouth like a beard. My face had a reddish hue. So did my chest, and stomach. I'd sunburnt my entire body, even my dick. I must have been lolling in the heat all morning, getting fried like a human wiener.

I didn't have any water – just beer. I opened the can and splashed some down my throat. It tasted warm and tinny but, if I had to, I could get by on beer.

As I eased myself behind the wheel, I noticed a scrap of paper pinned under my windshield wiper. He'd left me a note, scrawled in chicken-scratch: *I'll see you when you get there.*

I crumpled it up and left it at the roadside.

I drove. There were no cars going my way, and no cars going the other way. There were no cars out there, period. I had the entire road to myself. I started making use of it. First I swerved from lane to lane, slaloming between the road markings. Then I accelerated to top speed, and slowed to a crawl. Then I drove on the wrong side of the road – the left-hand side – just to see what it felt like. It felt exactly like driving on the right-hand side, only more daring. I decided I'd drive on the left-hand side of the road whenever possible from then on.

'Left is always right,' I said, chanting the words to myself.

I cruised along like that for about thirty minutes before I realised I had absolutely no idea where I was going. I eased up on the gas and my car inched to a stop, like a confused caterpillar. Ever since we'd turned off the highway to go to the hitcher's cave, I hadn't paid much attention to directions and navigation. He'd always seemed to know the way.

I got out my map, and tried my old trick of spreading it across the hood. But a map only works if you know where you are on the map. I didn't. I didn't even know if I was still in Oregon. I could easily have crossed the border into Nevada by that point. Or not. All the little squiggles and coloured symbols were meaningless. I hadn't seen any signs for a long time. I crumpled up the map and got back in the car.

I had a quarter-tank of gas left.

The sky crackled blue, like an arc light. Floating around up there were a few clouds in the shape of sheep. As I drove, I stared at the sheep. One of them detached from the flock, and drifted down to me – right in front of my face, right in front of my car.

I hit the brakes, fishtailing on to the gravel at the shoulder. My heart was going like a kettle drum: thrum, thrum, thrum. I looked around. The flying sheep was gone. I was still high, obviously. Not as high as last night, but still pretty fucking high. I had no idea how long peyote lasted. A while, apparently. I lit a cigarette. It quivered between my lips, causing the tip to dance. I smoked it to the butt in long, calming drags.

Then I kept driving. More slowly.

At about three o'clock – the hottest part of the day – my air-conditioning started to make a rattling noise, like an old lady with a chest infection. Then it emitted a hacking cough and died. I fiddled with the switches and knobs. Nothing happened.

I rolled down my window. The air out there felt like the backwash of a jet engine. My seat-rest was sticky with sweat and made squelching sounds whenever I moved. I was still naked – clothing chafed my skin and irritated my sunburn. All I had on was one shoe. My right shoe. I had to wear it to work the pedal. I didn't need the left, since the Neon was an automatic and there was no clutch. So I was driving along in my right shoe, going nowhere. But it was important, that shoe. Without it, I wouldn't even be going. I'd just be nowhere.

As I drifted along, I heard a humming in the distance. At first I thought I was having another hallucination. Then I saw the car. It appeared in my rear-view, emerging from a blur of heat and burning towards me. I slowed down. The other car was going fast. It must have covered the distance to me in about ten seconds, like a land-rocket, and then swung wide to overtake.

It was a blue sedan. Probably a rental, like mine. As it drew alongside, I caught a glimpse of the driver – this teenage kid, with freckles and a baby-face. He twisted his neck around to gawk at me, as if he was passing the site of an accident. I was still driving in the nude. My face was a pulpy mess and my upper body was pink as a lobster shell.

I raised a hand in greeting. He didn't wave back. He just floored it and barrelled on, hurtling towards the horizon. He was driving on the left-hand side of the road too. Maybe everybody did that, out there in the desert. I wanted to tell him to slow down and take his time. This was a dangerous place, full of unruly characters. He needed to be more careful.

But he was way ahead of me, now. The car dwindled to a blue disc in the distance. The way it gleamed reminded me of my visor. I'd taken it off before meeting those hunters, and I'd been lost ever since. Maybe it was time to get un-lost. I reached over into the back seat for the visor, pulled it on, and drove in the direction the kid had gone. It was possible that he was headed for Reno too, and might know the way. If nothing else, I figured I could warn him and keep him from picking up that fucking hitchhiker.

chapter 39

A diner popped out of the ground on the horizon. I only realised how hungry I was when I saw it waiting there, squat and square and garish, like a well-made cake. It had pink siding and a frosting of white trim. In front, anchored to a cherry-picker, was a big sign with those changeable marquee letters: *Kane 'n' Abel's Diner. All The Ribs You Can Eat.*

My belly gave off a low moan. I'd sampled some eagle, and tried those peyote buns. Maybe it was time to finish this fast of mine. While I was at it, I could ask them for directions out of the desert.

I pulled into the parking lot. It was full of vehicles, including a blue Chrysler sedan – the one I'd seen the teenager driving. I parked next to it and hopped out, forgetting that I was naked except for my visor and one shoe. The diner windows were bleached with sunlight, so I couldn't see inside, but I would have been in full view of anybody eating. I ducked down behind the car to get dressed, tugging on some jeans and slipping on a shirt.

Once I was ready, I crossed the lot and trotted up the steps to the porch. At the top I nearly tripped on a cat – a dirty white cat, tied to a leash in the sun. She was just lying there. I knew that couldn't be good for her. I'd had a white cat once, and both her ears had turned cancerous from being sunburnt too many times. It had killed her, eventually. And here was this cat who looked just like her, making the same mistake. I scooped the cat up and moved her into the shade. I stroked her back. Through her skin I could feel her ribs and the bumps of her vertebrae. Two bowls sat nearby. One was full of water, and the other was full of meat. I brought them over to her. She wouldn't touch the meat, but she lapped at the water, at least.

I left her there and went in. A bell hanging above the door dinged to announce my arrival. I stood beneath it, blinking as my eyes adjusted, piecing together an impression of the place: flesh-pink walls, lino floors, tables draped in red chequered tablecloths, settings laid with plates and cutlery, all of it clean and polished and gleaming.

Off to the left was the counter and till. Behind it stood a boy, plump and round as an apple. He wore chequered trousers that matched the tablecloths, a white apron, and a peaked cap. He waddled over, smiling. A burgundy birthmark leaked from the corner of his mouth.

'Will you be eating alone today, sir?'

I didn't answer right away. I was looking at all the chairs and tables. They were empty.

'Where are the other customers?' I asked.

'You're the first we've had today, sir.'

'But all those cars…'

'Those are for sale. My family runs a car lot, too. See the tags?'

He gestured outside. I hadn't seen before, but I did now. The other vehicles had price tags hanging in their front windshields. All except for the blue sedan I'd parked beside – the one I'd thought belonged to the teenager.

'Oh. Looks like it's just me, then,' I said.

He led me to a table in the centre of the room. I sat down at one of the place settings, and he cleared the others away. Then he brought me a menu. As I studied it, he hovered over me. The menu was a single laminated sheet. One side listed the buffet items: ribs, coleslaw, corn fritters, mashed potatoes. I turned the menu over. The other side was blank.

'All we do is the buffet,' the boy said. 'It's the Kane 'n' Abel special.'

'Are you Kane or Abel?'

He giggled – a high-pitched, squeaky sound, like dishes being scrubbed. 'Oh, no. Kane's my dad. He does all the cooking. Me and my brother just help out.'

'What about Abel?'

His smiled dropped. 'Abel doesn't work here any more.'

'Because he isn't able to?'

I laughed at my own joke. He didn't, so I stopped. I handed him the menu. 'I guess I'll order the buffet – if it's all you have.'

He made a mark on his pad and hurried over to the counter. Beside it was the buffet table. It had a glass canopy and heat lamps and aluminium warming trays. Apparently the buffet hadn't been prepared yet, because he had to fetch the food from the back. I sat and watched him go to and fro through a swinging steel door. Each time it opened, I caught a glimpse of the kitchen. A man was at work in there. He stood with his back to me, wielding a cleaver. It went up and down, making this thick, meaty sound: thock, thock, thock. He was cutting up ribs, I guess.

'All set,' the boy called. 'Come and get it.'

I stood up and walked over with my plate. They had huge racks of ribs, a mountain of mashed potatoes, fritters as big as my fist, and a tub-sized coleslaw bowl. I stood and stared at all that food. The heat lamps gave it a golden glow.

The boy rubbed his hands together, waiting. His face was sheened with sweat.

'Go on,' he said. 'Help yourself.'

Taped to the canopy was a handwritten note, partially covered by a stack of napkins. I moved the napkins aside. The note read *Take what you want, but you must eat what you take*. 'Must' had been underlined three times. I asked him what that meant.

'Oh, don't mind that old thing,' he said. 'Abel put that there ages ago. Just fill up your plate. That's the important thing. It's a buffet, remember. All you can eat.'

The mixture of smells – meat and grease, butter and barbecue sauce – worked on me like a narcotic. My stomach quivered. My hands trembled. I was tempted to pile my plate high, but I didn't know how much I'd be able to keep down, so I started with small portions.

The boy frowned. 'Are you sure you don't want more?'

'I can always have seconds.'

'But doesn't this look *good*?'

I agreed that it did. He kept offering me more, and I kept refusing. Finally he let me sit down. He stayed where he was, watching me. I tried the fritter first. It looked delicious: golden and crispy and fresh. But it wasn't. It was soggy with fat – the kind of fat that's sat in the fryer for days. I put the fritter aside. The rest of the food was the same. The coleslaw had gone sour, and the mashed potatoes tasted like play-dough. The ribs, though – the ribs were the worst. Beneath the gooey sauce, the meat was barely cooked. It was red and raw and clung to the bone. It didn't taste like pork, either.

'How is everything?'

The boy was standing right over me. I hadn't heard him sneak up.

'It's great, thanks,' I said. 'What kind of meat is this, by the way?'

'Pig meat,' he said. 'A special kind of pig, that we keep here.'

He went back to stand at his counter. I poked at my plate, and tried to nibble here and there. Each bite seemed to get worse, as if the food was deteriorating.

'Could I have a glass of water, please?' I asked.

'Sorry,' the boy said. 'The taps are bust.'

'What about pop?'

'Shipment's due in later today.'

I ate a bit more, pretending to really enjoy myself. You could tell that pissed him off. After another five minutes, I asked if they had a washroom. He nodded and pointed to a door in the corner. I stood up, taking my plate with me.

'Where are you going with that?'

I looked at my plate.

'I like to eat on the toilet.'

'Sorry. House rules. No food in the washroom. See the sign on the door?'

It was there, all right – and it really did say that. I left my plate at the table and went in empty-handed. The washroom was a tiny cubicle, the size of a closet. The toilet seat was broken, and brown stains streaked the inside of the bowl. The door didn't have a lock, so I shoved the garbage can against it. Above the sink, a window overlooked the parking lot. It had been nailed shut. As I fiddled with it, I saw movement outside. It was a chubby kid in dungarees. He looked just like the one who was serving me, only younger. He crouched next to the Chrysler. He had a hose, which he slid into the gas tank. Then he started siphoning the gas into a jerry can. When the can was full, he carried it across the lot to a big wooden shed.

Behind me, the garbage can shifted. Somebody had tried the door.

'All right in there?'

'I'm on the crapper. Do you mind?'

I rustled around a bit, pretending to take a dump. Then I flushed the toilet. When I came out, the boy smiled at me, as if he knew exactly what I'd been up to. I sat back down and stared at my plate for a long time, thinking. Then I stretched and faked a yawn.

'This is delicious,' I said. 'I'd love to take some home. Do you have a doggy bag or something?'

His smile widened. 'We don't do doggy bags. You have to eat what you take. That's the deal, remember?' He came up close to me again – close enough for me to smell him. He smelled sour and yeasty, like bad beer. He had both hands buried in the pocket of his apron. I could see he was holding something in there. 'But if you can't finish…'

'No – no. I can finish.'

This time he went to stand by the door, blocking my exit. In the kitchen the cleaver was still going, steady as a clock. Thock. Thock. Thock. I stared at the mess on my plate. There was only one way to eat this food: all at once, without thinking, so that my stomach didn't have time to react. I grabbed the fritter first, and swallowed it in a few bites. Then I shovelled back the mashed potatoes and coleslaw, holding my breath, trying not to chew or taste anything. Lastly I attacked the ribs. I tore at the meat, gnawed at the bone. Blood and juices dribbled from my chin. I was thinking, thank God I didn't take more than this...

I threw the final bone down on my plate and stood up. The kid gawped at me, his mouth half-open. In his hand he clutched a six-inch butcher's knife with a curved blade.

'All finished,' I said.

He rushed over to check the plate. 'He finished!' he said, practically shrieking. 'Daddy – he finished!'

The thocking stopped. A second later the door swung open. His father stood there, in a bloodstained apron. The cleaver dangled at his side, dripping red. He looked just like his son. He even had the same birthmark on his face. We stared at one another.

'Then he can go.'

Keeping my eyes on them, I backed towards the door.

As soon as I stepped outside, I puked up all the food in one clean shot. It was as if my stomach had realised what I'd given it, and decided to say, 'No, thanks.' A pink mix of meat and mash and coleslaw and fritter splattered on to the porch. The cat they had tethered out there noticed, and perked up. She crawled over to sniff my puke, then wrinkled her nose and drew back, disgusted. She knew what I should have known, this cat. No wonder she hadn't been eating the meat in her bowl.

I walked over to my car, popped the trunk, and got out my gun. They had knives, and cleavers, but I had a gun. I went back inside. The man was cuddling his son, who'd started crying and sobbing. 'He ate it all, Daddy. He ate it all and he got to go!'

'Shhh. I know, bubba, I know. It's okay.'

They stopped when they noticed me.

'I'm taking your cat,' I said.

'Now he's taking my cat!' the boy wailed.

'And I'm going to report this place. To somebody.' I waved my gun around – just to show that I had one. 'Don't try to stop me.'

They didn't. I tucked the gun in my waistband, adjusted my visor, and strode out.

The cat was waiting for me. I had a hard time unfastening her collar, but got it in the end. Then I scooped her up. She was so light – just a scrap of fur, like an old scarf. Cradling her in my arms, I carried her over to the Neon and lowered her into the passenger seat.

Across the lot, opposite my parking spot, was that shed I'd seen the other boy going into with the gas. He'd left the door ajar. I glanced at the diner – I could sense them in there, watching me – and went to check out the shed. Inside, it was packed with jerry cans. Some were full, some empty. I hauled two full ones back to my car and lifted them into the trunk.

Then I got the hell out of there – really flooring it. The cat cowered on the passenger seat. She was shaking. I was, too. I kept checking the rear-view until the diner disappeared. Even once it was gone, I could still feel it in my mind, lingering like a nightmare.

chapter 40

The cat stood in the passenger seat, stiff as a goat. I got the impression she couldn't believe how fast we were going. I don't think she'd ever ridden in a car before. It must have been like flying in a spaceship. The desert world that had always been her home was now whirling around us in a vortex – this colourful wormhole of scrub and sand and sky.

Once she recovered from the initial shock, she began to explore her spaceship. She hopped down and padded around in the footwell. She sniffed at the bag of eagle feathers. She slunk, eel-like, under the seat, and reappeared in the back. Then, for no real reason, she became insanely excited and raced back and forth across the seats, tearing the upholstery with her claws. At one point she leapt up on to the headrest, and perched there like a gargoyle.

Eventually she returned to the front. She crept down by my feet, and started rubbing against my ankle. It made it hard to drive. I scooped her up with my left hand and put her back on her own seat. She crawled into my lap. She was purring. It might have been cute, if she hadn't been so filthy. I placed her back on her seat a second time. She crawled into my lap again, and I put her back again. We played that game for a little while.

'Look, cat,' I said, 'I get that you're grateful. But we both need our space, if this is going to work. Trust me, I've been in relationships before. You've been tied to a stake at that terrible place your whole life. So I get to call the shots. You sit there, and I sit here.'

The cat looked at me. One of her eyes was weepy and cloudy, like a half-cooked egg. But at least she seemed to understand. She knew who was in charge.

'Attagirl. Good cat.'

As soon as I looked away, she crawled back in my lap.

Once she got accustomed to the car, the cat began to enjoy herself. She placed one paw on the armrest and held the other cocked, like a pointer hound, as she peered out at the scenery. Whenever something interesting flitted past, her head swivelled to track it. I rolled down the window a crack, and she put her nose right up there, letting the wind blast her whiskers back.

'What are you, some kind of puppy-cat?'

We drove along contentedly for a few minutes. Then something stung me on the leg. I looked down. I couldn't see anything, but I felt it, all right. It started itching immediately. Then there was another one. And another. I glanced at the cat. She was avoiding my gaze, but her fur seemed to be rippling and shifting.

'For God's sake, cat,' I said. 'You've got fleas?'

She pretended not to hear me. After a bit, she twitched and attacked her own leg – gnawing on it like a chicken bone. They were biting her, too. I couldn't believe I hadn't noticed before. They were everywhere: all over her, all over the seats, all over me.

I slammed on the brakes.

Leaving the cat in the car, I got the cooler out of the trunk and removed the lid. I emptied three cans of Lucky and a twixer of whisky in there. Then I opened the passenger door. The cat tried to make a break for it, but I grabbed her by the scruff of the neck, and hauled her over to the cooler. She squirmed and clawed at me, raking my wrist.

'Bathtime for bonzo.'

As I lowered her, she spread her legs apart, like a cartoon-cat, and clung to the edges of the cooler. I had to push her butt down to force her in. As soon as she hit the liquor, she went completely limp. I dunked her in up to her neck, and held her there. She whimpered at me.

'Look, cat,' I said. 'I know this sucks. But it's for your own sake. For both our sakes. And let's face it – you can't get any dirtier. Beer and whisky is an improvement.'

It wasn't much consolation. I could feel her trembling, but kept her in it for a few minutes. I spotted black specks in the beer bath. Some of the fleas were abandoning ship.

'Okay, cat,' I said. 'Up we go.'

I raised her out of the bath and let her drip, like an old washrag. Her coat had soaked up a browny-yellow hue. It reeked, too – a potent blend of beer and whisky. When I dropped her on her seat, she leapt into the back, behind the headrests and as far from me as possible.

I put the car in gear and kept driving, keeping one eye on her in the rear-view. She was sniffing herself. Then she started to lick and clean her fur. She had to get all that booze off herself, somehow. When she'd finished, she meandered back up to the front to join me. She wobbled a bit in her seat. She was obviously feeling pretty mellow.

'Looks like somebody's been hitting the sauce,' I said.

She leered at me, lay down flat, and passed out.

After she woke up, and sobered up, the cat got antsy. She turned in circles on her seat. She scratched at the side panelling. She meowed and mewled. I knew what that meant. I pulled over and shoved open the passenger door, but she wouldn't get out. She thought I was trying to ditch her. So I had to walk around, pick her up, and drop her in the gravel at the roadside.

'Okay, cat,' I said. 'Do your thing.'

She wouldn't. Not at first. She scratched at the dirt with a paw. Apparently it was no good, that dirt. She picked her way to another spot, like a princess looking for a jewel.

'Come on, cat!' I said. 'Hurry it up.'

To demonstrate how it was done, I unzipped and took a piss. That seemed to encourage her. She finally squatted down to give it a try. Her eyes narrowed and her whiskers trembled. That was why it had been such a big deal: she was doing a number two. It came out in stops and starts. When she'd finished she back-scratched gravel to cover it up. I went over and took a look. She'd left a runny puddle in the dirt. The puddle was filled with worms – little round worms, twisted up like croissants. All her scratching couldn't hide that.

I glared at her. 'You've got worms, too?'

She sat and nibbled on her front paw. I got a napkin from the car and wiped her ass. There were worms on her ass, too. I'd picked up a filthy, wormy, flea-infested cat with an infected eye. That was just like me.

'I ought to leave you here, you know.'

As I considered it, she rubbed against my leg, curling around it like a feather boa. I sighed, picked her up, and tossed her back in the passenger seat.

chapter 41

I unscrewed the lid of the jerry can, and sniffed at the spout to check the contents. It smelled like good clean gasoline. There was a flexible nozzle for pouring. I attached that, twiddled off my gas cap, then tilted the jerry can up to dump the gas into the tank. It was about ten o'clock, and already dusty and hot. We'd driven on until dusk, then parked and crashed out at the roadside. I hadn't wanted to drive in the dark when I had no idea where I was going.

'Well, cat,' I said. 'Let's see how far this gets us.'

She ignored me. She was crouched on the tarmac, with her head buried in a saucer that I'd made for her out of an empty beer can. That morning, I'd woken up with her stuck to my chest, like a limpet. She'd been drooling and purring and paddy-pawing me, as if to say, *Time to get up – I want some breakfast*. But I didn't have any cat food for her. I didn't have any food, actually. Or any water. All I had was beer, and we were even running out of that. At least she'd developed a taste for it. Maybe too much of a taste.

'Slow down,' I told her. 'Chew your food.'

I emptied both jerry cans into the tank. Then I replaced the gas cap and started the engine. The gauge had been in the red. I waited for it to adjust. It drifted up to about half a tank. By then the cat had finished her breakfast. I sat down across from her on the tarmac. I'd decided it was time for us to have a little chat, my cat and I. 'Look,' I told her. 'You don't have to ever worry about me abandoning you. When I took you with me, I was signing on for the long haul. I'm stupid and loyal in that way, like a dog. It's you cats that are the problem. You're like women. Fickle and self-centred. Nourishing yourselves from within.'

The cat licked her lips. She thought I was talking a lot of shit, obviously.

'Whatever,' I said, adjusting my visor. 'I'm just saying I'll look after you. But if we're going to find our way out of this desert I'll need your help, okay? We can't survive on beer and whisky and smokes. We have to get back to civilisation. Otherwise we'll wind up like that asshole hitchhiker, or those crazies in the diner. You remember them? Your old owners.'

She'd gone still. Maybe she did remember them.

'So I need you to think, cat. Think. Do you know of any way – any way at all – that we can get out of here?'

She started to lick her right paw.

I threw up my hands. 'You're useless, cat!'

The desert slowly dissolved into a wasteland. The roads were disintegrating. The pavement was cracked and buckled and, in places, half-covered by sand. There were no signs – just an endless series of unmarked forks, T-junctions and crossroads. Tumbleweeds pinwheeled alongside us, and dust devils shimmied at the roadside. As we rattled on, I noticed that every so often the cat's ears went flat and her tail puffed out. It only seemed to happen when the road turned a certain way, so I decided to try an experiment. At the next crossroads we came to I swung wide and wheeled the Neon around in slow circles. Each time we were facing one particular direction, off to the right, the cat would react. I parked and got out to take a look.

'What is it, cat?' I asked. 'What's got you spooked?'

Then I saw it. On the horizon, shimmering in the heat, stood a mountain with twin peaks. I knew that mountain. I'd spotted it way back at the gas station, before meeting the hunters. It had been on the other side of the plains. Maybe I could use it as a landmark. I hopped back in the Neon and spun her around, until the front bumper was pointed towards the mountain. The cat's fur flared out and she seemed to double in size, like a blowfish.

'Look, cat,' I said, 'I get that you're not exactly stoked to go to that mountain. But it could be a route out. Maybe the only one.'

I started driving. The cat still wasn't happy about it. She growled, low and deep in her throat, like a cougar. Then, when I ignored her, she pissed all over her seat. She did it secretly, crouching down, so I didn't notice until I caught a whiff of it. Then I looked over and saw the spreading puddle.

'Jesus Christ, cat!'

I slammed on the brakes and made a grab for her, but she darted under the seat. When I tried to pull her back out, she clawed and scratched at my hands. I gave up and pounded the seat with my palm, just to let her know how insanely angry I was. Then I got a pair of dirty boxers out of the trunk to mop up her piss. Some of it had already soaked into the upholstery. I sponged off what I could and left the sopping boxers at the roadside.

'That's just like a cat,' I said, starting the car. 'That's so typical.'

Even with the windows down I could smell the piss. At first, it wasn't so bad. But, as the day began to heat up, the stench got worse and worse – that sour-milk scent of cat urine. I knew from experience that it would never go away entirely. My poor Neon.

At one point the cat poked her head out from under the seat. I slapped at her and she withdrew like a tortoise. I could hear her under there, grumbling along with the engine.

'Don't you dare come out,' I yelled at her. 'Stay in your room, you little pisspot.'

chapter 42

From a distance, the mountain seemed to stand in isolation. But as we got closer I saw that it was actually part of a larger range – a jumble of jagged, saw-toothed crags that zigzagged off on either side of it. I'd spotted the mountain first because it was higher than all the others. It was also perfectly symmetrical – a pyramid thrusting up against the sky, with a notch cut into the apex that formed the twin peaks. The bowl-shaped rim resembled a massive crater. It must have been a volcano at one time.

The road stopped bending and winding and became perfectly straight, like a compass needle. I followed the needle, fixed on my mark. Inside the car it was quiet. I'd allowed the cat to come out from under the seat, but we weren't communicating in any way. She was still mad at me for going in this direction, and I was still mad at her for pissing on the seat. She lay on her belly, sphinx-like, with her paws in front of her and her hind legs hunched up.

I don't know how long it took to get there. Hours, probably. In the heat of the wasteland time melted away and became flexible and malleable, meaningless. As we approached the foothills the road narrowed and sloped upwards – steep and straight as an escalator, pulling us along. We were headed for a pass to the left of the mountain. The sun burned low in the sky. Its rays blasted through the windshield, as if I were driving into the flash of a nuclear bomb. I could feel the heat on my cheeks, my torso. I adjusted my visor, squinting against the glare.

The cat's tail began to twitch.

We entered the pass, with the twin peaks looming on our right. I thought I heard thunder rumbling among the mountains, even though there were no clouds. Then I spotted something on the road ahead. I took my foot off the gas, letting the Neon roll to a stop. My route was blocked by two wooden sawhorses. On the other side the asphalt had been dug up in preparation for repaving, and parked on the shoulder were various machines – excavators, wheel loaders, rollers – but they all looked rusty and derelict, long-abandoned. Beyond the construction site the road continued, dropping towards a plain similar to the one I'd crossed. In the distance, way out there, awaited a town. It wasn't much – just a cluster of low-lying buildings – but it signified the edge of the desert.

The only problem was this roadblock.

An arrow spray-painted on the sawhorse pointed to the right, up a side road. Next to the turnoff was a sign: *Roadworks Diversion This Way*. It had been hung on a post, over what looked like an older sign. I got out to check behind it. The original sign showed a picture of a handgun, above the words *North Nevada Shooting Range*. That explained the thunder, at least.

'Somebody was trying to hide this, cat,' I said.

I got out my road map. I also got out the instructions the border guard had scrawled for me. I thought it might be the same gun range she'd told me about, but it was hard to tell. The hitcher had mentioned one, too. Maybe they'd both been talking about the same place.

'What do you think?' I asked the cat.

I could tell what she thought. She was staring at the peak with her back arched, ears flat, tail flared. I stared with her for a while, trying to decide. Then I put my map away and turned the wheel, guiding the Neon towards the diversion.

The cat emitted this hissing snarl.

'I know, cat,' I said. 'But it's the only way.'

I wasn't sure if that was strictly true, but it felt true. Not that it mattered to her.

The detour was some kind of old mining road, gouged into the mountainside, with an overhang looming on the right and a straight drop falling away to the left. The roadbed was pitted with potholes and riddled with rocks. The Neon struggled on, whining and moaning like an old mule. Every so often the bellow of gunfire rolled down from the summit. The road cut back and forth in a series of switchbacks, higher and higher, until it levelled off at a plateau.

I'd come out at the gun range. If the mountain actually had been a volcano at one time, the range sat right in the crater between the twin peaks. Off to my right squatted a concrete hut, like a bunker. It must have been some kind of office or rental shop, but it wasn't open. The door had a padlock on it, and steel shutters were drawn across the windows. Adjacent to the hut were the shooting stalls, similar to the kind you'd find at a golf course driving range – all linked together and covered by a corrugated tin roof. We were approaching from the back, so I couldn't see who was in the stalls, but the parking lot was full of Harleys.

I pulled up, leaving the engine idling, and looked around. There weren't any other diversion signs, or any clear exits. I knew I hadn't missed a turn. I sat there for about three minutes, thinking. Through the windows, I could hear the intermittent reverberation of shots from the range. Boom. Boom. Boom.

'I'm going to have to ask them, cat.'

She meowed, to show me what she thought of that.

'It's not like they'll shoot me on sight.'

I killed the engine and opened my door. As I turned to get out, the cat pounced on my hand. She bit into it, hard, and hung on. I had to shake her off like a crab and shove her back into her seat. Twin pinpricks of blood showed up on my palm.

'Just chill,' I told her. 'I'm only getting directions.'

She hissed and took a final swipe at me. She knew that there was more to it than that. We both did. I turned my visor around backwards, rolled up my sleeves, and strutted over to the range. Gravel crunched and popped under my shoes. I made sure I had an unlit cigarette tucked behind my ear.

A doorway was built into the end stall. I cleared my throat, spat, and stepped through. From there I could see all the other stalls. Most of them were empty. In the whole shooting range there was only one customer. He stood way down at the far end: a guy in boots and a leather jacket and dark sunglasses. He was shooting at a target set up out on the range.

I walked up carefully, not wanting to startle him, and stopped about ten paces away to wait for him to finish. He fired six rounds, one after another. The reports resounded off the sides of the crater, like the pounding of a bass drum. Then he lowered the gun, looked back at me, and grinned – as if he'd known I was there all along.

chapter 43

It was the hitcher's brother, all right. It had to be. They looked almost identical, except this guy was older. His face was rough and weathered, and his lips were parched, as if he'd been out too long in the desert. Trail dust encrusted his hair, making it stick up in spikes. On the back of his jacket was a snake, curled up like a turd, and the words *Cobra Motorcycle Club*.

'Nice shooting,' I said.

He grunted and snapped open the cylinder to his pistol. He was using some kind of monstrous Magnum, even bigger than Pigeon's gun. As he reloaded, I stepped in closer to him. I couldn't tell if he really was the same guy I'd met in Vancouver. He didn't seem to recognise me. Or he was pretending he didn't.

'You come to shoot?' he asked.

'I'm a little lost.'

'Should have known. You don't look like you carry.'

I crossed my arms. 'Oh, I got a gun, all right.'

'Yeah?' He scratched at a patch of dry skin under his jaw, then reached for another slug and thumbed it into the chamber. 'You know how to use it? That's the *real* question.'

'I shot an eagle with it.'

'That's nothing. I've shot tons of eagles. I kill eagles for fun.'

He spun the cylinder, snapped it shut. On the counter next to his box of ammo sat a liquor bottle, blue and bulbous, with a corked top. The guy pulled out the cork, took a swig, then made that satisfied, lip-smacking sound and wiped his mouth with the back of his hand. Inside the bottle, coiled up on the bottom, was some kind of a snake, its skin all pale from pickling, like a tapeworm.

I asked, 'Do you know the way out of here? I'm following the roadworks diversion.'

'Depends where you're headed.'

'Winnemucca, first.'

'Going to the whorehouse, huh?'

'Maybe. You know it?'

'Course I do.' He leered at me, and made a pumping motion with his hips. 'I been there tons of times. I've fucked all the whores at that place, at least three times. In the ass.'

He was obviously one of those guys – the kind that's done everything you've done, only backwards and blindfolded.

'So which way is it?'

'What's the rush, kid? Go get your gun. Fire off a few rounds with me.'

'I don't have a lot of time,' I said.

'Hell – it won't take long. We're gonna lose the light in half an hour, anyways.'

He pointed up, towards the rim of the crater. Just above it hung the sun, fat and red and gaping, like a bullet hole blasted into the sky. The dying light trickled across the range.

'And then you'll tell me the way?'

'Of course. Ain't no secret.'

I couldn't read his expression. It was hard to see anything behind those sunglasses. It was as if he didn't even have eyes.

'All right. Half an hour.'

I went to get my gun. The cat was huddled in the space behind the headrests. She glared at me through the rear windshield as I dug the Glock and ammo out of the trunk. I didn't even bother trying to explain myself to her this time. She didn't want to hear it.

When I got back, the biker was out on the range setting up fresh targets for both of us. I took the stall next to his. Each stall had a counter, separating it from the range, that you had to shoot across. I laid my pistol and ammo box on the counter and began filling the magazine with cartridges. They tingled coolly between my fingertips.

He came back and watched me.

'What you got there?' he asked. 'A twenty-two? Only pussies use a twenty-two, kid. My mama packs a twenty-two. Hell, my *grandma* packs a twenty-two. Now *this* – ' he held up his revolver ' – is a real man's hand cannon. A Smith & Wesson .500 Magnum.'

'Well, you know what they say.' I jammed the magazine into the gun butt. It made a satisfying click. 'It's not the size that matters – it's what you do with it.'

I surveyed the range. It was about three hundred yards long, with a mound of earth raised at the far end, like the wall of a half-pipe, to absorb bullets. I could see solid targets down there, probably for rifles. Closer to us were some metal stands, like easels, that held paper posters. The posters showed a silhouette of a person, with a bull's-eye over the head and another over the chest. The two he'd set up for us were twenty or thirty yards away.

I purposefully took aim at the target, gripping my pistol in the way Pigeon had taught me, and pulled the trigger. The Glock barked and kicked. From that distance it was hard to tell what part of the target I'd hit, or if I'd hit it at all. But the guy was watching so I kept firing, casually squeezing off each round, as if I shot at a gun range every day.

After a minute he started shooting beside me. His gun was louder. Mine went bam, and his went boom. While we were shooting we pretended not to pay any attention to each other, but of course we were. It was like pissing at a urinal trough, when you avoid looking at the other guy's dick, but secretly you're wondering if it's bigger or smaller than yours. We shot off a full round together. As we reloaded, I asked him about the diversion again. This time he told me. Apparently there was a tunnel that took you down the other side of the mountain. The entrance was behind the bunker, past the bikes. I asked him about those bikes, too, and the owners – without letting on that I knew about his gang.

'Those are our bikes. Cobra bikes.'

'But where are the other Cobras?'

He gestured vaguely, waving his gun over his head. 'They're around. Don't worry about them. But tell me something, kid: where you gonna go after hitting Winnemucca?'

'On to Reno. To do some gambling. Then maybe over to San Francisco.'

'Nothing but queers and faggots in San Francisco.' He snickered, and flicked his tongue in and out at me, like a lizard. 'You a faggot, kid? You like sucking dick?'

'I'm going to see a chick I know, actually. A super-hot lesbian.'

'Oh, yeah?' He'd been fiddling with his cylinder, but when he heard that he stopped and looked at me. 'What's her name?'

'Why?'

'Because I might know her, dick-brain.'

I pretended to inspect my clip. I didn't like the idea of him knowing Beatrice's name. 'Trevine,' I said.

'Trevine, eh?' he said, taking aim. 'I'll remember that.'

We blasted off another set of rounds. Whenever he stopped to reload, he'd take a long swig from his bottle. He never offered me any, but at one point he noticed me eyeing it. He held it up, and sort of shook it to show it off.

'This stuff will put lead in your pencil, kid.'

The label on the bottle showed a lady in a red dress. She had inflated cartoon breasts and a serpentine body that tapered to a tail – like a cross between a mermaid and a snake. All the writing was in Spanish. The only word I could make out was 'agave'.

'Tequila, huh?' I said, removing my clip.

'Fuck no. This is the real deal, kid. Mezcal. A hundred and sixty proof. It'll make you animal-crazy, and ready to fuck.'

I began to reload, casually plucking bullets out of my box, pretending to be mildly interested in his little bottle. Really I was thinking, I need to get my hands on some of that.

'I wouldn't mind trying it,' I said. 'Want to sell some to me?'

'This shit is priceless. You can only get it in Oaxaca.'

I didn't know where Oaxaca was, but it sounded far away.

'Oh, well,' I said. 'Too bad.'

'Tell you what, kid. I'll give you the chance to win it. We'll have ourselves a little shoot-out. Six shots each. Best spread wins. If you win, you can have the bottle.'

It was exactly what his brother had warned me about. But it was still pretty tempting.

'What about if *you* win?'

'I get to pick something of yours. Sound good?'

I thought about all the junk I had in the car. None of it was worth anything.

'You can't pick my cat. Or my car.'

'Okay.' He offered me his hand. 'The cat and the car are out. Deal?'

'Deal.'

We shook. He put the bottle down on the counter between us. Then he reached up, plucked the visor off my head, and tossed it like a horseshoe around the bottleneck.

'We shoot for the mezcal and your visor.'

'Wait a minute – why do you want my visor?'

He was grinning now. Triumphantly. I hadn't even considered my visor. It was so comfortable and familiar that it was practically part of me.

'Do you know how rare that thing is?' he said. 'I been looking for one for years. I heard a guy was selling them, up in Trevor. But when I got there, some *fucker*,' he sneered, making it clear he knew that fucker was me, 'had already gone and bought it.'

'You tricked me.'

I reached for my visor, and he rapped me across the knuckles with his Magnum.

'You tricked yourself.'

'Whatever. The bet's off.'

I reached for it again. This time he pointed his gun at me, inches from my face. I went still and stared into the gaping muzzle. It looked big enough to swallow me whole.

'We shook, so we shoot.'

'Okay, man.' I let go of my visor. 'We shoot.'

Before we could shoot, first we had to put up fresh targets. He had a whole bundle of paper posters with him, rolled up in a tube. We took one each and walked on to the range. The sun was resting on the rim of the crater. The light had deepened to a rich blood-red that saturated the terrain and seeped across the sand. Our shadows, long and gangly, loped along beside us.

As we came up to the targets, I got a look at the bullet holes. All of his were packed close together, right over the target's chest – as if the poor bastard's heart had been torn out. My target didn't look like that. My target had holes scattered all over the place. I'd hit the silhouette in the neck, and the dick. I'd even shot him in the elbow. When the biker saw that, he chuckled and made some stupid wisecrack about me shooting wild and started whistling a little ditty. He kept whistling as we took the old posters down, and replaced them. To attach the posters, you used metal clips at the top of the stands. I fiddled with mine, buying myself some time. There was no way in hell I was going to win that contest. Not fairly, at least.

'Hey,' I said, 'Don't you think these targets are too close?'

'Twenty-five yards is standard.'

He'd tricked me. Maybe I could do the same to him.

'I'm no good at this close-range shooting. Any pussy can hit a target at twenty-five yards. I shot my eagle at, like, two hundred yards. At least.'

'Well…'

I shrugged. 'If you don't think you can hack it, that's fine. We'll just pussy-shoot.'

'Don't be a fuckwit. Whatever you can shoot, I can shoot.'

'Great. Here.' I handed him my target stand. 'You carry these out there, and I'll tell you when to stop.'

'Why me? Do it yourself.'

I rolled my eyes. 'Well, if they're too heavy for you…'

'Fuck that. I got this shit.'

Holding them high to show how light they were, he stomped off towards the rear of the range, then stopped to turn around. I backed up slowly, pretending to judge the distance.

'That's better,' I called. 'Go a bit further.'

He walked on, and I backed up some more. The next time he stopped to check, he was way out there, among the metal rifle targets at the back. I was almost at the shooting stalls. The visor and the mezcal were within arm's reach.

'A few more feet,' I shouted. 'Near the backdrop.'

As soon as he turned to walk away, I grabbed the bottle and visor and bolted for the exit. Just as I got to the door, I heard him shout. I tripped on the threshold, caught myself, and kept going. In the parking lot, I passed the bikes. They were all in a row. I tried that trick you see in the movies, and kicked the first bike over. It fell into the one next to it, and they all started going down, like dominos. Incredibly shiny and expensive dominos.

Then I leapt into the Neon. I threw her in gear and peeled out of there, spinning my wheels, spitting gravel, swerving wildly. We fishtailed past the bikes and around the bunker. Behind it, just like he'd said, was a tunnel. It had been bored into the crater wall between the twin peaks. The mouth of the tunnel was dark, and supported by wooden framework, like an old mineshaft. As I hurtled towards it, in my wing mirror I caught a glimpse of him storming out of the gun range. At first he gave chase on foot. Then, when he realised he wasn't going to catch me, he just stopped and pointed – as if he was marking me, or cursing me.

The cat, of course, was going absolutely ballistic.

chapter 44

We flew off that mountain, my cat and I. The road up had been full of twists and hairpins and switchbacks. The tunnel down was a straight drop, like the final section of a rollercoaster. For a moment we seemed to linger at the top, hanging in space. Then we were falling, falling, falling. The tunnel was narrow, barely one lane, and had granite walls lined with veins of iron. We swooped through it, feeling the G-force pull on our faces, pin us to our seats. At the bottom we shot out on to the highway, carrying all that momentum with us.

Up at the shooting range, evening had been lingering. But once we got down to the plains the sun fell from the sky like a buckshot bird. Day became night and the world went dark. We'd come out on a straightaway and I drove in the middle of the blacktop, straddling the centre line. It was marked by white dashes that streaked towards us like tracer bullets.

I watched the rear-view, the wing mirrors. I kept imagining I'd seen something back there, and then, finally, I did. On the road behind us the beam of a single headlamp appeared, slicing through the night like a knife. It was a mile or two back, and getting closer. The cat had seen it too. She arched her back and snarled her wildcat snarl.

'I know, cat. I know.'

I stomped on the gas, jamming the pedal to the floor. The speedometer crept up past a hundred and forty, a hundred and fifty, a hundred and sixty. Being a Neon, it maxed out at a hundred and seventy klicks. The engine began emitting this

202

weird, high-pitched mechanical hum. The whole car shook, rattled, shuddered. I clung to the wheel with both hands, keeping my elbows locked and my arms rigid. I wasn't even driving any more. I was just trying to hold on. It was like riding a giant missile that could explode beneath me at any time.

I checked the rear-view. The headlight was still there. It hadn't gotten any smaller, but it hadn't gotten any bigger, either. Apparently he could only go the same speed as me.

'Thank God he's got a Harley,' I said, 'and not some Kawasaki crotch-rocket.'

I kept flooring it. After half an hour of our deadlocked race, the headlight vanished. I figured he'd given up and turned around. I eased off the gas, dropping back to a hundred.

'That's it, cat,' I said, patting her back. 'He's gone.'

She let out a low growl.

We plunged on through the night, rolling over a series of camel humps that rose and fell like waves in a wine-dark sea. I power-puffed a cigarette to settle my nerves. Beside me, the cat sniffed at the stolen bottle of mezcal, sussing it out. In the dimness the blue glass glimmered magically, and the liquor inside sloshed around to the motion of the car, making the snake undulate. There was about three quarters of a bottle left. I told the cat what I'd done out on the shooting range to get it.

'How do you like that, cat?' I said. 'We tricked him good.'

She didn't seem impressed. She was still antsy. She kept lashing her tail around and turning in circles on her seat. Then she got up on her hind legs and braced her paws against the backrest, peering at the road behind us.

'We lost him, cat. Relax.'

She wouldn't, though. She started making a strange grumbling sound, deep in her throat. It got louder and louder. Too loud. I looked at her. It wasn't just her making the sound. I rolled down the window and the noise increased, like the drone of a lawnmower.

Or the engine of a Harley.

It was him. He emerged from the darkness behind us, his face lit up by the glow of my tail-lights, his features cast in red. He was still wearing his sunglasses. He must have been following us in the dark, driving blind – like a complete psychopath.

I screamed, making the kind of sound you only make when you're startled and terrified at the same time. The cat jumped down into the footwell to hide, and I hit the gas, hard, like a cowboy heeling his horse. The Neon leapt forward. I pushed her to one-seventy again, but he kept pace. I couldn't lose him. All he had to do was follow me until I stopped.

'Or until we run out of gas,' I whispered.

I had about a quarter-tank left. Our only chance was to hope he ran out first, or to reach a town. He wouldn't kill me in front of witnesses. At least, I didn't think he would.

'I saw that town from the pass, cat,' I said. 'We might make it.'

She glared at me from the floor as if she blamed me entirely – which was fair enough, considering I was entirely to blame. I checked my mirrors again. He was still there, all right. Since he was dressed in black, you couldn't really see his body. You could only see his face, malevolent as a demon's, hovering in the darkness. Also, in his sunglasses you could see the reflection of my tail-lights – these two little red dots, trained on me like laser-sights.

If I couldn't outrun him, there was no point in trying. I dropped down to seventy-five. I'd once heard that seventy-five is the most fuel-efficient speed. I had to conserve every drop of gas I had. It was on now: a war of attrition between me and the shadow behind me.

Beneath my palms the steering wheel was greasy with sweat. My neck was stiff and I had a brain-crushing headache. At some point I'd started huffing whippets, to keep me awake and alert. We'd been driving for hours. He'd stayed locked to my bumper the whole time, as if attached with a trailer hitch, accelerating or slowing down to match my speed.

Time was measured by the slow movement of the needle on my gas gauge. It crept counter-clockwise, like an hour-hand going backwards. It sank into the red, slowly, slowly, and my heart sank with it. Pretty soon the fuel light came on. That was it – the chequered flag of my fate. I slumped back in my seat. The cat made this plaintive mewling sound.

'I know, cat,' I said. 'I'm sorry. I'm sorry to have fucked things up for us in this hideous way. You were right and I was wrong.'

She clambered into her usual position on the passenger seat. I guess she wanted to go out with dignity, not cowering in the footwell. I reached over to scratch her ears. She licked my hand. Then she bit it gently, as if to say, *I always knew you were a hopeless loser*.

'We must be close, cat,' I said. 'We must be just out of reach.'

That was when I saw the lights. They appeared way out there in the dark, little pinpricks of colour against the matte black landscape.

'Holy shit, cat,' I said, leaning forward. 'You see that?'

She meowed. She'd seen it, apparently. The only problem was, the biker had seen it too. He shouted something I couldn't hear. Then he revved the throttle, making it rattle like a gattling gun, and tried to overtake us. As he did, I veered across, obstructing him, and he had to fall back to avoid being sideswiped. That pissed him off, all right. The next time I looked behind us, he'd drawn his Magnum. He waved it one-handed above his head, brandishing it like a sword. I was thinking, he can't really be crazy enough to start shooting at us, can he?

He started shooting at us.

I heard the first blast and saw fire blossom from the end of the barrel. It scared me so badly I nearly crashed the Neon. She lurched back and forth like a drunken donkey, while he kept shooting, before I got her under control. Maybe all that swerving made us harder to hit, or maybe he was only firing warning shots. I don't know. But he'd missed us. I half-turned in my seat to look back. He was fiddling with his gun, now, trying to reload it on the fly.

'We've got to distract him, cat,' I said. 'Mess up his aim, somehow.'

I started throwing things out the window. I threw beer cans and empty canisters of whipped cream and liquor bottles and basically anything I could get my hands on. He fell back a bit, forced to slalom between the obstacles, but eventually I ran out of stuff to throw. That was when the cat gave me an idea. She started scratching at a plastic bag tucked beneath the passenger seat. It was the one I'd stuffed full of eagle feathers.

'That's genius, cat.'

The biker was coming up behind us again. I grabbed the bag, held it out the window and shook it. All the feathers fluttered backwards, like a swarm of moths. He drove right into the swarm. Feathers smacked his chest and face. Some stuck to his clothes, and a few got caught right in his mouth – as if he'd swallowed a canary. He wobbled on his bike.

'Fall, you son of a bitch!'

He didn't fall.

We were close to the town now. I could see the shapes of buildings, the gleam of street-lamps. But my Neon was making strange noises, coughing and sputtering, running on fumes. Behind us, the guy had managed to steady the bike. He closed the gap again. He was no longer waving the gun around. He was holding it level, taking aim. His face was full of murder. I only had two things left on my passenger seat: the bottle of mezcal, and my visor.

'Goddamn it,' I said.

I picked the visor. I turned on the flashing lights, those beautiful lights, and flung it out the window. It spun in the air, twirling colours, like a flying saucer slicing across the sky. The wind caught it and carried it back at him. It settled in the middle of the road, right in his path. The guy wavered to avoid it, then dropped away and merged with the shadows.

'He fell for it, cat!'

By then we'd reached the edge of town. Above the road a yellow Shell sign appeared, with a digital display for the prices of diesel and propane and gasoline. I slowed down to turn off. As I did, I heard a staccato burst of engine-noise from behind us. It was him again. He roared past on my left, burning a wheelie and whooping like a coyote. He must have taken a final pot-shot, because my passenger window exploded. A shower of glass splashed over me, stinging my face. I was so shocked I misjudged the turn and hit the kerb. The Neon bucked wildly, tossing the cat up off her seat. The brakes locked, and we slid forward on tractionless wheels. Time stretched out, elasticising. I was aware of the cat hanging in the air beside me, as if we'd drifted into a field of zero gravity. A dumpster at the side of the gas station floated towards us. Just before we hit it, I thought, we're going to hit that dumpster.

Then something crunched, and a big white fist punched me in the face.

chapter 45

'What about the date?'
    'The date?'
'Do you know what day it is?'
'Sunday? No, wait – Monday.'
A man and a woman stood over me. They were both brown and thin and brittle-looking, as if they'd been put together out of twigs. They took turns asking me questions.

'Well, what month is it?'
I had to think about that one.
'July?'
'Close enough,' the man said.
They both laughed. Nervously. The man held a tyre iron at his side, and was wearing some kind of smock, spattered in black and ochre stains. His wife had a gummy smile, with most of the teeth missing from the lower front row. I was sitting at their feet, leaning back against a concrete pillar. I smelled stale gasoline.

'How many fingers do you see?'
The man held up three fingers. I could see them clearly.
'Three.'
He changed the set-up.
'Four.'
The man nodded and lowered his hand. Just beyond them, I caught sight of my Neon, nosed up against a dumpster. I asked them what had happened. They tried to explain, talking over one another. I heard something about coming too fast into the gas station, crashing, and being knocked out.

It took me a while to understand that I was the one who'd done all this.

'It's that turn,' the woman said. 'It's too tight. We know it. We're getting it fixed.'

'And the dumpster. Sorry about the dumpster. It shouldn't be there.'

The man pointed at the dumpster with his tyre iron. It trembled in his hand. He might have had some kind of palsy, or he might have just been incredibly jittery.

'It's not your fault,' I said. 'I mean, I crashed my car, didn't I?'

'Yes,' the woman said. 'But you crashed it into our gas station. So, in a way, it's our fault, isn't it?'

In my condition, that almost seemed to make sense. I reached up to touch my head, prodding for damage. It felt big and heavy and empty, like a hollowed-out pumpkin.

The man asked, 'You aren't going to sue, are you?'

I promised them I wasn't going to sue. Then I tried to stand. It wasn't easy. I got my legs beneath me, squatted for a minute, and lurched upright in one motion, like a weightlifter making his jerk. They stayed a few feet back, out of reach, watching me sway. I was starting to remember things, in flashes and snatches.

'What about the other guy?' I asked. 'The biker.'

They exchanged a glance. 'What biker?'

'The one chasing me. The one with the gun.'

'Oh, right,' the old man said, elbowing his wife. '*That* biker.'

'He followed me from the mountain.'

'I guess this is all his fault, huh?'

I rubbed the back of my neck and peered down the highway. The desert landscape I'd crossed was stained rose-red by the rising dawn. I could see for miles, but I couldn't see any mountain or twin peaks. Then again, we'd driven a long way, during our chase through the night.

'There was a shoot-out, and a terrible diner, and a hitch-hiker…'

'I'm sure there was, son.'

I shook my head, which hurt, and shuffled over to the car. The old people scurried along behind me, keeping their distance. The Neon's front bumper had crumpled on impact, and one of the headlights was cracked. The airbag dangled like a deflated balloon from the steering wheel. My cat lay on the passenger seat. Her left ear was bloody, and she wasn't moving. But when I reached down to touch her, she opened one eye, yawned, and stretched out her paws – as if she'd just woken from a long dream. Bits of glass, tiny as diamonds, were scattered all around her.

'See,' I said, pointing at the mess. 'He shot out my window.'

The woman smiled. 'Of course he did, dear. Unless it happened in the crash.'

'And I took this bottle of mezcal from him. It's priceless.'

I held it up as proof. They both peered at it, then nodded and shuffled their feet and made vague noises of assent and agreement. Neither of them would look me in the eye.

'What?'

'Well,' the man said, 'they don't put snakes in mezcal. Only worms.'

'But maybe yours is special,' the woman said.

I brushed the glass off my seat, slumped down facing them, and fumbled for my pack of smokes. I couldn't manage to light one. My grandpa's Zippo wouldn't work. It was out of flint, or fluid, or something. Eventually the man had to light the cigarette for me. While I sucked on it they hovered beside me. The man was still holding his tyre iron. He saw me looking at it, and tucked it into a loop on his toolbelt.

'We didn't know if you'd be friendly. Thought I might have to bean you.'

'But he didn't,' the woman added.

They still looked nervous, though. I guess living near the desert will do that to you – always waiting for the next nutball to stumble out of the wastes, or crash into your dumpster.

I gestured at my car. 'Can you do anything about this?'

The guy nodded. He patted the hood.

'The damage is mostly superficial.'

That depressed me, for some reason. I couldn't even crash a car properly.

Their gas station had a tiny garage, filled with tyres and oil drums and mufflers and hubcaps. It had a shop, too. The man worked in the garage and the woman looked after the shop. He said he could replace the airbag, repair the headlight and knock the dents out of my bumper, but he'd have to order in a new window, which would take a few days. I told him not to worry about it. I could do without the window.

While he worked on the car, I wandered into their little shop to get us a bottle of water. I splashed some into the cat's beer-can saucer, and drank the rest myself. It had been a long time since we'd had any water. I couldn't believe how good it tasted. I went back in and bought three more bottles for the road, along with some dry cat food, and a can of lighter fluid for my Zippo. It was that kind of shop – the kind that sells almost everything.

'Is that all?' the woman asked.

'I'll take a postcard, too,' I said, 'and a stamp.'

I sat by the gas pumps to wait for the Neon. While I did, I shook some food out on the ground for the cat, and refilled my lighter. Then I wrote on the postcard. I didn't write very clearly, or very much. I just needed to write something, so I wrote to Bea again.

Beatrice.

I'm still alive, still on my way. I don't know if any of this is helping or what. I got lost in the desert for a long time. There were no women out there and it was a terrible place, full of men and testosterone and loneliness and aggression. I'm out of it now, though. I found a cat, too. I'm bringing her with me, if I ever get there.

From Trevor, in the middle of nowhere.

That's what it said on the postcard: *The Middle of Nowhere*. The backdrop was a generic desert photo of cacti and tumbleweeds. I stuck the stamp on, stood up, and stretched. A few feet away, next to the gas pumps, was a squirming puddle. The cat had taken one of her wormy dumps.

'Goddammit, cat,' I said. 'You can't just shit anywhere you like.'

I went back into the shop to buy napkins to clean it up, and mail the postcard. On a rack near the counter they had a bunch of road maps for sale. That reminded me that I had no idea where I was. I selected one of the maps and flipped it open. The woman was watching me. All my coming and going and strangeness had made her even more nervous than usual.

I took the map over and unfolded it on her counter.

'Do you think you could tell me where we are?'

She studied it for a moment, pursing her lips in and out like a feeding goldfish. Then she pointed to a tiny road, almost an invisible road, in northern Nevada.

'Right here, near Denio Junction.'

'How far is Winnemucca?'

She slid her nail along the road.

'Just a few hours.'

I'd be there by mid-afternoon. Then it would only be a matter of finding the brothel.

'You don't have any condoms, do you?'

She shook her head. You could tell she found condoms, and the concept of selling them, completely appalling.

'What about worming tablets?'

She shook her head again. Those were the only two things they didn't carry in their shop, apparently. Instead she offered me a pamphlet, from a stack next to her till. The front showed a picture of a guy who looked like a bum, with a backpack and walking stick, hiking towards some hills. Way up in the hills was a giant cross. There was a caption at the bottom: *Saving Yourself – Advice & Wisdom from 'The Pilgrim's Progress' for Modern Christians*.

'You look as if you could use some guidance, dear.'
I took it. I didn't have the energy to argue with her.
'I sure could,' I said.

chapter 46

Since we were out of the desert, I had to drive at the speed limit, and on the right side of the road. It took me a while to get used to that. I kept drifting over the centre line. We'd been on our own for so long, but now there were all these other cars, and signs of life and civilisation. We passed barns and farmhouses and a country church, with a steeple that had been scorched black by lightning. We passed a makeshift windmill, built out of scrap metal, and we passed a barefoot girl selling eggs at the roadside. I honked and waved at her, and she waved back. 'Look at these people,' I said to my cat. 'They're living next to that wasteland, and somehow they're getting by. We're tough as rats, us humans. We can live almost anywhere: near a desert, up a mountain, in the snow. Except the Antarctic, I guess. Only penguins can live there. But anywhere else. We can take it. How do we do it, cat? What drives us on?'

The cat ignored me. She was busy nibbling on the scraps of the Christian pamphlet. I'd put it on the seat and she'd instantly shredded it into all these tiny pieces. She obviously didn't think *The Pilgrim's Progress* would be of much use to us, on this journey of ours.

'Maybe you're right, cat. Maybe we need new stories, new religions, new gods. But you know what?' I held up a fist, and solemnly proclaimed, 'God is just a metaphor for the human spirit – a metaphor for our ability to endure anything, like the people living out here.'

The cat spat out a bit of the pilgrim's arm. She wasn't interested in my philosophy, but I didn't care. I was having one of those bouts of euphoria that accompany starvation. I rolled down my window and leaned way out, opening my mouth to taste the wind.

'Hear that, America?' I shouted. 'I can take it! I'll endure!'

Just then, an oil tanker came roaring by in the opposite direction, and I had to pull my head in, super-fast. The vacuum left by the tanker's passing sucked at the car and rattled the windows. I held up my hand, palm out, in apology. She could be so damn tetchy, America. 'Okay,' I said, 'I get it. I wasn't trying to be lippy.'

A road sign floated by. We were less than forty miles from Winnemucca. It got me thinking about what I intended to do there. I checked my glovebox, to make sure I still had my map to the Pussycat Ranch. Then I picked up the mezcal from beside the cat, and studied the label as I drove. The guy had lied about the percentage. It was a hundred and fifty-four proof, not one-sixty – but it still looked pretty potent.

'I don't care what those old people say,' I told the cat. 'We went through some serious shit to get this twixer of elixir. I might have imagined some of it, but not all of it.'

I unscrewed the cap and took a sniff. It smelled rich and smoky, like wood chips.

'Think it'll put lead in my pencil, like he said?'

The cat sniffed and wrinkled her nose.

'In Winnemucca I'll put it to the test.'

She turned her back on me and stared out the broken window. Apparently she didn't want to hear about my plans for Winnemucca. I tried to pat her on the head, but she bit my hand and shied away. She wasn't that kind of cat. So instead I just chatted to her. I started telling her all about the other cat we'd had – the one with the cancerous ears.

'She was sort of wild, and hated being petted or stroked – a lot like you. She didn't trust people, and wouldn't let anybody touch her. Actually, that's not true. There was one person my cat trusted. They only met once, the first time she visited Vancouver...'

215

As soon as I said that, I stopped. I don't mean I stopped talking. I mean I stopped doing anything: talking, thinking, driving. It was as if I'd had a seizure. We rolled to the roadside and ended up parked at an awkward angle, beside a fallow field. Flies were buzzing around in the heat.

'I'm sorry, cat,' I said, turning off the engine. 'I just haven't thought about that person for a while. I'd managed to lose her in a haze of peyote and booze.'

A fly landed on the cat's ear. She shook her head, and the fly flew away.

'I'll tell you about her soon. Just not yet, okay?'

The cat lay down among the remains of the pamphlet, and lowered her head on her paws. I sat in a daze for a few minutes, gazing at the field. A scarecrow stood planted out there, crucified on a stick. He must have been on a swivel of some sort, because he would occasionally pivot in the wind, turning back and forth, as if he was looking for something.

chapter 47

'Do you take pets?'

The desk clerk peered at me. Shrewdly. He was a tall guy with a lazy eye. His scalp was completely bald except for this ring of shaggy red hair, encircling it like a clown's wig.

'What kind of pet?' he asked.

'A cat.'

We'd stopped at a motel on the outskirts of town. It was an innocuous stucco building, brown and weatherbeaten, laid out in a U-shape that enclosed the parking lot.

'Cat had its shots?'

'Yep.'

'It'll be ten bucks extra.'

I'm pretty sure he made that up. I paid it anyway. Our room had a water-stained ceiling and peeling wallpaper, but the sheets looked clean, at least. I left the cat on the bed, and switched the TV on for her. Then I went into the bathroom to get ready.

There was a mirror above the sink. For the past few days, I'd only caught the odd glimpse of myself, in the side mirrors or the rear-view. Now I had the whole picture, and I could see why those old people at the gas station had been so nervous. I still had cuts and bruises all over my face from my fight with the man-tiger. My nose was swollen and didn't look right, and the whites of my eyes were bloodshot and oddly yellow, like rotten egg yolks.

I stripped down and got in the shower. Water piddled over me. It created a brown puddle in the bathtub. At first I thought it was my own filth, but, once that drained off, the puddle stayed brown. Apparently the water in Winnemucca was as dirty as me. But it was warm, at least. I hung my head in the stream, letting it trickle off my hair. I opened one of those bars of cheap hotel soap and lathered myself up. It smelled bland and generic, like candle wax.

Afterwards I closed the curtains and got changed. I didn't have any clean boxers, so I went commando. My jeans and shirt still smelled of the road. I compensated by smearing on extra deodorant. The cat watched all these preparations with a dubious expression.

'What?' I said. 'I'm just going out for a drink, is all.'

She crept over to the stick of deodorant, sniffed it, and turned her nose up.

'Fine,' I said. 'I'm going to a brothel, okay? To get my groove back. My sex drive. It's no big deal. A lot of guys pay for sex. So don't give me any of that feminist bullshit.'

She narrowed her eyes, disgusted. I tossed a pillow at her and went into the bathroom to finish getting ready there – combing my hair and brushing my teeth and shaving my jaw.

By six o'clock I was good to go – except I was still sober. I hadn't even cracked open my twixer of elixir yet. I stretched out on the bed with the bottle resting on my belly. The snake inside was wound up on the bottom like a coil of rope. Its eyes were foggy and forlorn, and it had inch-long fangs. I guess it had been poisonous, at one time. In the liquor, flecks of snakeskin swirled around like soggy snowflakes.

I filled up a plastic cup and tried a sip, smacking my tongue to accentuate the taste. It had a bitter, smoky flavour – like a cross between tequila and whisky. It settled in my guts and started to smoulder. I imagined it going to work down there, warming up the engine that had quit. I drank two cups – maybe a quarter of the bottle – and chased with a beer. By then it was getting close to seven and I felt pretty loose. I sat with the cat a while longer. She was watching a game show in which people leapt around this obstacle course like complete idiots.

'Ha-ha,' I said, nudging the cat. 'What losers, eh?'

She shifted away from me.

Just before I left, I went back into the bathroom again. I took a piss and checked myself in the mirror. Also, I checked my dick. It was still limp and lifeless.

'Come on,' I said, jiggling it around. 'This is it. The big show.'

I tried splashing a bit of mezcal on the tip. I thought that might help. It didn't. It just burned and made my foreskin go red. When I came out, the cat stared at me in a revolted sort of way. I flipped her the finger and paced around the room, trying to figure out if I'd missed anything. The only thing I could think of was my visor. I felt naked without it, but there was nothing I could do about that. I poured some mezcal into an empty beer can to take with me.

'I'm going now,' I said. 'Wish me luck, cat.'

She wouldn't even look at me, now. She just gazed at the TV.

'At least I don't have worms,' I said, and walked out.

I followed the map I'd printed off the internet. It led me past a lumber yard and a vacant lot and a place called True Value Hardware, then down an unpaved side street that ran between two warehouses. Behind one of the warehouses was a dumpster stuffed with garbage bags, puffy and swollen and spilling over the sides. I stepped in a puddle, tripped, then stopped to check my map again. It was hard to read drunk and in the dark, but I seemed to be going in the right direction. The side street curved to the right and ended in a chain-link fence, and a gate – the kind of gate that slides sideways on roller wheels to allow vehicles through. The gate was open. I walked up to the threshold.

On the other side was a cul-de-sac. Around the perimeter, crooked buildings leaned and loomed at awkward angles, like the backdrop of a Tim Burton film. The entire area had been fenced off, ghetto-style. The ground was dusty and dotted with oil spots. There were a few different brothels: Villa Joy and the Red Light Lounge and Simone de Paris. But the one I'd come down for was the Pussycat Ranch. It was easy to spot: there were four neon signs in the shape of cats prancing along the edge of the eaves. The building was on the right side of the cul-de-sac. My old superstition – about left always being right – would have to be forfeited.

Tonight, right was right.

I walked over. The Pussycat Ranch had a paved area out front, like a patio, that was separated from the lot by a shallow swale-gutter. It must have rained recently because water – brown and foul-smelling – had puddled in the gutter. I hopped across it and approached the door. From inside, mournful country music leaked out into the night. I stopped to listen for a minute. It was some guy singing about Winnemucca, asking to be dropped off and left alone there. He knew his stuff, that guy.

I drained the dregs of my mezcal, tossed the can aside, and went in.

The front of the brothel was a saloon, with a bar, two pool tables and a tiny stage for stripping and pole-dancing. There were a couple of sofas and a chaise-longue covered in red velour, and – over the windows – purple drapes held back by tasselled curtain ties. I guess it was all supposed to be vaguely fashioned after those old bordellos you see in Westerns.

A woman stood behind the bar. She had grey hair that hung over her shoulders in greasy snarls, like an old mop. When she saw me come in she straightened up and blinked.

'Whoah,' she said. 'Hello there.'

'Hello, ma'am.'

There weren't any other customers in yet. The music I'd heard was coming from a jukebox in one corner. The tune sounded even sadder than it had from outside.

'What can I get you, lovebird?' the bartender asked.

'I'll have a beer, please.'

She got out a bottle of Bud. It was six bucks. She took my money and looked at me, waiting. Apparently the women were like beers at this place. You ordered them at the bar.

'And a woman. I'd like a woman, too, please.'

She smiled. Wearily. 'Let's do a line-up, girls.'

The women appeared: rising up from tables and stepping out of corners and emerging from the shadows. They formed a line in front of me. The bartender announced each of their names in turn. When a woman's name got called, she would strike a half-hearted pose. None of them were the sex-kittens I'd seen on the website. There was a towering black Amazon, with crimson lipstick and muscular shoulders. She looked as if she could break me in half. She looked as if she wanted to, too. Next to her was this peroxide blonde, wearing thigh-highs and a leather corset that squeezed her breasts together. There were others, as well: a pale girl with Celtic tattoos on her forearms, a middle-aged redhead in torn fishnets, and a dark-skinned woman who had a chubby, cherub face and a crooked smile. She got announced last.

'This is Sunita,' the bartender said.

I took a long pull from my beer – practically shotgunning the entire thing. They were all staring at me, uninterested and resigned, waiting for me to decide.

'I'll go with Sunita,' I said.

I don't know why. I think because she looked the least menacing. Also, I couldn't really remember the names of any of the others.

'Come with me, baby,' Sunita said.

She took my hand, and led me through a doorway.

chapter 48

To reach her room, we walked down a series of winding hallways. The walls were lined with wainscoting, and decorated with velvet paintings of naked women riding around on horses. Along the way, Sunita gave me a tour and showed me some of the extras that they offered. One of the extras was a suite with a king-sized vibrating bed. Another was the Jacuzzi. It was the only thing that resembled the pictures I'd seen on the internet – except there was an old, rat-faced man in it, and a woman with spiky hair. The man was leaning back, eyes closed, and moaning faintly. The woman must have been giving him a handjob under the water. She waved to us with her other hand. The water looked murky and the air stank of chlorine.

'We can come back here later,' Sunita whispered, 'if you like.'

'Great.'

She took me to her room. It was only a few metres wide, with a single bed, a closet, and a shower in one corner, sectioned off by a curtain you pulled across. There wasn't a lot of standing room. After shutting the door, Sunita squared up to me. 'I don't do anal,' she said, ticking off a finger, 'and I don't do pain.'

I told her that was okay, and asked her how much the basic stuff cost – the meat and potatoes. I called it that, too. She gave me a funny look but she knew what I meant.

'How much you got, baby?'

'A couple hundred bucks.'

I actually had five hundred. But three hundred were tucked in my shoe. I had thought I might get jumped or mugged, as soon as I got in the brothel.

'A hundred gets you a little. Not sex.' She had a soft accent, but it was hard to tell what kind. It was disguised by a lisp. 'Sex' sounded like 'thex'. 'A handjob or a blowjob.'

'What about sex?'

'Sex is two hundred. And you pay up front.'

I gave her two hundred. She seemed happier once she had her money. She told me to wait. Ducking into her shower cubicle, she pulled the curtain across. I heard clothes rustling. I sat on the bed and looked around. There were only a few personal touches in the room: a pink pillow with a butterfly embroidered on it, a postcard from Tucson, and a framed photo of people washing their clothes in a river. It looked like some place exotic. India, maybe.

Sunita came back out, naked. Her body was plump like her face. She had a pot belly and stubby legs. Her breasts dangled down like udders, and a ring of fat encircled her hips.

'You're still dressed, baby,' she said. 'You're making me self-conscious.'

I apologised, stood up, and peeled off my shirt. Then I unzipped my jeans and let them drop. But I'd forgotten to take off my shoes. I had to sit back down to lever them off, with my jeans around my ankles, like a guy on the toilet. One of the shoes got stuck in the hem of my jeans. Sunita watched with her hands on her hips. It would have been a lot more embarrassing if I hadn't drunk so much mezcal.

Finally I got the shoe off. I stood, and we faced each other. She only came up to my chest, so I had to stoop to kiss her. Her mouth had an artificial strawberry taste – like candy or chewing gum. As we kissed, I stroked her belly, and breasts. Her skin felt chilly as stone.

She made encouraging sounds, and guided my hand to her groin. I fingered her for a bit. She was sticky with some kind of lubricant, but I could tell she wasn't really turned on. I wasn't, either. My dick was hanging down, limp.

'Is everything okay, baby?'

I told her it was. But she was peering at my dick. Warily.

'It's all red,' she said.

Then I had to explain about pouring mezcal over it, because of my little problem. I don't know if she believed me or not. She said that we had to use a condom, anyways. She got one out from a box beside her bed, but I said, 'Maybe we could start with a massage.'

'What kind of massage?'

'Like a back massage.'

'It's your money, baby.'

I don't think she got to give massages very often, because she seemed pretty excited. She spread a towel over the bed and told me to lie down on my stomach. Then she climbed up on top, swung a leg over, and straddled me – riding me bareback. Her bristly pubic hair tickled my coccyx. Since she didn't have any proper massage oil, she used this moisturiser that smelled like peppermint. Her hands made slurping sounds as they moved over my back.

'You should be more careful, baby.'

'I'm usually pretty careful.'

'But you're all scratched and bruised.'

'Oh, that.'

I told her about meeting up with the hitcher, and the little prank he'd played on me. She giggled at the part where he turned up in the tiger mask. Then her hands slid down, around the sides of my ribs. She prodded them for a bit, as if testing their resiliency.

'You're too thin, baby. Don't you eat?'

'I'm on a fast.'

'If you fast any more, you'll waste away.'

My neck was getting sore, so I turned my head to face the other side. On the wall by the bed she had a big mirror. For customers to watch themselves, I guess. I could see her in it, frowning and grimacing as she worked over my shoulders. She wasn't quite as skilful as the masseuse at Madame Cleo's, but she was more earnest.

'Do you have a boyfriend?' I asked.

She shook her head. 'I have many boyfriends, like you. But no time for a real one.'

'They work you pretty hard here, eh?'

'I want to work hard. I'm saving up, to go to nursing school.'

'You could be a masseuse.'

'No – a nurse. Only two more years of this, and I'll have enough. I can move out and get my own place, and pay my tuition fees. My mother always said I'd be something.'

'Your mother must be proud.'

'She would be proud, if she was alive.'

'Oh. I'm sorry.'

After that, we stopped talking for a moment – out of respect for her mother. Sunita started getting a bit experimental with her massage. She tried chopping at my back, then dug her elbows in and rubbed them around. It wasn't exactly pleasant, but I could roll with it.

'What about your father?' I asked.

In the mirror, I saw her expression change.

'My father is a terrible man. He thinks I'm dead. He tried to have me killed.'

'Jesus.'

She explained that she hadn't wanted to marry the man her father had picked out for her, back in Bangladesh. She didn't love the man, and she'd seen what that kind of marriage could do to you. It had slowly killed her mother, she said, with each strike of her father's fist. Her mother's spirit had died first, then her body. Sunita didn't want to have the same thing happen to her. But, when she'd refused, her father had beaten her and broken her jaw.

'That is how I got this,' she said, touching her finger to her mouth. I assumed she meant her lisp, and crooked smile. 'But I still wouldn't obey him.'

She'd fled to another town. Her father had sent men after her, to kill her. As she told the story, her massage became more intense. She was working the story right into my back.

'One of the killers caught up with me, too. But it was my uncle.'

Her uncle had a soft heart, apparently. He'd always liked her. He couldn't bring himself to kill her. Instead he hid her in a cargo truck, which drove her to India. He said he was going to tell her father that he'd killed her and dumped her body someplace. She didn't know if the trick had worked. Her uncle had instructed her never to come back, or get in touch.

'Now, I am here,' she said. 'I have come far.'

I nodded. 'Like a fairytale.'

'And you, baby? You have come far, too.'

'Just from Vancouver.'

I was picking at the edge of her blanket. It was riddled with lint-balls.

'You had trouble there?'

'No,' I said. My troubles didn't seem like much, compared to hers. 'Not real ones.'

Now that she'd finished her story, her massage settled down again. She rubbed me in silence for a few minutes – first with her hands, and then with her hair. She shook out her hair and smoothed it across my back, spreading the strands between my skin and her hands. Lastly she pressed her body against mine and rubbed her breasts on me, sliding them up and down. They felt soft and warm, like balls of dough. Slowly, her movements wound down. We lay there, with her on top of me, cheek to cheek, looking at each other in the mirror.

'How are you, baby?'

'Good. This is good.'

We stayed in that position, playing piggyback, and dozed off. When I woke up, Sunita was snoring. She'd dribbled on the pillow next to my face. I wiped the saliva away before nudging her. She sat up, blinking, and yawned.

'Oh, no, baby,' she said. 'We didn't do anything.'

'That's okay.'

'Don't you want a handjob or a blowjob or something?'

226

'No – that was great. Just what I needed.'

She didn't believe me. She fussed and fretted over me as we got dressed together. She helped me put my clothes back on, and wrote down her phone number on one of their business cards, and told me to call her the next time I was in town, or if I just wanted to talk.

'Maybe we could have coffee together,' I said. 'Tomorrow.'

'Okay, baby.' But she looked a bit surprised. I don't think she had expected me to take her up on her offer so soon. 'You call me in the morning. I know a place.'

She checked her watch, opened the door, and ushered me out. I followed her down various hallways, in a different part of the brothel-maze. We reached the saloon through a door opposite the one we'd gone in. That was how it worked, I guess. You went in one side, and came out the other – maybe to keep the flow of traffic in one direction.

The music on the jukebox was livelier now. Other customers had turned up. A few guys were playing pool at one of the tables. When the bartender saw us, she frowned.

'That took a while. You got a friend waiting, Sunita.'

She nodded towards a scrawny guy sitting at the bar. He was wearing an oil-stained trucker's hat, pulled low on his forehead. A few empty bottles of Bud sat on the bar in front of him. He grinned at Sunita. His teeth were stained yellow and brown, like candy corn.

She gave my hand a squeeze and let go.

'Hello, baby,' she said to the other guy.

He seemed to know the drill. He got up and followed her towards the other door – the entrance. I lingered, hoping she would look back at me, but she didn't.

The bartender-lady was watching me.

'Anything else, cowboy?' she said.

I told her I didn't want anything else, and went outside. On the porch, I stopped to light a Lucky Strike. As I smoked, I studied the sky. The stars were bright blobs, smeared by mezcal. If I squinted I could make them drip threads of light – almost like at the peak of my peyote trip, only not as vivid.

I stared for a long time, trying to figure out how I felt. I was thinking, I go to a massage parlour and ask for a handjob, and I go to a brothel and ask for a massage. That was just like me.

chapter 49

I lay on my side, staring at the window. Dawn had come and gone. The hotel curtains were flimsy and full of holes, so I'd draped a blanket over the curtain rail to block out the sun. I had the TV on low, tuned into static. I'd been lying like that all night, sweating alcohol and basking in the glow of the screen. The mezcal had dried out my brain like a sponge. When somebody knocked on my door and told me it was checkout time, I dragged myself into the bathroom, turned on the tap, and lapped at the brown water. That didn't make me feel much better.

The cat was curled up in the corner of the room, where she'd slept. I tried to pet her in passing, and she took a swipe at me – a really vicious swipe across my wrist.

'Why'd you do that, cat?' I said.

She glared at me, as if to say, *You know why.*

'But I behaved myself last night. I didn't really do anything.'

Her eyes narrowed to slits. *So you came all this way to do the dirty, and you didn't even do it.*

'Because I didn't want to. Not like that.'

Because you still couldn't get it up, you mean. Mezcal or not.

I sank down on to the bed. The scratch on my wrist was beading into a bloody strand. I sucked at it absently, tasting iron. I said, 'It seemed kind of noble and poignant last night.'

She sniffed. *If there's one thing worse than paying for sex, it's paying for it and then not having it.*

I sat staring at my hands. They were empty.

'You're right,' I said. 'What a joke. What a fucking joke.'

Even the hookers probably thought it was a joke. Sunita would tell them all what had happened and they would retell it to each other. They would repeat the story of the bruised and beaten boy-man who'd paid two hundred bucks for a massage, just as the hunters would tell the story of the kid who'd shot a bald eagle. I was leaving a legacy behind me, all across America.

'Come on, cat,' I said. 'Let's blow this joint.'

I packed violently. I jammed my dirty clothes and shaving kit into my backpack, then carried the pack out to the car along with my bottle of mezcal. I hucked the bottle down hard. It bounced off the seat and clunked in the footwell. It hadn't done anything for me, that stuff.

Lastly I tried to grab my cat, but she slithered beneath the bed. 'Fine, cat,' I said. 'Whatever. I've got to make a phone call, anyway.'

I'd already decided I couldn't face Sunita. If she was going to laugh at me behind my back, with all her hooker friends, then I would break off our little coffee date. I trotted across the street to a payphone and called the brothel. Some guy answered. I had to wait for Sunita to come to the phone.

'I don't think I can do coffee,' I told her. 'I've got to get going.'

'Yes,' she said, lowering her voice. 'You've got to get going, baby. Fast.'

I was a bit disappointed – disappointed that she didn't sound disappointed.

'Why fast?' I asked.

'Men came here looking for you.'

'Oh, fuck,' I said. 'Bikers?'

'Yes. But I didn't say anything – not even when they threatened me.'

'Holy shit.' She hadn't been laughing behind my back. She'd been *watching* my back all along. 'I owe you, Sunita. Big time.'

'They don't scare me. They've come here before. The one idiot – he always wants to fuck in the ass.'

'But you don't let him?'

'Of course not. None of us do. Except Marcy.'

I should have known that the guy was a total liar – just like his brother.

She asked, 'What did you do to him, baby?'

'I stole from him. And knocked over all their bikes.'

'You've got to be careful, baby, or he might fuck *you* in the ass.'

I told her I'd be careful. Then it sounded as if somebody was talking to her. Her boss, maybe. She had to say goodbye and hang up. I stood for a while, resting the receiver against my shoulder. I wanted to call the old couple at the gas station. I'd say, I *told* you I was being chased by a crazy biker. But I didn't, obviously. I didn't even know their phone number.

Back at the hotel, I dropped off the key at the front desk. Everything else was ready, except the cat. She still wouldn't let me pick her up.

'I'm going,' I told her. 'You can stay here if you want.'

I walked out to the car. I sat behind the wheel, pushed open her passenger door and waited. She took her time. She tiptoed outside, sniffed the air. She crouched and peed in the parking lot. She paraded around for a bit. Then – finally – she stepped up into her seat, like a queen ascending the throne. She sat over by the door, as far from me as possible.

'I'm not proud of myself, okay? So cut me some fucking slack.'

On the way out of town, I saw a pet store and pulled over. I thought I could buy something for the cat, as a peace offering. Worming tablets, maybe. Or kitty treats. But the store was closed. It wasn't just closed for the day, either. It was closed forever. The rabbit cages in the window were abandoned, still spotted with droppings, and the water in the drip feeders had gone all scummy. I trudged back to the Neon and slumped in my seat.

231

'Sorry, cat,' I said. 'They didn't have any worm stuff. It looks like this is our lot in life. You're wormy, and I'm impotent, and that's just the way it's going to be for us.'

The cat mewled at me.

chapter 50

The I-80 ran southwest from Winnemucca. I hadn't driven on an interstate since Seattle. I'd forgotten what they were like. The traffic flow was thick and fast. Vehicles throbbed past us, as if everybody had a place to be, some vital purpose. We didn't. We stuck it out in the slow lane, doing about forty klicks, chugging along like a wagon through quicksand. Other drivers laid on their horns and shook their fists and screamed at me through the broken window. 'Learn how to drive, you fucking Canuck!'

The licence plates tipped them off, I guess. I was giving Canadians a bad name, but I couldn't get the Neon to go any faster. We'd entered some kind of industrial region, full of metal refineries and chemical plants and factories. Thin chimney stacks picketed the horizon, leaking ochre smoke that turned the sky the colour of burnt toffee. The air had a nasty smell of tar and melting plastic. Mileage signs crawled past, counting down the distance to Reno.

'Reno, baby,' I said, trying to psych myself up. 'Reno!'

The cat winced when I shouted. She'd been having a nap. A catnap, I guess.

'Hear that, cat? We're going to Reno, and we're going to win big.'

She yawned, as if to say, *How is that going to make any difference?*

'Because then we'll be winners, not losers, okay?'

The cat didn't seem too convinced. She crawled into the back seat and sprawled out with her head on her paws. She wasn't paying any attention to the scenery, or me. She just lay there and occasionally licked her belly or rolled over. I felt as if I'd become the chauffer of a listless and particularly unfriendly invalid.

'Look, cat,' I said, glaring at her in the rear-view, 'I know you think I'm just driving around aimlessly, doing all these irresponsible things, but there's more to it than that. This is about a girl, okay?'

The cat perked up. For a change, she actually seemed interested in what I had to say.

'That's right. The person I mentioned before. Her name is Zuzska.'

It seemed like a long time since I'd said her name. The foreign syllables sounded strange to me again, like when we'd met. I repeated them a few times, savouring the taste.

'She's got red hair – that shiny copper red. I don't know about cats, but in people that's pretty rare. She's a bit skinny, maybe, and wears fairly bizarre clothing – the kind of clothing that shouldn't look good but somehow does. Like those Russian fur hats and huge sunglasses and rubber gumboots decorated with pink polka-dots. Plus, she has nice ta-tas.'

The cat yawned, unimpressed. She didn't care about whether or not Zuzska was sexy or any of that superficial kind of shit.

'Okay – forget all that. It doesn't matter what she looks like. I'll tell you about who she really is. You'd probably like her. My other cat did.'

That got her attention. When I said 'cat', her head popped back up like a periscope.

'For one, Zuzska made me believe in love at first sight. I'd always thought it was bullshit. Then I walked into that Czech class and there she was at the front of the room in her teaching uniform – this weird maroon T-shirt that the school made them wear – and I was in love with her. Instantly. I was so in love with her that I sat at the back of the class and hid behind my textbook and tried not to stare at her because I knew she would be able to tell.'

I took the time to light a cigarette, for dramatic effect. My cat was watching me, wide-eyed. She still seemed to be listening.

'Then one day we had to partner up to do an exercise. I hadn't met anybody yet so I didn't have a partner. I was that loser who gets to work with the teacher. I had to sit with her and repeat all the things she was saying. The first thing she taught me was how to introduce myself and say my name. It was as if she gave me my name. Before her, I didn't have one. I didn't exist.'

The cat sort of snorted, and shook her head, as if she thought I was getting a bit overdramatic. She was a tough audience, my cat. I flicked ash out of the window, thinking.

'Okay, whatever, right? But here's the thing, cat. Zu grew up in a tenement in this shitty suburb, with her mum, who doesn't get out of bed, and her dad, who's a dedicated alcoholic. She still lives out there, looking after them, and only comes into the city to teach her language to idiot expats like me, with time and money to burn, who are looking for life experience or whatever. She's paying her own way through school. A psych degree. She has focus. I guess what I mean is that she's a real person. And being with her made me feel real too. My life up until then had been so easy, see?'

The cat had lowered her head on her paws and started to doze off. She'd lost interest, but I kept talking anyways. I told her about any memory involving Zuzska that came into my head. I told her about how she'd rescued me from some Czech skinheads on our first date, and I told her about carrying Zuzska to the First Aid hut after she'd broken her leg skiing out of bounds. I told her about the night Zu got drunk on Becherovka and took a swing at me, and about the time I'd leapt off Charles Bridge into the Vltava to prove my love. And I told her how my other cat, just before it died, had crawled into Zuzska's arms and started purring.

I must have talked for at least an hour. Maybe more. I guess I was hoping it would be cathartic or something. By the time I finished my cat was snoring away on the back seat. I tapped the brakes, just to mess with her. The shift in momentum made her flop over. She gripped the seat with her claws and leapt up, totally disorientated.

'I know you don't care about my romantic history,' I told her. 'All I really meant to tell you is that Zuzska is the reason I'm out here. Or why I originally came out here.' I took a long, steadying drag on my cigarette. 'I don't know why I'm out here any more.'

The cat made a chirruping sound, as if she agreed with me. I guess she didn't know why we were out there, either.

chapter 51

I drove beneath a big arch, with a sign covered in flashing lights. The lights spelled out *Reno – The Biggest Little City In The World*. On the other side of the sign, the street was lined with casinos. There was Fitzgerald's, which had a rain-stained marquee advertising nickel and penny slots, the Golden Phoenix, which was boarded up with sheets of plywood, and the Horseshoe, which had been converted into a jewellery and loan store. There were others, as well, all equally run-down. I didn't know if Reno had a strip, in the official sense, but apparently this was its equivalent – this cluster of dilapidated casinos.

It was two pm and stovepipe-hot. I felt as if I was melting into my seat. I pulled over in front of a food joint that sold ninety-nine-cent tacos. For a while I sat with my hands on the wheel and my foot on the gas, as if my whole body had cramped into that position from driving for so long. The cat was still flopped on the back seat. I riffled through the glovebox and found the notes I'd written back at the border. That guy Shooter had told me to try the Nugget.

'You stay here,' I said to her. 'I'm going to the Nugget, apparently.'

I pulled myself out of the seat. The upholstery peeled painfully off my back, as if it had taken a layer of skin with it. I didn't lock the car – there was no point, since the window was broken. On the back seat, in plain view, was the rat's nest of refuse I'd built up en route, but most of it was worthless, anyway. The only thing that looked even remotely alluring was my bottle of mezcal, glittering among the rest of the garbage. Whoever wanted that was welcome to it. There was also the cat, but only an idiot would take a mangy cat. I threw a handful of food on to the seat for her, and splashed some water in her beer-can saucer.

'Guard the car, cat,' I told her.

She hissed at me. Half-heartedly.

You couldn't walk through Reno. You had to wade through it. The heat had softened the asphalt, so your shoes seemed to sink into it. The gutters were lined with litter: napkins, chewing gum, chocolate bar wrappers, waxed paper, condom packets, coins, leaflets, pamphlets, parking tickets, everything. The sky was glazed with smog, the air noxious with exhaust fumes. On one corner, some city workers were tearing up the sidewalk to repair a burst sewage pipe, which made the entire strip smell like a cesspit, or a swamp.

The year before, Zuzska and I had gone to the *real* strip – the Vegas strip – with Beatrice and her then girlfriend. It had been on the same road trip that began in Oregon. After the sea lions and dune buggies and Redwoods, we'd meandered down the 101 and swung through Santa Cruz, Monterey and Salinas, then blazed a trail across the Mojave Desert to reach Las Vegas.

When we arrived, it was forty-two degrees Celsius and so humid that Zuzska burst into tears. Being Czech, she wasn't accustomed to that kind of heat. Luckily the hotel – a Motel 8 off the strip – had air-conditioning. We locked ourselves in there, basking in the AC cold and sucking on Coronas and playing cards and taking naps. When it got dark, we emerged from our refuge to test the temperature. It was still warm, but cooling. We set out for the strip – me and Zuzska and Beatrice. Bea's girlfriend had food-poisoning, and stayed behind.

It was peak season. The strip was packed with people and pumping with noise and all lit up with Day-Glo glamour. There were Texans in tuxedos, pensioners in Hawaiian shirts, strippers in sequined bikinis. There were frat boys and glamour girls, cowboys and Indians, Venetian gondoliers and Roman croupiers. There were pro wrestlers, Elvis impersonators, and this group of guys dressed like Mötley Crüe – or maybe it actually *was* Mötley Crüe.

Despite all those characters and distractions, we were the ones people noticed. That was nothing new with Beatrice. People always noticed Bea. But there was also something about Zuzska that night. She'd been too hot to wear anything but a black slip that clung to her like a shadow. It was the contrast between that slip and her moon-pale skin that set her apart. Her hair was still ruffled from the day's sleep. She wasn't wearing any make-up. She wandered around looking bewildered, wondrous, wild. She reminded me of a wide-eyed sleepwalker, or an escaped madwoman.

Outside the MGM Grand we passed a team of basketball players. They were all seven feet tall, with hands as long as my thighs. They were laden with bling: gold chains and rings and pendants in the shape of dollar signs. But even those giants fell silent and stepped out of our way, deferring to us. To the ladies, at least. I was just along for the ride. People must have assumed I was very gay, or very lucky, to be walking the strip between women like that.

It was hard not to think about Vegas as I wandered alone through Reno. The street simmered with heat. There were flies and gnats in the air, buzzing everywhere, feeding off the litter. I passed a few other people – mostly old men who had their pants pulled up to their sternums – but none of them looked at me or acknowledged me in any way. Reno had that effect. We were all a bit embarrassed to be there.

On the next block, I walked by the Cal Neva hotel, a Chinese restaurant called Hong Le's, and the Arch of Reno Wedding Chapel. In the window stood a mannequin of a bride, wearing a wedding dress. She didn't have any head, and her bouquet of roses had wilted in the heat, dribbling petals at her feet. It was fairly creepy. A little further on was a discount liquor store that had been closed down and gutted.

A *For Lease* sign hung on the awning. In the doorway sat a guy wearing a top hat and coat-tails, and nursing a forty of Old English.

I asked him, 'You don't know how to get to the Nugget, do you?'

'Of course I do, son. I'm the mayor, after all.'

'Could you tell me where it is, Mr Mayor?'

He took a swig, and burped. 'The old Nugget, or the new one?'

'I didn't know there were two Nuggets.'

'There are a lot of nuggets, if you know where to look.'

He said that the new Nugget – the Golden Nugget – was a big casino complex on the outskirts of town. The other Nugget was just down the strip. I thanked him and gave him five bucks and headed that way. It was exactly where he said it would be: near the big Reno welcome sign, between a place called Lucky 7 Gifts and another discount liquor store. I must have driven right by it on the way in. A sidewalk sign out front advertised something called the Awful Awful – this huge half-pound burger that came with a pound of fries. Above the doors, jutting out from the awning, hung a giant nugget, gilded and golden. The paint was tarnished and in places had started to flake away. Underneath, the nugget looked dull and brown, like a dried-up dog turd.

chapter 52

I lingered just inside the entrance, checking things out. The casino was small and cramped and had a strange smell, like a stagnant pond. I couldn't see any gaming tables, but in one corner they had a single roulette wheel that looked new. Other than that the floor was filled with video poker and slot machines. All the slots had a spin button, so gamblers didn't have to pull a handle or move in any way. They could just stand there, swaying like marsh plants, with one hand permanently affixed to the front panel. The diner was at the back. Over the doorway to the diner was a plastic sign: *9 out of 10 Vegetarians Don't Eat Here.*

A white-haired lady with a cane hobbled past me, on her way out. I asked, 'Are there any better casinos around here?'

I'd envisaged myself in some high-end joint, throwing money away on craps and blackjack, with one of those hot hostess-bunnies at my side and a crowd cheering me on.

'What do you mean, better?'

'Not so terrible.'

She frowned. 'Probably. But this isn't Vegas, you know.'

I figured Shooter must have meant the newer Nugget. I could have gone looking for it, but that seemed like a lot of work. Instead I trudged over to the bar. It looked like the counter at a convenience store. They sold hotdogs and popcorn and candy. They even had a slush-making machine. On a stool behind the counter sat a guy with one arm. His other arm had a prosthesis, which started at his right elbow and ended in a steel pincer instead of a hand.

'You got any drinks that pack real punch?' I asked.

'Well, there's the Asskicker.'

I could tell he wanted me to say, 'What's the Asskicker?' So I did.

'It's four shots of tequila,' he said, using his pincer to point at a chalkboard above his head. It had the prices of various drinks scribbled on it. 'A thirty-two-ounce margarita, for five bucks.'

'Hit me with it.'

He picked up a big plastic cup, designed specifically for Asskickers, and swivelled towards the slushie machine. He worked the lever with his pincer. The margarita mix came out thick and slow and reddish-brown, like rusted sludge. He filled the cup and gave it to me. It had a yellow lid and one of those bendy straws. On the side was a cartoon decal of a mule kicking a cowboy in the ass, above the word *Asskicker*.

'Do I get to keep the cup?' I asked.

'Sure. It's a souvenir.'

I tested the Asskicker. The slush was smooth, and went down easy. The ice hid the taste of tequila. I sucked it back, pausing to squint and wince whenever I gave myself a brain freeze. It hit the spot, that Asskicker. I plonked my empty cup on the counter and ordered another. The guy refilled it for me, took my money, and gave me change. 'Might want to pace yourself,' he said. 'There's a reason they call them that.'

'I'm immune to alcohol.'

'I'm just saying.'

I slid on to one of the barstools opposite him and kept drinking.

'First time in Reno?' he asked.

'Yeah – but I been to Vegas before.'

'Vegas is a hell of a town.'

'It was,' I said. 'It really was.'

In Vegas, the three of us had gone to dozens of casinos. We'd tried the high-end ones, like the Bellagio, and the gimmicky ones, like Circus Circus, and the famous old ones, like the

Flamingo. We'd ended up at a budget casino called the Sahara, with one-dollar blackjack and a Moroccan theme, near the end of the strip.

As soon as we got inside, I downed two Jägerbombs and started acting like a dildo. I refused to gamble with the girls. I'd decided they were cramping my style. Instead I played blackjack at a table with a bunch of frat guys, who were there for a bachelor party. We all sat with our elbows on the table and our sleeves rolled up. Whenever a hand paid out, we hooted and hollered and gave each other high-fives – talking big, betting big, losing big.

At the Sahara's blackjack tables they had a side bet called Madness. If you bet on Madness and got a blackjack, you won the usual payout plus a bonus. The bonus depended on this digital display that generated random numbers, ranging from one to a hundred. You multiplied whatever number came up by your Madness bet to calculate your bonus. It could pay out huge, but it was a pure gimmick. Side bets are for suckers. Everybody knows that.

Just before midnight, Zuzska drifted over and leaned on my shoulder, in that way girlfriends do. All the frat guys were eyeing her up and pretending not to.

'Bet on Madness,' she told me.

I laughed. The guys laughed too.

'Forget Madness, babe.' I'd never called her babe before in my life. 'It's a scam.'

'Bet on it anyways.'

'I'm not betting on Madness, okay?' I shrugged off her arm.

'Let me bet on it for you, then,' she said, and dropped a stack of chips on the Madness circle above my playing area.

I casually brushed the chips aside. 'Save your money, babe. No way is my chick betting for *me*.'

The guys all chuckled. That was the way to do it. They needed to be taught, these women. As the dealer shuffled, Zuzska crossed her arms and waited, smouldering like a match. The cards started coming. I got an ace first, then a jack of spades.

Blackjack. The Madness display cycled through its numbers, coming to rest on seventy-seven. It hadn't broken fifty all night. I would have won close to eight hundred bucks. Me and the frat guys were too shocked to speak. Even the dealer looked shocked, and it's their job to stay composed. The only one who wasn't shocked was Zuzska. She just shrugged and rapped me on the head – as if to demonstrate that it was empty.

After my third Asskicker, I told the Madness story to the bartender. He didn't seem all that interested, but he had to listen. It was part of his job.

'She's obviously a witch,' I said.

'It could have been a coincidence.'

'Of course it was a coincidence,' I said. 'But it was the kind of meaningful and synchronous coincidence that could only happen through witchery. Female witchcraft.'

'If you say so.'

He didn't sound too convinced, this guy.

'She did it in Monte Carlo, too,' I said. That was the only other time we'd gone to a casino together – when we were travelling in Europe. 'Not the exact same thing. It was even weirder, what she did in Monte Carlo. She'd been winning steadily all night. I'd been losing big. I was, like, three hundred euros down, and she was five hundred up.'

'Having a good run, huh?'

'But she didn't even know what she was doing!' I slapped the bartop with my palm, emphasising the point. 'She was betting randomly, blindly. Moving from slots to blackjack to craps to those super-risky games like Punto Banco and shit.'

'Only high-rollers play those games,' he said.

'That's what I'm talking about.'

He was polishing an Asskicker cup, using his fake arm to twist the towel back and forth against the base. It made him look more like a real bartender, which was cool.

'Then, at the very end of the night, after I'd blown my whole wad, she bet all her winnings on one spin of the roulette wheel: half on black, half on red.'

'That doesn't make any sense.'

'Exactly. We all thought she was nuts. The dealer, the pit boss, the other players. But she was just feeling things out. Once the ball was spinning, and just before the dealer stopped the betting, she moved her chips on black over to red, for no reason.'

The guy paused in his polishing, and squinted at me.

'And red came up?'

'Yep. She'd doubled her winnings on one spin. We waltzed out of there with over a thousand euros. Then she wanted to steal a pedal boat. We pedalled way the hell out. In the middle of Monte Carlo bay, I asked her why she'd chosen red. You know what she said?'

The guy said he wanted to know. He was a nice guy.

'She said, "Red is the colour of love, of life. Black is the colour of death."'

The guy put down his cup, next to the stack of a dozen others. 'Your girlfriend sounds like a real humdinger,' he said.

'She's not my girlfriend any more.'

'Too bad,' he said.

He didn't sound very surprised.

The casino got busier, which meant the bartender got busier and couldn't listen to me. Other customers came up to order Asskickers. He swivelled back and forth on his stool, taking money and giving change and dumping margarita mix into plastic cups. The only time I got to talk to him was when I ordered another Asskicker for myself. I did that frequently. I filled up on Asskickers. I must have drunk half a dozen, maybe more. Pretty soon I felt ready to kick some ass.

'She's not the only one who can bet big,' I said. The bartender was serving up a hotdog. He didn't pay much attention to me. Nobody did. 'I don't need Lady Luck, or even a lady, to luck out. I can show her. I'll top her. You just watch.'

I shoved off my stool and staggered over to the cash machine. Before leaving, I'd raised the cap on my account, which meant I was ready to dance. I withdrew two thousand dollars – almost all the money I had left from selling my camera – and stumbled, bull-like, towards the roulette wheel. Players were clustered around it. When they saw the look in my eyes and the cash in my hand they got out of my way. The betting surface only had a few chips scattered across it. I was thinking, look at these losers, gambling for chump change.

'Big daddy's here,' I said, slapping down my bills. 'Gimme two Gs' worth.'

The dealer – a thin Native kid with his hair in a ponytail – took the money and placed a monstrous stack of chips in front of me. I divided it in two and piled half on red and half on black. The other players watched, murmuring and whispering to each other. As the wheel started spinning, I let my hand hover over the stacks, like a magician about to perform a trick.

Then I pushed the chips on red over to black.

The dealer said, 'No more bets.'

The ball whipped around in whirring circles. We all watched, leaning closer and closer, waiting for the ball to drop. Eventually it did. It clattered around like a jumping bean. It popped off a red number, danced along the rim, and settled down in black. Then it seemed to change its mind and leapt two more places along to the green zero. The wheel slowed to a stop. Red or black wouldn't have mattered. I'd been destined to lose from the get-go. The dealer raked up the chips, in that apologetic manner they have. People were still murmuring, whispering. I was still standing there. I stood there for a long time.

chapter 53

While I was gone, the cat had been busy. I found her crouched on the driver's seat with her snout covered in black gunk. She must have been rooting around in the mulch that lined the gutter. She had something clamped between her jaws that looked like a dead animal. At one time it might have been a rat, or maybe a squirrel. Now it was just a soggy mess of flesh and fur. She'd opened up its stomach, too. Purple guts had spilled out across my seat.

'Jesus Christ, cat,' I said. 'No wonder you've got worms.'

I had to grab her by the neck and shake her before she would let the thing go. I used my notes from the border to scoop it up. The innards left bloody smears on the upholstery. I flung the remains towards a storm drain, and then shook out my hand and did a little shimmy – the kind of shimmy you do after touching something disgusting.

'Bad cat,' I said, bopping her on the nose.

I slumped into my seat and started fumbling around with the seatbelt. The metal bit slotted into the buckle, but wouldn't click shut. Eventually I gave up and threw the Neon in gear. It revved in place, refusing to go forward. I'd forgotten to release the handbrake. The cat was watching all this through slitted eyes. She could tell I was half-cut.

'I know, cat – I'm breaking a vow. But we have to get out of here. Before those bikers catch up with us. Before we get stuck in this fucking cesspit forever.'

I pulled out and wobbled down the strip. The Neon swung back and forth like a ship without a rudder. I took a corner too sharply and jolted over the kerb. The cat snarled at me, as if warning me to stop, and when that didn't work she flew into one of her feline freak-outs: hissing and spitting and leaping all over the place. She attacked the upholstery, and the door panels, and the cup-holders. She even attacked me. She pounced right on my lap and started clawing at my chest. Driving drunk was hard enough without her tearing at me like that. I smacked her with the back of my hand, catching her full across the ribs. She bounced off the passenger door – thump – and landed on the floor. Then she stayed down there, trembling.

I hadn't meant to hit her so hard.

'It's your own fault, cat,' I said. 'You were asking for it.'

An entry ramp appeared and I steered towards it. It tossed me over a hump and on to a highway. I merged blindly, hoping for the best. Somebody honked. I honked back. Then somebody else honked. Pretty soon we were all honking at each other, like a flock of geese. I flicked on my hazard lights. I was obviously a hazard, to them and myself. I kept hitting the brakes too hard, making the Neon lurch. Each time, my stomach lurched with it. I could feel the Asskickers rampaging around in there.

On the outskirts of Reno, I saw a rest area coming up. I aimed the car that way and swerved in. The drivers behind me honked good riddance. As I tried to park, my front wheel well came up against the guardrail and scraped along, shrieking like a buzz saw. As soon as we'd ground to a halt, the cat leapt out her window.

'Wait, cat!' I said.

I shouldered open the door and stumbled after her, but only made it three steps before I went down on my hands and knees, clutching my stomach. I retched a couple of times, as the Asskickers bucked their way up my throat. Then they leapt out and hit the pavement hard, bursting apart in a mixture of margarita, blood and mucus.

I knelt there a while, with streams of saliva trailing from my lips, staring at the mess I'd made. It seemed as if I'd been puking ever since I'd set out. Or ever since I'd found out. Anything I put into it, my body regurgitated. My oesophagus felt swollen and inflamed, as if I'd been drinking gasoline.

Eventually I stood up. My cat had disappeared.

'Here, cat,' I called. 'Here, girl.'

She didn't come, and I didn't know where to look for her. I perched on the hood of the car to wait. The paint was hot and seared my palms. Beside the car was an outhouse, and a phone booth. I stared at the phone booth for a few minutes without registering what it was. Then I remembered: a phone booth contained a phone. A phone could connect you to people, like a lifeline. I shuffled over to it, worked a few coins into the slot, and pawed at the buttons until I managed to dial Beatrice's number.

I don't think it rang. It seemed as if she picked up instantly, almost magically – in that way that happens sometimes.

'You've reached She-Ra, Princess of Power.'

'Beatrice?' I said. 'It's me.'

It came out as a croak. My throat was fucked.

'Trevor? Are you all right?'

'No. I don't think so.'

'Where are you, honey?'

'I don't know, Bea. I don't know what I'm doing. I killed this eagle and I met this fucking hitchhiker and I stole a bottle of mezcal and these biker guys are after me and I blew two grand on roulette so I've only got three hundred bucks to my name but the thing is, I don't really care about any of it. None of it's meant anything. And now my cat has run off. I hit her and I think she hates me.'

It must have sounded insane to Bea, but she didn't interrupt. She just waited for me to finish. Then she said, 'Everything's going to be okay, honey. But I need you to tell me where you are.'

'At a rest stop by Reno.'

'And you're drunk.'

'I'm shitfaced.'

'Okay. I'm going to come out there and meet you.'

'No!' I shook my head, like a belligerent child. 'I don't want you to do that.'

'Then this is what *you're* going to do.' She'd adopted that familiar feminine tone, soothing but firm. 'You're going to sober up. And you're going to get back in your car. And you're going to drive straight out here on the I-80, to see me.'

'I don't know if I can make it, Bea.'

I coughed a little as I said it. It was like the death scene in some shitty Western.

'You can make it. You're close.'

I rested my forehead against the glass of the phone booth. It was dotted with cigarette burns. In the background, at Bea's end, I could hear a swishing sound – like a broom being swept back and forth.

'Where are you?' I asked.

'At the beach, in Golden Gate Park. It's beautiful out here. Just wait till you see this city. It's like Xanadu. We'll surf perfect waves, and drink beverages with ridiculous names, and find a coastal cure for your desert blues. We'll party like we used to, like we did the year we met. It'll be epic.'

I closed my eyes, trying to imagine it. All I saw was the reddish shadow of my eyelids. 'I don't want to cause any trouble. For anyone. For her, for you. Anyone.'

'Don't be stupid,' she said. 'Promise you'll come.'

'Sure,' I said. 'Sure I will.'

I wasn't sure, though. If anything, I was pretty sure I was lying.

'If I don't make it…'

I wanted to say, 'Tell her I love her.' But, before I could, my money ran out and the line went dead. I slumped against the side of the booth, still clinging to the receiver. After a minute it started to beep and the automatic voice came on, telling me to hang up the phone. I left it dangling there.

I shuffled around the rest area, looking for my cat, working my way from one end of the parking lot to the other. Even though it was insanely hot, I was shuddering and hugging myself, like a guy in a blizzard. As I searched I made

250

little cooing noises. Then I thought I heard an answer, coming from the other side of the guardrail. I stepped over it to check there, among the dirt and litter and shrubs. And I found her. She hadn't made it far. She was under a sagebrush, flopped on her side. Next to her in the dust was a puddle of puke. Apparently we'd both been puking at the same time

'You goof,' I said, crouching down. 'Did that thing you ate make you sick?'

I scratched her ears. She was too weak and hurt to fight back, or fend me off. She let me stroke her, and even let me pick her up. I carried her to the car and laid her on her seat.

'I'm sorry, cat,' I said. 'I'm sorry I hit you and I'm sorry it's turned out like this.'

I reached for the crumpled pack of smokes on the dash and tapped out a dart. I didn't know how long we would have to wait for me to sober up enough to drive. Probably a while.

'If we're going to get through this rough patch, cat,' I said, 'I may have to break another vow: my vow of silence.'

I reached for the radio and pinched the knob. I was expecting to hear some kind of epic rock song about being on the road, about getting through tough times, about surviving.

'Here we go, cat.'

I turned the knob. The radio went 'click'. I fiddled with the buttons. I couldn't get any stations. I couldn't even get any static. The fucking thing was broken after all.

chapter 54

We lumbered on towards the evening sun, dragging our shadow on the tarmac behind us. I'd gone the wrong way out of Reno, and had to double back to find the I-80. From there the highway rolled west, up a series of gradual but steady inclines. We were leaving the Great Basin and entering the Sierra Nevada. At least, that was what it seemed to show on my map. The landscape changed, and the plant life changed with it. Shadscale and greasewood and other desert shrubs gave way to arid hillsides and woodland At first there were a lot of juniper and pinyon trees, and then, as we got higher, that changed to big lodgepole and sugar pines.

We passed the border into California. Rather than the usual interstate welcome sign, there was an actual border, with booths and checkpoints. The guards were searching for fresh fruit. You couldn't bring fresh fruit into California, apparently. You could bring loaded handguns, and sick cats, and all your personal baggage, but not fresh fruit. They gave the Neon a cursory glance and waved us through.

The steep grades were taking a toll on the old girl. She'd developed an odd clicking sound, as if something was stuck in the wheel. Also, any time I stopped paying attention, she veered left, drifting into the next lane. I guess I'd messed up the steering alignment when I'd hit that guardrail. As I drove I kept drifting and correcting, drifting and correcting, half-sick and half-asleep. The cat was no better. She lay sprawled on her side, eyes closed, breathing shallowly. We weren't going to get to San Francisco. Not before nightfall, anyways.

'We almost made it, cat,' I said. 'We got as far as California, even if we didn't reach the coast. That must count for something, right?'

She didn't answer. She didn't even raise her head.

'I would have liked you to meet Beatrice, though.'

Thirty miles past the border, near a town called Truckee, I saw a sign for the Boca Reservoir. The sign had a little green triangle on it, the symbol for a national park campsite. I looked at the cat. I was thinking of the way she'd crawled under that bush. Maybe Boca would be the same – a resting place for the both of us.

I turned off. The reservoir opened up before me. I pulled over at the welcome area and got out to take a look. The sides were shaped from sloping mud flats, soft and pale and stomach-smooth. The water was low, even for the dry season, but still looked appealing – winking like a sequin in the sun. I considered running down there, stripping off as I went. I'd hit the shallows going full-tilt, triathlete-style, and when it got deep enough I'd dive in.

'You feel like going swimming, cat?'

She didn't answer.

'I guess it's too much effort.'

The welcome area had an information board, with a map that showed where to find the campsite. I followed a one-lane road around the reservoir, then turned on to a dirt track that wound into the nearby hills. A few miles up I came to the campsite, nestled among a copse of Jeffrey pines. Parked near the entrance was a silver Airstream trailer. Its back-end was set on cinder blocks, and nettles and dockleaf had sprouted up around the wheels. Out front stood a big man in denim suspenders and a red undershirt. He was hitting pine-cones with a baseball bat. He hit one – smack – as I pulled up.

I got out and walked over. He waited for me with his bat raised, poised to swing again. He had a full head of white hair, like my grandpa, and a face tanned the colour of saddle leather. A set of dog-tags hung on a silver chain outside his shirt.

'Are you the warden?' I asked.

'That I am.'

He hit another pine-cone. Smack. It sailed off among the trees. Behind him, the door to the trailer opened, and a woman poked her head out, like a mouse.

'Can I camp here?' I asked.

'That you can.' He waved his bat in a sweeping motion. 'Plenty of space.'

Camping spots were interspersed among the trees. Most were empty, but in a few places dome tents bulged up from the ground like gigantic fungi. The dirt track carried on past the pitches and descended into a gulley. I nodded in that direction.

'What about down there?'

He rested his bat on his shoulder, like a club. 'That section is for overflow.'

'Oh, let him camp where he wants, dear.'

That was the mousy woman. The guy looked back at her. Sternly. It was enough to make her withdraw into her hole. He tossed another pine-cone up and caught it, one-handed.

'Guess it can't hurt,' he said, scratching at his chest. 'It's ten bucks, wherever you pitch. And open fires aren't allowed. It's forest fire season.'

I told him that was fine, and paid him the money. As I drove on he was still hitting pine-cones. Smack. Smack. Smack.

I found an isolated spot near a stream-bed. It was dry and the bottom was filled with smooth, rounded stones that looked like fossilised eggs. After scoping the place out, the first thing I did was check on the cat. She felt hot, feverish. Her fur was damp, her nose was runny, and her bad eye was weeping. I didn't know much about animal health, but all that couldn't be good. I placed a saucer of water on the seat beside her, and tried to get her to drink some. She wouldn't take any from the dish but she licked a few drops off my fingers.

My glovebox was hanging open. Inside it, I could see the pieces of my dad's cellphone. I'd forgotten all about that.

While I sat with my cat, I put the pieces back together, then gave the phone a try. The battery still worked, but there wasn't any signal. I took a road pop from the trunk, tucked my gun in the back of my jeans, and told the cat I was going for a walk.

'Don't die on me, okay?'

I hiked up a nearby hill, clambering over fallen branches and kicking my way through the scrub and underbrush. At the top I got a good view of the reservoir. I also got a sliver of signal on the phone. I hadn't really expected that. I tapped in Zuzska's number and stood with my thumb resting on the call button. I stared at the water below me. A wind was stirring the surface, and the reflection of the surrounding landscape looked both perfect and blurry, like an Impressionist painting.

I didn't press call. Instead I stuffed the phone in my pocket and got out my Glock. I couldn't fire it that close to the campsite, so I removed the clip. Propping my beer can on a nearby log, I took aim and fired. Click. I kept doing that, practising mechanically and firing blanks, as night came on. The sky turned black and the reservoir turned black with it. In the blackness I looked up at the stars. There were no star-threads tonight, no mezcal visions or tricks of the eye. The stars were cold and distant, indifferent as diamonds.

After a while I returned to our campsite. The cat hadn't moved, but she was still breathing. Barely. The sweat had cooled to clamminess on her fur and she was shivering. She had the chills. I wrapped her in one of my shirts, but she needed more than that. She needed real warmth. Our camp spot had a fire pit. So long as I kept the fire small, I figured the old man wouldn't notice. From the surrounding forest I gathered moss, bark and twigs, and built a little teepee in the centre of the fire pit. I lit it with my grandpa's Zippo, then added larger branches. The wood was dry as old bones and burned clean and smokeless.

I carried the cat over and laid her next to the flames, all bundled up. With her head poking out of my shirt, she looked like one of those moles in the 'whack-a-mole' game you play at the arcade – waiting for the hammer to fall. I sat and talked to her for a while. I told her about how I'd almost given in and called Zuzska.

'But what would I say to her, cat? That I'm a fuck-up, a nothing. That she was right to screw around on me and break up with me. She's better off with this new guy, whoever he is. He probably has a real job and can provide for her and will know how to take care of her and make her happy. He's probably a real person, like her.'

The cat emitted a little sigh. She already understood everything I had to tell her.

'So I didn't call her, obviously. I'd rather kill myself than admit all that.'

I got out my phone. Zuzska's number was still on the display. I deleted the digits, one by one, then tossed the phone in the fire. The plastic case bent and cracked apart, and the screen started to melt. Then the whole thing exploded like a cherry bomb. The battery must have blown.

'Sorry about that, cat.'

I stroked her for a while. I couldn't tell if she liked it or not. She wasn't purring. I knew my other cat – the one who'd died of cancer – had wanted to be left alone at the end. She'd crawled into Zuzska's arms to say goodbye, and then she'd crawled under our couch to die. Maybe this cat was the same.

'Remember we're in this together, cat,' I said. 'If you die, I'll die. And if I die, you'll die. Like Butch and Sundance. So you'll just have to pull through. You got that?'

She opened one eye, and squinted at me, as if to say, *You are so full of shit*. She didn't believe in my pact. She was a cynic, my cat, hard and jaded till the end. I walked over to the Neon and popped the trunk. The only supplies I had left, apart from the mezcal, were two cans of beer, a few packs of smokes, and a single bottle of bourbon. Everything was running out, coming to an end. I cracked open the bourbon and took two long slugs. It didn't help much. I tried to think of something to do, something to prove how serious our pact really was.

'I got it, cat,' I said.

I flipped back the trunk mat and checked beneath. Along with the spare tyre and car jack, I found a shovel – one of those emergency snow shovels that come in three pieces.

I assembled that, and started digging our graves.

chapter 55

Digging graves, even with a shovel, was difficult. The shaft of the shovel was short – about the length of my arm – so I had to stoop real low to get any leverage. The dirt was hard, too, on account of it being summer and the dry season. But I tried. I dug a small cavity for the cat, and a wider depression for me. It took a while. After an hour my palms were blistered and stinging with sweat. The graves didn't look like much, but they would have to do.

'It's been nice driving with you, cat.'

I dropped the shovel and picked up my gun. Standing over the graves, I gave a mock soldier's salute, and pressed the gun muzzle to my temple. The steel felt cold and made me shudder. The safety was still on. I slid it to off, and imagined pulling the trigger. I could see the bullet driving through my skull, and dragging everything out the other side in a streamer of blood and brains. I wondered if I'd feel anything, or if it would just be like falling asleep.

Then I heard a sound behind me. I lowered the gun and turned around. A shadow, tall as a sasquatch, rippled across the trees. At the base of the shadow was the warden. He hadn't seen me yet. He was carrying his baseball bat with him. I slipped the pistol into my pocket and stepped away from the graves, into the campsite clearing.

He saw me then. He stopped and pointed his bat towards the fire. 'Thought I told you fires weren't allowed.'

I agreed he had told me that, then tried to explain about my cat being sick, and how she'd needed a fire to keep warm.

He didn't seem too interested in the cat. He was looking at the bottle of booze next to her. He'd spotted that, straight away.

'Whisky?' he asked.

'Bourbon.'

He nodded and stared at me. You could tell he was waiting for me to offer him some. Apparently he hadn't noticed the graves behind me. They were fairly shallow graves, really.

I picked up the bottle. 'You want a drink?'

'Don't drink much these days.'

He swaggered in a circle around the fire, twirling his bat in this casual, one-handed fashion. When he got to my side he took the bottle from me. At first he didn't drink any. He just rotated the bottle by the base, studying the label. Then he capped it and held the mouth of the bottle under his nose and inhaled deeply, as if smelling a bouquet of flowers.

'Ahh,' he said. 'We don't keep none in the trailer no more.'

I waited. Eventually he had a small sip.

'That's good stuff.'

'For sure,' I said, even though it wasn't. It was bargain-basement rotgut. But I guess any liquor would taste good after being dry for so long. 'You want to sit down for a bit?'

'Might as well.' He scratched at the collar of his shirt, making his dog-tags jingle. 'Seeing as you're asking.'

'Hold on. I'll get you a seat.'

At the edge of the clearing was a chunk of tree trunk, which had been sawn on both sides to form a slab. I rolled that over to the firepit, laid it flat, and brushed it off for him. I had the notion that he might give me some sage advice – the kind only an old man can give.

'There you go,' I said.

We sat down across from each other – him on the slab, and me on the ground next to my cat. I added more fuel to the fire. He didn't seem to mind it now. We passed the bottle back and forth and stared at the flames.

He said, 'Car looks like it's got some miles on it.'

I glanced at the Neon. She was speckled with dead bugs and spattered with mud. The sparkling maroon paint-job was now obscured by layers of grime. Then there was the missing window, the dented bumper, the scraped wheel well. I explained about where we had come from, and where we were going – without telling him why.

'And you?' I said. 'You look after this place permanently?'

'Nah. We move around in the trailer, from year to year. By acting as warden, I get to stay for free. We're trying all the different campsites. Mainly in California.'

'On the road, eh?'

'For the past ten years or so. Came from back east, originally. But it's warmer out here. Good for old bones.' He shrugged and took another sip. 'The wife likes it, anyhow.'

'She seems nice.'

'She behaves herself.'

He still had the bourbon, throttling the bottle by the neck. For a guy who didn't drink much, he could really put it away. He kept licking his lips, making them glisten, and his face had a liquor-flush to it.

'What about you?' he said. 'You got a lady-friend?'

'No.' I was looking at the flames. 'That's why I'm out here, really.'

He offered me the bottle, as if he could tell I needed some courage to say what I said next. 'Had a lady.' For some reason I'd started talking like him, in that hokey and humble way. I took a swig, wiped my mouth with my hand. 'But she cheated on me, the bitch.'

The fire popped, like a cork coming out of a bottle.

'That sure is tough, son.' He scratched around his collar again. It looked as if he had some kind of scar under there. 'But a woman will do that to you, when your back is turned. Unless you keep an eye on her, keep her in check.' He looked at me. Significantly. 'Were you doing that, son?'

'It was tricky. She lived in the Czech Republic.'

He slapped his knee, as if he was trying to kill a fly. 'Shoot – no wonder she cheated on you. You let a filly roam, she'll start looking for a stud. That's just nature's way, son.'

'If you say so.'

'I do say so.' He snatched the bottle back from me again. Each time it was his turn, he held on to it longer and took bigger swigs. 'Trust me, son. You got to corral that filly if you want to make it work.'

'Guess it's all over now, anyways. There's no coming back from something like that.'

'Not necessarily.'

I looked up from the fire.

'Take me and my wife. We had our problems. One problem in particular. Similar to *your* problem. You understand me?'

I told him I did.

'I'd been working long hours back east, for the army vets. Both our boys had left home. They run off someplace. So my wife, she had nothing to keep her occupied. She got to roaming. I'd been too lenient with her, see? I'd let her have free rein of the house and home. She put it to good use, all right.'

He laughed – a dry, hacking sound, like a cough. He held up the bottle and tilted it back and forth. The remaining bourbon ran one way, then the other, glinting like oil in the firelight.

'But I took care of that. Took care of the guy, too. That was when we came out here.' He tapped his nose. His eyes were heavier, now, the lids weighing down. 'That was all she wanted: a little attention. When a woman acts up like that, she's asking to be put in her place, begging to be punished. It's hardwired in their systems, see? Like cats.' He gestured with the bottle towards my cat. A bit of whisky spilled out and sprinkled on her, and she made a confused sound, as if to say, *what the hell?* 'You ever seen cats hump, son? It's vicious, is what it is.' He nodded, and repeated the word, savouring the sound: 'Vicious. But sometimes you got to be a bit vicious, to get what you want from them.'

'Cats?'

'Don't get smart, son.'

By then, he'd started to sweat from the booze and the heat. He hooked a finger in his collar to loosen it, then undid a couple of buttons, and I could see the scar on his chest more

261

clearly. It was a burn scar, a bad one – the kind of scar that itches and peels, no matter how long it's left to heel. He saw me staring and smiled, craftily, as if he'd wanted me to see it.

'All your girl needs,' he went on, 'is a bit of a heavy hand. You show her you're in charge, and she'll bend to you. You got to break her in. And then she'll be yours for life.'

'What if she doesn't want to be broken?'

'Oh, she does. She might put up a fight, but that's just to test you. Even now, once in a while, my wife needs to be reminded. Of her place, I mean.' He stroked his bat, running his palm over the hard, varnished wood. The flames gleamed in the whites of his eyes. 'And I give her exactly what she needs. Exactly what she deserves.'

I looked away, cleared my throat. I was thinking, so much for that sage advice…

'Where are your sons these days?' I asked.

He waved a hand, as if they didn't matter. 'Somewhere out here. Running with a bad crowd, last we heard. They were never no good, anyways. Didn't listen. Always butting heads with me, shirking their responsibilities.' The guy took a final swig of bourbon, draining the dregs. He'd guzzled the last quarter of the twixer, fast – without offering me any. He held up the empty bottle. 'Got any more of this?'

'That's the last of it.'

'Too bad.'

He stood up. He was a big man, in height and girth. He loomed above me, lit from below by the flames, holding his bat in one hand and the bottle in the other. He tossed the bottle and caught it, tossed the bottle and caught it – like one of his pine-cones.

'Watch this, son.'

Flipping the bottle up, he took a full swing. The bat caught the bottle cleanly, and it exploded in a shower of shards. They went everywhere: all over me, all over my cat, all over the campsite. They went all over him, too. A few even caught in his hair.

'Wow,' I said.

He was cackling and wheezing, hacking out laughter. Then he stopped, and his face got serious – so fast it was as if he'd changed masks. He poked around in the fire pit with his bat. The glass that had fallen among the coals was beginning to glow yellow, like brimstone.

'You put that shit out now, son.'

'What about my cat?'

'Forget the cat. You can put her out, too. Out of her misery.' He hefted the bat, gripping it mid-shaft, and made a hammering motion. 'I'll handle it, if you ain't got the balls.'

I stood up, and stepped between him and my cat. 'You're not going to touch that cat.'

He pointed the bat at me.

'You telling me what to do, son?'

I removed the pistol from my pocket, making sure he saw it. 'I'm not your son.'

We faced each other in the firelight. Then he laughed his hacking laugh, turned, and lurched off. He headed into the woods in the direction of his trailer. As he went he swung the bat randomly, using it like a machete, smashing branches and cracking tree trunks. He didn't have a flashlight. I listened to him getting further and further away, until it got quiet.

I walked around my campsite, gathering up the bigger glass shards. I tossed them in the flames and put another log on the fire. Then I went to get my sleeping bag, unrolled it, and stretched out beside my cat.

'I swear, cat,' I said, 'I haven't met a single normal person on this trip.'

She mewled in agreement, and I patted her. She wasn't shivering as much any more.

'Maybe there aren't any normal people left.'

As we dozed off, I kept one hand in my pocket, on my gun.

At some point I woke up. Or I might have dreamt I woke up. It's hard to say, since I had no frame of reference. The fire had burned itself out, and the stars were hidden by clouds. I couldn't see the forest. I couldn't see anything. I was surrounded by darkness, silence and empty stillness, like sleep. But coming from up at the campsite I heard noises: banging and pounding, shrieks and screams. I listened for a long time, wondering if I should go up there and do something. Finally the noises seemed to reach some sort of climax, and died down.

In the quiet that followed, my cat meowed.

'Go back to sleep,' I told her. 'It was just a dream.'

chapter 56

When I set out the next morning, the old man's wife was in the yard, hanging laundry on the clothes line. She'd done a load of underwear: off-white ginch and wire-rimmed bras and a few pairs of wrinkled granny panties. I drove past the trailer, parked, and walked back to her. I guess I just needed to see.

She was wearing sunglasses that hid her eyes. They didn't hide the bruise on her cheek, or her puffy lip. Her face had a pinched look, and her whole body seemed to have shrivelled in on itself like a dried flower.

'Sorry about the noise last night,' she said.

'I'm sorry I gave him that booze.'

'Weren't your fault.'

Neither of us was really looking at the other. We were both staring at the ground, the trees, anything. I'd started fiddling with my keys.

'Well,' I said, 'guess I should get going. I'm headed for the coast today.'

'I never been. I never seen the sea.'

'But you're so close.'

'He don't like the sea.' She had one of his undershirts in her hands. She twisted it slowly, wringing it like the neck of a chicken. 'You'll enjoy it, though. Travelled far?'

'Not so far.'

'There are a lot of kids on the road these days. Both mine are. My boys.'

'He told me.' I was shuffling my feet, feeling sheepish. 'You must miss them, eh?'

'I miss them plenty.'

She draped his shirt on the line, pegged it, and then looked at me directly for the first time.

'Say – you haven't seen them, have you? My sons? Last we heard they was around these parts.'

I shook my head. 'That would be pretty unlikely, but you never know. I might've.'

She put a hand to her throat, took a step towards me. She looked ready to cry. 'Do you really think so?'

'Sure,' I said. 'I mean, I met a couple guys along the way. One was hitchhiking. The other was biking around with his friends.'

'That's wonderful – just wonderful. I been looking so long, hoping to find them. If only he'd…' She glanced towards the trailer. The door was open and I could hear the nasal grind of the old guy snoring. She lowered her voice and asked, 'How are they both doing?'

'Good, you know. Getting by, anyways.'

I didn't mention that one of them had attacked me wearing a tiger mask, and that the other wanted to kill me for stealing his mezcal. She didn't need to know the truth about her prodigal sons.

'That's something, at least.'

'It sure is.' I hitched my thumbs in the pockets of my jeans, trying to think of something else I could tell her. 'One said he was going to Sausalito.'

She raised her eyebrows. 'That's a nice place. Maybe he's doing well.'

From inside the trailer came a low grumble-groaning, like the sound of a grizzly bear shaking off hibernation. We both went still. In the silence I could hear her laundry dripping.

'You better go on now,' she whispered.

'I'm going.'

I tiptoed away, trying not to step on any twigs. Halfway to the car, I stopped and glanced back. 'Where is Sausalito, anyways?' I asked.

She mouthed the answer to me: 'San Francisco.'

I smiled. It made perfect sense – in a synchronous kind of way.

I headed out along the road that circumnavigated the reservoir. The cat lay in her usual position on the passenger seat. She was still with me, and still alive. I hadn't had to bury her in her grave after all. I placed a palm on her belly. Her sweats and fever-chills had passed and her breathing was steadier.

'You've got a lot of spirit, cat,' I told her. 'Enough spirit for the both of us.'

She yawned, displaying her canines.

The sun hadn't cleared the surrounding hills, and the moon was still up – slender and white and curled like a soap shaving. The right side was lit, and you could see the rest of the moon's shape to the left, in a faint outline. It had been ages since I'd seen the moon. The last time I could remember was back in Trevor, with that Slovak girl.

As I passed the information board, I pulled over again and got out to look across the water. The morning was calm and windless, the water perfectly still, reflecting the trees, the hills, the moon. It looked like an alternate world, a looking-glass realm. I could even make out a tiny version of myself down there, standing beside his Neon. Nobody else was around.

'What do you think, cat?' I asked. 'Ready for a dip now?'

She blinked at me, bleary-eyed, as if to say, *I'm feeling better, but not that much better, buddy.*

'You watch the car, then.'

I stripped down to my boxers and set out across the mudflats. At first the ground was hard, but as I got closer to the water the mud softened, becoming smooth and clay-like. It squelched up between my toes, coated the soles of my feet. I padded over it like a monk. At the water's edge I stepped in and kept going. The water was cold and shivered over my skin, rising to my calves, my knees, my groin. When it reached my waist I dived in. Since the water level was so low, the reservoir was only about half a mile across. I put my head down and broke into a front crawl and swam out to the centre, then stayed there. I tried lying on my back, but the fresh water didn't buoy you up as well as the sea. It wanted to draw me down, so I let it. I took a breath, tucked into a ball, and dropped. I sank deeper and deeper, away from the light, feeling the pressure in my ears, the ache in my chest. When my oxygen ran out I clawed my way back up, one stroke at a time, climbing an invisible ladder. I broke the surface, gasping. The sun had just crested the hills and the water around me was lit up, flickering like a lake of fire. I pulled myself through it towards shore.

Back at the car, I perched sideways in the driver's seat, with my feet on the tarmac. Water dripped from my hair and the tip of my nose. As I sat there, I felt something brush my knuckles. The cat was licking droplets of water off me. I went back down to the reservoir to fill our bottles up. I drank half a litre myself and poured some in her beer-can saucer. She lapped away at it, gulping every few seconds. It was good water – what we needed. But it wasn't nearly enough.

'This is just a taste, cat. Wait'll we get to the coast.'

By the time she finished I was dry. I stood up to put my clothes on. In the window of the Neon I caught a glimpse of my reflection. My sunburn had faded to a tan. The bruises on my face and scratches on my torso were healing. All the fat had melted off me, like candle wax. I was lean as a wick, burnt down to the quick.

I got back in the car, adjusted my rear-view, checked the side mirrors. The cat was licking her paw and using it to rub behind her ear. It was the first time I'd seen her clean herself properly.

'Better find some flowers for your hair, cat,' I said. 'Today, we're heading to San Francisco.'

I turned the key in the ignition. The Neon sounded all right. The rattle was gone, at least. As we rolled out on to the highway, the cat's tail was twitching in anticipation.

PART III

PART III

chapter 57

I smelled San Francisco before I saw it. Somewhere past Sacramento the air grew heady and thick with the scent of sea. I knew that smell. It was the same here as at home: a mix of surf and sand and landed fish and dried-out crab shells and kelp-whips and suntan lotion and sex on the beach and tidal pools and seine nets and herring roe. The old Pacific.

'Smell that, cat?' I said. 'We're getting close.'

From there the I-80 swooped west into Solano County. The land was low and flat and divided by a gridiron of irrigation ditches. We passed through a series of sprawling orchards, where all the trees were evenly spaced and laden with fat-ripe fruits – plums and apples and nectarines – that weighed heavy on the branches. Further on lay wineries, and vineyards. The grapes glowed gold in the sun, their skin tight and translucent. There were swallows bobbing back and forth between the rows. When the cat noticed them, she perked up and put her paws on the window to watch, and made a strange bleating sound – a kind of cat-squeak.

Then came Vacaville, and Vallejo, where the highway was lined with these big, forty-foot birch trees. The I-80 carried us, smooth as a conveyer belt, past a Safeway and a Motel 6 and strip malls and suburban sprawl, and on into Richmond and Berkeley. In Berkeley we caught our first glimpse of the bay – a swatch of green water stretching out to the right. On the opposite side, hidden in the horizon haze, were the hills and towers of a distant city.

'That's where we're headed, cat!' I cried. 'This is going to be an epic moment – our entrance into a fabled, legendary city. We might even get to cross the Golden Gate Bridge.'

The cat looked, and yawned. It took a lot to impress my cat.

We lost that view as we entered a tangle of spaghetti junctions, where the I-80 and the I-580 joined for a few miles. Cars swerved from lane to lane, merging and exiting, slinging around the loops and ramps in a kind of orchestrated chaos. Then all the traffic was slowing, and we were approaching what looked like a big concrete barricade. It was a toll, which I hadn't expected. It kind of marred the momentousness of our entrance.

We got in one of the lines, and waited behind a big yellow school bus. The kids were all leaning out the windows to escape the heat, letting their arms dangle down. When it was our turn we pulled up to the booth and a burly guy in a high-vis bib asked me for six bucks.

'What's the toll for?'

'The bridge.'

'The Golden Gate Bridge?'

My voice cracked when I said it. I was getting a little bit excited.

'The Bay Bridge.'

'I was hoping to go over the Golden Gate.'

He had his palm out, waiting for my money. 'You'd have to turn around, scoot over to San Rafael, and come in from the north.'

'Oh.' I thought about that. It seemed like a lot of trouble. 'I guess I'll just cross here.'

I handed him the six bucks.

On the other side of the tollbooths the traffic was all sluggish and congested. This wasn't what I'd imagined at all. I wanted speed, freedom. I wanted that rush of arrival. I wanted a helicopter shot tracking us as we sped towards our ultimate and final destination.

'Goddammit,' I said, 'we should have doubled back, cat.'

We crawled on to the bridge and entered a long section of trusswork, with beams and girders overhead, riveted together, creating a kind of canopy. It was like driving through the skeleton of a giant caterpillar. We were moving as slowly as a caterpillar, too. It was only as we approached a mass of land in the centre of the bay that things began to pick up. I saw a sign for a turn-off to Yerba Buena Island, and Treasure Island, which I'd thought was just a fictional place in the book.

'See, cat,' I said. 'I told you this city was legendary.'

Even the cat had to grant me that. As we approached we both peered at the island – so mysterious with its forests, its breakwater, its secluded cove – and then we plunged into a tunnel bored through the centre of it. Everything seemed outrageous and new: a bridge that led to a fabled island and into a tunnel. Traffic was thinning and we were going faster, faster. We accelerated through the tunnel and emerged into a glare of daylight, like a flare-out in a film, so bright I couldn't see, as if I'd driven right into the afterlife.

Then the world faded back into view and I saw we'd come out on to another bridge, a suspension bridge, stretching across an expanse of blue. We were driving on air, through the sky, flying. We blazed like a plane, low over the bay, and up ahead was the city – towers and skyscrapers, steel and glass, parks and piers and stretches of grass – and, inflated with a giddy, vertiginous feeling, we swooped in to land in the mystical, mythical city called San Francisco.

Beatrice lived on a houseboat in a place called Mission Creek. Before I'd left, she'd given me directions. We should have been fine. But when I came off the highway I must have taken a wrong turn. Instead of the waterfront we ended up among the famous San Francisco hills. We went up and down, up and down, feeling our stomachs do that familiar rollercoaster flip-flop. No matter where we went, the bay always seemed to be in view. It was like driving around in a retro video game, with a backdrop that never changes.

'What does the map say, cat?'

The cat was navigating for me. By navigating I mean she was sitting on the map and attacking it, shredding it with her claws. The wind coming through the window kept making the map flutter, which drove her absolutely bonkers.

'We better not be lost, cat!'

We were lost. For about half an hour we cruised around and around, like a boat with a broken rudder. Then I pulled over at a payphone and called Beatrice. When she heard my voice, she let out a cowgirl whoop.

'Trevor! I dreamt you crashed your car and died in my arms.'

'I did crash my car. Twice.'

'I knew it!'

'But I'm not dead. I'm just lost.'

She got me to describe where we were. I'd stopped at an intersection between a public park and a big sports complex, called the George R. Moscone Recreation Center.

'You went north from the bridge instead of south. Go back a couple blocks and take a left on Lombard Street. Follow that to Columbus.' She paused, then added, 'You'll have to go down the hill.'

She sounded happy about that.

'What hill?'

'That famous hill from *Bullitt*. It's the crookedest hill in the world.'

I thought she was joking, but it really is the crookedest hill in the world. I found that out when we got there. It was paved with red brick, and so steep that they'd had to put in seven or eight hairpin turns to make it passable. It looked ridiculous and cartoon-like and suicidal. The cat meeped.

'Buckle up, catnip.'

We nosed over the edge and dropped off, spiralling down. At each switchback, the Neon bottomed out and the muffler ground against the bricks. Ever since going up to the twin peaks her suspension had been shot to shit. We scraped our way to the bottom and levelled out. From there we coasted down Lombard, and followed the rest of Beatrice's directions:

Columbus to Stockton, and Stockton to Fourth Street, which took us right back to where we'd started – at the base of the Bay Bridge.

'We were nearly there, cat!'

Mission Creek was just a few blocks further south. A wide access road snaked past a park and down to the water. We could see the houseboats, moored to a dock running parallel to shore. The roadside was lined with parking spaces, and in one of them, halfway down, she was waiting for us. She was wearing a blue bandanna on her head, and around her waist a red sarong that snapped and fluttered like a flag in the wind. She was shielding her eyes from the sun with one hand, watching us approach. In that pose, surveying her terrain, she looked like the daughter of a Basque freedom fighter and an Indian healer – which is exactly what she is.

'That's her, cat,' I shouted. 'That's Beatrice Carmen!'

I honked and skidded over there and parked at an angle and jumped out. When she saw me, Bea clamped a palm across her mouth, as if holding in a laugh.

'What?' I asked.

'Honey,' she said, 'you look like hell.'

'I've been through hell, in a way.'

'You've made it to heaven now. Come here.'

She grabbed me in a huge bear-hug and held me. I relaxed against her, resting my chin on her shoulder. We're the same height, and our bodies seemed to fit together.

'Oh, my God,' she said, looking past me at the car. 'You really have a cat.'

I tried to explain about finding the cat in the desert, at the diner – but the story sounded completely nonsensical, even to me. It didn't matter. Beatrice let go of me and scooped up my cat, who squirmed around in Bea's arms, and started nuzzling at her hair.

'I need to get her de-wormed,' I said.

'We've got tablets,' Bea said, scratching the cat's chin. 'What's her name?'

'She doesn't really have one.'

Bea pressed a finger to the cat's forehead, as if anointing her. 'We'll call you Sprite.'

She waited as I dug my backpack and dirty clothes out of the trunk. I also gathered up the various souvenirs I'd gotten along the way: my Asskicker cup, my last eagle feather, the *Wizard of Oz* tape I'd bought in Trevor, and the soother keychain those clerks had given me. I stuffed them in a bag and followed Bea towards the water. We had to cross a gangplank to reach the dock and houseboats. Hers looked just like an old-fashioned cabin, with board-and-batten cedar siding and a gabled roof. She stopped out front, still cradling Sprite in her arms.

'Here,' I said, holding out my bag. 'I brought offerings.'

She peered inside, and pulled out the soother. 'Just what I need.'

'Did you get my postcards?'

'I got the one from Trevor. It was hilarious.'

'The second is probably still on its way.'

Bea opened the door. Waiting in the entrance hall was a big black Labrador – as high as my waist, and built like a bull. It whimpered at us and wagged its tail.

'This is Belle,' Bea said. 'Belle, say hello to Trevor, and Sprite.'

She put Sprite down on the floor.

I asked, 'Is that a good idea?'

The two of them stood and faced each other. Sprite arched her back and let out a low hiss, but in return Belle just lay down and panted at her. After a minute they touched noses and started sniffing around each other, in that way animals do. We left them to it and Bea led me into their living area. It was the same as a regular house, with a breakfast bar dividing the kitchen and lounge. In the centre of the lounge stood a wooden coffee table carved in the shape of an elephant. A set of sliding doors led to the back deck, which sat level with the water.

'Does this thing have an engine?' I asked.

'Some do – but most are floating homes, not real house-boats.'

'I didn't know there was a difference.' I was peering out the side window. There was a dried starfish dangling from the eaves. 'This is so you, Bea. What a place to live.'

'Beats being landlocked,' she said, and put my gifts on the table. 'You hungry?'

'I'm not really eating. I'm on a kind of fast.'

'Cool – me too.'

'What for?'

'Me and Venus are on vacation, so we're doing a ten-day cleanse. All we've had is maple syrup, lemon juice and cayenne pepper.'

'Oh.' I let my bag drop. It slumped over and laid flat, like a dead badger. 'Well, my fast isn't like that. Mine's a reverse cleanse. All I've had is beer and hardbar and cigarettes.'

'For how long?' she asked.

'On and off for a couple of weeks, I guess.'

'That's long enough.'

Placing her hands on my shoulders, she guided me to the sofa and pushed me down on it, then went to get two glasses out of her kitchen cupboards. She poured us both a drink from a pitcher on the counter. 'Your detox starts today.'

She handed me a glass. The liquid inside was cloudy. I took a sip. The mix of citrus and syrup didn't sit well together, and the cayenne left an after-burn on your tongue.

'Nice.'

'You get used to it.'

From upstairs, I could hear music – wailing vocals and the thrash of guitar chords. I looked at the ceiling.

'That's Venus, rehearsing. She's got a gig this weekend.'

Bea went to the bottom of the stairs, waited for a break in the song, and called up, 'V? My friend is here.'

I heard the whine of feedback, followed by the sound of heavy footsteps. Then Venus appeared on the stairs. She looked stocky and squarely built, like a block of ice. She was wearing black jeans and a black tank top, and had a lot of piercings on her face: in her nose, her lips, her eyebrows. Just as she reached the bottom of the stairs, Belle trundled by, and

Sprite scampered after her. They were playing tag, chasing each other around the place.

Venus wrinkled her nose. 'What's with the cat?'

'Trevor brought it. Trev, this is Venus.'

We didn't bother pretending to hug. She held out her hand, and I shook it. Her fingers felt cold, her grip brittle. She had a band of thorns tattooed around her bicep.

'Nice to meet you.'

'Same here.'

We both let go. Venus slumped into a lounger by the kitchen, stretched, and took a sip of my drink. She saw me looking at it and smiled.

'Sorry – was this yours?'

'No, go ahead.'

She took another swig. 'How long are you staying, Trevor?'

'Not long.'

Beatrice smiled. 'You can stay for as long as you want.'

'Thanks,' I said.

I was smiling too. We were all smiling.

chapter 58

The first place they took me was a juice bar in the middle of the Mission. Out front it had a small balcony, shielded by an awning, with chrome tables and chrome chairs. Inside, pieces of origami dangled from the ceiling on fishing line. When you opened the door, the breeze sent all the origami spinning: cranes and insects and dragons and giraffes and butterflies and flowers. The air in there was ripe with the scent of pulped fruit and vegetables.

While Venus got us a table, I followed Bea to the till. She marched right over to it and scissor-kicked her foot up on the counter. She wanted to show the clerk her new shoes. They were high-top sneakers with flat white laces – similar to old-school Converse.

The clerk wolf-whistled. 'I'm jealous. Where did you get them?'

He cupped his hands around her shoe, cradling it like a glass slipper. He was a beefy guy who looked like a surfer: tanned skin, sun-bleached hair, big delts and shoulder muscles.

'Thrift Town. Five bucks.'

'You are such a bargain-whore.'

She let her shoe drop, cocked her head to one side, and adopted a Valley girl accent. 'Tell me about it. Now are you, like, going to serve me some juice or what?'

'Of course.' He twirled a blending-cup in his palm, like a cocktail artist. 'Are you and V still on your fast?'

'The last day. But we can juice. What do you want, Trev?'

The guy looked at me for the first time.

'This is yours?' he asked. 'Did you get him at Thrift Town too?'

'Yeah,' I said, 'I was lying in the bargain bin, naked. It was nuts.'

Bea laughed, and so did the guy. After that I was all right by him. Bea ordered us a round of strawberry-alfalfa iced smoothies. While the guy diced and ground our ingredients, she leaned on the counter and chatted to him, one leg bent back at the knee like a character in a Fifties film. She had his complete attention, and the attention of all the other customers, too. She was like a miniature sun, with her own gravitational pull. You couldn't help getting drawn into her orbit.

The guy asked, 'Are you going to Burning Man this year, gorgeous?'

'Of course, gorgeous,' she said, imitating his surfer-drawl. 'We're taking a play.'

Venus was waiting for us on the patio. The table she'd chosen was divided in half by a shaft of sunlight, and she was sitting on the shady side, with her arms crossed, staring at the street. I went out there to join her.

I said, 'Thanks for letting me stay.'

'I'm used to it. Everybody comes to Beatrice.'

'Like pilgrims or something, eh?'

'Yeah. Or something.'

After that we sat in silence, not looking at each other, until Bea strutted out. She had a tray flat on her palm, waitress-style, balancing three tall glasses filled with reddish slush.

Venus said, 'What about our fast?'

'It's the last day. You're allowed to juice on the last day.'

'No – you juice *after* the last day. After ten days.'

'I wanted Trev to try this.'

She placed her tray on the table, took the seat between us, and handed out the smoothies. At first Venus wouldn't have any of hers – she took her straw and gripped it like an ice pick and stabbed repeatedly at the slush in her glass. I ate mine in slow spoonfuls, savouring the tongue-numbing taste, and studied my placemat. It was a piece of paper with folding patterns and instructions written on it, so customers could make their own origami figurines.

Between sips, Beatrice said, 'Your phone call scared me.'

'Sorry. It's been a rough ride.'

'Tell us.'

I poked at my smoothie, scooped up a bit, and let it slither off my spoon.

I said, 'For starters, I'm impotent.'

Bea nodded, concerned, accepting this as if I'd told her I'd broken my wrist.

Venus said, 'Only old men get impotent.'

'That's what I thought.'

'For how long?' Bea asked.

'Ever since she told me. Nothing happens down there – not even when I went to a hooker.'

'Oh, God.' Bea lowered her head and covered her eyes, as if shielding them from something very bright. Or very embarrassing. 'I was worried about you going a bit wild.'

She actually seemed kind of impressed. Not Venus. She slammed her glass down on the table, making the chrome ring. 'Those girls get treated like slaves. You know that, right?'

I held up my hands.

'I know. But it wasn't what you think. We really bonded, me and Sunita. Remind me to send her a postcard. I owe her – for helping me get away.'

'From the brothel?' Bea asked.

'From these guys that were after me. These bikers.'

Venus rolled her eyes, but Bea wanted to hear the whole story. I tried to explain about the hitcher and his brother, about stealing the twixer and the chase through the desert, about the Cobras tracking me to the brothel. But it was the same as my story about Sprite and the diner – it came out all wrong and sounded far-fetched and unbelievable.

'Sure,' Venus said. 'You stole whisky from the Hell's Angels and now they're chasing you all around the coast.'

'They're not really Hell's Angels. And it's mezcal, not whisky. I can show you the bottle – it's in my car.'

'Awesome,' Bea said, pointing her straw at me. 'We're sampling it later.'

'I've been through some really weird shit.'

She patted my cheek. Affectionately. 'I know, Trev. But maybe it was…'

'What?'

She hesitated, and Venus answered for her. 'Totally imaginary.'

I thought back, but none of it was clear to me. Ever since crossing the border I'd been drinking so much, and sleeping so little. Then there'd been the hitcher and his fucking buns.

'Well,' I said, rubbing my temples, 'I was pretty high on peyote a lot of the time.'

Even Venus laughed at that.

We sat in the juice bar all afternoon. Sunlight poured down over the street and sidewalk, but beneath the awning the patio was sheltered and shady and porcelain-cool. I was dying for a real drink – an alcoholic one – but kept that to myself. We ordered a few glasses of lemon water to wash down the smoothies, and talked about the work Bea was doing for the woman's shelter. That was how she and Venus had first met.

'V's been doing it longer than me. It's really harsh, Trev. Some of the women who come in are just broken. Venus is a rock for them.'

She reached out and squeezed Venus's hand. Venus's nails were painted black, and glistened like the minor keys on a piano. I stared at their fingers, at the way they interlocked.

'Have you heard anything from Zu?' I asked, trying to sound casual.

'She's called me a couple times. She feels awful.'

'She should.'

I picked up my placemat and studied the origami instructions. They looked pretty complicated. I gave it a go anyway. I bent the paper in half, and folded it along the dotted line down the centre. I had no idea what I was making, but I needed to be doing something.

Bea said, 'You have to at least talk to her.'

'What's the point?'

Venus yawned, deliberately, and said, 'The point is, you have to decide what you want. You either want to fix things and make it work, or you want to end it and move on.'

I focused carefully on the next fold. It was a tricky one – a kind of inverted triangle that doubled back on itself, like a lightning bolt.

'It's not that easy,' I said, running my forefinger over the crease. 'Just imagine if Bea cheated on you. You'd still love her, but you'd also be bitter and hurt and infuriated.'

She shoved the rest of her smoothie aside. 'That would never happen.'

'I'm not saying it would. I'm just using it as an example.'

'It's a stupid example.'

We bickered back and forth while I tried to figure out how to do the next few folds. Bea listened and smiled, letting us butt heads, making a neutral comment every now and again. We were still at it when the clerk came over to clear our glasses and spoons away.

'Hey, bunnies – you dig the shakes?'

'Unreal, Tao.' Bea touched his wrist. 'Come sit with us, if you're not busy.'

He put down his tray, turned a chair around, and sat straddling it with his arms folded across the backrest. His features – aquiline nose, full lips, dimpled chin – all fitted together perfectly, like a Roman bronze. He was probably the best-looking man I've ever seen.

'And this is…?' he said, nodding at me.

'This is Trevor. We were just talking about his issues.'

'You want to share?' he asked me.

'I think I've bored these ladies enough.'

'Good. Then we can talk about my favourite subject.' He touched his fingers to his chest, intentionally effete. 'Me.'

He started telling us about a guy he'd picked up on the weekend, at a gay bar called Mystique. The guy had fallen in love with him and wouldn't stop calling. He wanted Tao to pee on him, apparently. Or that's what the guy had said when he was drunk. Tao related all this in a matter-of-fact, deadpan manner that was ridiculously funny. Stand-up-comic funny.

'It's not that I have anything against watersports,' he said. 'But it all seems a little too soon. I need to know a guy pretty well before I'll give him a golden shower.'

I was giggling so hard I gagged up a bit of smoothie. My stomach was still adjusting.

'I can't believe he asked you that,' Bea said.

'Yeah,' I said. 'What a total fag.'

Everybody went quiet. Tao looked at me. 'Oops,' he said. 'Sorry.'

Bea patted my hand. 'You're still learning.'

I took a sip of water. After that, I kept quiet and let them talk and concentrated on my origami. It turned out to be a horse. Or it was supposed to be a horse. I'd made the legs too short and it looked more like a donkey. I put it down in front of me on the table. The others were discussing a party cruise, which was being hosted by one of their mutual friends the following night. Tao wanted us to come along, but Bea wasn't sure about it. Venus didn't seem to care. She was rocking in her chair, balanced on its back legs, with her hands laced behind her head. You could tell she was a lot happier now that I'd made an ass of myself.

chapter 59

'This girl turned up the other week. About our age, maybe a little younger.'

Beatrice and I were sitting on the sofa in their living room. Venus was in the kitchen, making peppermint tea. Since it was still technically the last day of their fast, we couldn't drink. They couldn't, anyways. Instead we'd decided to watch the *Wizard of Oz* tape I'd brought them, since I'd never seen it. While we waited, Bea was telling me about her job.

'Her name was Alison,' she said. 'She'd left her boyfriend, and come to us to hide from him. Like a lot of our girls, her bruises were hidden: on her ribs, her back, her thighs.'

I winced, imagining it.

'But she also had these raw red marks on her wrist. Her boyfriend had been handcuffing her to the bed whenever he went out, to prevent her from running away.'

'Jesus.'

From the kitchen, Venus called out, 'Fucker deserves to be castrated.'

I sighed and let my head flop back on the sofa. It was a big three-seater, with those beanbag cushions that mould to your body. I said, 'That kind of thing makes me ashamed to be a man.'

'You could always turn tranny,' Bea suggested, 'or get a sex-change.'

'Sure – just call me Trevine.'

'You should move down here, and become our sister.'

'I will, just so I can break the news to Zuzska. Imagine

that. I'd be like, "Look what you've done to me. I'm a woman now."'

Bea laughed. 'As if it's her fault.'

'Of course it's her fault.'

On the coffee table in front of me was one of those digital photo frames. It cycled through various photos of Venus and Bea: huddled in a tent during a rainstorm, and sitting rinkside at a hockey game, and leaning over a birthday cake, their faces lit from below by the candle-glow. There was a photo of them with Tao, too, during some kind of costumed race.

I said, 'I need to go to the bathroom.'

I went in and locked the door and sat on the toilet for a bit. Then I splashed water on my face, and took a quick slug from the mickey I'd picked up on the way back from the juice bar. It was a cheap Chinese rice liquor that tasted a bit like sake.

When I came back out, Bea asked, 'Okay, honey?'

'It's funny,' I said, and sank down beside her, 'but I can't be mad at her any more. All that rage burned through me on the road. Now I just feel empty and ashen, like an urn.'

'That's probably a good thing.'

Belle and Sprite came in from the hall, and curled up at our feet. Entwined like that, black and white, they looked like a living yin and yang symbol – except in this case the yin was a lot bigger than the yang.

'Is that normal?' I asked.

'It's natural,' Bea said.

Venus brought out the tea. They had a Japanese teapot and matching cups. She put them down on the elephant table, then dropped between us – plonk – like an icicle that had fallen from the ceiling. She poured the tea and offered me a steaming cup. I scorched my tongue on the first sip, and had to spit it back out.

Seeing that, Venus grinned. 'Careful, it's hot.'

'Thanks.'

Beatrice used the remote to start the movie. The MGM lion appeared on the screen, roaring and snarling. Sprite looked up, her ears stiff, and didn't relax until the lion faded to black.

Venus had wanted to do the Pink Floyd thing, and watch the film while playing *Dark Side of the Moon*, but Bea had insisted that my first viewing experience be a pure one.

'It's hard to believe you've never seen this, Trev.'

'I know – it's weird.'

At the same time, it was one of those stories that I already seemed to know, somehow. Maybe from hearing about it so much, or seeing clips of it. Either way, it was exactly what I expected it to be: Dorothy and her journey, the yellow brick road, her magic red slippers, the various obstacles she faces, and the characters she meets.

'Hey,' I said. 'Isn't that the guy from before?'

We were at the bit where she first comes across the Tin Man, all rusted up.

'Obviously,' Venus said. 'Shhh.'

Until then, I hadn't understood that most of the people from back in Kansas – like her bitch of a neighbour, and those helpful farmers – are the same actors that turn up in Oz as the witch and the wizard and her three companions. They all appear as reflections of themselves.

The whole thing was a lot more subtle than I'd imagined.

chapter 60

A pelican swooped in over the creek, dipped a wing to pinwheel, and dived straight down – spearing into the water and disappearing. When it resurfaced it had a fish in its gullet. I was watching from Bea's back deck, leaning on the railing. I'd woken up early and come outside to hack a morning dart. In the pre-dawn stillness the creek was as cool and pristine as an ice rink. There was no breeze, no traffic, no people. I was feeling calmer, and almost composed. On Bea's sofa, I'd had a full night's sleep for the first time in weeks.

As I stood there, soaking up the serenity, I heard a strange sound behind me. I looked back. Sprite and Belle were lying together just inside the deck doors. Sprite was suckling one of Belle's teats – nursing off her like a kitten. It was fairly unsettling.

'What are you doing?' I asked.

Sprite paused and looked up at me, as if to say, *What does it look like I'm doing?* Then she went right back to it.

Beyond them, I saw movement in the kitchen. Somebody was up.

'Beatrice?'

'In here. I'm making fruit salad.'

'You've got to see this.'

She came out carrying a big knife and wearing an apron over her pyjamas, which were decorated with pictures of She-Ra, in various poses. Bea had a rolled, unlit cigarette behind her ear. Seeing the animals, she stopped and put her hands on her hips.

'Well,' she said, 'I'll be darned.'

'But Belle isn't lactating, is she?'

'I've heard it can happen. Or maybe Sprite just needs comforting.'

'She's too old for that.'

'Guess it's a case of arrested development.'

Bea went back into the kitchen, and I heard the steady staccato rap of knife against chopping board. Sprite kept on nursing, eyes half-closed, totally blissed out.

'Watch her, Belle,' I said. 'She'll suck you dry if she can.'

Belle lifted her head up, gave a bear-snort, and lay back down. She could handle it.

I went over to shut the deck doors.

Blades of grass prickled my neck. I lay on my back, staring up at a stonewashed sky. After breakfast they'd taken me down to Golden Gate Park, and we'd ended up in this Japanese tea garden near the centre. The grounds contained paths and ponds and rock gardens and bonsai trees and pagodas. There were a lot of tourists wandering around, but we'd managed to find a secluded spot near one of the ponds to get baked.

Beside me, Bea dipped her hand in the pond, scooped up a palmful of water, and let it trickle through her fingers. Then she flicked the last drops in my face, as if casting a spell.

'Speak,' she said. 'Play me a memory.'

'This reminds me of Amsterdam,' I said.

I told them about the trip Zuzska and I had taken there. I told them that she and I had gotten stoned in a pot café and collapsed next to one of the canals. I told them how she'd laid her head in my lap, and how I'd been stroking her hair, feeling it hot and silky with sunlight.

I told them what she'd said, too.

'She claimed these were the things we'd remember. Not the big moments, but the in-between moments. And I guess she was right, since I do.'

'Boo-hoo,' Venus said. 'Enough with the broken-hearted sonata.'

'Venus, be nice,' Bea said.

'I'm just saying. If you guys had problems, you had them for a reason.'

'It might help if I knew what that reason was.'

Bea sat up. She had bits of grass in her hair, like green tinsel.

'Maybe we should ask the I Ching.'

Venus groaned. 'Please, no.'

'What's the I Ching?'

Bea was already rooting through her purse. She brought out a pocket book the size of a cigarette case, and a set of coins – these three bronze coins with holes in the centre. She told me that the I Ching was a fortune-telling system, like the Chinese version of Tarot cards.

'You flip the coins six times,' she said, tossing them in the air to demonstrate. They bounced and settled in the grass. 'Then use them to build a hexagram – a sequence of lines.'

'And it works?' I asked.

'It's total bullshit,' Venus said.

'It never works for Venus because she's a sceptic.' Bea picked the coins up one at a time, and held them out to me. 'But if you believe me, and trust your unconscious, it works.'

'I believe,' I said, and took the coins.

'I'll guide you through it.'

Venus snorted and started rolling another joint. Bea and I sat cross-legged, facing each other. She spread her scarf on the grass between us, like a miniature picnic blanket.

Bea said, 'What do you want to ask?'

'Why she did it, I guess. Why she cheated on me.'

Bea got me to toss the coins on the scarf. She had a pen and an old shopping receipt to write on. She told me that one side of the coins had a certain value, and the other side had another value. You added the values up to create part of the hexagram. I didn't really get it but she seemed to know what she was doing. She counted my coins and drew a line on her paper. I had to toss the coins five more times, and she drew five more lines, and that was it.

'This is very portentous,' Bea said. She sat back and put her fingertips together, steeple-like, playing up her part as soothsayer. 'A perfect example of the I Ching in action.'

'Action, my ass,' Venus muttered.

'The hexagram you made,' Bea said, brandishing the receipt, 'is standstill.'

There was a long pause. I could hear water burbling from a fountain in the pond.

'Is that good?' I asked.

'Let me check.'

She flipped through her little book. Venus had sparked up her joint. She leaned over to offer it to me, and I took a huge hit that turned my tongue numb and made my ears pop.

'Don't listen to her,' Venus whispered. 'That book is pure hocus pocus.'

'It's a bit mystical,' Bea said. 'But it was good enough for Carl Jung.'

When I heard that, I choked on the smoke in my lungs and had a huge coughing fit. I waved the joint towards Venus, giving it back, and thumped my chest with a fist like an ape.

'Carl Jung?' I said.

'The guy who came up with individuation and synchronicity and everything.'

'I know. My hitcher mentioned him.'

We looked at each other, and I felt the ground shudder, as if a tremor had passed beneath us. Venus was blowing smoke, oblivious, but you could tell Bea had felt it too.

'Did you find the meaning of the hex-thing?' I asked her.

She nodded, and read out, '"It's a time of stagnation and decline. This hexagram is linked to the eighth month, August, when the year has passed its zenith and decay settles in."'

'Holy shit,' I said. 'It *is* August!'

'See?' she said. 'It's already working.'

I gave her a high-five. We started seeing all these parallels between my reading and my situation with Zuzska: how our relationship had stagnated, and decayed, since neither of us was willing to move or emigrate to be with the other.

291

'All we did was fly back and forth and have sex,' I said.

'No wonder she cheated on you!'

'Let's ask it something else.'

Venus shook her head and flicked her roach in the pond. It landed with a sizzle. A second later a fish snapped it up, thinking it was food. There were various breeds of fish in the ponds – mostly those giant carp with bulging eyes.

'I'm going for a walk,' Venus said.

We said goodbye to her without looking up. We were totally focused on the oracle. Bea rearranged her scarf while I gathered up the coins. The second time, I asked it if what I was doing – running away, the whole road trip idea – was a good plan or a total waste of time. I threw the coins again, and Bea jotted down the lines again. I waited for her to decipher it.

'Hmm,' Bea said. 'Youthful folly.'

'Damn.' I'd started picking blades of grass. 'That one's pretty self-explanatory.'

'It's not all bad. Listen.' She put her finger on the page, and traced it along the print as she read out, '"In a time of youth, folly is not evil. One may succeed in spite of it."'

She explained a bit more, emphasising the positives, but you could tell she was just trying to make me feel better. I threw all the grass I'd plucked into the air, like confetti.

'Forget it,' I said. 'I've got a better question: what should I do now?'

We ran through the coin-tossing and line-drawing ritual a third time. We were leaning together, with our foreheads almost touching. Some of the lines were solid, others broken. She didn't recognise the next hexagram, and had to look it up in her book.

'It's deliverance,' she said.

'Like the film?'

'It can mean getting out of danger, clearing the air, or a release of tension. It says if you have something to do, then do it. If you don't, then it's probably time to return home.'

'But I just got here,' I said.

'Wait. One of your lines is moving. That changes the reading. It means…' She thumbed to another page, and recited solemnly, '"Shoot at the hawk on a high wall."'

Neither of us laughed. This seemed fucking serious.

'How do I do that?' I asked.

'Apparently something – or someone – is standing in the way of your deliverance.' Bea glanced around, as if the person might be lurking nearby. 'He must be overcome first.'

We sat in silence for a while, tripping out about that. A cloud of gnats rose up around us in a frenetic tornado. I saw Venus coming along one of the paths. She had a unique walk – a kind of bow-legged swagger. When she reached us, she spat in the pond and sat down.

'Are you still doing that shit?'

'It says I'm being delivered,' I said.

'Delivered like a letter?'

I thought of the hitcher, and his envelope.

'Could be,' I said.

chapter 61

We skimmed over the water like a stone, barely touching the surface. The bay was simmering with waves that juddered against the underside of the hull. You could feel the reverberations in your tailbone and rattling up your spine. Each time we hit a big wave, flecks of sea-spray splashed up from the prow and showered our faces – cool and sweet and exhilarating.

'Yee-haw!' Bea shouted.

She was standing in the wheelhouse beside the driver – this beefy Ukrainian guy, built like a tree trunk, with gold teeth and pockmarked cheeks. Venus and I had been consigned to the back, where the passengers were supposed to sit.

'Tao will be there tonight,' she called across to me. 'So you'll know somebody.'

'Tao seemed cool.'

'Tao *is* cool.'

We'd decided to go to the party cruise after all. Or Venus had, and she'd convinced Beatrice that it was the best way to celebrate the end of their fast. Since we'd been running late, Bea had ordered a water taxi to take us straight to the pier. In San Francisco there's a company that does that kind of thing. But it's not cheap.

'That's twice as expensive as a regular cab,' Venus had said.

'It's also twice as fast, and twice as awesome.'

It was, too. The guy had navigated his boat right into Mission Creek, and docked at the back of their float home.

His taxi wasn't like those dinky water taxis you see puttering around Vancouver. It was a sleek white speedboat, low and long, with a sheltered seating area and twin 275-horsepower motors. The thing really went. We were torpedoing along about fifty yards from shore, beneath the Bay Bridge, and it felt a little like flying.

'Where you go tonight?' the driver yelled at Bea.

'A party cruise.'

'Forget cruise. You come with me to our Ukrainian Centre. We do folk dancing.'

'I love folk dancing – but not tonight.'

Like everybody else, he'd fallen for Beatrice, instantly. In rapid-fire broken English, he started telling her about himself: how he'd fled the Ukraine after the collapse of the Soviet Union, how he'd met his wife in an opium den, how his son was playing baseball for a triple-A team and his daughter was a concert pianist. He was so engrossed with Bea that he wasn't watching the water at all. A buoy – one of those big triangular ones – was racing towards us.

'Heads up, buddy!' I shouted.

He casually swerved around it, throwing up a huge rooster-tail of spray.

'Maybe I should drive,' Beatrice said.

'You want to drive? You drive.'

He let her take the wheel, and stood behind her to help her steer. It was always like this with Bea. In Rome, the chief of the *polizia* had taken her on a personal tour of the city.

'Hold on to your girdles, girls,' she said, leaning on the throttle.

'You one crazy lady.'

Me and Venus brooded in the back and stared at the scenery. It was near sunset and the sky above the bay was flamingo-pink, dotted with cotton-candy clouds. On Venus's side we had a good view of shore. We were skipping along parallel to a sea-wall, past a series of piers that supported waterfront bars and restaurants and amusement arcades and flea markets.

'What part of the city is that?' I asked Venus.

'The Embarcadero.'

'Looks funky.'

'It's pretty mainstream.' She pecked at the window with her nail. The outside of the glass was spattered with beads of saltwater. 'There are a few okay bars, but most of them are overrun with tourists and straights. Luckily that won't be the case on the cruise tonight.'

'What do you mean?'

She grinned. Wickedly. 'It'll be a boatload of gays.'

'Oh. Wow.'

'Don't worry – it's not exclusive.'

Further along, Venus started rooting around in her handbag. She pulled out a mickey of rum, and glanced at the front. The driver was still chatting away, distracted by Bea. He'd put on some kind of funky Ukrainian rap, which throbbed through the boat's sub-woofers.

'Here,' Venus whispered.

She offered me the mickey. I went over to join her, and took a quick swig.

'Thanks,' I said.

'No prob.'

We handed it back and forth in stoic silence – like two soldiers from warring factions who'd called a temporary truce. Ahead of us, way across the bay, a fog front was moving in. Amid the haze I could see another bridge, the lights on the uprights glowing like gas lanterns.

'Is that the Golden Gate Bridge?'

'No,' Venus said. 'The Richmond Bridge.'

I was beginning to think the Golden Gate was a myth, like the Golden Fleece. It didn't actually exist – it was a just a trick they played on tourists to draw them down here.

'Where *is* the Golden Gate, anyways?' I asked.

'Around to the west. It connects San Fran to Marin County and Sausalito.'

I reached for the rum. 'What do you know about Sausalito?'

'Lots of waterfront property and five-star hotels and rich yuppie pricks. Why?'

'That's where the hitcher I picked up said he was headed.'

'Oh, sure. Your *hitcher*.' She mimed making little quotation marks as she said the name. 'The brother of the *biker*.'

She laughed – this cackling laugh like the wicked witch in Oz. Beatrice looked back, and Venus had to explain what was so funny. Then, of course, the driver wanted to hear all about it: about my imaginary friends and desert hallucinations, about my wingnut road trip and zany experiences. There was a lot of laughing and joking at my expense. I laughed and joked along with them, feeling that rum eating away at my belly.

The truce was over, obviously.

chapter 62

The party ship looked like an old steam ferry, with three levels, two bars and dance floors, and an upper deck open to the sky. Our driver dropped us off right next to it, at a pier on the northeast corner of the city. He gave Beatrice his card, and told her if she called he'd come back to pick us up later.

'Remember,' he shouted, as he pushed off, 'you ask for Captain Victor!'

'Aye-aye, captain.'

To reach the cruise ship, you had to cross this wobbling gangplank. A woman in thigh-highs and fishnets welcomed us aboard and punched our tickets. Then the gangplank went up and the ship's horn sounded and we chugged out into San Francisco Bay. The decks were packed with people in nautical-themed outfits: pirates and sea gypsies and sailors and various types of marine life. There were also a few hardcores in fetish wear and bondage gear. It was a costume party – which Bea hadn't known about, and Venus hadn't bothered to mention.

'This is pretty wild,' Bea said to me.

She and I were sitting on the middle deck, next to a table of transvestites dressed in skimpy mermaid costumes. Venus was at the downstairs bar, getting us a round of drinks.

'We're the only ones not dressed up.'

'We'll just have to improvise,' Bea said.

'You can't improvise a costume.'

Bea was already knotting her blouse between her breasts, cowgirl-style. Then she dug a scarf out of her purse, and tied it around her neck like a kerchief. She pointed at me with both forefingers, miming a pair of six-shooters. 'Stick 'em up, Huckleberry.'

I held my hands up. 'You got me, doc.'

She started pulling the imaginary triggers, and I pretended to get shot, clutching my heart and sinking down in my seat. I was lying like that, half-dead, when Venus returned, carrying a tray laden with drinks.

'What's with him?' Venus asked.

'He's pissed you dragged him out here.'

Venus sat down and distributed the drinks: three highballs and a round of shooters. 'I only brought him because I thought he'd like it.'

I popped right up, like a corpse coming back to life. 'Really?' I said. 'I thought you only brought me because you think I'm an uptight straight who's too macho to handle it.'

She crossed her arms and we stared each other down. Then somebody shouted in my ear, 'Hey, breeder!' It was a guy dressed as a skin-diver, except his snorkel was a giant dildo. He prodded me with the dildo, danced a little jig, and pranced off. It was fairly intimidating.

'See?' Venus pointed at me. 'You *are* an uptight straight.'

'We'll see about that.'

'Them's fighting words,' Bea said, in her cowgirl drawl, and raised one of the shot glasses. 'Now listen, children. We are going to play nice, and have a toast. We're going to toast the end of Trevor's journey, and the end of our mutual fasts. To endings.'

Me and Venus joined her, clinking glasses, and chimed, 'To endings.'

We tossed back the shooters. It was sambuca, which I hate.

The two of them hadn't had a drink for ten days, and the alcohol hit them hard – especially Venus. After a few rounds she was getting all loved up. She wrapped her arms around Bea and they entwined like a couple of octopuses. The music had fired up – electric bubble-pop – and it was too loud to talk, so eventually we stopped trying. While they cuddled and kissed, I slid an empty shot glass back and forth on the tabletop, leaving slug-trails of condensation.

'If I go for drinks,' I asked, 'do you think anybody will hit on me?'

They stopped nuzzling to look at me. Venus shook her head. 'Not looking like that.'

I was wearing my road-worn jeans and a green T-shirt, limp and wilted as a piece of old lettuce. Then there was my swollen nose, my orphan look, my whole lovelorn demeanour.

I said, 'I guess I'm pretty unappealing.'

Bea said, 'Not to me, Trev. But gay men are notoriously superficial.'

'Well,' I said, palming the tabletop to push myself up, 'what are you ladies having?'

'Drinks!'

'Alcohol!'

As I slunk away, they'd already started making out again.

There must have been nearly a thousand guests on that boat. All the decks were full, and the downstairs bar was packed, sweaty, heaving. I waited in line behind a guy in a pair of leather chaps, with a bare ass. I was stuck with that ass for half an hour, and when I finally got to the bar I made the most of it. I ordered a twixer of Cutty Sark and a two-litre bottle of soda to help wash it down. The bartender – a hairy bear in a mesh top – grinned knowingly. 'How many glasses?'

'Just one.'

He whistled. 'Somebody's having a party.'

'I'm lovesick, okay?'

It cost me seventy-five bucks, which was a big chunk of what I had left after the cruise ticket and the wad I'd dropped on roulette in Reno. Carrying a bottle in each hand, I wormed and wiggled through the crowds. The only place on the ship I could find any privacy was the back deck, right above the propeller. I sat and straddled a post of the safety rail, with my legs dangling off the stern. Directly below me the wake churned and frothed and bubbled like a cauldron. I set to work on the Cutty, drinking mechanically, taking no satisfaction in it. That went on for a while – until somebody found me. A pair of bronzed legs appeared on my left, and I heard a voice booming down from above. 'Behold, the lonely straight man.'

I looked up. It was Tao. He was dressed as a surfer, in a shorty wetsuit with no sleeves, unzipped to the midriff. His chest was waxed and burnished and looked absurdly buff.

'Is it that obvious?'

He lowered himself down, joining me at the stern, and I offered him the twixer.

'I'm guessing,' he said, taking a straight slug, 'that you're still having issues.'

'They're not real issues. Just girl troubles.'

'Girls *are* trouble. Boys are so much better.'

I told him a little about what had happened. Not the whole story – just enough to fill him in. As I talked, we shared the Cutty Sark, passing it back and forth, drinking from the bottle.

'Seems weird they brought you here, when you're all over the map emotionally.'

'It was Venus's idea. She's feeling threatened.'

'By you?'

I nodded. 'She thinks I'm in love with Beatrice.'

'*Are* you in love with Beatrice?'

'Who isn't?'

He laughed. 'I know. I'm gay and even I'm in love with her. But listen, man.' He grabbed me by the neck, pulled me close. 'You can't let V get away with that. You've got to show her that you're not as uptight as she thinks. You've got to loosen up, relax, go with it.'

'You sound like a masseur.'

'I am a masseur. I just work in the juice bar to make ends meet.'

'Oh.'

'Come on,' he said, slapping me on the thigh. 'Let's cut up the rest of this Cutty Sark and then go join the fun. They're playing all kinds of ridiculous games on the upper deck.'

'I haven't dressed the part.'

'We can take care of that. But first you need to chillax a bit. Here.' He held out his hand, palm up. There was a small white pill in the centre. 'This'll help.'

'Ecstasy?'

'You know what they say. A halfer for a laugher.'

I didn't know people said that – but apparently they do. I took the tab, placed it delicately on my tongue, and washed it down with a swig of whisky.

'In an hour you'll be rolling,' Tao said. He got up and stood behind me and started massaging my neck and shoulders, working out the knots. 'In the meantime, let's try to get rid of this mad-gruesome vibe you're carrying around.'

I closed my eyes, feeling my muscles relax.

chapter 63

'Remember,' Tao said, 'if you're feeling uncomfortable at any point, just say so.'

'I'm feeling uncomfortable now.'

'It hasn't even started.'

We were on the upper deck, in a circle of revellers. About twenty people were taking part. There was a lot of skin on display, including my own. Tao had made me strip down to my boxers. He'd said that I could pretend to be a swimmer, and that would be my costume. All of our bodies were sweat-sheened and glistering. The boat was drifting into the fog bank but it was a muggy kind of fog – almost tropical – and the night was still hot as a lobster pot.

'Look at these scabs,' Tao said, spider-walking his fingers over my back. By then the E was kicking in, and his touch tingled on my skin. 'They'll think you're into some really hardcore S&M.'

I swatted his arm away.

'I lost a fight with a man-tiger.'

'I'd like to hear that story.'

'I bet you would.'

A whistle sounded. The hostess with the thigh-highs and fishnets was in charge. She cracked a bullwhip and told us that the first game we were playing was called 'pass the berry'.

'All you have to do is take the berries from your neighbour and pass them to the other side...' She paused, letting us hang, then added the kicker. 'Using nothing but your mouth!'

When she said that, everybody cheered, and I felt a slap on my ass. I assumed it was Tao, but it wasn't – it was the diver with the dildo-snorkel.

'Looks like I'll be passing to you, breeder.'

'Oh, boy,' I said, and inched away from him.

'Ready, people!'

The hostess strutted up to a blonde girl on the far side of the circle, and popped a strawberry into her mouth. I watched the berry make its way around, from girl to guy to girl to girl to guy to guy. Then the snorkeller had it. By that point the strawberry was pretty chewed up. He bared his teeth, dribbling red, and leaned towards me. I puckered up and tried to take it, but I was so sketched out that I dropped it. It splatted to the floor.

Everybody hooted.

'Uh-oh!' the instructor said. 'Looks like somebody gets a strike.'

I grabbed Tao's bicep and asked him what that meant.

'The receiver always gets the strike. Three strikes and you lose.'

By then the next strawberry was coming around. I really went for it, snapping it from the diver guy's mouth. Then I turned and offered it up to Tao. He leaned in. I felt his lips brush mine as he took it. After passing it on, he wiped his chin and gave me the thumbs-up. 'Now you're dancing.'

As the game continued, it got faster and faster. To keep things interesting, the hostess switched from strawberries to cherries to raspberries. The raspberries were tricky. They had a tendency to fall apart. I dropped one of them and got my second strike. But other people were dropping them too. If I could hold out for a few more rounds I might scrape by. Then came the clincher: the blueberries. They were so small you couldn't really bite them. You had to deliver them to the next person with your tongue. Tao was a gentleman about it but the dildo diver tried to take advantage. As he made the pass, he slipped his tongue inside my mouth and wiggled it around, like a persistent little slug.

'Easy, man,' I said, jerking back.

The blueberry dropped out and plopped on the deck. It bounced once, like a marble, then stopped. The whistle shrieked, right in my ear. The hostess had been waiting beside me, ready to pounce.

'That's THREE strikes!' she shouted.

The rest of the contestants went crazy, stamping their feet and shaking their fists in a kind of primal dance. I stared at the blueberry. I couldn't look away from it. The lady blew her whistle again to get everybody's attention.

'All right,' she said. 'He'll have to hook up with the winner. How many people have NO strikes?'

The snorkeller's hand shot straight up. He wanted me bad, that guy. But there were a few other contenders, including Tao. To decide between them, the hostess had them all draw a condom packet from a bag. Most of the packets were blue. Tao's was pink.

'That means it's you!' she announced.

He smiled at me. Ruefully. 'Sorry.'

'It could've been worse,' I said.

The other participants encircled us. The fog had thickened, hanging over us like a veil. You couldn't see the shore any more. You couldn't even see the water. But you could feel it – rolling and roiling beneath us, as if the whole bay was set to a low boil.

Me and Tao stood in the centre of all that, facing each other.

'You can always make a break for it,' he said. 'Jump overboard.'

'I can handle it.'

The lady cracked her whip again, right next to my ear. 'Okay, people,' she shouted. 'Let's count them in. Five... four...'

Tao put his hand on my hip. His touch felt hot, scalding. 'Three... two...'

The fog swirled and shifted, obscuring the circle of onlookers.

'One… kiss!'

I froze and he leaned in and kissed me. Hesitantly, to start. Then more hungrily. His mouth tasted of vodka and tonic and a faint hint of mint. At first he was mostly kissing me. Then I started kissing back. His palm found its way to the small of my back and slid up my spine. I clenched him in a kind of headlock. Around us, the voices of the onlookers rose up in one of those steady crescendos that goes *whhhoooooo*!

When the lady blew her whistle, we kept kissing.

chapter 64

Later the boat hit a shoal, or a sandbank. We weren't sure which. We just felt the lurch and heard the low, vibrating groan as the vessel ground to a halt. Me and Tao were sitting at the bow, cuddled up. I had my legs stretched across his lap, and an arm draped around his neck.

'What was that?' I asked.

'We hit something.'

People were peering over the sides, excited. The captain made an announcement on the PA system, telling everybody to stay calm. He said we were stranded, but not sinking. Another cruise boat was coming out to pick us all up.

'I guess that means more boy-time for us,' I said.

'I told you boys are better.'

'Let's see what toys the boys got.'

For participating in the berry game, we'd been given a prize pack – a sealed plastic bag with a label on it that read *Warning! Contains Sexual Contents*. We opened it up and went through it together. Inside was a cock-ring, a silver dildo, some condoms, a battery-powered buzzer for shocking nipples, an eye mask, and this glass vial labelled *Rock Hard*.

'Is that a shooter?' I asked.

'Poppers. A lightweight aphrodisiac.'

'Just what I need.'

He raised his eyebrows, and I had to explain about my limp-dicked dilemma.

'You mean, even when we were kissing…?'

I shook my head. 'Nothing.'

'That's terrible. Here.' He unscrewed the cap, and held the vial beneath my nostrils. 'Breathe deep.'

I inhaled. The gas slipped up behind my eyes and pressed out from inside. There was something familiar about the sensation. 'Hey,' I said. 'It's kind of like huffing whippets.'

'It's exactly like huffing whippets.' Tao took a sniff himself. 'It's the same gas, only more so. Any joy?'

We both looked down at my crotch, as if we expected my dick to leap out of my pants and do a little dance.

'Nothing doing.'

'Maybe you need more.'

We kept sniffing and inhaling, inflating our brains like balloons. Between huffs we cuddled and kissed and played around with the nipple buzzers, giving each other shocks. We stayed there a long time, hidden in the mist, electrified by Ecstasy. Other party-goers floated dimly past, immaterial as ghosts. We were still at it when I heard somebody call my name.

'Trevor!'

It was Bea. She pointed at me, then took three steps and surfed over the deck towards us. Venus straggled up after. They were both sweaty and sloshed and liquor-logged, but Bea managed to make that seem somehow glamorous.

'We've been looking for you.'

I smiled at her. Coyly. 'I was with Tao.'

I was still cuddled on his lap, still half-naked. Beatrice looked from me, to Tao, and back to me. 'Okay, Trev,' she said. 'Time to get dressed and say bye-bye. We're leaving.'

'It's not even midnight yet. Besides – we're stuck here.'

There was still no sign of the rescue ship. Apparently it had been delayed.

'I called Victor. He's picking us up.'

'He's driving his water taxi all the way out here?'

'He already has. It's tied up at the stern.'

She gestured that way. If it was anybody other than Bea, I wouldn't have believed it.

'You go ahead,' I said, leaning my head on Tao's shoulder. 'I'll stay with Tao. It's boy-time, right, Tao?'

'That's right,' Tao said, kissing my forehead.

Beatrice covered her face with a hand. 'I can't believe I'm hearing this.'

'Oh, let him stay.' Venus gestured expansively with her cocktail glass. Liquor slopped out on to the deck, and she nearly lost her footing. 'It'll do him some good.'

'No,' Bea said. 'Trevor's coming with us – and that's that.'

I looked up at Tao, and shrugged.

'I guess that's that, then.'

We started kissing goodbye, but Bea interrupted and hauled me up and dragged me towards the stern. The taxi was there, all right. Victor stood on the gunwale, with both arms crossed, grinning his gold-toothed grin. He extended a hand to help Beatrice aboard, and then Venus. When it came to me, he took a look at my half-naked state and held up his palm to stop me.

'You have no clothes.'

'I have them,' I said, showing him the bundle. 'I'm just not wearing them.'

'On my boat, you wear them.'

I started getting dressed as Victor undid his tie-lines. People had gathered round, whispering and muttering, watching us launch. Tao had come to see us off, too. He called out to me, 'Can we hang out again some time?'

'I don't know.' I hopped aboard, and looked back. 'My life's complicated right now.'

Venus snorted, in that way of hers.

As Victor fired up the engine, Beatrice strode to the prow, and stood surveying the bay with her hands on her hips and her feet shoulder-width apart. Then she pointed dramatically, like Christ in that famous Caravaggio painting.

'To Alcatraz!' she shouted.

I thought she was joking, and maybe she was, but Victor obeyed her. He took us on a personal tour of the island, circumnavigating it twice. At night, in the dark, you couldn't see much – just a hunk of rock, rising from the fog like a Leviathan, dotted with a few glinting lights. We all huddled in his wheelhouse, and knocked back shots of Ukrainian potato vodka.

'Nobody ever escape here,' Victor said.

'That's because they never locked me up,' Bea told him.

She went to stand on the front deck, and Venus followed. Their figures blended into the fog. Me and Victor stayed inside, gazing up at the island fortress looming on our left.

'She sure something, yes?' he said.

I didn't know if he meant Alcatraz, or Beatrice.

'She sure is,' I said.

chapter 65

When we got back to their place, I flopped down on the living room floor and lay with my legs together and my arms extended straight out at my sides, as if I'd been crucified. I was babbling about how Beatrice had prevented me from expanding my sexual horizons. I told her I'd been ready to experiment.

'No, you weren't.'

'Maybe it would have cured me. Maybe I've been gay all along.'

'Honey – you're the straightest man I know.'

'I'm sick of being straight!'

Bea patted my head and went to put the kettle on. I sat up and made an extravagant stretching gesture with my arms, like a prima ballerina. Venus was rolling a joint on their elephant table, but she was doing it furtively, with her back to me, shielding her stash from view. When she finished, she offered me the joint first, pinching it between her thumb and forefinger. 'You want to christen this?'

I took it and lit it. Two tokes got me totally blitzed, as if the inside of my skull had been whitewashed. It was so potent I hardly remember what happened afterwards. I just remember doing handstands, and parading around. Then I had this deck of cards. I was on the floor, playing poker with Sprite. Five card stud, I think. She was pretty good, for a cat. She had a great poker face. You couldn't read her.

'Goddammit, cat,' I said, throwing down my cards. 'Another straight flush!'

Venus and Bea were behind me on the sofa. I heard Venus whispering something.

'What was in that joint?' I demanded.

'Only weed,' Venus said.

'I've smoked weed my whole life. That wasn't weed.'

'Don't be paranoid.'

I played another hand with Sprite, just to show them I was in control. Then I put the cards down, carefully, and sipped my tea. I told them I wanted to go to bed now.

'Okay, cardsharp.'

Bea patted the top of my head. 'See you in the morning, honey.'

They went into their room, leaving me to arrange my sofa bed. As soon as I lay down, it seemed to levitate and swivel in circles, like Aladdin's magic carpet. I held on and closed my eyes, willing it to settle. Sprite watched all this curiously.

'She tricked me, cat,' I said. 'The party cruise didn't go as she planned, so she resorted to sabotage. That was a loaded joint.'

Then I heard noises coming from the bedroom – a soft moaning, faint but distinct. I lay still for a minute, eavesdropping, until Sprite caught me at it and took a swipe at my foot.

'Okay, okay,' I said. 'I'll be a gentleman.'

I rolled over and mashed my ear to the pillow and tried to ignore the noises. It wasn't easy. The moans were getting louder. Sprite was stretched out on the floor among the pile of scattered playing cards. She raised her head and peered at me and sniffed, as if to say, *You can act like a broken-hearted gay-boy all you like. She's still the one in there, getting laid.*

I threw a sock at her. 'At least I'm not suckling off a dog.'

I don't know if I fell asleep that night. I was drunken-dozing when Sprite leapt on to my chest – scaring the hell out of me. She flexed her claws into my shirt and crouched with her face in front of mine, breathing cat-food fumes on me. Her fur was less scruffy than it had been, and her rheumy eye was clearing up. Bea had given her some eye drops and a worming tablet. 'You almost look like a real cat,' I said, petting her.

She mrrred at me. We were lying like that, lazing, when I heard the rasp of Bea's mail slot. Something dropped to the floor. I checked my watch. It was two twenty-two am. No mailman delivered mail that early. No normal mailman, anyways. Sprite had tensed up, staring at the door like a pointer hound. I pried her off my chest, put her down, and crept over to the entrance hall. On the floor was the postcard I'd sent to Bea, after getting out of the desert – the one that said *The Middle of Nowhere* across the front. I slid it aside and opened the door. Halfway down the block, a shadowy figure was power-walking away. As he passed beneath the sodium glow of a street-lamp, I saw that he had a mailbag slung over one shoulder.

'Hey, you!' I called.

He looked back. It was him, all right. When he saw me, he took off, sprinting away down the street. I chased after him. I hadn't undressed to go to sleep, but I'd taken off my shoes – so I was booting it barefoot.

'Hold up!'

We ran for half a dozen blocks. My feet slapped against the warm pavement. I was faster than him on the sidewalks, but whenever I crossed a street I had to hop and hotfoot it, mincing my way over the prickly asphalt. Eventually he gave up and waited for me. As I drew level with him, I threw up my arms in a kind of exasperated, bewildered gesture.

'What the fuck?' I said.

We both doubled over, bracing our hands on our knees. We stayed like that for a bit, sucking wind and trying to catch our breath.

'Why did you run?' I asked, still panting.

'Why did *you* run?'

I shook my head. I'd forgotten how annoying he could be.

'What are you doing in San Francisco, anyways?' I asked.

'I told you before that I was going to Sausalito.'

'This isn't Sausalito.'

He looked around – as if he'd only just realised that. Then he shrugged it off. 'Of course it's not. I'm still on my *way* to Sausalito. But I needed to give you a message first.'

We'd stopped in front of an all-night diner. A few of the patrons were watching us through the windows. I asked the hitcher if he wanted to get a cup of coffee or something.

'On you?'

He was such a natural mooch, that guy. 'Sure. Whatever.'

Since I'd offered to pay, he ordered a full meal for himself. I only had coffee. Our waiter was an old guy with a jaundiced face and a ducktail comb-over. He didn't say much. He didn't say anything, actually. He just took our orders and plodded away.

'Still not eating?' the hitcher asked.

'I had a smoothie yesterday, and a fruit salad this morning.'

'Not quite as exotic as eagle, eh?'

We stared at each other across the table. He looked better than he had in the desert. His face had filled out a bit and his skin had a healthy sheen. He'd finally gotten around to washing his clothes, too. Making it to the coast had obviously done him some good.

'I'm surprised to see you again,' I said, 'after that mauling you gave me.'

'Oh, that.' He became overly interested in a black spot on the tabletop. He tried to wipe it away with his thumb, but it was stain of some kind, or a burn mark. Finally he gave up and said, 'I might have gone a bit far. But I wanted to give you a spiritual experience.'

'You put on a tiger mask and kicked my ass.'

'We were both deathly high, remember?'

The waiter returned. He had a way of walking without taking his feet off the floor – a slow, half-step shuffle. He gave us our coffees and went back to slump behind his counter. It was an L-shaped counter with tarnished chrome trim. The place reminded me of the diner in that Hopper painting – except, instead of a redhead and two guys in fedoras sitting on the stools, there were three mechanics in greasy coveralls.

'How did you find me, anyway?' I asked.

'I'm a postman. You put the address on your postcard.'

That made sense, I guess – on some kind of bizarre, irrational level.

'You're not a postman any more.'

'I've still got contacts in the mail room.' He blew on his coffee, took a slurp, and smacked his lips. 'I needed to give you a message, so I scribbled one across the card.'

'You wrote on *my* postcard?'

'Now it's our postcard.'

I let that slide, and we drank our coffee in silence. Mine was speckled with grounds, and tasted stale and bitter and old. Eventually the waiter brought over the food. The hitcher had ordered a beef dip – one of those roast beef sandwiches in a Kaiser bun, that comes with a side bowl of thin gravy. He noticed me eyeing it up.

'Want half?'

'I haven't had much luck sharing buns with you.'

He grinned and took a big bite – so big he couldn't fit it all in. A strand of excess meat hung from his mouth, as if he'd swallowed a mouse. While he chewed, he asked me how my trip had been since we'd split up. I told him about some of the things I'd been through, and about facing his brother at the shooting range. He didn't seem surprised.

'I knew he'd dupe you,' he said. He was still attacking the sandwich, and talking with his mouth full. 'Even though I warned you. You really fucked the dog on that one.'

'I didn't expect him to want my visor.'

He shook his head. Wistfully.

'I did.'

'I know you did.'

'That visor's one of a kind.'

'I still got away with his mezcal.'

I expected him to mock me for that, but he stopped eating and looked up.

'You did? Where is it?'

'Back at my friends' place.'

'Right. Your *friends*.' He sneered. There were bits of beef between his teeth. 'You mean those dykes you're hanging out with. I wouldn't trust them. They're not real friends.'

'They don't think you're real, either. They say I imagined you.'

'Women are always saying stupid shit. That's why I left mine.'

'No – you left because you got her pregnant and weren't man enough to handle it.'

He winced, pretending to be wounded, but didn't deny it.

'Have you found her and given her your letter yet?' I asked.

He shook his head. 'I will when I get to Sausalito.'

'It's only across the bridge.'

'It's a big fucking bridge, okay?' He spat out a piece of fat. 'Besides – who are *you* to tell *me* how to act? I'm not the one getting naked on cruise ships, hooking up with guys.'

'How did you know about that?'

'Everybody knows! You were showing off and making a spectacle of yourself, like some homosexual superstar. You've obviously forgotten what I taught you in the desert.'

'You didn't teach me shit,' I said. Then I laughed, remembering. 'Except how to wrestle naked. As if there wasn't anything homoerotic about that.'

'You better hope you learned something out there, because you're going to need it.' He glanced around, as if he was worried about being overheard. It was all very theatrical and put on. In a stage whisper he said, 'Did you tell my brother you were coming here?'

'Maybe. Why?'

'He's in town. Looking for you.'

I picked up my spoon and stirred my coffee, starting a slow whirlpool.

'It's a big town,' I said.

'He'll find you. Or you'll find him. One way or another. It's…'

'Synchronicity.'

'See? You did learn something. And, when you meet him again, you're not going to be able to trick your way out of it. That was the main thing I wanted to tell you.' He dunked his bun in the dip and swabbed it around. 'It's all in the message I wrote. You can read it on our postcard.'

'I'll have a look.'

I gulped the dregs of my coffee. As I put the cup down, it rattled against the saucer. Coffee always makes me jittery. The hitcher shoved the last bite of sandwich in his mouth, tossed his napkin on his plate, and stood up. I figured he was going to take a leak, or wash his face. He still had gravy glistening on his chin. But instead he slung his postbag over his shoulder, and strode regally towards the door. I could tell he wanted me to ask him, so I did.

'Where do you think you're going?'

He paused in the doorway, and patted his bag.

'Where do *you* think I'm going?'

He stepped outside, letting the door swing shut behind him. It was a glass door and I watched him through it as he walked away, fading into the dark. The waiter slogged over to clear our dishes and top up my coffee. I sat a while longer. I don't know how much longer. The next time I looked over, the waiter was asleep at his counter. All the other customers were asleep, too. It was like that scene in *Sleeping Beauty*, where everybody passes out because of the witch's spell. I left twenty bucks on the table and got the hell out of there.

chapter 66

I heard instrumental music, made up of plucking and strumming in a minor key. I lifted my head to peer around. Beatrice was standing in the middle of the living room. She had on a shorty wetsuit, sleek as sealskin, emblazoned with the boned hand of the Body Glove logo. She breathed in and held out her arms, as if to encompass the entire world. She was running through what looked like some kind of Kung Fu form – each movement slow, deliberate, refined.

I groaned and mashed my palms against my eyes. It was still dark outside.

I said, 'It's not even morning yet.'

'That's the point.'

'I feel like a dead man walking.'

'And you look like a casualty of war.'

'I love that you can match my cinematic references.' I managed to sit up. My body was still buzzing from the cocktail of toxins I'd dumped into it, and I had the shakes – as if I'd been drinking endless coffee. 'I also love that you're immune to hangovers, apparently.'

From in the kitchen came the clink of metal on glass. Venus was over there, stirring a spoon around a jug. She poured some blue liquid into a tall glass and brought it over to me.

'Here you go, Casanova.'

'What is it?'

'Kool-aid, apple juice and Tabasco sauce.'

'Thanks. I think.'

She flopped down beside me on the sofa. Together we watched Beatrice perform a complex set of backhand strikes. I sipped Venus's concoction – which tasted like a spicy popsicle – and tried to figure out what was going on.

'Is this wake-up call a punishment for my antics last night?'

Bea smiled, pulled back into a crane position, and swept both arms across her body, as if disposing of a negative vibe. 'Punishment sounds a bit harsh. Think of it as an antidote.'

'Or a therapy,' Venus added.

'Hydrotherapy.'

I'd finished drinking her brew. I put the empty glass on the table beside me.

'Isn't that where they throw you naked in a shower and blast you with a firehose?'

'Not in this case.' Bea swept one foot out and sank into a horse stance. 'In this case it's where we take you to our secret surfing beach and ride killer waves in the dead of night.'

With a monkey's paw, she gestured towards the front hall. By the door, propped against the wall, were three longboards – freshly waxed and gleaming like gigantic fishing lures. I stood up and went over there. I'd remembered something else about last night. On the ground, at the foot of the boards, was a stack of mail from the last few days. I gathered it up and flipped through the letters and flyers.

'It's really here,' I said, holding up my postcard. 'I thought I might have been dreaming.'

Beatrice took it from me and turned it over, and read out what was written on the back.

'"Watch out – he's coming after you. Women aren't the answer. Neither are men. You're the answer. You are it. When all else fails, blind luck will see you through."' Bea looked over at me. 'Hmm. Thank you, Trevor. It's like our own personal fortune cookie.'

'I didn't write that!' I said, grabbing it back from her.

The bastard had scribbled over my message, making it illegible, and added his own.

'Who did, then?' Venus asked. She was acting polite, but you could tell she was incredibly pleased that I'd made a fool of myself again. 'And who's coming after you?'

'The hitcher.' I flopped back on the sofa, arms out. 'And his brother, the biker.'

Beatrice took my postcard and placed it on the mantelpiece. Delicately. 'Well,' she said, studying it like an art critic, with her hands on her hips, 'it's a very nice picture, Trev.'

'Maybe I've gone loco,' I said.

There was a fairly long pause, as we all pondered the possibility that I was losing my mind. Then Bea said, 'That's why we're going night-surfing: to clear your head of clutter.'

The moon had swollen to a half-circle and looked unnaturally huge, hanging so close to the water. Its reflection spilled glossily across the waves – these sleek black swells about seven or eight feet high. As each one rolled in it would crescendo steadily, like an incoming bomb, and then detonate with an explosion of spray and a concussive boom, echoing across the bay.

'Whoah,' I said. 'Those are big rollers.'

Bea said, 'You've ridden bigger.'

'Not at night.'

'That's why I'm preparing you.'

We'd driven to a secluded beach south of the city, along a stretch of coastline called Half Moon Bay. Bea had us kneeling at the water's edge, three abreast, with Belle and Sprite sitting obediently on our right and the longboards laid out on our left. We'd coated the boards in a layer of fluorescent green latex paint – waterproof and glow-in-the-dark – and smeared the same stuff on our faces, necks, and forearms. We looked like the ghosts of tribal warriors.

'The latex is dry,' Venus said. 'Surf's up.'

'I haven't baptised Trevor.'

Bea stood up, scooped a palmful of water from in front of us, and emptied it over my head. It trickled down my neck. She repeated the same thing three times, saying, 'Take care of Trevor out there. I pray for his protection, and I ask for permission to enter these waves.'

Venus started doing up her leash, ignoring the ceremony.

'Who are we praying to?' I asked.

'The sea-gods. It's a Hawaiian tradition.'

Venus yawned. 'It's more inch-deep beatnik bullshit, is what it is.'

'I pray for Venus's protection, too, even though she's a cynic.'

Then we were ready.

We waded into the shallows, which were as warm and frothy as a bath full of Epsom salts. The animals sat and watched from shore. When the water got deep enough we lay on our boards and stroked towards the break, paddling over the smaller waves and turtle-rolling through the larger ones. Ahead of me I could see their boards glowing like Kryptonite in the darkness, vanishing every so often as they sank into a trough.

At the break, we swivelled around and pulled up alongside each other, facing towards shore. For a minute we floated in reverent silence, rising and falling as waves swept beneath us. There was no real way to differentiate between the sky, the sea, and the land. It was just a sprawling morass of black, awesome and fathomless. A kind of primal oblivion.

I said, 'It's like we've stepped off the edge of the world.'

'We have,' Bea said. 'Or the edge of the continent, at least.'

Her face was luminous, eerie. She started paddling – deep strokes to either side of her board – and slid smoothly away from us, melting into the dark. I could hear a wave coming.

She called back, '*Vaya con Dios!*'

'See you in the next life!' I shouted.

'What are you talking about?' Venus asked.

Before I could tell her, a large swell rolled under us and seemed to envelop Bea and she vanished, spirited away into the night. About ten seconds later the glow of her face and arms reappeared, but much smaller – an apparition hovering near shore.

'Magic,' I said.

Venus was already looking behind her, gauging the waves. 'This one's mine,' she said.

She paddled off ahead of me, and another phantom wave came to carry her away, her whoops fading with distance. I was left alone. I felt like the last paratrooper on an aircraft, flying a night mission – facing that leap of faith into the void. I looked back and saw a dark mound moving towards me, vacuuming in a backwash of water. I paddled furiously and felt my board tilt as the wave surged beneath me, and then I was sliding down towards the abyss. I popped up into a crouch, wobbling and almost falling, but I held my stance as I cut across the face, the water gliding beneath me like black glass, like obsidian, glinting. I rode blind, guided by my board, until the wave folded over me in a shroud and buried me underwater.

I came up gasping, disorientated, exhilarated.

'How was it?'

It was Bea's voice. I could see her ghost-face, glowing off to the left.

'Like surfing the afterlife.'

They were already heading back out. I flutter-kicked to catch up. For the next half-hour we dedicated ourselves to the rhythms of the ocean: riding in and paddling out, and waiting for the next set of waves. Everything else was washed away in the dark. Between sets, we bobbed at the break, lying on our bellies, with our legs dangling off the ends of our boards.

As we were doing that, Venus said, 'We should have a surfing contest.'

'Isn't that an oxymoron?' Bea asked.

'Come on. It'll be wicked.'

'V,' Bea said, 'don't ruin it.'

'Okay – Bea's laming out.' Venus turned to me. 'What about you?'

I shrugged. I was kind of sick of contests and competitions, after the stuff I'd been through with the hitcher and his brother in the desert. I thought I'd left all that behind me.

'What kind of contest?'

'We'll see who can ride their next wave closest to shore. I'll go first.'

I didn't really agree to it, but she was already looking back, waiting for the next good swell. The sky had lightened to grey and the stars were going out, one by one, fading away into the dullness of day and taking the magic of the night with them.

'Here she is. This one's mine, you wave-whores.'

She paddled off. When the wave came she caught it and rode it ferociously, thrashing back and forth across the face. As the crest began to break she adopted a low crouch, milking her momentum. Eventually, close to shore, she stepped off and waved to us in the half-light.

'Guess it's my turn,' I said to Bea.

'You don't have to.'

There was another roller coming. I couldn't resist.

'Might as well humour her.'

I caught the wave and rode it in, but it was just a mushy little ankle-buster. I didn't make it as far as Venus – I lost my balance and bailed out, about ten yards short of her.

She flipped me the finger. 'Sucks to be you.'

I waded over to her. We both turned to look at Bea, who was bobbing out amid the swells, which had gone teal green in the growing dawn.

'I don't think she's into it,' I said.

'Wait,' Venus said, 'here she goes.'

A giant wave, like the back of a whale, rose up beneath Bea and carried her forward. She slid smoothly down the face, but she didn't get into the usual surfing crouch. Instead she adopted a kneeling position, riding it that way, with both arms out at her side, palms up, as if asking the water to elevate or uplift her. Her hair snaked out behind her in a Medusa tangle.

'That doesn't count,' Venus said.

The wave carried Bea past us, and further, without ever really breaking. It just settled and slowly dissolved, effectively landing her right on the beach, where Sprite and Belle were waiting. She stood up majestically, hefted her board, and walked off without looking back.

'I guess she wins,' I said.

'Come on,' Venus said, turning away, 'let's catch a few more without her.'

I followed her out and we kept riding, but the moon had gone down, the sun had come up, and other people had started to arrive. It began to feel like just another day at the beach.

chapter 67

When I emerged from the water, my eyes were slitted against the sting of salt and my limbs felt loose and gelatinous, like the arms of a jellyfish. Beatrice was stretched out on her towel, with one arm draped across her face to shield it from the sun, and the cat and dog curled up at her feet in their funny yin-yang position. She'd taken off her wetsuit to suntan in a bikini top. On her torso was a string of tattoos – Cantonese symbols, delicately etched in black ink, like calligraphy. They ran from her solar plexus down to her belly-button. I knew the top three meant freedom, vitality, and creativity. She'd had two more added since the last time I'd seen her. I didn't know what they meant and I didn't study them for long.

I eased down on the towel beside her. She must have heard me. She lifted her arm, opened one eye, and smiled.

'How you feeling?' she asked.

'Like I've been reborn.'

'Where's V?'

I pointed. 'She didn't want to come in yet.'

Bea shifted on to her elbow, shielding her eyes to look out. Venus was bobbing near the break. The offshore wind was picking up, and the waves were getting choppier, but she was still making out all right.

'She's pretty good,' I said.

'She fights the water too much.'

As we watched Venus catch the next wave, I asked Bea about her new tattoos.

'That one,' she said, pointing to her midriff, 'is sex. And this one is energy.'

The energy was just above her belly button. The skin surrounding the symbol still glowed faintly red. It was recent, I guess.

'Where'd you get it done?' I asked.

'This place up the coast in Mendocino – Voodoo Ink. I want one more big one.' She placed a hand below her belly and above her bikini line, where her womb was. 'Right here. The symbol for goddess.'

She started telling me about a statue she'd seen, in this tiny rural museum, while travelling through Central America. She said the statue had been made by a lost civilisation that pre-dated the Aztecs. It depicted a woman with big hips and big breasts and a big belly. Lines had been carved into the stone of the stomach, signifying stretch marks. Bea traced a line across her own stomach to demonstrate.

'It was their way of showing that she'd given birth,' she said. 'Isn't that incredible? That's what these people used to worship – birth and life and nature. The earth mother.'

'What happened to them?'

'Same old. The Europeans massacred them and imposed Christianity. All that's left now are a few statues like that, and we're stuck with shitty patriarchal religions. Why did we have to get rid of our goddesses? Chicks like Nike and Athena and Isis totally kicked ass.'

'You should bring them back,' I said. 'Start your own religion.'

'Totally. Like the scientology guy.'

'I could be your first disciple.'

Bea stuck her forefinger in the sand and traced a circle. 'I would demand utter, monk-like devotion.'

'I'm part monk already. I've got the celibacy thing nailed.'

She laughed and added some lines to her circle, radiating out from the centre like wheel spokes. I stared at the design for a few seconds, trying to place it.

'What is that?' I asked.

'A mandala – a symbol of wholeness.'

'Shit. I knew it.'

I told Bea about the vision quest the hitcher had forced me to go on, and the pattern he'd made in the sand, and what he'd said to me that night: lose yourself and find the key.

'You can't lose your self,' Bea said. 'That's the whole of your psyche, and the goal of individuation. He must have meant lose your ego and you'll be free.'

'Could be. That guy had a tendency to mix things up.'

'Did it work? Do you feel free?'

'I'm single for the first time in years. That's freedom, right?'

'It's a kind of freedom.' She wiped out her mandala with her palm. 'A kind I miss.'

'You seem fairly settled, these days.'

'I am settled. It's good.' She gazed out at the water, to where Venus was struggling among the waves. 'But I wonder about us in the long run. You know me.'

I nodded. I'd seen her flutter through so many lovers' lives, elusive as a butterfly.

'When I was little,' she said, 'my dad used to tell me all the old stories of the Nez Perce – our tribe's myths and legends. My favourite was this one about the picky princess.'

I lay back on the towel, feeling it hot against my back. 'What was she picky about?'

'Basically, all the braves in the village wanted to marry her. They each took their turn going over to her teepee and trying their luck. She'd string them along for a while but always got bored eventually. She wouldn't pick one. She was looking for something else.'

I rolled on my side and closed my eyes, listening to her voice. Down at the surf the waves pounded on as steadily as tom-tom drums, acting as a kind of backdrop to her story.

'Finally her father – the chief – got tired of this. He announced that he'd make her pick her husband blindfolded. On the big day guys came from all over, hoping to be the one.

She was allowed to touch their faces and torsos to size them up.' I felt Bea's fingers on my face, tracing my cheeks, my nose, my lips. 'Finally, she found one she liked, and made her choice. But nobody had ever seen this guy before. He said he came from a tribe far away.'

I opened my eyes. 'A real mystery man, eh?'

'Yep. But she couldn't change her mind. She had to go back with him to live with his people. And get this – they were all wolves. This guy was a wolf spirit. If she wanted to marry him, she'd have to become a wolf spirit, too. So she did, and she lived a wild life forever.'

'That's so you.'

'I know.' She sighed, leaning back on her arms and turning her face up to the sun. 'Sometimes I think that's what I'm waiting for. My wolf spirit. Does that make sense?'

'Sure. You were obviously traumatised by your father's stories.'

She threw a handful of sand in my face. I was already laughing, so the sand went right in my mouth. It got in my eyes, too. Then, when I was choking and blinded like that, Bea attacked. She started using all these Kung Fu moves on me: elbow strikes and knife hands and hammer fists. She even kneed me in the ribs at one point. I wrestled and squirmed, trying to fend off the assault. I kept apologising over and over. At the same time, I couldn't stop laughing.

'Bastard,' she said, and gave me a final punch.

Our battle had left the towels all tangled and sandy. We straightened them out and flopped back down, side by side. We were both breathing hard, and my skin had that sticky, sweaty, after-sea feeling. As we lay there, recuperating, I heard the scuffle of feet on sand. Venus was trudging up the beach, dragging her surfboard. I'd been lying on her towel, so I shifted over to make room for her. She was dripping brine and shivering like a shipwreck victim. She wedged her surfboard upright in the sand, tombstone-like, and leaned against it.

'Hey, baby,' Bea said. 'You were out a long time.'

'Good waves.'

Venus sat with her back to the board while she caught her breath. Then she started digging a hole in the sand. I don't know why. I guess she had a hard time sitting still. Belle went over to check it out, as if wondering why a person was doing what a dog was normally supposed to do. She poked her nose in the hole, and Venus pushed her away.

'What do you guys want to do tonight?' Bea asked.

Venus grunted. 'I've got my gig.'

There was a long pause. It was fairly awkward.

'Of course,' Bea said. 'Cool.'

'It would be wicked to see you play,' I said.

Venus made a non-committal sound in her throat, and kept digging.

We decided to head back at noon. By then we were all sun-seared and water-weary, and it was a long trudge with our boards up the wooden steps to the parking lot. As we approached the Neon, I noticed odd markings all over it. Somebody had keyed up the doors and hood, making jagged scrapes in the paintwork. We stood looking down at the damage. Bea had Sprite cradled in her arms. The cat twisted around to look at me, and meowed.

'What shitheads,' Venus said.

'Must be out-of-towners,' Bea said. 'Locals would never do that.'

'Luckily she's already pretty beat-up.'

While they lashed the surfboards to the roof, I leaned over the hood and examined the scratches more closely. I couldn't be sure, but a few of the markings seemed to be connected, like a constellation, in the shape of a snake.

After we got in, I asked Bea, 'Is my mezcal bottle still there?'

She had to root through the litter in the passenger footwell, but found it eventually. 'This?' she said, holding it up.

'Guess they didn't see it.'

She peered into the bottle, turning it back and forth. 'Is that a *snake*?'

'A cobra, I think.'

'We definitely have to try this.'

'I did,' I said, starting the car. 'It doesn't work. It's supposed to be an aphrodisiac.'

Venus said, 'You sure didn't need an aphrodisiac last night.'

They both laughed. I didn't. I was still thinking about those marks on my car. Then, when we were pulling out of the parking lot, I heard a familiar chainsaw buzz in the distance. It came from somewhere down the highway. I waited, listening, with my signal ticking – but no motorbikes appeared. The sound faded, like a hornet meandering away.

'You okay?' Bea asked.

'Sure. Fine.' I peered down the highway, to make sure it was all clear, and pulled out into the northbound lane. 'I was just thinking it might be time for me to be moving on.'

Venus leaned forward, sticking her head between the seats. 'You're going?'

'I should probably head back some time tomorrow.' The damage to the Neon might have been a coincidence, but I wasn't about to risk it.

Bea said, 'You only just got here.'

'That's true.' I nodded stoically, doing my best imper-sonation of the hitcher. 'But you know what they say about guests. They're like fish.'

They both looked at me, and waited for the punchline.

'After three days, they start to stink.'

chapter 68

'You could at least phone the venue.'

'You phone them.'

'It's your fundraiser. I've got no clout.'

The voices coaxed me out of sleep. My skin felt all crusted with salt. I was on the sofa, my makeshift bed. After the beach we'd come back to their place and I'd crashed out. Now Venus and Beatrice were in their bedroom, having an argument of some sort.

'One guy won't matter,' Bea said.

'It defeats the whole point of ladies' night.'

'Who would care?'

'My band would care. The audience would care.'

I smiled. They were arguing over me. Then I noticed Sprite. She lay on the floor by the sofa, watching me through narrowed eyes. She knew exactly what I was up to.

'You're so goddamn pious,' I said.

I started doing that thing you do, when you want to let people know you're waking up. I rolled over and thrashed around on the sofa. I stretched. I mumbled. I yawned and smacked my lips – like a big, lazy lion. The argument stopped. They'd heard me.

Bea came out first, followed by Venus. Venus had changed into jeans, torn at the knees, and combat boots. Her hair was spiked, her lips black, her lashes layered in mascara.

'Hey, guys,' I said, rubbing my eyes with my knuckles. 'What time is it?'

'Just after six,' Bea said.

'I'm heading off to set up,' Venus said. 'For my gig.'

'Good luck.'

I waited for them to tell me whatever it was they weren't telling me.

'The thing is,' she went one, 'the gig is a fundraiser for our shelter, with karaoke, and it's a one-off ladies night. No men allowed.'

I had to think about that. 'You're a karaoke singer?'

'No.' Venus frowned. 'The karaoke is just part of it, to raise money.'

'Oh. I get it.'

I sort of did. It still seemed weird, though.

Bea said, 'I was hoping Venus might be able to pull some strings and get you in…'

'But I don't think the organisers would go for that,' Venus said.

She crossed her arms, as if waiting for me, or Beatrice, to challenge her verdict. I leaned back, sinking into the sofa cushions. 'Honestly,' I said, 'don't worry about it. You go without me, Bea. I mean, I'd love to see Venus do her karaoke thing – ' I only called it that to piss her off, obviously ' – but if not we can all just meet up after, right?'

'Trevor.' Bea lowered her head, fixed me with a stare – that no-nonsense, matter-of-fact, Beatrice Carmen stare. 'I'm not ditching you on your last night in San Francisco.'

Venus checked her watch. 'Whatever,' she said to Bea. 'I've got to go. Don't feel like you have to come to my gig or anything. You can hang out with him if you want.'

'No, really,' I said.

We both looked at Bea, waiting on her decision. It had come down to that. She looked from me, to Venus, and back to me.

'I have an idea,' she said.

'Hold still.'

'It tickles.'

'If you keep smirking, it will smudge.'

I puckered up for Bea again, ready to be kissed. She ran the lipstick, firm and slick, across my lips. Her face was right in front of mine. As she worked I studied her iris. It was dark green, gleaming like jade, with a delicate star-burst pattern around the pupil. When she paused to twist the lipstick case, I asked her, 'Do they call it an iris because of the flower?'

'It's Greek. It means rainbow, or eye of heaven. It's a goddess, too.'

'How do you know this stuff?'

'I know everything. Now close your mouth.'

I did. She rubbed my bottom lip one more time.

'Okay,' she said. 'Try smacking them. Like this.'

She demonstrated how, and I imitated her. She stood back to examine me, assessing her work. I was sitting on a chair in the bedroom she shared with Venus. T-shirts and bras and panties lay scattered about the floor. The bedsheets were all twisted up and entwined.

'Can I see?' I asked.

'Not yet. I haven't done your mascara.'

She selected a rectangular make-up case from among the clutter on her dressing table. She told me to look up and keep my eyes open. I felt the stroke of the mascara brush.

'You've got such long eyelashes,' she said.

I shivered. 'It feels like a butterfly kiss.'

'What's that?'

'When somebody flutters their eyelashes against yours.'

'That's beautiful.'

'Zuzska taught me.'

Bea nodded. Solemnly. Anything to do with Zuzska had to be solemn.

'All right – just one more thing.'

She'd already done my foundation, and my eyeliner. Last she added a dash of blusher. By that point she was pursing her lips, trying not to laugh. We were both three drinks deep. They were stiff drinks, too – double mojitos – or I would never have agreed to it. But Bea said it was the only way to get me into the place on ladies' night.

'Come on,' I said, 'let me see.'

'Just a sec.' On her dressing table she had one of those circular mirrors that you can swivel vertically. She'd flipped it away from me so I wouldn't get distracted as she did my make-up. Now she turned it back, presenting me to myself. 'Ta-dah.'

'Wow,' I said. I touched my face. Testing.

'Don't mess it up.'

I wasn't pretty. But I wasn't all that ugly, either. My lips were full and glistening. And she was right about my lashes. I had long lashes. The mascara had brought them out. My jaw was a bit too square, though, and I had prominent cheekbones. That couldn't be helped. The combination was vaguely European – like a butchy villainess from a Bond film.

'My hair,' I said. 'What about my hair?'

'On it,' Bea said. She rooted around in her closet, first on the top shelf, then in shoeboxes on the floor – yanking off lids and tossing them aside. The boxes were full of trinkets and dress-up props: outlandish hats and Venetian masks and feather boas and handcuffs and wigs.

'Here!' She held up one of the wigs, shaking it like a pom-pom. 'You're too pale to go brunette. But I think you could pull off a redhead.'

She came over and fitted the wig on me, tugging it down to my ears. She adjusted the loose strands and brushed them away from my face. Then she bent to peer over my shoulder, studying my reflection. The hair on the wig framed my face in a bell-shaped bob.

'Oh, my God,' she said, covering her mouth. 'You look like…'

'Zuzska,' I said, flatly. 'You made me look like Zuzska.'

Bea doubled over, laughing. She laughed so hard she nearly puked.

chapter 69

The venue for the fundraiser was across town. We caught the Muni train over, got off at the nearest stop, and walked from there. Bea walked, anyway. I hobbled. I'd put on a pair of Venus's heels. They were low heels – only an inch or so – but they were still heels, and all the things you hear about heels are true. My ankles kept rolling and I felt completely off-kilter, like a kid in his first pair of ice skates.

'Remember,' Bea said, 'men walk from the shoulders. Women walk from the hips.'

'From the hips. Got it.'

En route, I asked Bea about the venue. She said she'd never been. It was a dive-bar called the Peaks. Apparently the organisers of the fundraiser had screwed up the booking.

'They were supposed to book out this gay bar, called Twin Peaks Tavern…'

'Wait a minute – why are both bars called that?'

'Because of the Twin Peaks in the middle of city.'

When she said that, I stumbled in my heels, but managed to stabilise.

'There are actually Twin Peaks *in* San Francisco?'

'Sure.' She pointed. They were right there, rising above the rooftops – a pair of twin peaks like the ones I'd driven to in the desert. 'This whole area is named after them.'

'Oh, man,' I said.

I stopped walking. Bea looked back, waiting for me.

'What's up?' she asked.

'Nothing, hopefully.'

But I could feel it – both in me and in the air, like the first stirrings of a storm.

The Peaks bar had a faux-stone façade – styled like a Spanish taverna – with swinging saloon doors and, above them, a neon sign showing an image of a cartoon hiker. The bar was right at the base of the peaks, which loomed impossibly behind it. I still couldn't quite believe it – that there was this giant, thousand-foot mountain in the geographical centre of San Francisco.

'How come that thing hasn't been developed?' I asked Bea.

'It's a municipal park – why?'

'Just wondering.'

Out front people were lining up. The all-female crowd looked fairly random. I saw a couple of punks with their hair frosted into Liberty spikes, a hippy-chick burning a fat one, and this bleary-eyed emo whose mascara was already running. On the sidewalk was an A-frame sign with a publicity poster for the event. It showed a killer plant, like the one in *Little Shop of Horrors*, with a big mouth and jagged teeth. A man was caught between the teeth. His blood dripped down to form the words *Venus & The Flytraps – Karaoke Fundraiser*.

'That's them,' Bea said.

She led me past the line to the front door. I stood clutching my handbag while she motioned the bouncer over, and explained that we were VIP. He checked his guest list for our names. He was scrawny and anxious and had an amateur tattoo of a rattlesnake, all smudged and smeared, crawling up his neck. He didn't look like much of a bouncer.

'We're on the guest list,' Bea said. 'Beatrice and Trevine.'

We'd decided that would be my name for the night. It seemed appropriate.

He said, 'There's no Trevine on here.'

'We're with Venus,' I said, raising my voice to a falsetto.

The guy looked me over. 'You got ID?'

I rooted around in the handbag Bea had lent me, angling away from him because I didn't want him to see what else I had in there. I'd brought my bottle of mezcal along. I'd also brought my gun. That's the great thing about handbags – you can fit almost anything in them. It was only after I'd withdrawn my wallet that I remembered about being a woman. By then it was too late – I had to hand it over. He checked my licence. At first he looked confused. Then he looked disgusted. He handed it back.

'Go ahead, Trevor. Sorry – I mean, Trevine.'

'Classy,' Beatrice said, and pushed past the guy. I scuttled after her.

The interior was really something. There was an old-school jukebox, a backlit Sierra Nevada beer sign, an antique cash register that opened with a hand-crank, and, in one corner, a vintage wooden phone booth. But along with that retro décor they had all kinds of racing memorabilia: pennants and trophies and posters, and even lampshades in the shape of cars.

'This place is a trip,' Bea said.

'It's reminding me of my trip, with all this weird para-phernalia.'

'Let's get you a drink, Trevine.'

The drink special was a cocktail called Dragonfire – basically a margarita souped up with spices and Tabasco sauce. We ordered two each and went looking for some seats. The bouncer had started letting people in but there was still plenty of space. We got a table near the front, right by the stage. It wasn't actually a stage – just a raised platform set up near the rear exit, with a few PAR lights rigged on stands. The band had already prepped their amps and microphones and drum kit and speakers. They weren't scheduled to start for another hour.

While we waited, I kept fiddling with my wig and adjusting my bra.

'Relax, darling,' Bea drawled, stirring her drink. They each came with one of those little plastic swizzle-sticks. 'Just pretend you're a *femme fatale* from some *film noir*.'

'I don't have the seductive powers.'

'Sure you do, sweetheart.'

The tables around us were filling up. I gulped my drinks and studied the women as they sat down. A big-nosed Goth on the next table caught my eye, and smiled. Her smile seemed to say, I can see right through that little outfit. All her friends were looking at me, too. I was terrified that one of them would whip off my wig and denounce me as a man. Hordes of rabid females would descend on me, like a pack of Bacchae, and tear me apart.

'You want another drink?' I asked Bea.

She looked from my glasses to hers. Mine were both empty. Hers were both full.

'Take it easy, Trevine.'

I was already up, moving off. I concentrated on walking from the hips, the way Bea had told me. I sashayed up to the bar and leaned against it. While I waited to be served, I caught sight of this red-headed chick in the mirror behind the bar. She looked all right, actually.

'Excuse me?' I said, wiggling a finger at the bartender.

He waddled over to me. He had a bald head, gleaming like a cueball, and there were two nicotine patches stuck to his bicep. He spread his palms on the bartop and grinned at me.

'What can I get you, miss?'

'Two Dragonfires, please,' I said.

He shook them up and poured them out. I thought he might be giving me the eye.

'Lucky you,' I said. 'All alone on ladies' night.'

He winked at me. 'It's a first, all right.'

I tipped him big, and told him to keep the change. As I walked away, I glanced back to see if he was watching me. He was. He was checking out my ass. It was my best feature.

Back at our table, I twirled my swizzle-stick around in my drink. 'I think I'm getting the hang of this,' I told Bea.

The band came on with a bang. They did that thing bands do, where they launch straight into the first song without any introductory bullshit. They just walked out, grabbed hold of their instruments and fired it up. It was a three-piece band:

drums, bass, and guitar. Venus was the frontman, or front-woman. She sang and played lead guitar. She was good, too – quick-fingered and kinetic, attacking those strings, moaning and wailing and swearing. She'd run her voice up high and then just let it hang there, quavering, like a flag in the wind.

'*You're my fix, my addiction, my white nurse in a needle.*'

Most of the seats were taken, except a handful at the back. There were maybe fifty or sixty women in there. When the first song ended, they all applauded and pounded the tables.

I leaned over and shouted to Bea, 'She's awesome!'

When the applause died down, Venus gave a little speech – welcoming us to ladies' night and thanking the venue and introducing the band. Then she told a story about the next song. It was a song about rape: the rape of the land, the rape of a friend. It was called 'Seed of the Tillerman'. As a nod to Cat Stevens, I guess.

'*Old Mother Nature, she's been abused. Ploughed and pillaged by the tillerman...*'

All the women nodded along. Trevine nodded along with them.

'*The soil is soiled,*' Venus sang, raising her voice to a fever-shriek, '*there's blood on the grass, blood on your ass...*'

The crowd shrieked back, and Trevine shrieked too. She shrieked and screamed and shook her hair and stamped her feet. She kept that up all through the first set, becoming more and more hysterical. At one point she even fell out of her chair, but nobody seemed to care. It was that kind of gig.

At intermission, Venus came over to say hello. Beatrice stood up and gave her a hug, then stepped aside to introduce her to Trevine. Apparently Venus hadn't recognised me from up on stage, because she looked completely dumbfounded. I twiddled my fingers at her and offered her my hand. The nails were painted an off-red that matched my lipstick.

I said, 'You're blowing them away, baby.'

Venus laughed, clasped my hand, and pulled me into a sisterly hug. Her shirt was clammy with sweat, and I could smell her cologne – a musky, man's scent.

'I like you this way,' she said.

She liked it so much that she dedicated a song to me – the first one after the break.

'This is a Martha Wainwright tune,' she told the crowd. 'It's for my new friend, Trevine.'

Everybody applauded. I held up my hand in acknowledgement.

Then she started singing. About being a chick with a dick... I lowered my arm, sliding down in my seat. I wanted to slide right under the table and hide under there, like a troll. Bea pushed her drink over to me.

'Take it as a compliment,' she said.

After that number, Venus switched to an acoustic guitar. The lights dimmed, and her bandmates put down their instruments. Sweaty and worn, Venus clutched at the mike. She whispered. She moaned. She crooned. The room settled to a lullaby-hush. In the midst of that intimacy, I heard a faint buzzing noise. At first I thought it was feedback from the amps. But it seemed to be coming from outside. I cocked my head, listening.

'What?' Bea asked.

I made a dismissive gesture. At that point I still wasn't sure. Then I heard the door bang open, followed by shouting and what sounded like some kind of scuffle. Beatrice and the women at the other tables turned around to see what the hell was going on. I didn't. Not at first. I was staring into my glass, and thinking, it can't be them.

Then I looked back, and said, 'Oh, shit.'

There were bikers shoving in past the bouncer. They were all dressed in matching leather jackets, lathered in trail dirt. The one leading the way was wearing a pair of super-dark sunglasses. I had the same feeling I always had when I saw that guy, or his brother – that feeling of uncertainty and unreality. This time I knew it was him, though. It had to be.

He was wearing my visor.

chapter 70

They swarmed in like a sandstorm, filling the place with laughter and shouting, high-fives and back-pats, burping and swearing and dust and testosterone. They settled on the seats at the back, moving tables around and dragging chairs into place. The chair-legs scraped across the floor, like fingernails on a blackboard.

'Where did these assholes come from?' Beatrice said.

'The desert, unfortunately.'

The bouncer hovered in the doorway, as if hoping somebody else would handle it. Nobody did. Eventually he shuffled over to face them. I couldn't hear what he said, but whatever it was didn't work. The head biker palmed the bouncer's chest and shoved, so he fell back on his ass. The rest of the Cobras howled. It was like a scene from a pantomime play. Venus was still singing her solo, but it was hard to hear over the commotion.

After a moment, the bouncer picked himself up and slunk over to the bar, where he spoke to the bartender I'd flirted with earlier. They conferred with their heads tilted towards each other. Then it was the bartender's turn to try. He looked like a capable man. He had both sleeves rolled up, displaying his flabby biceps and his nicotine patches.

But, as he swaggered up to their table, he grinned and extended a hand. He and the head biker shook. They did one of those tricky guy handshakes – a grab and a clasp and a knuckle punch. They chatted for a bit, while me and Bea and the other women watched.

'What the hell's he doing?' she said.

'He's kissing his ass!'

By then the bartender was already strolling back to his bar.

'Let's have us some beer,' the biker called.

The barmaid started ferrying pitchers of beer over to their tables. On-stage, Venus shielded her eyes and peered out at the audience, trying to see what was happening. It was probably hard to tell, with the lights shining in her face. So she did the only thing she could do: she carried on with the next song. The first few bars were off-key, though, and the band had to stop to re-tune. At the back, the bikers chuckled and mock-applauded the mistake.

'This is such horseshit,' Bea said.

She shoved back her chair and strode over to the bar. I hurried after her. She crooked a finger at the bartender to beckon him over. He waddled towards us, twisting a towel around in a pint glass with his fist.

'I thought it was ladies' night,' she said.

The guy held up the glass, considering it. 'It is.'

'So what's with those assholes at the back?'

'Yeah,' I said, shimmying my shoulders a bit. I'd seen chicks doing that when they were getting all bitchy. 'What's with those jerks coming in when it's ladies only?'

'They know the owner.'

'Goddammit,' Bea said.

'And the stage is only booked for another half-hour. Ladies' night finishes at eleven.' He went back to his polishing. The towel made a soapy squeaking against the glass. 'Look – I'm sorry or whatever. But you know how it is.'

We retreated to our table and slumped in our chairs. The band had kicked off a more upbeat number. The drummer was shaking her tambourine and stomping the drum pedal. I sucked on my Dragonfire. The tequila dregs tasted bitter.

'This is all my fault,' I said.

'How could it be your fault?'

'It's him. The biker guy I told you about, and his gang. The Cobras.'

Bea gazed at me. Appraisingly. 'That's why you were worried about the peaks?'

'It's too much of a coincidence. It had to be synchronicity.'

'Whatever it is, they better settle down.'

They didn't. They were getting noisier, and rowdier. Venus switched to harder numbers, trying to drown the bikers out. She wailed on her guitar and shouted into her mic, but the louder she played, the louder they got, cackling and braying like a pack of hyenas.

Then, in the silence between songs, the head biker burped – one of those extended, deliberate burps that lasts about five seconds.

Venus smirked and said, 'Looks like somebody ate too much.'

'Yeah,' the guy called back. 'I ate too much pussy!'

All his cronies laughed on cue. It was as if they were a single organism with a hive mind, led by him. Venus blanked on the comeback. There wasn't much she could say, to a comment like that. Instead she started singing her next song – a punked-up pop cover. '*You didn't want a real girl, you wanted me to be your dream girl...*'

'You can be my dream girl, baby – my wet dream!'

That was the guy again. But pretty soon the others joined in the heckling.

'Time to get off the stage.'

'Yeah,' another shouted. 'Get off, or take it off!'

Venus missed a chord change. She was flustered now, and singing out of sync.

'Time's up, girlie!'

'Is it a girl or a guy?'

'Let's have some karaoke!'

They all started chanting. 'Ka-ra-ok-e! Ka-ra-ok-e!'

The band members looked at one another, blinking and sweating beneath the lights. A few of the women in the audience tried to counter-heckle, and shouted insults back at the bikers. They loved that, of course. It was exactly what they wanted. Next to me, Bea was trembling – actually trembling with rage.

'Fuck this,' she said, and stood up.

'Wait.' I grabbed her wrist. 'What are you doing?'

'I'm going over to tell those shitheads to be quiet.'

'Not a good idea, Bea. The guy's dangerous…'

I trailed off, withering like a worm under her glare.

'Trev,' she said. 'I'm just going to ask them to keep it down. If you're scared of him you don't have to come.'

'It's not that.' I lowered my voice. 'But he might recognise me.'

She rolled her eyes, pulled her hand away, and started walking off. I was thinking, if you let her go alone, you're not a man, or a woman. You're a non-thing, a nothing.

'Beatrice – hold on.'

I slurped back the rest of my drink, feeling the ice chill my teeth, and stood up. I tugged down my skirt, checked my wig and tits. Then I picked up my purse. Bea was waiting for me.

'With you,' I said, 'I'd face a hundred of those fuckers.'

We strutted over there. I focused on my chick-walk, rolling my hips and putting each heel in place. I told myself, you're not Trevor, you're Trevine. He won't recognise Trevine.

Bea marched us right up to the table of the main guy. He was obviously the one in charge. All the other bikers were clustered around him, like lackeys in the king's court. To his right sat a beefy guy who reminded me of a walrus. He even had a walrus moustache.

'What do we got here?' the biker said, grinning at Bea. He looked more weathered than the last time we'd met. His nose was peeling, his whole face was worn and parched from sun, and that patch of dry skin under his chin had spread – almost as if he'd developed eczema. My visor was fairly battered, too. He was wearing it at an angle, like a wannabe gangster.

'What we got,' Bea said, 'is a problem. Because that's my friend up there. And you're making her uncomfortable. So I'd appreciate it if you could keep it down until she finishes her set. Please.'

The biker lowered his sunglasses and looked Bea up and down, in that way guys do – as if he was picturing her naked. She stared right back at him, not blinking.

'And who are *you*, babe?'

Bea grinned, as if she wanted to tear out his throat with her teeth. 'I'm Bea.'

'Bea, huh? Like a honeybee. You got some honey for me, little bee?'

He used his foot to push a chair towards her. There was mud caked on his boots.

'Have a seat.'

'We have seats, thanks.'

'So I guess a blowjob is out of the question?'

The big walrus sort of chortled, and something shifted in Bea's face.

'Good one,' she said, giving them the thumbs-up. 'But I'll leave that to your friends here. You guys look like you spend a lot of time circle-jerking and sucking each other off.'

The women at nearby tables had turned to stare. The music was still going on in the background – feeble and limp as a deflating blimp – but the real performance was back here.

'Watch it, honeybee. Play nice unless you want a spanking.'

'I think you're all talk, tough guy.'

The biker said, 'All talk, huh?'

He leaned back in his chair, resting one elbow on the shoulder of his walrus sidekick. The movement pulled aside the front of his jacket, revealing a shoulder holster. The butt of his Magnum gleamed in there. He flaunted it for her, like a flasher flaunting his dick.

'Come on, honeybee. Have a drink with me.'

'Is this how you pick up women?' Bea said. 'By threatening them?'

But for the first time she sounded uncertain – you could tell that the gun had thrown her a little. I'd seen it all before, though. Not just his gun, but his entire tough-guy routine.

Maybe I could use that to our advantage.

'Nice piece,' I said, in my fluttery Trevine voice. I stepped up beside Beatrice and struck a bimbo-pose, with my head tilted and one hand on my hip. 'What is that? A thirty-eight?'

He gave me the once-over. Then he licked his lips. They were so parched that they'd started to crack and split, like waxed paper. 'It's a .500, sugar,' he said. 'You like guns, huh?'

I flicked my hair, trying to look nonchalant. 'Maybe.'

'Wanna see mine?' he asked.

'Ooh,' I said. 'Are you really going to show me your big gun?'

That drew some laughs from his men. Bea leaned over and whispered, 'I think you're getting a bit carried away, Trevine.' But the guy was already easing out his Magnum. There was a collective gasp from the women sitting nearby. I heard chairs being pushed back, and the scuttle of heels. Some of them were getting out of there. Others sat rabbit-still, waiting.

'Pearl-handled and nickel-plated,' he said.

Then he laid the gun on the table. I took the seat he'd offered Bea, and touched the pistol, running my nail along the barrel. I pretended to shiver. At some point the music had stopped. I guess the band must have realised that something crazy was going on. Now the place was silent as a sound stage.

'Is it loaded?' I asked.

'Sure. But the safety's on. Go ahead. Pick it up.'

I did, making a big deal about how heavy it was. I posed with it, pointed it, blew on the muzzle. 'It's big,' I said. 'But are you any good with it, or are you just shooting blanks?'

His cronies chuckled again. They loved my gun-slut routine.

'Sugar,' he said, 'I'm so good with this thing, I can shoot it backwards, blindfolded or riding on my motorcycle. Or all three. You name it.'

I giggled. Girlishly. 'No, you couldn't.'

'Yes. I could.'

He said it as if he actually believed he could shoot it backwards and blindfolded while riding his motorcycle – which gave me an idea.

'Show me, then.' I put the gun down in front of him. 'Show me how good you are.'

'What – in here?'

'No, silly. Out back.'

He laughed. 'I can't just fire this thing for no reason, sugar. Not in the city.'

'Why not? Gonna get reported?' I leaned forward, put my hand on his knee. I lowered my voice, too – making it all husky. 'I *love* seeing a man shooting off his pistol.'

The biker cleared his throat. His men were looking at him, waiting to see if he'd rise to the challenge. Eventually he picked up his gun, spun the cylinder and snapped it shut.

'Okay, sugar. Whatever turns you on.'

All the Cobras whooped it up in appreciation, and I clapped my hands like a little girl – with the fingers spread wide. The guy stood to address the whole bar. 'If any of you ladies are interested, we're going to have ourselves a firearm display. Out back in the yard.'

Then he bowed to me, stepping aside to let me go first. As me and Bea passed him, he slapped my ass, the way you would to get a horse going. It stung like hell, but I pretended to like it. The rest of the bikers, and some of the women, fell into step behind us. We led the way towards the rear exit, behind the stage.

'You're out of your depth, Trevine,' Bea said, under her breath. 'We need to leave.'

'No – we need a scarf. Do you have one?'

Bea always had a scarf – up her sleeve or in her purse or in her pocket.

'Sure I've got a scarf. But he's got a fucking gun, okay?'

I held a finger to my lips. The biker guy was only a few steps back.

'Tonight, I'm hoping scarf trumps gun.'

chapter 71

Everybody piled outside: the bikers and the women, Venus and her band members, the bartender and the barmaids and the bouncer. Everybody. The yard was dark and cluttered, like the back of somebody's mind. They had a large patio out there, littered with cigarette butts, broken glass and bits of paper. A low-watt security lamp glowed above the fire exit. It didn't give off much light, but you could see fairly well because of the moon. It was past the halfway point now – going gibbous – and hung directly above the Twin Peaks, coating the slopes with a dreamy, hallucinatory hue.

At first nobody knew what was going on. We just milled about, nervous and excited as a herd of cattle before a stampede. Then a semi-circle began to form around the sides of the patio. All the women were on one side of the semi-circle, and all the men were on the other. The head biker stood at the centre. He started doing fancy tricks with his Magnum. First he twirled it around his trigger finger like a gunslinger. Then he palmed it into his holster, and whipped it out – super-fast. From the sidelines the other Cobras cheered him on.

'Where's sugar?' he yelled, looking around.

I was standing in the crowd with Bea. When I stepped forward, she came with me. Since the guy had his walrus sidekick as back-up, it only seemed fair that I got to have her.

'*There* you are,' the guy said. 'Come here.'

He wrapped an arm around my waist and managed to slip his hand under my blouse, palming my hip. Beside us, Beatrice plucked up the sides of her skirts and performed a slow-dip curtsy for the walrus, who looked absolutely flabbergasted by this.

'So,' I said to the biker, 'what are you going to shoot for me?'

'What do *you* want me to shoot, sugar?'

He wasn't much different from his brother, that guy.

'Hmm,' I said, nibbling my fingernail. 'Let me see…'

As I considered, I could feel him staring at me from behind his sunglasses.

'Hold on,' he said. 'Have we met before?'

'Of course – in your dreams.'

He was still studying me. Closely. I had to choose a target, fast. His walrus sidekick was sipping from a bottle of beer. I pointed to it.

'How about that?'

The sidekick looked down at his bottle, as if he'd just noticed he was holding it.

'Perfect, sugar,' the biker said, and motioned with his gun. 'Put it over there, Fatty.'

The fat guy's nickname was Fatty, apparently. That made sense.

'No,' I said, in a spoiled-child voice, 'let *me* do it.'

I took the bottle from Fatty and held it up, presenting it to the crowd with a showgirl flourish. Somebody wolf-whistled. Carrying it like that, I strutted across the patio, striking my heels on the concrete and swinging my hips. Around the yard was a concrete wall, about head-high. That was the place. I went over and balanced the bottle on top. As I adjusted it, I noticed the label for the first time. It showed the head of a black bird with a hooked yellow beak, beside the words *Black Hawk Stout*.

'Let's hope you're my hawk on the high wall.'

I kissed it for luck, then sashayed back to the centre of the horseshoe. The biker and Fatty were chuckling and nudging each other – as if Trevine had done something silly and female.

'I thought you were going to give me a challenge, sugar. That's easy.'

'Even if you do it blindfolded?'

'Don't be stupid. Why would I do that?'

I looked at him with big doe-eyes. 'I thought you said you could shoot backwards and blindfolded and riding your motorbike.'

One of the women, who was obviously pretty hammered, called out, 'You did say that. I heard you.' A bunch of the other women muttered and nodded their agreement.

'Ladies,' the guy said, like a teacher explaining to a group of children, 'that's just a saying. Nobody could ever really shoot a target blindfolded. It's impossible.'

I looked at him coolly. 'Want to bet?'

He laughed. His men laughed, too. Even some of the ladies laughed.

'What kind of bet is that?'

'I bet I can hit it, even if you can't.' Dipping one hand in my purse, I slowly pulled out my pistol, like a stripper teasing off a piece of clothing. When she saw that, Bea made a little sound, as if to say, what the hell is Trevor doing with a gun? The biker looked as if he was wondering the same thing, and around us the crowd started whispering and murmuring.

'How about it, sugar?' I said. 'A shoot-out. Me against you.'

I pursed my lips, blew him a kiss. He blinked, as if the kiss had caught him right between the eyes. He didn't answer immediately. I think he must have suspected a trick.

'And what if you win?' he asked. 'What then?'

'Then,' I said, raising my voice and addressing the whole crowd, 'you and your buddies have to leave, and my friend gets to finish her set. It'll be ladies' night, all night!'

When they heard that, the women all started cheering and whooping and stomping the ground. Among them, I caught sight of Venus – looking absolutely stunned. I winked at her.

'And if *I* win?' the guy said. 'What do I get if I hit it first?'

I levelled him with my sexiest Trevine stare. I padded around behind him, ran a hand over his chest, and whispered in his ear, 'What do you think, silly? If you win, you get me.'

The Cobras standing nearby, who'd overheard, all went, 'Oooohhh.'

'Do it, boss,' one called out.

'Go for it!'

The guy looked around. You could tell he was still trying to figure out my angle, my plan. He couldn't, though – mostly because I didn't have one. Not a rational one, anyway.

'Okay, sugar,' he said. 'Let's do this. How many shots do we get?'

'I don't know how many you'll need,' I said. 'But I'll only need one.'

'Like hell you will.'

We picked a spot to shoot from, and Fatty scratched a line in the gravel with his toe. Then we flipped to see who would shoot first. I won the toss and told the biker he could go. He made a big deal about taking off his jacket and checking his gun. He spun the cylinder, cocked the hammer, and sighted along the barrel like a pro. Then he stepped up to the line.

'All right,' he said. 'Where's the goddamn blindfold?'

Bea already had her scarf out – a green silk scarf with red and blue floral patterns on it. She waved it above her head, displaying it, then stepped up behind the biker. The silk was thin so she folded it twice to make sure he couldn't see through it.

'Could you give me a hand, honey?' she asked Fatty.

Fatty hurried over. He seemed incredibly excited to be helping her. He held the scarf across his boss's face while Bea tied it carefully at the back. In his hair you could see white flakes of skin, thick as snake scales. 'Somebody needs Head and Shoulders,' she said, under her breath.

'What's that?'

'I said you're all ready to go.'

Fatty, who was grinning, turned him in the right direction. 'It's dead ahead, boss.'

Fatty moved back, and motioned for us to move back, too. The chatter of the crowd lowered to a hush. In the stillness you could hear the traffic in the Castro. There was a park behind the bar, and from one of the trees an owl hooted.

'This is so fucking stupid,' the guy muttered.

He did that thing you do, where you tilt your head up and down, trying to peek out the top or bottom of the blindfold.

'No cheating,' I said.

'Yeah, yeah.'

He raised his Magnum, and hesitated. Holding it like that, he looked stiff and awkward as a scarecrow. While he adjusted his aim I leaned over to whisper to Beatrice.

'You know to only fold the scarf once for me, right?'

'Of course, darling.'

Then the biker pulled the trigger, and his Magnum thundered. The echo resounded in the confines of the yard, but the bottle didn't break – the bullet had gone clean over the wall.

'Fuck,' he said, yanking off his blindfold.

Fatty went up and patted him on the back. 'Nice try, boss.'

'As if this chick is going to hit it, anyways.'

He tossed the scarf down at my feet. Bea gathered it up and took my handbag from me. Together we crossed to the shooting line. I checked my clip, thumbed the safety, and spat on the palms of my hands, playing up to the crowd a little. Then I gave Bea the nod. She stepped behind me to put on the blindfold. I could smell the biker on it – this stale, musty smell.

He called out, 'Make sure those sluts aren't cheating.'

Fatty came over to check, feeling the front with his fingers.

'Looks legit, boss.'

It wasn't, though. Bea had only folded the scarf once, so the blind was thin enough for me to peer through. Not perfectly, but partially. I saw the outline of Fatty's head as he finished inspecting me. Then he stepped aside, and I could vaguely discern the yard, and the wall at the back. It was like looking at everything through a veil.

'This is harder than it looks,' I said.

They all laughed. Nobody actually expected me to hit it. As my eyes adjusted, I could make out the wall a little better, but not the bottle. I took a few deep breaths. I was thinking, the hitcher had said his wife did it, somehow. Through blind luck and feminine intuition – like Zuzska in Las Vegas, and Bea's Indian princess. Maybe I had it in me, too.

I raised my gun.

'Good luck,' the guy said.

I ignored him. Bea called for quiet. I stood for a long time, holding my pistol lightly, like a divining rod, and feeling for the target. I imagined taking aim. I imagined squeezing the trigger. I imagined the bullet sliding from the barrel. I imagined being the bullet, on a beeline for the target. I imagined burrowing into that bottle, like a sperm into an egg, and I imagined being that bottle, accepting the inevitable impact. And, as I imagined all that, I saw a faint glimmer atop the wall, like the glint of moonlight off glass, and felt my arm float up.

Then the pistol fired. I didn't consciously pull the trigger – it just went off. There was that familiar gunshot-yip followed by a sound like a light bulb popping. I still wasn't sure what had happened until, in the shocked silence, I heard shards of glass tinkling down.

chapter 72

The crowd went absolutely wild. They didn't care that they'd just witnessed something that should have been impossible. I'd made it possible, by doing it. From a distance, the reaction must have sounded like a riot. An extremely happy riot. People were shouting, screaming, cheering, jumping around, laughing in disbelief, pumping their fists in the air. Even Fatty joined in. He roared and seized Bea by the waist and twirled her around. The only one not whooping it up was the head biker. He couldn't believe it.

'But – that's *impossible*,' he kept saying. 'Impossible!'

I guess some people can accept the impossible, and some can't.

'Looks like Lady Luck was smiling on me,' I said. Then, while everybody else was still celebrating, I leaned over to kiss his cheek, which felt dry and coarse and leathery. In my regular voice, I whispered, 'Does this mean I get to keep your bottle of mezcal, sugar?'

He drew back to look at me. His nostrils flared and his eyes quivered wildly, like a horse on the verge of going berserk.

'You!' he said. 'You fucking queer-bitch!'

He grabbed me by the throat, with both hands, and started choking me. I kicked and squirmed and tried to break free, but his grip was as solid as a hose-clamp. I couldn't speak, or breathe, or do anything, really – except make this weird gurgling noise. His face loomed in front of me, all twisted up and demented-looking, like the reflection in a distorted mirror. My vision began to flicker, flaring white, and I figured that was it. I was finished. Then I heard a dull, hollow sound, which seemed to reverberate in my skull, and he let me go.

I doubled over, coughing and clutching my throat. On the ground in front of me the biker was sprawled flat, with one arm folded awkwardly behind his back. He was out cold. It took me a second to figure out what had happened. It was Bea. She was standing beside me, holding my bottle of mezcal like a club. The bottle hadn't broken. She brandished it above her head and glared at the other bikers, her eyes flashing like fucking Athena.

'So are we going to party and play nice,' she shouted, 'or are the rest of you assholes also the kind of men who would hit a lady?'

All the bikers muttered and looked at each other – trying to figure out whether or not they were the kind of men who would hit a lady. It fell to Fatty to decide. Since the boss was down, he was the new boss – and you could tell he was already a little in love with Beatrice.

'Hell, no!' Fatty roared, thumping his chest. 'I've never hit a lady in my life!'

Then he kicked his old boss, right in the guts. That clinched it. Everybody cheered: me, Bea, Venus, her band, the ladies, the bikers. Even Fatty started cheering, for himself.

Then one of the woman – the drunk one who'd called out before – screamed, 'Let's get this party started!'

Even though I'd won the bet, we didn't make the Cobras leave. We piled inside, en masse, and the bartender served up a round of drinks on the house. Venus and the Flytraps got back on-stage to finish their set. The rest of us gathered near the front. At first the men and women were standing apart and sitting at separate tables. But after a few songs, and a few rounds, people started to mix and mingle, stirred up by the music.

The Flytraps rocked out for another hour. We kept demanding encores. Whenever they tried to wrap things up, we would pump our fists in unison and chant, 'More! More! More!' We wanted more music, more booze, more revelry. It was as though the single bullet I'd fired had set off a race to see who could party the hardest. Pitchers were poured, corks were popped, bottle-caps were snapped, cans were cracked, and shots were lined up like dominoes. People kept bringing me random cocktails, too: Mai Tais and Grizzly Bears and margaritas. They wouldn't let me get my own. They all wanted to buy me drinks, and they all wanted to know the same thing: 'How did you *do* that?'

Whenever they asked, I would tell them I didn't know, which was true. I didn't. Not in any way I could explain. The only one who didn't ask was Bea. She had a question of her own, though. She waited until we were alone in the women's bathroom, checking our make-up, before laying it on me.

'Trevine,' she said, 'what the hell are you doing with a gun?'

'That's a long story. Literally.'

We were looking in the mirror, talking to each other's reflections.

'Don't get all mysterious on me. I had your back out there.'

'Good point. I'll take you as my wing-woman, any day.'

'You think you're so crafty, with your wily ways and gun tricks.' She turned and tapped my nose with her forefinger. 'I want to hear the whole story. Later.'

'That could take a while.'

'We'll stay up to watch the sunrise.'

'Deal.'

When the band was finally allowed to finish, the bartender asked for a volunteer to kick off the karaoke. One of the Cobras hopped up there, right on cue, as if he'd been waiting for the chance. He was wearing a NASCAR racing cap that he'd grabbed off the wall. He held it high and waved it at us, then started crooning that old-school Willie Nelson track, 'On the Road Again'. The other bikers knew all the words, and sang along. It was their gang's anthem, apparently.

The ladies got into it, too. This butch chick tore through a couple of indie classics – Modest Mouse and Arcade Fire – and managed to blow one of the speakers. Afterwards Bea and Fatty took over, belting out a supercharged rendition of 'Life is a Highway'. They had to holler the final chorus to be heard over the rampant cheering. It was followed by more duets and group singalongs. Almost everybody got in on the action, except Venus. I spotted her sitting at a table near the back, drinking. Her band members weren't with her. One of them had passed out, and the other was playing pool with three Cobras.

I went over and told her, 'You guys rocked tonight.'

'Cheers.'

She didn't look up. She was staring across the room, to where Beatrice was arm-wrestling Fatty amid a circle of onlookers. They'd both rolled up their sleeves. Their arms, hand-locked at the top, tilted to and fro like a slow-motion metronome.

'The latest member of the Beatrice Carmen fan club,' I said.

Venus grunted. I sat down with her and poured us both a glass of mezcal. I'd cracked open the bottle to share it around. We'd been pounding it back, but that stuff never seemed to run dry. It was like a magic fountain.

Venus asked, 'How'd you pull off that stunt, anyway?'

'Your girl helped me cheat.'

'That figures. Thanks for stepping in like that.'

'It was my fault that guy showed up in the first place.'

A cheer erupted from the arm-wrestling table, and we both looked over. Bea had won. She stood up and flexed her bicep. Fatty was shaking his wrist out, exaggerating the pain for the onlookers. Venus toasted them with her empty glass, then tipped it back and dumped the ice cubes into her mouth. I listened to her crunch and crack them like candy.

'Want another?' I asked.

'No,' she said, shaking her head. 'I'm about done.'

A few minutes later the bar got lit on fire. The bartender did it. He doused the bar top in sambuca and set it alight.

People got up to dance in the flames, scorching their shoes and skirts. It was fairly extreme. The heat triggered the smoke detectors, which set off the sprinklers. Then everybody was parading around in the showers of water. The floor became as slippery as a waterslide. You could barely stand up. My wig had fallen off somewhere, but nobody seemed to notice, or care that I was actually a guy. People were trading clothes and costumes, tearing props off the walls. Men became women, and women became men. A lesbian wearing a Cobra jacket organised some kind of piggyback race. Then one of the bikers took to the stage in a pink dress and did a little striptease to 'I'm Too Sexy'.

At around midnight I ducked out to check on the head biker. Amid all the celebrating I'd forgotten to get my visor back. It was lying in the centre of the vacant lot, on top of a pile of dust. I picked it up, whacked it against my thigh to clean it, and looked around. I couldn't see him anywhere. I guess he'd slunk off to nurse his wounds.

'You're missing a great party,' I shouted.

I heard muttering and scuffling to my left. Behind the garbage bin one of the punk chicks was making out with a biker. I apologised and told them to ignore me – I was just talking to myself. Then I went back inside. Our party raged on into the night, like a demented lion.

chapter 73

Back at their place we staggered and stumbled around, crashing into the furniture: chairs and tables, lamps and bookshelves. I even managed to knock a plant over. The floor was tilting wildly, as if the waters of Mission Creek had flooded and risen up and washed their houseboat out to sea. We were floating on an ocean of booze, and nothing would stay still.

'Stop this floor from rocking!' Beatrice shouted.

'The table,' I said. 'Get to the table.'

We made a heroic effort to reach the kitchen table and clung to it, trying to steady ourselves. The entire place was bobbing up and down and spinning around in circles, like Dorothy's house on the way to Oz. Venus couldn't take it. She emitted a low moaning sound, like a sick cow, and lowered her head face-down on the table.

'Baby?' Bea said.

She was out. The houseboat listed to one side, and Venus began to slide off her stool. Bea managed to catch her in an armpit hold. I got up to help, lifting her feet, and together we carried Venus into the bedroom. As we were tucking her in, she opened her eyes and looked around, fraught and frantic as a fever victim. 'Don't leave,' she said, clutching Bea's blouse. 'Don't leave me.'

'I'm right here, honey.'

'Don't...'

Her moment of clarity passed, and she conked out again. We left her lying on her side and shut the bedroom door. The house was still spinning, so we took what remained of the mezcal on to the deck. Out there, they had a set of deckchairs, a Moroccan table, and a hammock strung between the railings. We sank into the chairs, and Bea stretched her legs across my lap. I removed her shoes, handling them as gently as glass slippers, and placed them on the table. The raging waters that had carried us along subsided to a gentle seesaw lilt.

'I haven't tried your mezcal yet,' Bea said.

'Everybody else did. But it seems to be bottomless.'

She picked up the bottle and studied the label. I'd never been able to decipher it, but Bea understood a little Spanish. She understood a little of everything, really. At the base of the bottle was a slogan, which she translated and read out. '"For everything good, mezcal. For everything bad, also."'

'Go ahead, *señorita*.'

She dutifully took a swig, handed the twixer to me, and smacked her tongue against the roof of her mouth – in that way you do to accentuate the taste.

'It's like drinking liquid smoke,' she said.

'I could do with a smoke.'

She opened her pouch of American Spirit and rolled one. I lit it for her with my Zippo. Before taking a drag, Bea pointed with the cigarette towards each of the four horizons, dipped it down at the deck, and then held it up to the star-splattered sky.

'Great Spirit,' she said, 'we offer this smoke to begin our ceremony tonight.'

'Is that a West Coast thing?'

'A Native thing.'

For a few minutes we smoked and swilled in silence, and took in the view. Since it was so late, the condos across the creek were dark. I could hear the water slopping against the sides of the houseboats, and some animal rustling around in the reeds that lined the bank. The air smelled wet and foetid, almost fen-like. It felt as if we were somewhere in the wilds – the bayou, maybe – rather than the centre of a major American city.

Then Beatrice reached over and tapped the brim of my visor.

'This,' she said, 'is possibly the most radical fashion accessory I've ever seen.'

I tipped it at her, like an old man doffing his cap. 'Are you jealous?'

'Insanely so. Where'd you get it?'

'In Trevor. It's like my equivalent of Dorothy's slippers.'

'You,' she said, jabbing her cigarette at me, 'still haven't told me about any of that. You and your visor and your biker and your gun. The whole crazy story of your road trip.'

'I tried. You guys didn't believe me.'

'Try me again.'

I sat back in my chair, adjusted her legs on my lap. 'Where should I start?'

'Wherever you want.'

'The road trip – the actual road trip – started when I picked up the rental car at the airport. But really it all started before that, when I was working on this independent film.'

I told her about Zuzska's phone call and crossing the border, about meeting the hunters and shooting the eagle, about Seattle and Sprague and the other places I'd passed through. I told her all of it, but not always in the correct order. I jumped around a bit at first, since I was so excited. I exaggerated here and there, too. I turned the girl I met in Trevor into a kind of Slovakian witch, when really she'd just been a rich chick with a weird family. And I made the father and son in the diner more psychotic than they actually had been. There were a lot of details like that – little tweaks and alterations to make it seem more exciting. I wasn't lying, exactly, but I was stretching the truth, turning my long story into a tall tale.

'That's harsh,' Bea said, when I got to the bit about the old man in the trailer park, with his baseball bat. 'What a son of a bitch.'

I nodded. I hadn't had to exaggerate much about him. 'I felt guilty about getting him hammered.'

'Booze is just an excuse for assholes like him.' She twisted her cigarette in the ashtray, as if she was imagining grinding it into the guy's eye. 'And after that? Tell me the rest.'

'You know the rest. I showed up on your doorstep, like a penitent pilgrim. I came to prostrate myself before you and worship at your altar and kiss your feet, looking for a cure.'

Bea raised her foot, very seriously, pointing it like a dancer. I cradled it in my hands and kissed the bridge, just below the ankle.

'Has it helped?' she asked.

'Well, there's still the impotence thing…'

She threw back her head and laughed – this braying coyote laugh. 'You and your fucking impotence. You're so melodramatic.'

'Trevine's a drama queen, all right.'

We gazed at each other for a while. Her eyes were shining in the dark like a cat's.

'You still haven't called her.'

'*Mañana*,' I said. 'I'll call her tomorrow.'

'Is that how the story ends?'

'If she answers.'

Bea took the cork for the mezcal and pushed it back into the bottle. There were only a few ounces left, and I guess she didn't want to drink it dry.

'It's a good story,' she said.

'I made some of it up, for you.'

'I know.'

I sat with my fingers laced behind my head, smiling reminiscently. I told Bea that I thought the story of my trip was one I was destined to retell – the definitive tale of my life. And each time it would get a little more grandiose, a little more incredible, until, when I reached my grandpa's age, it would have taken on almost mythic proportions.

'The strangest part is,' I said, 'the things that actually happened seem the most outrageous. I mean, who's ever going to believe I had a shoot-out in a karaoke bar?'

'I know I sure as hell don't,' she said.

'Me neither.'

As we considered that, I saw something flash behind her head. Then came another, and another – like bright streaks of chalk against the slate-black sky. They were shooting stars.

'Oh, my God,' Bea said. 'The sky is falling!'

'It's the end of the world!'

'I remember hearing about a meteor shower.'

We gazed skyward, hypnotised, until our necks began to ache. Then Bea said that if we were going to watch the world end we should at least be comfortable enough to enjoy it. The hammock seemed like the best solution. We stretched out on the netting together, lying side by side. She kept one foot on the deck to swing us back and forth. It was like being in a cradle. As we hung there, Sprite and Belle crept out – obviously wondering what the hell we were doing. They sniffed around before curling up beneath us, in their yin-yang position.

'You might have a hard time separating those two,' Bea said.

'How would you feel about having a cat?'

She reached down to scratch Sprite's ears. The cat emitted a little meow.

'I like that the name of my pets together would mean "Beautiful Spirit".'

A huge star skittered across the sky, as if to seal the decision. After the initial burst, they'd settled into a slower rhythm, flashing every few minutes – sometimes bright and glaringly obvious, other times so faint you wondered if you were imagining them.

'There's another,' I said, pointing.

We shared a cigarette and watched the stars dart left and right, pointing them out to each other. Eventually we stopped doing that – understanding that we could both see them.

Bea said, 'They look like aircraft contrails.'

'They remind me of my vision quest.'

In relating the story of my journey, I'd kind of skimmed over that part – about how on my peyote trip I'd seen threads of light dripping from the sky. My lame little hallucination hadn't seemed like an important detail, but Beatrice wanted to know, so I explained it to her. I said, 'I guess I was trying to have some kind of epiphany.'

'You did,' she said. 'That's just like Black Elk's vision.'

'Whose vision?'

Apparently Black Elk was an Indian chief her dad had told her about. For Black Elk's vision quest, he'd climbed to the top of this mountain. When he got up there, he saw threads of smoke or light coming from all the trees, all the stones, all the animals, all of everything.

'Holy shit.' I drew back to look at her. It was hard since our heads were so close, and the curve of the hammock kept pulling us together. 'Did he figure out what it meant?'

Bea traced a circle of smoke with our cigarette. 'Each of the threads was tied to the others. He'd found the place where all things join together and become one. Everything in the universe, the seen and unseen, is related. It's a lot like Indra's net of gems, in Buddhist philosophy, and interconnectedness. Or Jung's synchronicity. It's all the same shit, really.'

'In my vision, one of the threads was attached to me.'

'Of course. You're connected to the universe, too. You're part of it.'

'You are it,' I said. 'As my hitcher said.'

'Or thou art that, as the Hindus say.' Bea yawned, stretching her jaw and baring her teeth, like a lioness. As she finished she added, 'It's supposed to be the key to Nirvana.'

'If the key is that simple, why doesn't everybody know it?'

'Everybody does. The hard part is understanding. That takes a lifetime.'

'I don't think I'm that dedicated.'

'That's okay – us hedonists have more fun, anyway.'

She shifted around in the hammock, trying to get comfortable. I lifted an arm for her to slip under. She was a little too tall to fit, but we managed it. We were all tangled up in the mesh. Holding one side in each hand, I wrapped it around us, like our own personal cocoon.

'It's tragic that you're leaving,' Bea said.

'How will we start your new religion?'

'You'll just have to go forth and spread the word.'

She slid her hand across my chest, angling herself towards me. I held her like that. I could feel my heart beating, and I could feel her heart beating, too. The rhythm was the same but the timing was completely opposite. Mine would beat, and then hers would beat, like two small animals communicating with each other.

'Remember,' she said, 'we're staying up to watch the sunrise.'

'I don't know if I'm going to make it.'

'Don't bitch out on me, Trevine.'

Her head was tucked under my chin, so that I was breathing through her hair. It smelled of smoke and honey. I closed my eyes. Some time after that we seemed to be back in the karaoke bar, with the bikers from the biker gang, and the ladies from ladies' night. Except this time the hitchhiker was with us, too, and his brother, and Sunita, and Pigeon and his hunter friends. All the people from my road trip were at the party, even that one-armed bartender from Reno, and the old couple from the gas station. A big space had been cleared in the centre of the floor for me and Bea. We seemed to be sparring with each other, and dancing at the same time. Everybody else stood in a circle around us, clapping their hands.

chapter 74

Then came a falling sensation, followed by an impact that jolted my whole body. I was lying on the deck, with one arm folded awkwardly behind my back. Above me hung the hammock, swinging gently. I'd tipped out of it somehow.

I got up, massaging my collarbone. The table was set with three plates, a jug of orange juice, and sun-silvered cutlery. In the water by the deck I could see a bunch of moon jellyfish, hovering just beneath the surface. From out in the bay a freighter moaned, low and mournful, a monstrous rooster announcing the start of a new day.

Beatrice came out with a coffee pot and mugs.

I smiled at her. Shyly. 'We missed the sunrise.'

'You did. I figured I'd let you sleep.'

'I dreamt me and you were doing this weird dancing-fighting thing.'

'Like *capoeira*?' she said.

'Almost.'

'I wondered why you were twitching and kicking me.'

We sat down to eat, blinking and bleary-eyed. Bea had bought a paper. We divided up the sections. She read the arts, and I read the sports. We sipped our coffee. We smoked. For a few minutes we were like a married couple.

Then Bea said, 'Trevor?'

'Yeah.'

'I think you just ashed in my coffee.'

We looked. It was true. My ashes were floating around in there – even though I had no recollection of doing it. I guess

I was just incredibly tired. We both started laughing, and Bea asked, 'How about some breakfast?'

'I'm about ready to eat again.'

She brought me toast and an organic free-range egg, poached to perfection. The white was firm, and the yolk bright and yellow, like a miniature sun on my plate. I sawed off a bite-sized slab, slid it on to my fork, and lifted it to my mouth. The yolk was warm and gooey and leaked over my tongue. My stomach shuddered. I doubt I'll ever taste another egg that good.

Halfway through breakfast, Venus appeared, looking leaden-eyed and bed-headed and completely dishevelled, like a revenant back from the dead.

'Morning, baby,' Bea said.

Venus shuffled over and fell into a chair and lowered her forehead to the table. We treated her very delicately. I poured her some coffee. Bea brought another egg out. While Venus hacked away at it, Bea told her about the meteor shower, and how she'd decided to keep the cat. Venus didn't seem all that interested. She kept rubbing her eyes and massaging her temples. Every few minutes she hawked and spat into the water.

'What's the best route north?' I asked them.

'Take the Number 1 highway,' Venus told me, her mouth full of toast. 'Less traffic at this hour. Better views, too.'

Afterwards, while Bea and Venus were clearing the table, I said goodbye to Sprite. I scooped her up and sat with her on the sofa and stroked her until she started purring. Her coat had a soft sheen to it now, like ermine. I buried my face in it and blubbed for a bit.

'You goddamn cat,' I said, sniffling. 'You were all I had out there.'

She eyeballed me, in that way of hers, as if to say, *Keep it together, buddy. We had our time. Now that time is over. I'm happy here.*

I put her back down. She strode away with her tail in the air. 'Don't get all snooty with *me*,' I said. 'I used to wipe your wormy ass!'

I didn't have much to pack – just a few clothes and the dregs of my mezcal. Bea gave me a couple of her rollups for the road, and Trevine's wig as a souvenir. She said it would keep me in touch with my feminine side. I put it on, then put my visor on over it. 'How do I look?' I asked her.

'Like a complete psycho.'

'At least I'm complete.'

Then there was nothing to do but say goodbye, and go. Bea and Venus followed me out to the street. Beatrice had Sprite cradled in her arms. Even big Belle came, bouldering down the front walk, wagging her tail. At the car Venus gave me a hug. I held her gently, as if she were an ice sculpture that might break in my arms.

'Look after yourself,' she told me.

'You, too, eh?'

Then I turned to Bea. I didn't hug her because the cat was in the way. I didn't know what to say to her, either. I just thanked her, lamely, and got behind the wheel. 'Well,' I said, adjusting my visor, 'there's no place like home, right?'

'Drive safe, Dorothy,' Bea said. Then she slapped the door with her palm, making the metal ring. 'Now click your heels and get a move on, you hear?'

'As you wish,' I said, and put the Neon in gear.

As I rattled away I could see them in my rear-view. They were strolling back inside. Then, just as I was about to round the corner, Bea turned and raised her hand and made the heavy metal sign – the devil's horns. I honked and did the same out the window.

Two blocks down, I saw a news stand. I stopped and hopped out and bought one last postcard. I'd figured out what I should have told Bea. On the back of the postcard I wrote: *I love you like the sun – for your light, your warmth, your generosity.* Then I dropped it in a mailbox, got back in my Neon, and kept going.

On the way out of town, I crossed over a bridge. It was a long suspension bridge, with two sets of upright supports, imposing and monolithic. They looked like giant doorways, painted red. Stretching between them were strands of cable, also painted red, gleaming in the sun.

'No way,' I said.

I looked over at the passenger seat, to where the cat should have been. That was the first time I really missed her.

'This must be Golden Gate Bridge,' I whispered.

I passed through the second set of supports and felt a shiver of shadow – as if I'd gone through a portal. By the railing I saw a sign: *Marin County Line*. That was where Venus had told me I'd find Sausalito. At the far side of the bridge, I expected to see the actual golden gates, but there weren't any. There was just a lookout called Vista Point.

I turned in at it.

The lookout had a visitor centre with a parking lot, surrounded by a waist-high stone wall and a circular walkway that overlooked the bay. From there you could see the whole of the bridge, arching back towards the city. I found an information board that explained they'd named it the Golden Gate Bridge because of the waterway it spanned: Golden Gate Strait.

A set of steps led down to another platform, with those tourist telescopes you can pay to use. I saw an old couple peering through one, and a pack of schoolkids playing freeze-tag. Then I noticed this family: a man, a woman and a boy. They were strolling along, taking in the view. The man had his back to me, and was wearing a bomber jacket and baseball cap, but I still knew it was him – even without the mailbag.

'Hey!' I called out, and waved to him.

He looked back, hesitated, and raised his hand. He didn't seem all that stoked to have been recognised, but I trotted down to meet him anyway. The woman and boy walked a little further on, giving us space.

'Nice disguise,' I said.

'I'd worn out my travelling clothes.'

We shook hands and man-hugged. It was fairly awkward.

'So,' he said, 'you finally put my brother in his place.'

'Only through sheer blind luck, like you said.'

'I'm glad. He deserved it.'

He had both hands in the pockets of his jacket, and was moving them back and forth – making the jacket flap like bat wings.

'And you?' I said. 'You finally made it to Sausalito, and delivered your letter?'

He nodded. 'That's my ex and our kid.'

The two of them were waiting, watching us. The kid was about twelve, and dressed like a rapper: gold chains, baggy black jeans, and a huge LA Lakers jersey that hung down to his knees. His mom was an Oriental woman with long black hair and a serene, serious face.

'They look nice,' I said. 'How's the whole family thing going?'

'We're not back together or anything,' he said. 'It's complicated. She's got this new boyfriend. But I can see them, at least. It's a start, right?'

I agreed that it was a start. He glanced over at her, and held up a finger to signal that he was almost done. I noticed a strip of bandage wrap poking out from under his baseball cap.

'What happened to your head?' I asked.

'Oh.' He reached up to feel it. 'I banged it on the sink, trying to fix the toilet.'

I stared at him, sceptically, and he started to fidget.

'Anyway, man,' he said, 'it's been good seeing you.'

'Sure. Take care of yourself.'

'Take care of *your* self.'

I smiled. I was going to miss his little parroting trick. I told him to look me up if he ever made it to Vancouver. He said he would, but we didn't exchange phone numbers or anything. Then, as I turned to go, he asked, 'Hey – did you sort things out with your girl?'

'Not really. But I'm coming to terms with it.'

'Well, there's plenty of other – '

'I know, man. I know.'

I couldn't bear to hear him say it. I hadn't driven halfway across the continent just to learn what I already knew. He hustled to catch up with his ex and kid, and I kept walking. I looked back once but couldn't see them. They'd slipped away, like his brother at the bar.

On my way to the car, I passed a phone box. It gleamed like a beacon in the sun. I circled it a few times, trying to decide, then locked myself inside and filled the coin slot with quarters. The booth was quiet and secluded as a cloister. I picked her number out on the keypad. On her end it rang and rang. Then, just when I'd decided she wasn't going to answer, she did.

'*Ahoj?*'

'It's me.'

I heard some fiddling and rustling on her end, as if she was adjusting the phone.

'I'm glad you're okay,' she said, lowering her voice. 'Your parents called. They couldn't get in touch with you.'

'I incinerated my cellphone.'

I was gazing out across the bay. The flare of sun off water hurt my eyes, making me squint and grimace like a wounded soldier. I was feeling fairly cinematic.

'I miss you,' I said. 'I guess I always will.'

'I'm glad. Can you hold on a sec?' She must have covered the mouthpiece. I heard some muffled voices, and then she came back on. 'Sorry – but I can't really talk right now.'

'Are you with him?' I said. I was trying to sound casual, but of course I sounded jealous, and probably a little insane. 'Just tell me if you are.'

'With who?'

'This guy you're fucking.'

She sighed. 'No – I'm still at work. It's not like we're together or anything. It was just a stupid thing that happened.'

'Oh.'

I twisted the phone cord, trying to decide how I felt about that.

'I'm in San Francisco right now,' I said.

'Bea told me.'

'She did? What else did she tell you?'

'Not much. She said I'd have to hear it from you.'

That was a relief. At least she didn't know about Tao and Trevine and everything.

I said, 'Maybe I could call you when I get home.'

'That would be good. We need to talk.'

There was a pause. A gust of wind rattled the phone booth door.

'My evening class is starting,' she said. 'I should probably go.'

'Hold on,' I said. 'Just hold on a second, will you?'

I closed my eyes and listened to her breathing. The credit on the phone was counting down, down, down. Then it ran out, and we got cut off.

chapter 75

North of the city, I took the Number 1 highway like Venus had suggested. It wound its way along the waterfront, like a crooked spinal column, linking the vertebrae of coastal towns and communities. I drifted through San Rafael, Tomales and Bodega Bay, floated on through Jenner and Stewart's Point, and washed up in Mendocino. I recognised that name, but didn't place it until I took a wrong turn and passed a tattoo parlour – Voodoo Ink – down one of the side streets. It was the spot Bea had mentioned, where she got all her ink done.

I pulled over and walked back to take a look. The place had a country cottage feel, with white siding, blue trim, and slatted shutters. Hanging beneath a wooden arch out front was a painted sign, which depicted that symbol of a hand with an eye embedded in its palm.

The door was open, and I went on in. An overhead fan churned the air, the blades rattling as they rotated. The floor was divided into black and white linoleum squares, like a chessboard, and the far wall was covered with photos of various tattoo designs: flowers and daggers and skulls and serpents and Cantonese characters and countless others. Nobody was at the front desk. For a few minutes I stood and studied the tattoo collage.

'Can I help you?'

Behind me, a person had appeared – a person with short hair, prominent cheekbones, and a slim crane's neck. She looked like a woman, but she could just as easily have been a man. She was wearing a sleeveless top and her arms were wrapped in well-toned ink.

'My friend Beatrice comes here, to get her tattoos. Beatrice Carmen.'

She smiled. 'Of course. Bea.'

Like everybody else, she loved Bea. She let me wander around for a while longer, studying her photo displays, before she asked, 'Do you want to get something done?'

'Yes,' I said, 'I think so.'

Pinned among the more colourful pictures, I found a black and white charcoal sketch. It depicted a circular pattern, like an iris or starburst, with lines extending from the centre out to the circumference.

'Is that a mandala?'

'It's a form of mandala.' She came to stand beside me. 'It's an image they found on the Dead Sea Scrolls, or my rendition of it. I've been waiting to do it for somebody.'

She had a low, throaty voice, sexy and masculine. I was sold.

'I'm your somebody,' I said.

She took me into her studio, which had the same chessboard floor. In the centre of the room stood a padded tattoo table, with a doughnut-shaped headrest at one end. Peeling off my shirt, I lay down on my stomach and lowered my face into the hole. I'd decided to get the tattoo at the base of my neck, just below the collar line. For some reason it seemed important that my body stay symmetrical.

'I want to be balanced,' I told her.

She seemed to understand. She came to stand next to me, and started doing things to my back. First she wiped it down with a damp pad, which smelled of soap and alcohol. A disinfectant, I guess. Then she patted the spot dry.

'I'm going to put the stencil on now,' she said.

The stencil was similar to the decals you stick on model planes. She smoothed it on to my skin, before peeling the paper backing away. Next she snapped on a pair of latex gloves and picked up her tattoo iron. It rested between her thumb and forefinger, slender as a pen. She turned it on and the needle started to vibrate.

'It's a wonderful pattern,' she said.

'Do you know what it means?'

'What does it mean to you?'

'It's a reminder, I guess.'

She ran a finger down my spine, as if to prepare me or reassure me. I stared at her feet. They were nice feet, smooth and tanned. She'd painted her toenails a speckled blue, like tortoise shells. The sound of the needle got louder, and louder.

'Is it painful?' I asked.

'Some people think so.'

Then I felt the needle prickling my spine, stitching ink into my skin.

'How's that?' she asked – so close that I could feel her breath on my ear.

'It hurts,' I said. 'But in a good way.'

The vibrations tingled along my spine like low-voltage electricity. It flowed into my lower back, my tailbone, my ass, and further – right into my colon and balls. The sensation made my dick twitch, and I felt a stirring down there. I had to shift around a bit and adjust my jeans. Then, when the implications of that hit me, I pushed myself up off the table.

'Easy,' she murmured. 'Is that bit sensitive?'

'No, no,' I said. 'It's just…'

She looked at me, but I couldn't really explain it. The whole impotence thing had been a bit of a charade, anyway.

'It's perfect,' I said. 'It's exactly what I need.'

'You also need to stay still for me.'

She waited for me to settle back down. Then I felt the arousing prickle of the needle again. I lay there, savouring the sensation. I was thinking, maybe that mezcal worked after all. I'd just had to drink it under the right circumstances, and in the right company.

'How's Beatrice doing?' she asked.

'As stellar as ever,' I said.

Then, more gravely, she asked, 'And Venus?'

'Not so good, I don't think.'

She waited, still tickling my chakra.

'It might not last.'

'I suppose it's inevitable.'

We both knew it was coming. On some level, even Venus must have known.

chapter 76

The Number 1 meandered north, and I let the Neon meander with it. The road was carved into a series of steep cliffs and hillsides, and filled with sweeping curves. To my left the Pacific stretched on and on and on, surging and undulating in the sun. The breeze blowing through the broken window made my shirt ripple, like a slack sail. I coasted through Fort Bragg and Westport and Leggett. At Leggett the Number 1 merged back with the 101, and a few miles further on I hit a place called Eureka.

In Eureka, for no real reason, I started fiddling with my radio. I didn't actually expect it to work, but it did. It was like a minor miracle. This kitten-voiced DJ came on and purred to me. All she was playing was Nirvana: Nirvana live, Nirvana unplugged, Nirvana B-sides, Nirvana whatever. They were having a Nirvana marathon, apparently.

'Listening to all these tracks back-to-back,' she said at one point, 'I feel like I'm really understanding Nirvana for the first time. Does anybody else feel like that?'

'I do,' I told her. 'That's me.'

'Next up, a tune from *Nevermind*: "On A Plain".'

By mid-afternoon I'd reached the redwood forests. I was back on the terrain that me and Zuzska and Bea had driven through together the previous year – the section of America I'd deliberately avoided on the way down. Now I ventured into the forests, and circled twice around Hyperion, the world's tallest tree. I drove past Paul Bunyan, with his big-balled bull, and I drove past the famous, enormous redwood stump. I'd taken a photo of Zuzska lying on that stump, spreadeagled like a human sacrifice. Beyond the redwoods lay Oregon, with all the campsites we'd slept in, the bars we'd partied at, the beaches we'd surfed. At each spot I would pull over and have a little sentimental moment. Then I'd keep driving.

Night came on suddenly, like a screensaver. I stopped at a rest area near the Oregon sand dunes. We had been there, too. We'd rented dune buggies and quad bikes and zipped around like particles, smashing into each other, altering the course of our trajectories. I parked the Neon among the dunes. From there I could hear the shush of waves, and see campfires flickering on the beach. I closed my eyes and rested. I wasn't really sleeping – just recharging at the wheel. When the eastern sky turned grey, I set out again. If I drove steadily, I could get the car back by the end of the day – exactly two weeks after I'd left.

That early in the morning, the coastal highway was empty. I held the wheel with one hand, and let the Neon steer herself. By then I knew that car so well it was practically an extension of my body. At Newport we banked inland, wiggled along a one-lane back road, and emerged, magically, on the I-5. The HOV lane was clear. We slipped into it, gliding over the asphalt like a luge in a chute. I'd lost the Eureka radio station and DJ a while back, but other DJs rose up and faded out, keeping me company. They were playing Nirvana, too. A new box set was being released, apparently. Again. When 'All Apologies' came on, I cranked it up until the speakers started shuddering. Before then, I'd always listened to the final chorus – about all in all being all we are – without really hearing it. This time the words seemed to resonate indefinitely, echoing in my head. As the track faded out, I lit one of Bea's American Spirits, took a deep drag, and sighed smoke.

'You knew the key too, Kurt,' I said. 'But I guess it just wasn't enough.'

Somewhere past Salem a squad car latched on to me and started riding my tail. I was doing eighty in a work zone. I slowed down to let it overtake, but it didn't. After a minute or two, the lights spun blue and the siren emitted an angry squawk, so I pulled over, and the squad car pulled in behind me. We sat there. The patrolman didn't get out immediately. I guess he was running my licence plate through his computer. I turned down my radio and finished my cigarette. Then I gazed out the window, resting my palm on my belly, feeling peaceful and patient as a Buddha. I was thinking, he won't hassle me, now that I've discovered Nirvana.

Finally the patrolman got out and approached the passenger side. That confused me. Cops don't do that in Canada. He bent down and peered through the broken window. He had terrible sunburn. It was so bad his face had gone completely purple, like a plum.

'Licence and registration.'

'Sure thing, officer.'

My calf was itching, so I bent forward to scratch it.

'Keep your hands where I can see them!'

His was holding the butt of his gun, ready to draw. I raised my hands. Slowly.

'Sorry about that, officer,' I said. 'I've just got a mosquito bite on my leg. Those darned skeeters, eh?'

I said 'eh' loudly – to let him know I was Canadian. When I reached for the glovebox, I sensed him tense up again. I opened it as cautiously as a safecracker, then carefully extracted the registration papers, which I handed over along with my licence.

As he flipped through them, he asked, 'Where you headed, sonny?'

'Back home to Vancouver.'

'What are you doing in the States?'

'Originally I just needed to get away. My girlfriend cheated on me, see.' I half-turned in my seat, so I was facing him. 'But my trip became something more than your regular, run-of-the-mill trip.'

'How can a trip be more than a trip?'

'When it's an epic journey.'

'I see.' He scratched his sunburnt nose and peered around my car. 'You aren't high, are you?'

I exhaled, deflated. That was just like a cop.

'No, I'm not high.'

'You got any drugs on you?'

'No, I don't have any drugs on me.'

'Then you won't mind opening the trunk.'

When he said that, my newfound sense of Nirvana completely vanished – like a genie back into its bottle. I stared at the cop for a few seconds. His nostrils flared, as if he'd caught a scent of my fear.

'The trunk?' I asked.

'That's what I said.'

I still had my gun in there. An unlicensed firearm.

'It doesn't pop from inside,' I said. 'I've got to get out.'

'Go ahead.'

I opened the door, put my feet on the pavement, and stood up. As I zombie-walked to the back, I offered up a prayer. Not to God, though. I prayed to America, this motherland I'd crossed in pilgrimage, and the birthplace of Beatrice Carmen. I prayed for a little bit of luck.

'Here we go,' I said, fiddling with the lock.

The trunk rose up, revealing my cooler and dirty clothes and backpack and sleeping bag and empties. The cop used his nightstick to poke around among all that junk. The Glock was tucked to one side, half-hidden behind the cooler. I could see it clearly from where I stood.

'Any reason you were doing eighty just now?' he asked.

'I'm in a kind of zone today.'

'You sure are. A speed zone.'

He wrote me out a speeding ticket. He also wrote out two other tickets: one for the broken window, and one for a cracked tail-light. I didn't argue. I just stood and smiled and accepted his tickets as if they were hundred-dollar bills.

'Thanks, officer. I know you're only doing your job.'

'Don't give me any of that lip, sonny.'

'No, really – I mean it.'

I kept thanking him and congratulating him. I even stood by my car, waving at him as he drove off. Once he was out of sight, I did a little dance of joy, hopped up on the hood of the Neon, and shouted at the sky, 'I owe you, America!'

At the next rest stop, I pulled over. I removed the clip from the pistol and wiped my fingerprints off the grip, using some dirty underwear. Then I dropped it in a garbage can, underwear and all. At another rest stop, and another garbage can, I got rid of the bullets and extra clip. Afterwards, to thank America for watching over me, I knelt down and kissed her grass. It tickled my lips and tasted a bit wet. I hoped a dog hadn't pissed on it.

chapter 77

'Have a nice trip?'
  'I had the kind of trip I needed.'
'Glad to hear it.'

At the rental car agency, the same guy who'd been working when I'd set out was on duty – the Asian guy with the hoop earring. I don't think he recognised me at first. He didn't look as if he recognised me, anyways. He didn't look very well, either. His eyes were puffy, his uniform was crumpled, and his quiff was flopping around all over the place.

I hated to add to his troubles.

'But there was a bit of a problem,' I said, 'with the car.'

'What kind of problem?'

'You better come look.'

We walked out into the underground parkade. In the drop-off bay sat my brand-new Neon, covered in dust, spattered with mud. The replacement bumper was dented and the wheel well was scraped and the window was shattered and the panelling was covered in key-marks. I'd gotten used to all that, but now I was seeing it through his eyes. She looked pretty battered. The clerk was absolutely baffled. He walked around the car, gawking, then poked his head inside to check the odometer. I'd put over four thousand kilometres on the clock.

He asked, 'Where did you *take* it?'

'A town called Trevor. Then Oregon, Reno, San Francisco. And back up the I-5.'

'In two weeks?' he said, shaking his head. 'Fuck.'

I slapped him on the back. 'Good thing you sold me that insurance, eh?'

We stood and stared at her. You could tell he was impressed, which made me oddly proud – as if I was presenting a work of art. I patted her hood affectionately, in farewell. 'If I could afford to buy you,' I said, 'I would, old girl.'

Back in the office, I had to fill in some forms, explaining the damage. I was going to lose my deductible – which was almost as much as the rental – but I'd expected that. While I scribbled, he took his phone out of his pocket and fiddled with it, as if checking to make sure it still worked.

'How's your fiancée?' I asked.

'I don't have a fiancée,' he said. Then he tugged on his earring. I guess he must have remembered that he'd told me about her before, because he added, 'Not any more.'

'Girl troubles, eh? You want some advice?'

You could tell he didn't, but he didn't have a choice, either.

'Go on a road trip. That's why I went on mine.'

'Did it make a difference?'

'It made all the difference. Distance gives you perspective.'

'Bet you saw some things, huh?'

'I saw things you wouldn't believe.'

'Really?' He slid another form towards me – he had a whole sheaf of them – and pointed to the spot where I was supposed to fill in my details. 'What kinds of things?'

'Well,' I said, signing my name with a flourish, 'I saw a desert plain on fire, like a landscape in hell. I saw a diner where they serve human flesh, and a darkness that's never seen the sun. I kissed a girl from a distant land, who had escaped her fate, and I slept with a witch in a waterbed. I had a shoot-out at the Twin Peaks – twice – and I surfed the afterlife. I got deathly high on peyote, and saw the luminescence behind existence, but I didn't know what it meant until I drank mezcal with a goddess and she interpreted my vision for me.'

I thought all that sounded pretty impressive, but he was only half-listening, and kept checking his phone discreetly.

When I got to the bit about my vision, though, he looked up.

'It meant everything is connected,' I said. 'Everything in the entire universe.'

'Connected by gravity?'

'By invisible rays of light, that run between all the physical phenonema you can see. Between plants, animals, the landscape. Between distant stars and planets. And between all the people, too. Even me and you.'

He looked at the space between us, as if expecting to see something there.

'You mean like the Care Bear Stare?'

'Not exactly. Never mind. The point is, you're part of it, and it's part of you.' I tapped him in the chest, with my pen. 'You are it, or thou art that. Understand?'

'I think so.' But he had that frozen, service-with-a-smile look on his face now. 'Sounds like you had quite the experience out there. Did you bring any souvenirs back?'

'Actually – hold on.' I unzipped my backpack, pulled out my bottle of mezcal, and plonked it down on the counter in front of him. 'Check this out.'

He peered at the snake. 'Harsh.'

'You can have it, if you want.'

He looked from the bottle, to me, and back to the bottle. Only a few ounces of liquor remained at the bottom. The snake, half-exposed to the air, had started to rot and fall apart.

'That's the mezcal,' I said. 'Practically a magic elixir.'

'Thanks very much.' He pinched the bottleneck with three fingers, as if he thought it might be infectious, and placed it to one side. 'Now, let's finish off this claim, shall we?'

He tapped the final form. You could tell he didn't believe me – about the mezcal or anything else – but it didn't matter. I'd done all I could for him. He'd have to figure out the rest on his own. I signed off that last form, and handed it over along with the others. I told him again that he should really consider going on a trip, if he wanted to get his head together.

'The road heals all wounds.'

'I'll keep that in mind.'

'Easier said than done.'

I turned to go, hoping I looked appropriately wise and sage and mysterious.

'Wait,' he said.

I looked back. I half-expected him to thank me for my gift and advice.

'You have the key.'

I smiled. Knowingly. 'We all have the key.'

'No – the car key. You still have it.'

'Oh. Right.'

He held out his hand. I dug the key out of my pocket, and lowered it into his palm, as if I were performing some kind of sacred rite. Then I folded his fingers around the key, held on for one more moment, and let go.

Acknowledgements

Many people have helped make this journey possible, and I would like to specifically thank a few of them: Naomi, my first and ideal reader; Becky, for believing in this book before it was even a book; Matthew, who has critiqued too many drafts to count; Angela, my San Francisco advisor and correspondent; Vicky, for all the editorial guidance; Holly, Candida, and the rest of Team Myriad for backing and supporting the novel; Linda, the best copy-editor this side of the Sierra Nevada; Anna, who designed the stand-out cover; my friends and family back home for the geography and vernacular checks; Douglas Coupland, who kindly gave me permission to quote from *Life After God*; and lastly America – yes, America – because she is such a big country, with so many smooth and well-maintained roads, waiting to be traversed by a young man in search of something.

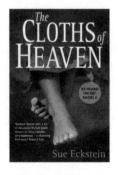

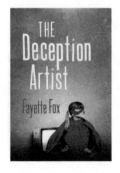

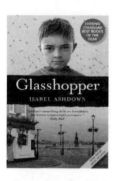

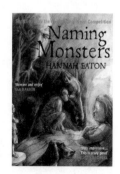

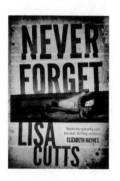

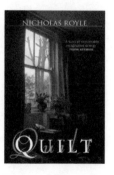

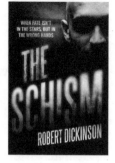

MORE FROM MYRIAD EDITIONS

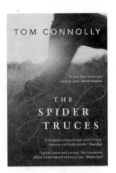

www.myriadeditions.com